PIECES

A Novel From

Patrick Heffernan

ISBN 10: 0-9975794-1-2

ISBN 13: 978-0-9975794-1-3

Cover by N.D. Taylor.

Table of Contents

ONE..1

TWO 8

THREE 14

FOUR 21

FIVE 25

SIX 31

SEVEN..39

EIGHT..53

NINE...57

TEN 66

ELEVEN 70

TWELVE...74

THIRTEEN 77

FOURTEEN..87

FIFTEEN 93

SIXTEEN 96

SEVENTEEN 101

EIGHTEEN 108

NINETEEN 117

TWENTY 121

TWENTY-ONE..129

TWENTY-TWO 134

TWENTY-THREE..153

TWENTY-FOUR 159

TWENTY-FIVE 164

TWENTY-SIX...169

TWENTY-SEVEN...176

TWENTY-EIGHT...179

TWENTY-NINE...196

THIRTY..210

THIRTY-ONE..216

THIRTY-TWO...219

THIRTY-THREE...227

THIRTY-FOUR...233

THIRTY-FIVE...237

THIRTY-SIX...243

THIRTY-SEVEN...249

THIRTY-EIGHT...257

THIRTY-NINE..265

FORTY...273

FORTY-ONE...279

FORTY-TWO..286

FORTY-THREE..290

FORTY-FOUR..299

FORTY-FIVE..304

FORTY-SIX...311

FORTY-SEVEN..314

FORTY-EIGHT...324

FORTY-NINE...337

FIFTY..345

FIFTY-ONE..350

FIFTY-TWO 358

FIFTY-THREE 364

FIFTY-FOUR 370

FIFTY-FIVE 374

FIFTY-SIX 376

FIFTY-SEVEN...394

FIFTY-EIGHT 400

AFTERWORD 409

ACKNOWLEDGEMENTS...410

ONE

Mike Lowe had been promoted to sergeant four months now. But his promotion had seen him transferred from Narcotics to Homicide, working under Lieutenant Darrell Capps. He and Capps had known and cordially hated one another for over twenty years, although each would very privately acknowledge the other was a good cop. They just didn't get along well.

Consequently, Lowe was routinely shunted to the supervisory position on night shift. In his four months in Homicide he fielded eleven cases and had nine airtight arrests, certain to eventually lead to conviction and probably someday two or three executions. The other two were drive-by shootings, which were often solved more by dumb luck than good policing, most often when the morons were arrested for something else, months later, still carrying the murder weapon. In both cases, the murders were done with .38 Special pistols, gaining in popularity with the scarcity of .22-caliber ammunition, and both were cheap Saturday Night Specials. He wasn't worried about those cases, though. The truth was, nine arrests out of eleven cases was an excellent record, and in one of those he had even received an official letter of commendation. He looked on that matter with dubious eyes. Sure, it was a nice shiny spot on his record, but it probably doomed him to finishing his career putting up with Capps in Homicide, unless Capps retired first. But this was unlikely since Capps was younger than Lowe. Lowe had entered the force twenty-three years before, at the age of 30 after growing sick of the Army and taking discharge rather than a crap recruiting assignment he didn't want.

He was finishing a report the DA was demanding on a case he'd closed three weeks before, one that saddened him, truth to tell. 77-year-old Margaret Connors had turned up dead, and the coroner had pronounced it a murder. Her husband, 79-year-old Daniel, had gone to a farm supply company and secured a syringe and needle, then came home, drew up 1,200 units of insulin and injected it into her vein, killing her quite handily. The problem was that Margaret was dying of pancreatic cancer and had asked her doctor, and others, about help killing herself. Daniel had performed a mercy killing but was being held without bail, and would probably die behind bars before he ever came to trial. Like so many, Lowe was deeply conflicted about "right to die" matters, and found himself empathizing with Daniel Connors and even hoping the old man somehow beat the rap on this one, but he knew that was a pipe dream. Connors would never be a free man again.

His work was interrupted by the phone ringing. "Homicide, Sergeant Lowe," he answered.

"Sergeant, this is Sergeant Ann Knox," he heard. "We have a … it's a huge mess at a vacant house. 15833 Drew Estates Road is the address. We already have Crime Scene on the way to start processing, but the death count in the house looks like at least eight, and quite possibly more."

"Jesus Christ, what happened?" Lowe asked, the report on Daniel Connors instantly filed aside in his mind.

"We got an anonymous call for a welfare check at the address, someone calling from a dispose-a-phone," Knox said. "Officers Landry and Suarez responded. The house was vacant, not even curtains or blinds on the windows, and they looked through a window and saw body parts scattered all over the place, like some kind of B-movie. They went around all the windows of the house and saw body parts scattered from Hell to breakfast. On my orders, they have not entered the house. I have a warrant on the way just to cover our ass, and once Crime Scene arrives they can enter the house and an untrammeled crime scene."

"Good news," Lowe said. "15833 Drew Estates Road, you said?"

"That's the one," Knox confirmed. "I'm on scene right now and we have it all taped off. So far nobody's called the press, but you know how it is. It's a sure bet someone will."

"Jesus," Lowe said and put the address in the GPS of his cell phone. "Okay, I'll be there in twenty, Sergeant Knox."

Lowe wandered out to his car, sensing this was going to be a nightmare case, and drove first through a convenience store for a tank-like cup of hot coffee, and then to the scene. Lowe was pleased to see that none of the – he counted – eleven police cars scattered about had red-and-blues on. It was 3:04 of a Wednesday morning in a relatively quiet lower-middle-class neighborhood, and there was no sense in waking up the entire block and drawing a herd of lookie-loos to get in the way and then draw a flock of news vans. Lowe had no illusions that something this spectacular would escape the notice of the local Fourth Estate, but he'd rather this scene be clear or near to clear before the newsies got wind of it.

He found Sergeant Knox, a thirty-year-old go-getter who seemed energetic and bright as could be, and instantly decided he liked her. Ten minutes later another car arrived, this with a police officer bearing a search warrant signed off by a notably irritable Judge Marisol Rivera, who was cooped up in bed with a raging case of intestinal flu.

With the warrant in hand, an officer checked the front door, found it unlocked, and opened it. "Jesus Motherfucking Christ," the officer said. His name was Paul Morris. He was 22 years old and barely out of the academy. Indeed, his FTO (field training officer) had only signed off on him ten days before.

Lowe looked into the living room and groaned. He saw parts of bodies and four human heads at first glimpse. "Okay, back out of here and let's wait on the Crime Scene Unit to do their thing," Lowe ordered. "I think this one is officially my case, Officer Morris."

"Jesus, you're welcome to it," Morris said, and then darted to the porch railing and hurled a huge spew of vomit into the flowerbed before walking away on unsteady legs. Moments later the crime scene team arrived with a huge Dodge Sprinter van piloted by one member while four others arrived in an Expedition. They entered the home with cameras and began their task while Lowe waited.

But twenty minutes later the house exploded. A call from one disposable phone was placed to another disposable phone, but this was wired to a little transmitter that sent a signal to a dozen thermite devices scattered about the house, several conveniently centered near gas lines. The explosion and fire were cataclysmic.

One CSU member near a second-floor window leapt from the window to the ground, breaking three vertebrae and sustaining a closed head injury on impact. Three others were killed in the explosion. The fifth, near the door, burst out of the door with his clothes ablaze, and two cops blasted at him with fire extinguishers while Knox got on the radio for two ambulances and for the Fire Department to send in the world.

Four local news vans arrived at the same time as the fire department, which spent eight hours putting out the flames. With nothing to do, Lowe considered his options and returned to Homicide, buying another monster coffee on his way. He knew it would be a long damn time before he would be able to go home and sleep. At the station he texted his wife Lisa to tell her he would be working late. She always put her phone on do-not-disturb until 8:00 in the morning, so he knew she would see the text after she woke.

He drank the coffee at the station as he prepared the initial report, wondering what, if anything, the CSU people had salvaged before the house blew up. He wondered what happened. The blaze looked initially furious, so he figured these were military-grade incendiaries, and wondered what the hell was going on. But he knew until the blaze was out and he'd gotten more information, he was more or less akin to a dog chasing his own tail. At the same time, like or not, he knew he would have to report this one to Capps. He had briefly considered and then discarded the notion of calling Capps on his way back from the scene, but decided there was no upside to that beyond annoying the asshole. So he sat and drank cup after cup of coffee, but managed to finish the report to the DA before Capps came in at 7:00.

"I need to talk with you, Lieutenant," Lowe said formally when Capps arrived, which got the lieutenant's attention.

"Let me use the john and get some coffee, Lowe," Capps answered. The truth was, while Capps didn't particularly need to use the bathroom, he did need coffee to start fueling his brain, but one way or another he figured it illustrated to Lowe where he stood in the pecking order. Right as Capps ducked into the men's room, Sergeant Natalie Price, the day-shift Homicide sergeant, arrived. "Hey, how was the overnight, Lowe?" she asked, smiling. Lowe and Price enjoyed a good relationship, and genuinely respected and liked one another. Price, at forty, had recently taken the examination for lieutenant, and Lowe thought privately that Price would be promoted within the coming six months, probably three or four months. In his heart of hearts, Lowe suspected that if he was still with the Department in fifteen years, Price would very possibly be a deputy inspector and maybe even chief of police.

"Okay, what do you have, Lowe?" Capps asked a moment later, ushering Lowe into his office.

"A total fucking mess," Lowe said. "You'll start catching heat any moment on this one, I'm afraid. A welfare call came in this morning, round 1:30 or so, I think it was. The first uniforms on scene looked through the windows – the house was vacant – and saw several dismembered bodies. The first patrol sergeant on scene got a warrant. We waited on that. The warrant arrived a moment ahead of CSU, and they went in first since they're best at keeping a crime scene intact. Moot point, I guess. They'd been in there only a few minutes when the house blew up. Two of the CSU people got flown to the trauma center. I understand neither is expected to live. When I left the scene, the FD was still putting out the fires and the news stations were crawling all over the place. I have a call into the tax office to find out who owns the place, but I expect to hear from them in the afternoon, probably."

Just then, Capps' phone rang on his desk and he answered. He didn't say much other than "Yes, Sir" several times, and then hung up the phone. "Why didn't you tell me the news was in on this?" he asked Lowe.

"That was next on my list, Lieutenant," Lowe said. "They got there about the time the firemen did."

"That was Inspector John Johnson," Capps said. "I hope you have a nicer suit than that, Lowe. He wants to see us in his office in thirty minutes."

"What you see is what you get with me, Lieutenant," Lowe said. "I think there might be another tie in my locker, but I was never a clothes horse one way or another." Lowe wasn't telling the whole truth here. He indeed had in his closet at home eighteen very nice suits, none older than five years, and no less than fifty neckties. But he'd always liked this battered sports coat and he managed to wear it once weekly. That he was wearing it now was luck of the draw, but he wasn't altogether interested in running home to change suits just to appease Capps' worries about Commissioner Johnson's ideas of decorum and high sartorial standards. To Lowe's way of thinking, detectives would be far more effective in sneakers and jeans, like the average John Q. Public wore. Suits could be off-putting to people who lived more casually, perhaps even more off-putting than uniforms with pistols and nightsticks.

"Maybe I'll imply to him that you're a retard or something," Capps grumbled. "Let's go.

TWO

"What in the red, white, and blue bleeding fuck happened out there?" Johnson demanded.

"Inspector, we were set up," Lowe said. "Once the fire is out the arson investigators will have some answers for us. The house itself was vacant with a Keller-Williams sign in the yard and we'll follow up with the Realtor and the tax office to learn who owns the house. But right now, until the fire is out and we have some answers, I'm in the dark. Two of the CSU people were flown to the trauma center, and three were killed. Sir, I've been around house fires before, but this was different, one hell of a lot hotter for one thing. Terrorists? With that many body parts I doubt this was a one-man job. But right now – I only got the call four hours ago on this – all I have are questions. CSU had only begun their part of this when the house blew up."

"Jesus Christ, the press is howling for information or a statement on this, and you want me to tell them jackshit? Seriously?" Johnson glared at Capps. "Is Sergeant Lowe your best man for this, Capps?"

"Inspector, to be fair he's earned a good arrest record and has the right instincts," Capps allowed. "He's certainly not my most experienced detective, but he's the best I have available right now. I have one detective in the hospital and another on leave for a month —"

"Son of a bitch, a month?" Johnson snapped. "What the fuck is going on in Homicide, Lieutenant?"

"Sir, Detective Jenkins is on FMLA leave," Capps said. "To be honest, I don't know if he's returning or not. His wife had a baby two weeks ago —"

"Touchy-feely bullshit," Johnson grumbled. "I'm glad you're single and I don't have to hear tales of your own snot-nosed kids."

"Yes, Sir," Capps said carefully. The truth was that he was homosexual and had been in a committed relationship twelve years with a man named Jim Fisher, who owned a used car lot. Equal rights be damned, Capps knew that if his sexuality came to light, his career would be incinerated in days. "The situation with Jenkins is a bit different, Sir. His wife died in childbirth, and her parents and his live a long way off. But right now we're wait-and-see on him."

"Okay, Sergeant Lowe," Johnson said. "You are hereby anointed lead investigator in this matter. Nothing against you personally but I think this is one hell of a lot more than you can handle alone. I have to go see Chief Watts, but the flat fact of the matter is we're probably going to have to assign a task force to this one. What will probably happen then is you'll be 'under' a lieutenant, maybe even a captain, and unless that luminary is psychic or has a working crystal ball, your 'commander' will probably seldom see you."

"Yes, Sir," Lowe said, and stifled a yawn.

"You worked all night, didn't you?" Johnson asked.

"I had a court appearance yesterday that lasted almost the entire day," Lowe said. "And then I had to be in last night at 8:00 to meet with one of the prosecutors on a case."

"Okay, Capps, assign at least two good detectives under Lowe," Johnson said in a kinder voice. "Lowe, go your ass home and get sleep. I'll be setting wheels in motion, but details that won't really affect you. I'll want you back here at 2:00, but Capps will throw you out of the building and take you home in handcuffs at 6:00 if he must. And then I think you're on day turn, Sergeant. Is this the first you've been in a supervisory role?"

"I was an E-6 in the army before I joined the police," Lowe said.

"Then I don't have to bend your ear about delegating duties," Johnson told him. "Get your asses out of here. The chief is about to chew mine to shreds and I'd rather you two weren't on-hand to witness that merry event."

"Look, you look like hell," Capps said a few minutes later in Capps' car. "But I think it's time we talked, Mike. So I'm going to buy you breakfast and we'll talk, and then I'm going to personally drive you home. I'd rather not have to go to Johnson and tell him my sergeant fell asleep at the wheel of a Department car and plowed it into a school bus full of blind orphans." He parked at a Denny's and the men went inside. Lowe wasn't hungry and didn't like Capps, or to socialize with someone he didn't like, but Capps was his commanding officer, and Lowe had never really escaped the military mindset.

At Capps' request, the men were seated away from the other diners after Capps showed his badge to the hostess and told her they would be discussing gruesome things that other diners didn't want to hear. As they sat, Capps' text alert dinged, and he looked at it, frowning. "Damn, one of the CSU people died in surgery, and the other, the one who was burned, isn't expected to survive the day."

"Goddammit," Lowe muttered.

"Friends of yours?" Capps asked.

"No," Lowe said. "I knew them vaguely but hadn't worked directly with any of them before. But the two survivors were young, I think in their 20s. What a waste. Christ, I don't know if the department has ever lost five officers at once."

"Yeah, we usually see only six or seven dead in a year, and that's too damned many," Capps remarked, and then shook his head. "Okay, you and me, Mike. I've spent a lot of time thinking about you for the past couple or three weeks, and I can't come up with a single reason for the animosity we have except that it's chemical. But we need to fix this somehow or another. I guess I could have ignored it for the next ten years if you'd been on routine cases like you've been doing. But this one … this is high-visibility, Mike." He paused and looked over Mike's shoulder. "Christ, it's on TV now." Mike turned and looked, seeing the press room at headquarters and Sergeant Anna Moss, who was the department spokesperson. She spoke a few minutes, only saying that the case was under review at the highest levels of the department and that a task force was being assembled as she spoke.

"I feel sorry for you on this one, Mike," Capps said. "I feel sorry for myself too, because the chief will be looking for sacrificial offerings if we don't close this case in a hurry. Could be we both get transferred to a rubber gun squad out in the ghetto somewhere. And lieutenants are juicier sacrifices than sergeants, so I'll probably be put out to pasture at the 22nd and then to an inglorious retirement." He snorted.

"This one is going to take tons of legwork, Darrell," Lowe said. The waitress came by and the cops ordered breakfast, just bacon and eggs for Lowe, with orange juice. Capps ordered a stack of pancakes and a Denver omelet.

"Look, I don't think we're ever going to be best buddies, but do you think we could at least try?" Capps asked.

"Of course," Lowe said. "I've thought about the same, Darrell. And one way or another, we're glued together now, and it's better if we try to like each other."

"As a token of this reset, I'm going to let you pick your two detectives," Capps said. "The only ones off-limits are Gene Placer – he's on an assignment with the state attorney general – and Starla Cunningham, who's about to be flying out of town for probably two or three weeks on a case that had a change of venue, so she'd be unavailable one way or another."

"Bob Neely for one," Lowe said. Neely had been in homicide twenty years and knew how the whole system worked.

"He's yours," Capps said. "I'll notify him as soon as I'm at the office. Who else?"

"That's where I need your help, Darrell," Lowe admitted. "You've been in homicide longer than me, far longer, and I'm smart enough to know I'm the rookie."

"Jay Walker," Capps said, chuckling. "Jesus, the jokes that poor fucker has to endure. His parents must have hated him even in his crib to do that to him. But he's smart, an up-and-comer. He just took the sergeant's exam and will probably place high enough to be promoted soon, but even so, that's probably six months off, and if we don't have this case closed by then, well, I expect we'll be in duties we'd rather not consider."

"Walker it is, then," Lowe agreed. The food arrived. Lowe picked at his, but drank down the orange juice.

After they ate, Capps ran Lowe home and told him a detective would be at his home with his car. Lowe entered his house and stumbled to his bedroom, which he and Lisa had darkened to coal-mine levels, and in a moment he was undressed and sound asleep.

THREE

While Lowe slept, much was happening outside his knowledge. Inspector Johnson met with Chief Aaron Watts, and it was decided a task force was indeed indicated. "I think it's best that I'm tight in the loop on this one, John," Watts said. "This man Lowe … he's competent?"

"According to his lieutenant, he's a bright one, with a good clearance record, but a relatively new sergeant. He was transferred to Homicide when he was promoted," Johnson said. "I asked a few questions and it seems he's a smart one. His former lieutenant flat told me that if Lowe wasn't addicted to overtime pay and had taken exams as soon as possible, he would very possibly be a captain by now, maybe even an inspector. Most everyone I talked to seems to think he's a great cop through and through."

"Yeah, that happens too much," Watts grunted. "He comes back on at 2:00?"

"Yes, Sir," Johnson said.

"Bring him to my office," Watts decided. "What I am going to do is put this task force under Lieutenant Holmes, but Lowe will be running it unless he trips over his dick. I know he's going to need one hell of a lot of support, so you put the word out to the inspectors and captains that what Lowe wants, Lowe gets. What about an office for him?"

"I have people on that," Johnson said. "There's a suite of offices on the third floor, hopefully bigger than he'll need, but it should suffice. People are in there now cleaning the carpets, and then I put in the order that I don't care if they work all night, I want it furnished and phones in there, the whole electronics package. It should be ready tomorrow."

"Okay, good," Watts said. "Right now I want you to levy every lieutenant for three officers to detail to Lowe. Anyway, I have to go meet the mayor. I'll be back in a while."

Johnson got on his tasks to support the task force, and worked right through lunch.

"You set off the incendiaries too late, and killed five innocents," the man said to the trembling woman. They were at a remote spot just outside town. "Worse, you killed police officers! They won't rest until we're in prison for the rest of our lives. We'll continue our work, but you may as well know sooner or later we're going to be caught because of your stupidity."

"I am sorry," the woman said. "I got there late and wanted to see it when it happened."

"Just like Lot's wife," the man said as he stood. "You know what to expect for this."

"God help me," the woman breathed. "I ... I know." She stood and walked out to the barn, and offered her wrists to a post. Using iron shackles, he bound her to the post and ripped her blouse away, dropping the tatters to the dirt floor. And then he uncoiled a whip.

"Be glad this isn't the flagellum," he said, and then stood several feet back and began horsewhipping her while she screeched in agony. It wasn't her first time for this. Indeed, her back was decorated with scars from four earlier sessions of his discipline. The whipping lasted a long time, over a hundred lashes, until he coiled the whip and poured antiseptic on her bleeding wounds, making her scream anew and then faint. He woke her and undid her shackles, and then told her to pick up her blouse and toss it in the trash. Once done, the woman went to a cell in the barn, much like a big dog kennel, and entered, knowing she would be confined for at least a day, maybe a week. He locked her in and returned to the house while she curled up and sobbed, hating herself for being such a disappointment.

In the house, the man sighed, annoyed with himself but knowing what had to be done. He went into a clinical-looking room, tiled on the floor and all the walls, but otherwise furnished only with whips hanging from hooks on the wall, and fetters along the opposing wall. There, he stripped from his clothes and picked up a flagellum. He'd grown an erection out there with the woman on the whipping post, and that was unacceptable. It wasn't the first time for him either, and he sentenced himself to forty lashes, and then swung the heavy whip sidearm, wrapping it around to strike his back, and cried out at the fresh agony. In all, it took nearly an hour for him to build the courage to endure the sentence before it was done. He poured antiseptic on a huge towel and rubbed it across his bleeding back, fighting to remain conscious, and then put on a shirt he had lined with cotton trauma dressings and then falling into a fitful sleep.

Lowe's alarm went off at 1:00 and he hurried into the shower, and then deciding it was wisest, put on his newest suit and polished his shoes hurriedly. Detective Walker arrived in Lowe's car and Walker drove them to headquarters, where they rode to the chief's office on the 11th floor. There, he was ushered right in to the chief's office and gaped as he saw the mayor, Sanford Youngblood, sitting on one chair and the DA, Blake Hamlin, on another, apparently waiting for his arrival.

"Sergeant Lowe reporting as ordered, Sir," Lowe said.

"Sergeant, we looked into you and have yet to hear a bad word about you," Watts said. "I'm sure you will make us proud with your task force."

"I hope so, Chief Watts," Lowe said.

"Sergeant, you have the entire support not only of Chief Watts and Blake Hamlin, you also have my support," said Mayor Sanford Youngblood. "I want you to understand fully that I'm closely monitoring this case as well."

"Thank you, Sirs," Lowe said.

"I know you're just returning to duty after catching a bit of a nap to wipe out a 20-hour day," Watts said, probably for the benefit and edification of the DA and mayor and to cover Lowe's ass. "This lady is Lieutenant Miranda Holmes. She is my aide, but she is also your commander for this task force. But this one is your baby, Sergeant. She's here to provide you high-echelon support. An office suite is being handed off to you and I have levied every precinct for people, as well as the entire detective bureau. Additionally – since many of us suspect this is some kind of Satanic cult – you also have free access to the Narcotics unit and even IAB for undercover people, if needed. We basically just wanted to meet you today, Sergeant. Inspector Johnson will take you downstairs and show you your office suite. Your command should all be around tomorrow morning."

"Thank you, Sir," Lowe said.

"Come with me," Johnson ordered.

Lowe and Walker went with Johnson to the elevator and down to the third floor, which seemed relatively vacant. "This is where you'll work," Johnson said, handing keys to Lowe and Walker. Johnson unlocked the door and the men could see a buzz of activity with laborers moving desks and technicians wiring the place. The suite was huge, probably 8,000 square feet, Lowe considered. A glassed-in office was in the middle of it, where he could oversee his kingdom until he got relegated to a nowhere job for falling on his face in this one.

"I'm going to leave you and Walker to it," Johnson said, and shook hands with both men before returning to his own office on the sixth floor.

"So what developed while I was catching forty winks?" Lowe asked.

"Not much," Walker said. "We got in touch with the Realtor and the county tax office. The house has been on the market not quite a month. It is owned by The Church of God's Law over on Durango Boulevard."

"I don't think I've heard of them," Lowe said.

"Neither had I," Walker agreed. "I looked into them and terms like 'lunatic fringe' instantly rise up. It fits in if a coven of Satanists wanted to twist their tail. These people are into all of God's laws. They keep Kosher, for instance, but worship Jesus quite vigorously. A big part of their doctrine sounds Mormon, the body is a temple and all that, and there was even the implication that they are into the whole polygamy thing. Their website even has a section detailing – I hope it was photoshopped – the torments Christ suffered. Sergeant —"

"This ain't the army, and as long as you know I'm in charge, I'd as soon you just call me Mike," Lowe interrupted. "God knows you and I are going to be spending most of our lives shoulder-to-shoulder for the foreseeable future, Jay. And in token of my respect for you, I won't offer up any of the 10,000 jokes you've already heard about your name."

Walker chuckled at this and sat comfortably. He wasn't sure if he'd like this guy Lowe, with whom he was only acquainted, but the chemistry felt good, and he sat easily in one of the chairs in Lowe's office. "Mike, then. Anyway, I'm like you. I've seen ten tons of gruesome in this job, and that section of the website made me fight my gorge."

"Oh boy," Lowe groaned.

"I looked into them, their minister is a guy named Isaiah Quinn, fifty-four years old, clean record without warrants," Walker said. "As best I can tell he's never even had a jaywalking ticket." The men both chuckled at the wisecrack.

"So he's a fruitcake but a law-abiding one just the same," Lowe said.

"That seems to sum it up, Mike," Walker answered. "In any event, the church has a board of elders, all men – women must remain silent in church, you see – and an attorney who appears to be on the board, a guy named Walther Kurberg. Legal questions are to be directed to him, apparently."

"Fuck that," Lowe said. "I want you to investigate that church inside and out. I'm going to go meet this Quinn guy and get a feel for him."

FOUR

"Do you have an appointment?" the secretary asked in the outer office. She looked to be in her late twenties, red-headed and pretty, wearing a long-sleeved white blouse and otherwise seeming sane. The desk plate indicated her name was Shannon Bridger.

"I sure don't," Lowe said, and showed her his badge. "But it's police business."

"Let me see if he's available," she said. She picked up her phone and pushed a button, and then spoke in low tones before hanging up.

A man came out of the office and looked curiously at Lowe. He was dressed simply in black ministerial attire, and Lowe looked for and saw no signs of him living high off the hog, so to speak. "I'm Shepherd Quinn," he said with a grin. "Have I somehow run afoul of the law?"

"Oh, no Sir," Lowe said and shook hands. "But can we talk privately for a few minutes?"

"Certainly," Quinn said, and ushered Lowe into his office.

"Sir, there was a gruesome scene last night, a murder, and the house that caught fire," Lowe began. "Perhaps you saw it on the news."

"I don't own a television," Quinn said. "It's all sin and depravity and a celebration of the same."

"I understand, Reverend," Lowe said.

"It's 'shepherd' if you don't mind," Quinn returned.

"I'm sorry," Lowe said. "Shepherd Quinn, then. In any event, the house was entered and right as techs began processing the scene, several incendiary devices went off. The house burned to the ground and five officers from Crime Scene Unit were killed."

"God protect their souls," Quinn breathed. "I'm very sorry, Detective Lowe. How does this involve me, though?"

"Your church owns the house," Lowe said flatly.

"How terrible," Quinn said. "The church owns a number of houses, Detective. When God calls parishioners home, many leave the houses to us in their wills."

"I see," Lowe said. "What information can you give me on the house?"

"You're welcome to copy the entire folder on it," Quinn said. "What's the address?"

"15833 Drew Estates Road," Lowe said.

Quinn picked up his phone and dialed his secretary, and told her to look up the address and copy the entire folder for him. She came in a few minutes later with a big manila envelope. "Sergeant, this is what I found," she said. "Hiram Sturgis died three years ago and left the house – three houses, actually – to the church in his will. It took until three months ago for it all to clear probate. The elders then put all three on the market. The other two sold quickly but this one … it's not in the best neighborhood … isn't going fast."

"Well, it won't go anywhere now," Lowe said, standing. He opened the envelope and glanced inside, and saw an envelope paper-clipped to it with his name on it in feminine script, but kept poker-faced. "Thank you very much for this, and we'll be in touch. If you carried insurance on it, you can notify your insurer and they can get with our arson investigators."

"Thank you, Detective Lowe," Quinn said, rising and offering his hand.

"And thank you, Shepherd," Lowe said.

Ten minutes later he stopped in a diner and opened the envelope with his name on it, curious as to its contents.

Sergeant Lowe,

Please call me tomorrow after 5:00 at 555-7921. I have information that might be helpful to you, Sir. I look forward to hearing from you.

S

Lowe ordered a refill of his Coke to go, looked at his watch, and drove to his new office. Something about Quinn and his church raised Lowe's hackles, and he wondered about looking deeper into it.

At headquarters, a phone rang and a very senior policeman answered. "This is Isaiah Quinn. Look into a detective named Mike Lowe for me," Quinn ordered.

"It will be done, Shepherd," the officer promised.

Lowe's file was called up on the computer, and the officer grunted a couple times as he saw between the lines the records of a very good cop who was now trying to advance on the ladder as he neared retirement. Lowe probably would make captain before retiring, conceivably even inspector. There was no dirt on him, nor even unofficial communication that he was trouble. He closed out the inquiry and used his desk phone to call Shepherd Quinn to report what he had found.

"Apparently a murder and arson took place in a house we were trying to sell," Quinn said, and explained what he knew.

"I'll do what I can, Shepherd. It's a high-profile case spread all over the news." The call ended.

FIVE

The next morning, Lowe was in his office at 6:30, after staying up late the night before, until around midnight, thinking of various facets of the case. The funeral for the officers was still pending but promised to be a huge matter. Already, he had learned through the grapevine, several police departments and benevolent societies, some from as far as 2,000 miles away, were planning to send officers to the service. In a way, Lowe felt responsible for them. It was his case, and they were arguably under his command, but who could have predicted the outcome?

He opened a preliminary e-mail from the arson investigators and saw that the devices were indeed devastating. The report said they were devices disguised as bug bombs, but had been full of homemade thermite, which the report went on to say were basically a blend of iron oxide and aluminum oxide with a magnesium kicker. Lowe, who had never gotten much into munitions, was amazed to read about thermite, which had been around since before World War II, and was easy to make from items from one's own garage with maybe a trip to a sporting goods store for the magnesium. Iron oxide was simply rust, and could be sanded from any rusty item around, or culled from a brake lathe at an auto shop. Aluminum oxide was a highly common abrasive in sandpaper, available at most hardware stores. Magnesium was readily available as a starter for campfires, and available at any sporting goods store. To Lowe, this was a double-edged sword of good-news-bad-news. On the good news side, it meant he wasn't facing real professionals but a talented clown probably with a battered and dog-eared copy of *The Anarchist's Cookbook*. This was not an Al Qaeda IED. The downside of it was these materials were commonly available, easily obtained, and impossible to trace, so if his adversary was clever at concealing himself he could do this shit for years on end.

The phone on his desk rang. "Sergeant Lowe," he answered.

"Sergeant, this is Captain Paul Luden," he heard. "I need you to come to my office to discuss something with your case. I'm in 534. Get up here."

Curious, Lowe left his office and boarded the elevator, then went to 534. There was a male secretary in the outer office, who ushered him right into Luden's office. Lowe was baffled some by the office décor, but left that lay as he came to attention and studied Luden. He guessed Luden's age at around sixty. The man wore his hair in a military-style high-and-tight, and had a mustache that was right at the edge of breaking regulations. Even though Luden was sitting, Lowe could see he was tall, maybe 6'3", and the man looked all-around hard and tough, out of sync with the office itself, which was decorated on all four walls with Christian memorabilia. Lowe searched his memory and remembered several years ago that a Christian movement upsurged throughout the department, and that Luden had been the ramrod of it. He filed that thought away.

"Sergeant Lowe reporting to Captain Luden as ordered, Sir," Lowe said.

"Have a seat, Sergeant," Luden said, smiling. Lowe sensed something amiss in the smile, but sat. "Sergeant, I understand you visited Isaiah Quinn yesterday as part of your ongoing investigation?"

"I did, Sir," Lowe said. "His church owns the house that was our crime scene. But I suppose now they own a lot of ashes."

"Tragic mess," Luden remarked. "Sergeant, this church … I've met Shepherd Quinn on many occasions … they're good people. But they're also largely wealthy people used to getting their own way, and Quinn was already remarking that he suspects the police are about to persecute his church for being out-of-step with mainstream Christianity. Or perhaps being politically incorrect in today's cultural climate. I assured him nothing of the sort was going on, but I don't think he's entirely convinced. I am going to suggest, Sergeant, that you route your inquiries of them through me. I don't think any of us want Quinn calling the mayor and building fires there. These people are quiet but very politically active, if you take my meaning."

"I see, Sir," Lowe said in a calm and unconcerned manner, but alarm bells were ringing all over his brain. "Captain, is Chief Watts on-board with this? My chain of command was described to me as Lieutenant Holmes and then Chief Watts. I hope I don't sound insubordinate, but your name never came up, Sir."

"No, I'm unofficial, and I didn't give you an order, Sergeant," Luden said. "It's just a friendly suggestion that these people, absent damning evidence of their guilt, must be handled with kid gloves."

"I'll keep that in mind, Sir," Lowe said.

"That's all I had, Sergeant," Luden said, standing and offering his hand. The men shook hands and Lowe wondered if he needed to count his fingers as he departed for his own office, changing his mind and going up to see Lieutenant Holmes.

"What's up, Mike?" Holmes asked when he entered her office.

"Not much, but … I figured I needed to talk with you," Lowe said. "I visited the church that owned that house that burned, spoke with their minister, a guy named Isaiah Quinn, who titles himself 'Shepherd.' Anyway, his secretary gave me copies of the folder on the house and I'll go through that in my office. But I got a call from a Captain Luden —"

"God save us from the Apostle Paul," Holmes groaned. "Dare I ask what that jackass wanted, Mike?"

"His office did seem more like a chapel, come to think of it," Lowe chuckled.

"Yeah, he was one of the two-fisted drinking party cops until I guess fifteen years ago," Holmes said. "His wife was diagnosed with cancer and that made him grow up. She died a couple years later, and along the way he went and got a huge dose of Jesus. In truth, it's an improvement but you go into his office and start wondering if you cuss, if God will strike you dead on the spot." She grinned and Lowe laughed.

"Yeah, that's the sense I got too," Lowe agreed. "Anyway, he summoned me to his office to tell me this preacher Quinn called him, and Luden suggested these people are rich and politically powerful and I should route my inquiries of the church through him."

Holmes held up a hand and picked up her phone. "I think you need to hear something," she said, and then, "Yes, Sir." She stood and ushered Lowe into Watts' office.

"What's going on?" Watts asked.

"I was summoned by a captain named Paul Luden ..." Lowe began, and told the tale while Watts' face grew red with anger.

"I've already summoned Inspector Johnson," Holmes said, hanging up a phone.

"That's what I like about you, Miranda," Watts said. "You're a superior mindreader."

Johnson appeared a moment later, and Lowe recounted the tale for the third time while the inspector nodded with a contemplative expression. "Inspector, I want Luden routed into the most shit-tastic assignment you have for a captain," Watts said. "Let's hope he gets the hint and files for retirement once and for all."

"The night patrol captain of the 22nd Precinct is retiring in a few days," Johnson said. "I was going to transfer ... well, another captain who's disfavored ... to the job, but I can certainly move Luden there instead, Chief."

Lowe remained quiet but understood the enormity of the wrath. The 22nd was always a problem precinct. Officers were routinely sued for their excesses there, the crime rate was sky-high, and at least two captains and a lieutenant assigned there over the years had opted for suicide. One captain fifteen years before got into full dress uniform on his first day, marched into his office like a man with a purpose, and blew his brain all over the wall. Ballistics tests later confirmed the round of ammo was a reload the captain had made in his own home, with roughly twice the powder charge a .45 should have. The barrel ruptured, in fact. And no captain (or for that matter, lieutenant) assigned to the 22nd left the 22nd for another assignment. It was Durance Vile for the brass, and the only way out was retirement. Lowe thought Luden was a smart man and would get the message quickly. He was surprised the punishment was so ruthless, but Watts wanted a lid kept on everything with this case. Lowe was even smart enough to understand Luden wasn't being taught a lesson with this. No, this lesson was for the sole edification of Sergeant Michael Lowe, he understood. Message received.

SIX

"Captain Paul Luden, reporting to the chief as ordered, Sir," Luden said, standing at attention. That snotnosed aide of his, Holmes, was sitting easily on a chair, but stood and exited the room. Luden wondered what Inspector Johnson was doing here.

"Captain Luden, I asked you here to tell you you're being reassigned," Watts said. "As we speak a couple of officers are going through your office downstairs and rounding up your personal items while a maintenance man changes the lock on your door. You are the new night patrol captain at the 22nd Precinct, starting tomorrow night at 10:00. That is all and you are dismissed."

"Sir … why?" Luden asked, stunned.

"Paul, do you really have to ask?" Watts wanted to know. "I know you're a member of that God's Law Church. I know Sergeant Lowe went to meet the preacher, and I know the preacher called you. Every call coming in is identified. And I know you then tried to put heat on Lowe, telling him to route his inquiries through you. Captain, if I was in a less charitable mood, you would be leaving here in handcuffs and charged with obstruction of justice. So you can contemplate your sins against the department there, or you can retire. One way or another, you're dismissed."

Luden left the office, red-faced and fuming, and Holmes was in the outer office. "I'm sorry, Captain, but you won't have an unmarked unit in your new assignment, and I have to ask you for your keys, Sir," she said. "An officer is in the lobby to give you a ride home, Sir."

Luden didn't want to lower himself to talk to this rude woman who didn't understand her place, so he merely handed her the keys to his four-year-old Impala sedan, in which he'd left no personal belongings, and wandered down the stairs to the lobby, and then rode home with an officer, one who looked old enough to know Luden was being run out of headquarters in disgrace. The officer, fortunately, was quiet and said nothing for the entire route to Luden's farm, but Luden, lost in woolgathering, didn't realize where the officer had taken him, and redirected him to an apartment in the city, only four miles from Headquarters. He owned the farm outside town but didn't live there. There were too many memories of his wife Ruth and his estranged sons, Joseph and Dillon, who both told him they never wanted to see him again as they left Ruth's funeral.

He had two garage spaces at his apartment, one for the Department unmarked he'd driven for years, and the other for his personal car, a relatively simple Chevy Cobalt he'd purchased used four years before. He got into the Chevy and drove to the church to confer with Shepherd Quinn, a thousand worries suddenly on his mind at Chief Watts' overreaction to the situation.

"Well, hello, Paul," Quinn said after Shannon escorted him into the office right at the dot of 5:00. Quinn turned his attention to his secretary. "Head on home, Shannon. I'll see you in the morning."

"Yes, Sir," she said, relieved. She rounded up her purse and strode out to her battered Pontiac and started toward home. Five minutes into her drive, her phone rang and she answered.

"Ms. Bridger, this is Sergeant Lowe. I got your note. Can we meet somewhere?"

"Yeah, I think that would be good, Sir," she said, beginning to fret.

"Name the place," Lowe said.

"Tully's," she answered immediately. "It's on —"

"Turner Boulevard at 3rd," Lowe interrupted. "I'll be there in ten minutes."

As Capps had done earlier, Lowe asked for a remote booth and flashed his badge at the pretty hostess, who led them to a far corner of the restaurant and pub, certain this was another cop cheating on his wife with some pretty floozy young enough to be his daughter. In fact, Lowe's oldest daughter was but six months older than Shannon Bridger, but the hostess couldn't have been farther from the truth.

"So what is it you'd like to tell me?" Lowe prompted after they got drinks delivered to their table, a Scotch and soda for Lowe and a margarita for Bridger.

"I don't know everything that went on, Sergeant, but you need to know that is a psychotic church, and I shudder to think what would happen to me if they knew I was talking out of school to you," she began. "Quinn … the hell of it is, he's kind and I like him … but

33

he and that church are so narrow-minded I think their ears blister against one another. Quinn doesn't approve of me. Their doctrine is that women are to be barefooted and pregnant, and taking care of home, husband and kids, but here I am, 24 and unmarried and working. On the other hand, it's difficult to find men willing to be secretaries. I'm somewhere between secretary and personal assistant, so I know more about those nutcases than I want, and I'm warning you I think they're dangerous. Christ, if they knew I'm a lesbian and my 'roommate' is … well, you get the picture, right?"

"I understand," Lowe said.

"Sergeant, they're heavy on law and discipline," Bridger said. "Their law and their discipline. One of my duties is maintaining records on all the members. Across the last year, they have charged nine women and six men with various offenses. Five of the six men were horsewhipped at assemblies of the all-male elders and the sixth was excommunicated. All nine of the women were horsewhipped at Sunday services in front of the whole congregation. All of the events were recorded on video as examples for people to see, and I took the time to watch the women. The ones of the men are only for the men to see, and password protected even from me. One woman last year got fifty lashes for it being her third offense over the last fifteen years. She had no voice when it was over and … if I had to guess I'd guess she's scarred for life from that one."

"Jesus Christ," Lowe muttered.

"Yeah, Him," Bridger said. "Eight months ago – I didn't think I'd ever tell this to anyone but my partner, but here goes – eight months ago one of the elders blew up at me first thing in the morning over a mistake I made. I admit I was in the wrong and totally owned the initial fuckup but I snapped back at the asshole, a guy named Dale Rawson. He raised hell with Quinn about me and stormed out. Quinn called me into his office. He looked regretful but told me I had two choices. I could be fired on the spot, or come to his office after hours and be paddled. I chose the paddle."

"Why?" Lowe asked, shocked.

"A number of reasons starting with who would believe me if I reported it, for one, since all I had for proof was my word and a purple ass and I'm sure he and Mrs. Rawson would deny it and testify I'd walked out at 5:00 when he fired me and I probably had someone do it to me to cook up a cock-and-bull lawsuit. Meanwhile, I'd have been unemployed with few skills in a shitty job market," she said. "You can look up my criminal history, Sergeant, but when I was 17 I got busted for having a quarter-ounce of marijuana. A plea bargain was worked out that saw me in jail every weekend for six months, but the judge was a real bastard and put ten years of probation on me with deferred adjudication. So that's hanging around my neck for the next three years, which makes me hard to employ. In a bad job market, employers can be very intrusive and picky. But once that's off my record, I'm getting a new job, maybe even with the city since the benefits are good." She shook her head. "So anyway, I came into his office after we closed. He told me I wouldn't be punished with the horsewhip on my naked back like a parishioner but called on Mrs. Rawson. She took me to the ladies room and made me strip out of my pants, and gave me only a thin scrub pants to wear, not even underwear, and then she returned me to Quinn. To be fair, he looked remorseful about it, but he bent me over his desk and paddled me thirty times. I was a wailing mess, and Mrs. Rawson had to hold me down for the last half of them, but ... this is the kind of mentality you're facing there, Sergeant. Be damned careful around them." Throughout her tale she took steady sips of her margarita, and hailed the waitress for a second one while Lowe took a healthy swallow of his drink. "Mr. Rawson is a pure hateful asshole, but he's at least more or less sane. His wife – Sergeant, she's looniebirds, and I really wonder when she's going to go off the deep end and be a star on the 10:00 news."

"I'm very sorry," Lowe said.

"Don't be," Bridger returned. "It's not your fault. I liked Quinn before he did this, and I honestly still do. But compared to so many of his parishioners, he's the sane one. In his mind, he did what was necessary to enforce discipline at his church. He ... he's otherwise fairly kind to me. I've been there three years, and he always gets me a little something for my birthday and a little something at Christmas, along with a hundred dollar bill every Christmas from his own pocket. As I said, we like one another. I don't think Quinn is capable of murder on his own, but some of those people ... a whole different tale, like a Christian Al Qaeda. One of the elders is even a cop in your department."

"Luden?" Lowe asked, but it wasn't quite a question.

"Yeah, him," she said. "He's a pure holy-rolling jackass, that one. I hate his guts. He hates women, for whatever his reason, and acts like he's the sergeant major of the entire place. I think he was a soldier or something once."

"He was a Marine," Lowe said, remembering one shadow-box on display in Luden's office, with Marine corporal's stripes and his Purple Heart with an oak-leaf cluster and a Bronze Star. "A decorated Marine, in fact." Lowe himself had both of those medals but no cluster on his Purple Heart. As a young buck in the Middle East, an IED had gone off near a truck he was riding, and shrapnel pierced his left arm. Fortunately, it wasn't a serious wound, but required eight staples, and he had the scar to prove it.

"I don't care what he did, he's still a hateful son of a bitch, especially to women," Bridger said. She dipped into her purse and gave him a DVD in a case. "Please be very discreet with this, Sergeant. I think I'd be killed by someone if word of this came to light."

"Thank you for meeting with me, Miss Bridger," Lowe said, deciding that the church needed to be watched closely, and so did Captain Luden. Lowe paid the tab and went back to headquarters, where he found Capps at his office.

"I was told to send your ass home at 6:00," Capps said. "It's 6:20. Scram, Mike."

"Yeah, no sense sticking around, is there?" Lowe said, knowing there wasn't much he could do until morning.

"Inspector Johnson was dead serious, Mike," Capps said. "You know as well as I do that you can't afford to kill yourself with 20-hour days. You'll have a huge crew here in the morning to boss around."

"I guess I'm showing my years, but Johnson's right," Lowe agreed. "Time to go home and have a beer or ten and hit this fresh in the morning. Adios, Darrell."

Lowe departed for home but called Lieutenant Holmes on his way, telling her he absolutely needed to meet with her first thing in the morning. She told him he was penciled in for 8:01, and then he got home to Lisa to give her a brief outline of his new duties, and then took her out to dinner, a rare occasion with the hours he typically clocked. They even made love that night, something that hadn't happened in nearly four months. But sleep was a long time coming for Lowe, who fixated on the case, turning it over and over in his mind, trying to find any hint or clue that would lead him toward a solution. But no inspiration or insight came.

SEVEN

Lowe's phone went off at 6:30, right as he was waking, and he answered it in a slurred voice.

"Mike, this is Miranda," Holmes said. "First, wake your ass up. Second, another similar murder got called in about an hour ago. The building is in flames so there's no sense going to the scene. But you'll have to hit the ground running today. Third, we're having a big breakfast with the chief and some other bigwigs, so wear a nice suit. It'll be at the chief's house. It's 8201 Golden River. Be there in an hour."

"Yes, Ma'am," Lowe said. "Ma'am, am I about to be sent to a rubber gun squad?"

"Hell no," Holmes said, surprised. "Look, we know the obstacles you're facing, and you're about to find a great deal of support heading your way. Get on over here, Mike." She ended the call and Lowe hurriedly showered, and then donned his best suit, one he'd bought three months before, a Savile Row on sale but still expensive, at Macy's, and donned a tie he'd bought the same day that had set him back another hundred dollars. In truth, he'd only worn it two other times, to court appearances. He hated doing dirty work in such nice clothes, and often thought the Department would be wiser giving detectives more discretion in how they dressed, but he knew that was an uphill battle that he'd never win.

The chief's driveway looked about like a used car lot, but one of the vehicles was a Cadillac limousine with exempt tags, that told him it was all but certainly the mayor. He approached the door and Holmes answered, and led him to the huge dining room of the house. Lowe came to attention as he entered, seeing the chief and mayor there. Captain Chuck Rivers, the Mayor's driver and chief of security, was there with Mayor Youngblood, as well as Inspector Johnson, and then the doorbell rang again, and Holmes admitted Walker, who looked tired and bedraggled in jeans and a t-shirt under a sportcoat, and smelling a bit of smoke.

"And who is your assistant?" Johnson asked.

"Sir, this is Detective Jay Walker, who is my deputy and adjutant," Lowe said. "I believe he was at the second scene."

"I was," Walker confirmed.

"Jay Walker?" Captain Rivers snorted. "Jesus."

"Yes, Sir," Walker said, straight-faced, but the mental eye-roll was plain as day in his tone of voice.

"Be seated, gentlemen," the chief said. "We're waiting on three more. This case is rapidly expanding. Sergeant, it's no fault of yours. One way or another, one of the technicians was able to identify two of the victims from the first fire. The second one … I know it's too soon to know diddly about it, but there are associated developments that we need to investigate."

Just then, the doorbell rang, and Holmes admitted Inspector Amanda Reese and Inspector Jim Parker. Lowe knew both by reputation. Reese was in charge of Internal Affairs. Parker was in charge of Science and Technology, indirectly the commander of CSU. They sat at the table and the chief's cook came out with bowls of scrambled eggs, bacon and sausages, as well as a platter of pancakes and two quart-size bottles of syrup. She returned a moment later with two pitchers of orange juice. "Gentlemen, there's a big urn of coffee in the kitchen for who wants it," she said. "Is there anything else you need, Chief Watts?"

"I think that's all, Louise," Watts said. "We're all grown up and can serve ourselves. Thank you for doing all of this."

"Then I'll be back tonight, Sir," Louise said, and departed.

"Inspector Reese, why don't you begin?" Watts asked.

"The angle on Captain Luden is unsettling," Reese said. "So we will have him under surveillance later today, to see if he and his church have a hand in these events. I —"

"Begging your pardon, Ma'am, but before you go deeper into this, I have something to offer that might deepen this," Lowe interrupted. "I came into new information last night. It was too late to get it to Chief Watts since Inspector Johnson put a curfew on me yesterday." He grinned and Johnson snorted in amusement.

"Go on, Sergeant," Reese said, looking genuinely curious.

"Ma'am, I met with a … I'll just say a CI," Lowe began, taking care not to identify Shannon Bridger. "Among other things I learned that Captain Luden is an elder with the Church of God's Law. But I've also learned that they're … I was told the church routinely horsewhips members who break with their rules."

"You're shitting me," Reese said.

"No, I am not," Lowe said. "The CI gave me a DVD yesterday that I've had no chance to view."

"Why not?" Reese asked.

"Ma'am, Inspector Johnson was worried that I wasn't rested enough," Lowe said. "I worked a 20-hour turn and when I initially met with the Inspector I was at the end of my rope. He told Lieutenant Capps to remove me from the building at 6:00, and Capps did exactly that. It has remained in my possession. I decided not to watch it at home since my wife was there, and I try to shield her from the more unpleasant aspects of my job."

"Well, why don't we go into the living room and put it in my DVD player?" Watts suggested.

There was a note in the case that Lowe read. It was from Bridger:

Sergeant,

This lady, Emma Thorne, was punished when no less than Elder Luden came to visit her and found her wearing shorts and a halter top in her house. She was alone at home waiting on an A/C repairman on a day when her A/C was totally out and the temperature outdoors was over 100 degrees.

Lowe read the note aloud to the assembled brass, and then put the DVD in the player. The video began with the end of a hymn, and then Quinn stepped into the pulpit. "Brothers and sisters, I'm afraid today must include some unpleasantness," he said. "Emma

Thorne was found in a state of immodesty, in very revealing clothes, when an elder stopped in to visit her, and he had no choice but to charge her with her offense. The elders recommended a punishment of 30 lashes, and I have agreed this sentence is appropriate. Emma, will you please come to the dais?"

A pretty woman, blonde and probably in her mid-twenties, nervously approached the dais. Two other women approached her and led her to a sturdy cross. Ensuring her back was turned to the congregation, they had her remove her blouse and bra, and offer her hands to cuffs dangling from the arms of the cross. Once the woman was cuffed, Quinn removed his coat and uncoiled a horsewhip.

"Sister Emma, this is an earned punishment," Quinn said in a somber tone. "I want you to consider how much more Christ suffered for your sins, and how disappointed He must be that you were strutting about your house like a strumpet, and how disappointed your husband Darren must be that you have humiliated him so." Without further preamble, he popped the whip on the air twice, and then began whipping the woman. From the first lash, she screamed piercingly, the echoes ringing through the chapel. She fainted on the eleventh stroke and was roused with ammonia, and then the whipping continued until the poor woman endured all thirty of her lashes, with several of her welts weeping blood. The two matrons approached and put a dressing on her back, then helped her from the post and put her blouse on her, and then half-carried her out a side door.

"Holy shit," Holmes breathed.

"Goddamn, I didn't need to see that," Walker said.

"Luden is a party to this?" Reese asked.

"Yes, Ma'am, he is, according to my CI," Lowe said. "Ma'am, I'd like to bring in undercover people to try to penetrate that place and learn what they can."

"I think that's wise," Reese agreed, looking deeply unsettled. She picked up her phone and dialed a number, wandering off to speak quietly with whoever she called, and then returned to the living room while Lowe was returning the disc to its case.

"Okay, it's probably going to take a couple or three days," Reese said. "The internal affairs units of several local agencies have pooled resources in a federally funded project. What we're going to do is send in a man and a woman to pose as a couple. We can create thorough backgrounds on them very easily but want time to train them up into character. Lowe, may I speak privately with you for a few moments?"

"Yes, Ma'am," Lowe said, and followed her down the hall to Watts' combined home office and man cave, a beautifully paneled room redolent of pipe and cigar smoke, with a monster of a television dominating one wall of the room.

"Lowe, what's the story on your CI?" Reese asked. "And can he help with the case, with getting our officers trained up?"

"Ma'am, I'm reluctant to risk burning this CI," Lowe said. "There's genuine worry of being murdered or … well, you saw the DVD."

"Think on this," Reese said. "Here's what I'm proposing …"

They talked for twenty minutes and Lowe nodded some, and then said he would contact his CI and get consent. Reese left the room and Lowe dialed Bridger.

"Shannon, we have an idea here," Lowe began. They talked for five minutes, and Bridger agreed to the suggestion. She was slated to work a half-day anyway, she said, and Lowe made a mental note to ensure she was paid well for her cooperation and risk.

At 9:15, as Lowe was getting to his office to meet his fresh-assembled squad and start their assignments, two patrolmen showed up at the Church of God's Law. "Are you Shannon Bridger?" one of them asked.

"Yes, Sir," she said. "What's wrong, officers?"

"Miss Bridger, we have a warrant for your arrest from a parking ticket," the officer said.

"A parking ticket?" she asked, sounding baffled.

"Yes, Ma'am, it was issued six months ago, when your car was ticketed parked and blocking a fire hydrant," the officer said.

"I never got a ticket," Bridger said truthfully.

"Ma'am, that's between you and the judge," the officer said. "I'm sorry, but you're under arrest."

"What's going on here?" Quinn said, coming out of his office.

"Police business, Sir," the second officer said. "It seems your secretary neglected to pay a parking ticket, and we have a warrant for her arrest."

"Look, I need her here," Quinn said. "How much is the ticket and can I simply pay the money to you? I can cut a check in just a moment."

"I'm sorry, Sir, but that's just not how it works," the first officer said. "Miss Bridger, please stand and put your hands behind your back."

"Shannon, call me as soon as you can and I'll get you out of jail," Quinn said, glaring at the officers.

"I'll get to the bottom of this," Bridger said. "I'm sorry, Shepherd. I'll call as soon as I'm able."

The officers helped her into the car and then drove sedately away to the jail, in case Quinn was following. At the jail she was led to an interview room and uncuffed, and a moment later, Reese walked in. "Okay, the cover story to give to Quinn is the car ticketed was one you'd sold a month before this happened," Reese began. "We looked at your records and it was a Nissan Sentra, and you drive something altogether different anyway. It's plausible."

"Thank you," Bridger said.

"Ma'am, we need to know everything about your church that you can tell us," Reese said. "We don't know what, if any involvement, they've had in these events, but from what we've learned by our own investigations and through you, we think the Church of God's Law needs close watching."

"And you're Inspector Reese?" Bridger asked. "Where is Sergeant Lowe?"

"Sergeant Lowe is meeting his task force but should be along soon," Reese said. "And yes, I am Inspector Amanda Reese."

"What are ... what do you do for the police?" Bridger asked.

"Miss Bridger, I am in command of the Internal Affairs Division," Reese said. "This first came to our attention because —"

"Because Elder Luden finally showed his ass," Bridger interrupted, chuckling.

"I think it's fair to say that he's in hot water," Reese allowed. "He had a job here in headquarters, but got transferred to an assignment generally recognized as one of the worst in the Department, an assignment from which he can only retire. He might last a few years in it spinning his wheels to get in the Chief's good graces, but ... yeah, he's doomed. Ma'am, it's still possible he could go to prison just for what he's done."

"What did he do?" Bridger asked.

"I'm not at liberty to discuss that, except to say he stuck his nose in where it wasn't wanted," Reese said. Reese personally knew Luden and was dubious about him. To be fair he'd always conducted himself in a gentlemanly fashion and his religious leanings didn't bother her, but he was known to be mean to subordinates, notably the women. It wasn't anything she could take to Human Resources to have him fired, but he'd been the subject of several internal complaints. Reese also realized just then that most of the complaints had come from officers who weren't Christian. At least seven of the names were Jewish and two were Islamic. She made a mental note to look into it.

"But you ... I'm going to guess you're going to send undercover people to the church," Bridger stated. "It's something where Shepherd Quinn says many are called but few are chosen. Church attendance is for members only, and there is a vetting process ..." Bridger and Reese spoke for an hour while the conversation was recorded, and Reese used a legal tablet to write a flurry of notes for later reference. After the hour, Reese suggested that Bridger phone Quinn.

"What's happening over there, Shannon?" Quinn asked, sounding genuinely concerned.

"Oh, do you remember that blue Nissan I had when I first came to work there?" Bridger asked.

"Yeah, I remember it," Quinn said.

"Well, the person who bought it didn't register it in his name, and a month after I sold it, the car was ticketed," Bridger said. "I called my roomie to raid my filebox at home and bring the bill of sale here. Fortunately I copied the signing of the title and had a notary stamp all of it, so once they have all of that, they'll bring me back to the church. They're being very nice about it. It'll just take a couple more hours to straighten out. A lawyer from the DA is here and tells me once I present the bill of sale, he'll drop the charges and go after the guy who bought the car."

"Well, I am delighted to hear you are not a scofflaw," Quinn said, and chuckled. "I know you have a half-day today anyway, but when you get back, look in and assure me they didn't use a rubber hose on you or something."

"I will, Sir," Bridger said. "I need to go now."

"Inspector, the trouble I have with this is that Shepherd Quinn really is a genuinely nice man," Bridger said. "He doesn't approve of unmarried women, or working women, but in spite of that he's mostly treated me well."

"He paddled you," Reese pointed out, looking and sounding irritable.

"He even hated doing it, but I guess Sergeant Lowe explained that to you," Bridger said.

Just then, Lowe entered the room and smiled at Bridger. "Thank you for coming in to help, Shannon," he greeted her. "If it means much, I understand your conflict. When I was a corporal in the army I had to report a sergeant, my superior and a good friend, for dereliction of duty. He lost two stripes and never spoke to me again, and it still hurts. But ... it had to be done."

"I've been twenty years in Internal Affairs," Reese contributed. "But when I was a lieutenant in this division, an officer came under investigation who had been my FTO when I was a rookie. He was like a father to me, but he'd started taking bribes. His son was ill with cancer and he was trying to fund the treatments. But I had to investigate him, and had to testify against him. He was lucky enough that his lawyer got him probation, but his career was shattered. He was a year shy of earning his pension, and the last I heard he's driving for a local freight company making a bit more than minimum wage. I feel guilty about that, but at the same time I have no question I did the right thing, Ms. Bridger."

"Call me Shannon, please," Bridger said. "I'm too young for people to call me Ms. and Ma'am." She chuckled sardonically. "I get what you're saying and I'm going to cooperate. I saw on the news that there were multiple victims in the house and five officers were killed. It needs to stop and whoever did it, and I don't care if it turns out to be my saintly old grandmother, needs to go to Death Row for it."

"Then we're in agreement," Reese said.

"We are," Bridger agreed. "Okay, let's get to brass tacks here …"

Two hours later, an officer drove her back to the Church of God's Law and she poked her head into Quinn's office, surprised to see Luden in there, looking tired and drawn. "It's all good, Shepherd," she grinned. "Hello, Elder Luden."

"Do you have a moment, Shannon?" Quinn asked.

"Sure," Bridger said.

"Have a seat, please."

"What's wrong?" Bridger asked.

"Miss Bridger, the church has recently come under some unfair scrutiny over that fire," Luden said. "I'm going to look into this 'warrant' for your arrest and learn if it was just coincidence – I don't tend to believe in coincidences in my career – or if you were singled out for police harassment. A detective was here and the

Shepherd thinks, with good reason, that the church is about to face persecution. Can you tell me, please, what happened?"

"In short, I sold a car a while back —" Bridger began, but was silenced when Luden held up his hand.

"I heard that tale from Shepherd Quinn," Luden interrupted, not unkindly. "What happened at the jail?"

"The details were laid out to me and I told them I sold the car before it was ticketed," Bridger lied, trying to stay calm. "I called my roommate and asked her to bring the file I kept on the sale of the car. A lawyer from the DA came to look at it, and then dropped the charge against me." Bridger knew the police were busy forging supporting paperwork and knew that when Luden looked into it he would find all in order and accordance with her tale. "They were very nice. Honestly, at least I can entertain friends with my exploits as an outlaw." She grinned, and even Luden smiled a bit at this.

"Even so, I want to take steps to ensure this wasn't a put-up or an attempt to harass the church," Luden said. "Did any church matters come up while you were there?"

"No, not really," Bridger said. "The attorney asked what I did at the church, but I just told him I was the secretary, and he nodded and wrote that on a legal pad. He asked if I liked the job and I told him yes, of course. But it was more about ... frankly, when I told them I'd sold the car long before the ticket was written, they seemed more embarrassed than anything."

"As well they ought," Luden remarked. "Miss Bridger, thank you for talking with us. I'll see if there's more I can learn about this."

"May I go?" Bridger asked, looking at her watch. "I have a doctor appointment in thirty minutes."

"Yes, you may," Luden said. "Thank you again for your time."

Bridger indeed had an appointment with her gynecologist, and had been warned she was likely to be followed, so she didn't even make a stop. Her appointment was at 1:45 and she got called to an exam room at 2:30 and didn't get out of the office until nearly 4:00.

EIGHT

"Shepherd, I don't like this," Luden said. "I'll admit being a policeman as long as I have has made me suspicious and maybe even paranoid, but this coincidence is a bit much to swallow."

"So look into it," Quinn said.

"I'll do the best I can, Shepherd, but … Chief Watts already told me he was on the verge of charging me for obstruction of justice," Luden said. "He's whistling in the wind on that, but it would mean I'd be fired. I could get reinstated after six or eight months of unions and lawyers posturing, but by then, this matter would be said and done, so I have to be more circumspect and careful. And I'm persona non grata at headquarters, back in a uniform working … well, you don't want to hear me whine … but I'm being watched and Watts is looking for any excuse to fire me. The precinct where I'm assigned is known throughout the Department as the place where captains are sent to die."

"What happened?" Quinn asked.

"I summoned that impudent Lowe to my office and suggested that I coordinate any further contacts from him with the church," Luden said. "He instantly reported me to Chief Watts, and a short time later I was more or less drummed out of headquarters in disgrace. I suppose in an earlier age they'd have cut off my epaulets and shattered my sword, and then marched me out while the drummer played the Rogues' March. I was told on no uncertain terms that I was not to touch this murder case. I was trying to protect the church, though. Looking through their eyes, I can admit they should have read me the riot act, but I think sending me to the 22nd was just cruel and unfair. Unfortunately, I have no recourse. But no captain ever got transferred back out of the 22nd, not in seventy years now. Captains there retire or die. I understand one of them even committed suicide. Sooner or later I'll retire and they'll move someone else there who's fallen into disfavor."

"I'm sorry to hear that," Quinn said. "Paul, I need you where you are, at least until this matter of the murder and arson is concluded. I'm sorry it has ended your career, but God works in mysterious ways, and I'm certain He'll take good care of you no matter your duties."

"I understand, Shepherd," Luden said. "All I'm telling you is that for me to remain with the police, I need to be far more circumspect moving forward, and I can do you absolutely no good from a prison cell. But … I have some ideas nonetheless."

"What can you tell me about this Detective Lowe?" Quinn asked.

"Under other circumstances I think I would like him," Luden said. "He's a veteran over 20 years, well-respected, spotless record. He made sergeant recently and was transferred to Homicide, and has been a fireball there. He and his superior, Lieutenant Darrell Capps, don't get along well at all. Just one of those personality conflicts, I'd suppose. But I looked into Capps and learned he's a sodomite, and hiding it so his own career doesn't wind up in splinters. I might be the only man in the department who knows this about Capps. One way or another, though, Lowe will get support from Capps, but answers to the chief's lackey, a woman named Miranda Holmes, his aide. But it means he answers, honestly, to Chief Watts. I heard a rumor the mayor is hot on this one too, since it's an election year and he'd rather look effective and tough on crime." Luden sneered a bit at this, his distaste obvious.

"How sad that even the police are infiltrated with such perverts as this man Capps," Quinn said. "And women belong at home with children and husbands."

"I agree, Shepherd, but the laws of this country protect them like a sow protects her cubs," Luden said, his expression showing his distaste. "Holmes ... to be fair she has three sons. One is an engineer with Halliburton and the other two are in college. She lost her husband – he owned an electrician company – about three years ago. A drunk in an 18-wheeler ran him over one afternoon. Rumors fly and who knows what's true, but the word is the trucking firm settled quickly with her and for a ton of money, and his cousin bought the electrician company from her. I do know her personal car is a BMW 7-series, and you don't buy that on police pay. I think even the deputy chief would struggle buying a car that expensive."

"Well, I know you need some sleep before your shift," Quinn said.

"I ... yes, Shepherd," Luden said, and stood, wincing.

"Are you okay?" Quinn asked.

"Yes, Shepherd, just some pain in my back," Luden said, and walked gingerly to his car, and then drove to his apartment.

NINE

"Ladies and gentlemen, for those of you who don't know me, I'm Chief Watts," Watts said to Lowe's flying squad. "I want you all to know that Sergeant Lowe enjoys my complete confidence, and despite departmental regulations, this flying squad will be run on his terms. He answers to Lieutenant Miranda Holmes and she answers to me. He has announced that Detective Walker is his second in command and that's how it is. I suspect that some of you may be senior to Walker and think you're entitled to be second in command here, but I don't care. I really don't care. You should all understand that regulations are not carved-in-stone law but only for guidance. Those of you who might be disgruntled at this can go to the union and find out I'm 100% correct, and those of you who find this state of affairs unacceptable may go to Detective Walker, who will arrange your transfers back to your routine duties with the appropriate remarks in your files that will see your careers taking unhappy turns. Additionally, I put out the word to your commanders that this assignment was not an opportunity to get rid of officers who weren't up to the job, and if any of you are seen by Sergeant Lowe or Detective Walker to be lacking, you will be returned forthwith to your routine duties, again with the appropriate remarks in your jackets.

"This is a critically important job," Watts continued. "I won't go into everything, but the simple fact is the death toll now is at least twenty, and quite probably more, and that includes five good police officers burned to death Are there any questions?"

Several hands went up and Watts pointed to one. "Sir, I'm Corporal Janis Lewis, from the 10th Precinct, a patrol officer. What are we supposed to be doing in this job?"

"I'll take that one, if I may," Lowe said, and Watts nodded. "Officer Lewis, right now we're working on identifying the victims and hoping there's a link we can find. We also need a lot of shoe leather on the ground around both crime scenes to see if anyone saw anything, any place where we can hang our hat. Right now we know practically nothing except that one of the CSU agents texted a few pictures to the CSU computers, and from the photos of the heads from the first crime scene, two were identified using facial recognition software. One was Roger Kurtz, on parole these last three years from a murder conviction. The other was Theodore Washington, on parole for rape. I'm going to assign one of you to see if these two can be linked together somehow, and others to learn all you can from their neighbors, employers, anyone who might have even ridden an elevator with either of these men. I will use you in whatever capacities I find necessary to breaking this case. People, this is a high death toll, and I'll repeat to you that five officers of this police department were killed in the first scene. Their funeral is in a few days at the football stadium, and we're expecting over two thousand officers from other agencies, one from 2,500 miles away, to be in attendance. It would be nice if they saw that this squad cares about those officers as much as they do."

More hands went up and Watts pointed to another officer, this one in his late-40s. "Sir, I'm Detective Jim Costlow from Robbery Division," the man said. "I'm not certain what a robbery detective is supposed to do in a case like this."

"Without sounding facetious, what Sergeant Lowe orders you to do," Watts said. "Look, detective work is detective work, Costlow. You know as well as I do that detective work is largely wearing out your shoes, knocking at doors and asking questions, and I am certain Sergeant Lowe will have plenty for you to do. I understand about twenty of you are detectives from one division or another."

"Yes, Sir," Costlow said, but didn't look happy. Watts took note of this, and saw on Lowe's face that so did he. An hour later, Costlow was detailed back to Robbery, and Lieutenant Holmes left remarks in his jacket that would see to it that Robbery was the best assignment he would ever have. Six months later, after a dispute with his sergeant that almost saw him coming to blows with his lieutenant, he was transferred to patrol in the 22nd Precinct. Four months after that, he hit his 20 years with the Department and filed for retirement.

After the meeting concluded, Lowe went to meet with Reese and Bridger. Once Bridger left, Lowe returned to his office and met several of the officers, including a corporal assigned to patrol in the 14th Precinct, a man named Tom Lemon, who seemed bright and motivated. Another corporal from the 6th Precinct, Gerald Tarkin, also seemed quite intelligent. Lowe named Lemon the evening supervisor and Tarkin the night supervisor, and randomly assigned 25 officers to each shift. This left him with 38 officers on day turn, but Lowe and Walker knew it was likely the other shifts would need more officers than they had.

A short time later, Lowe got a call from Inspector Reese. He drove to the local shopping mall, went into Sears and then came out of JC Penney, and entered a blue Caravan. The driver of the Caravan drove him to a house in a quiet neighborhood, and there, Lowe entered the rear of a cube van, where he sat in a seat much like that on an airliner, and rode to another location he couldn't identify, only knowing it was a biggish warehouse with a mock house inside it. He entered the house and met Reese, who was with several people, including a man and woman who both looked to be in their late 20s.

"Sergeant Lowe, meet John Morrow and Sarah Foster," Reese said, pointing to the young officers. "We're working on backgrounds for them as we speak, but as of now they are John and Sarah Avery. They're going to be trained intensively for several days – this house is an identical mockup of a house that will be their home, about twenty minutes from the Church of God's Law. John really is a veteran, so John Avery is too, complete to a purple heart and a few other medals for his work in the Middle East. John took his discharge from the Army, where he worked in disarming IEDs, and now he works for a private contractor under contract to the military. He works indirectly for the Department of Homeland Security, which has flagged his records to notify them, which in this case means us, of any and all inquiries. Sarah Avery is simply his housewife. John grew up in a church in Alabama much like the Church of God's Law, which is now defunct, and is delighted to find a similar church out here, where he will take his wife this Sunday to attend services. He will, of course, be sent away since he is not a member, and will then contact Shepherd Quinn Monday and arrange to meet with him and begin the membership process."

"You two listen to me," Lowe said. "Someone has already murdered five good cops in this case, and they will suffer no more penalty for killing more and more. It's like the Wild West outlaw who remarked he could only be hanged once. My CI tells me these people are, kindly, out-of-step with current culture, more aligned with Torquemada or the Puritans than with the likes of Billy Graham. They do routinely horsewhip women on their bared backs at Sunday services. I'm not sending you two in to be heroes, and I'd rather you blow your cover than get hurt or killed in this assignment. Is this understood?"

"Yes, Sir," both undercover officers said.

Reese pointed to two of her people. "Start drilling them," she ordered. "Lowe, come with me, please."

"I'm glad you reinforced that to them," Reese said a moment later in a spot remote from the two-story mockup house. "Your CI told me that they're thorough with new members, including home inspections and complete physical exams. Tattoos, in violation of holy writ, aren't allowed, for instance, and neither of these officers is tattooed anywhere. I honest-to-God hope they're safe in this one, but I also told them the moment a horsewhip comes near one of them to break cover and walk off. We have a house – this mockup is identical right down to the last detail of that house – for them, but you're better off not knowing it in case this case somehow brings you into contact with Mr. and Mrs. Avery. I hope they're in no danger, but this one worries me, Lowe. I'm suspicious of churches like this in any event, and these people seem almost a cult. Hell, I got a report a short time ago that Luden showed up at the church an hour after we got Shannon Bridger, and was on hand to meet her, and I would assume interrogate her, when she got to the church. Someone else, unidentified, came out of the church while Bridger was in there, and planted a tracking device on her car. We picked up the signal of the device, but I don't think she's being monitored otherwise. One way or another, her doctor appointment was legit, so that's fine and dandy.

"Meanwhile, John Avery just wrote a check to the local Ford dealer for two vehicles, a brand-new big pickup truck for himself and a run-of-the-mill car for his wife, both Fords. They refuse to buy foreign labels and Ford didn't need a government bailout, so they will only buy Ford, if anyone asks them," Reese continued. "We've backdated paperwork for the house where they'll be living and those papers were signed three days ago. They have receipts for a weeklong stay in a local motel and meals and the like. The movers should be at the new house in an hour, and we have receipts for all that as well."

"Wow, that's a lot of details to hold together," Lowe said, giving a low whistle of approval.

"Sometimes we even impress ourselves," Reese cracked, and chuckled. "The thing is, if they've suborned Luden to the point that he fucks himself over investigating them, he's going to have to dig damned deep until he hits a dead end. Sarah Avery stayed at home while her husband went overseas as a contractor with an oil company, doing security work and defusing IEDs. She stayed with John's parents in Birmingham, helping take care of them. We have those agents in place to verify and confirm these elements of the story. Basically, a lot of street cops hate the FBI with good reason, but for what we do, they can be an amazing resource, Mike. They have thousands of bios ready to rock, only requiring updated photos of the subjects. I'm kinda bending some of the rules here since our investigation is more about this church of psychos than Captain Luden, but I don't think I'm going to run into any trouble here since they handed the bios over to me and sent an agent from DC to work on intensive coaching of these officers. From here until the end of the investigation they're like method actors, trained to never step out of character. The car and truck will be delivered here and they will drive them home and pick up their lives. We have a team in a house across the street from them who'll monitor the comings and goings 24 and 7.

"Shannon told us one hell of a lot about this church and its expectations," Reese went on. "Among other things, women are utterly chattel to these people and sex is only for procreation, so any kind of birth control is an utter no-no. We've decided – these two only met today anyway – that John will have the master bedroom in the house, king-size bed, the whole schmeer, and Sarah will be in a small bedroom down the hall from him on a twin-size bed. She's getting the shit end of the stick through and through this assignment, but it's also that way when we've had to penetrate bike clubs with a couple and the female has to be the bitch to her old man. I keep reminding myself that this is far less dangerous than an undercover narcotics assignment, but still I worry."

"I do too," Lowe said. "I do too."

Just then, his phone rang and he answered. "Mike, this is Jay," he heard. "The S&T people have more for us and asked us to run to their area for them to show us what they've got."

"I'll be there in an hour," Lowe said. He rode back to the mall and his car, and drove to headquarters, and then to S&T's secure area, which was pretty much the entire fourth floor of the building.

"Okay, we're a long way from having all the parts identified," said Rodney Forrest. "But here's what we have so far. Facial recognition software identified a couple of the victims and you already have that information. But two of those parts had artificial joints. Few know this, but those are all serial numbered, a lot like a VIN on a car. So I introduce you to the artificial hip of Raphael Corrubias, who received the hip while in prison – Jesus, those jailbird assholes get better health plans than we do, all on our dime – and got paroled two years later. He served fifteen years of a twenty-year sentence for murder. The other is Catherine McCloud. She was —"

"I remember," Lowe interrupted. "She ran a string of bordellos around here, had about two hundred girls on the string. She got convicted for that, but the Feds really hammered her for the tax evasion angle. I think she got ten or so years, didn't she?"

"She did indeed, and served every day of it, and was released four years ago, and has an artificial knee from about two years ago," Forrest confirmed. "So far, everyone we ID'd has been a criminal of some sort, Sergeant. Make of that what you will, but from my chair I don't think Satanists would go around killing sinners."

"No, I don't think so either," Lowe agreed. He went straight to Holmes' office with this new information, and then called Reese with the new heads-up. One way or another, while a jury wouldn't buy it, the whole thing made the church look more suspect.

The fire marshal called and reported that the incendiary in the second fire was the same thermite as the first one. He also reported that he had spoken with the chief and that every station would have a truck full of sand nearby. As hot as thermite got, it fractured water into hydrogen and oxygen and only caused the flames to grow, so watering the flames wasn't going to help in these fires. Lowe wondered what the hell kind of situation was going on here. He spent the rest of the day going through reports, which all amounted to nobody saw or heard anything. With amused annoyance, he went on Amazon and ordered a totem pole of the see-no-evil-hear-no-evil-speak-no-evil monkeys to be delivered to his office. It reminded him of the Kitty Genovese story from long past. People didn't want to get involved. He figured it would make a nice desk ornament when he talked with frustrated officers. That done, he decided to call it a day when Holmes called.

"Come to Chief Watts' house in an hour, please," she said.

TEN

"My spokesperson started getting a lot of heat about these arson-murders," Mayor Youngblood said when Lowe arrived. "I figured I'd best bring you in on the political aspects of this situation, Sergeant. Yeah, I see your look of distaste and I entirely understand it, but you need to understand the stakes. This is an election year. In four months voters will go to the polls and choose from four contenders, and there will probably then be a runoff election. Now, I don't know how much attention you pay to all this, so if I seem like I'm going Dick-and-Jane, please forgive me.

"I flatter myself to think I'm a huge supporter of the police," Youngblood continued. "My opponents ... not so much. DeMarcus Washington has been a thorn in my side for the whole three years he's been a City Councilman. He wants oversight of all the police see, say and do. He's even opined that you should be armed only with tasers and has suggested, seriously, gutting the Police Department by about a third and use the money on social programs. And then there's Leo Suarez, who's seriously proposed firing every cop who can't speak Spanish. He wants to turn this all into a sanctuary city for all the wretched refuse coming north from Central America, and sees to it that every illegal arrested here is undercharged for their crimes. About a third of the Hispanics in the department think he's the Second Coming of our Risen Lord and Mexico uber alles and all that bullshit, while the rest of them see him as another blowhard, which he is. And then there's Lydia Marson, who also wants to gut the police and hand off many of the duties to the county or even the state. She thinks we should all be uniformed Officer Friendly, no detectives, and at most we should be armed with .38 Special revolvers, and certainly no body armor, SWAT units or tactical gear. I hope you shudder to think of any of those clowns being in power here, Sergeant."

"It would be damaging, I agree," Lowe said. The truth was, while Youngblood was mostly supportive of the police, he had also reduced the pension plan in his first term and had stricken many items the police asked for in their budget, including a huge reduction in vehicular purchases, which meant many patrol cars were being held together with spit and baling wire. It was growing more and more common for officers to be doubled up in cars because the motor pool was full of vehicles requiring this repair or that. But he agreed that Youngblood was the best of a bad lot of options. Washington was their own homegrown variety of Marion Berry. Suarez, also on the City Council, was no better. Marson, an academic so left-leaning that she needed jackstands on that side to keep her from falling over was, simply, a lunatic. But very few took her seriously and she was unlikely to win the election anyway. Lowe figured the black community was bigger than the Hispanic, and had enough votes to force a runoff, so he figured the runoff would be Youngblood versus Washington. But he knew enough about Washington to know it would be disastrous if he won.

"City Council meets tomorrow at noon, and they're going to turn the heat up," Youngblood continued. "In truth, Washington and Suarez will be delighted to see these murders continue until Election Day to get rid of me. So I'm going to reiterate to you that what you need is yours for the asking, Sergeant. I'll even call the governor and ask him to send the National Guard in here if you think you need them."

"I don't think we're to that point yet," Lowe chuckled. "Sir, we do have some leads and information developing and it just takes time. Unfortunately, the real world isn't an episode of *CSI* where the crime is solved in an hour, including commercials. Christ, I really do wish I could get DNA information in ten minutes."

"Sergeant, you're being entrusted with extraordinary authority in this case," Watts said. "The truth is, I'm about to put out the order to double the size of your task force, and that's the size command that would be handed to a captain if not an inspector. It's a lot of spaghetti to put on one fork. To that end, I looked into the latest sergeant exam, and your man Walker made fourth. I am going to hold a ceremony tomorrow and promote the top seven since we have spaces for them. But that will give Walker a bit more horsepower as your deputy. I'm also going to detail a half-dozen S&T officers just to you and this matter, as well as your own 5-officer CSU team, who will be on 24/7 call for your cases. Something in my gut tells me this is going to get one hell of a lot worse."

"I think so too, Sir," Lowe said. "One interesting facet is that we've identified four bodies, two from facial recognition software and two from surgical implants, and all four were convicted felons, including Catherine McCloud."

"Implants?" Watts asked.

"Cloudy Cat?" Youngblood asked simultaneously.

"Yes, Sirs," Lowe said. "Ms. McCloud had an artificial knee. Apparently they're all serial numbered, and that's how she was ID'd.

Another had an artificial hip emplaced at taxpayer expense in the prison system."

"Are you thinking vigilantes, then?" Watts asked.

"It seems likely," Lowe allowed. "We're taking a very close look at —"

"I think Mayor Youngblood would rather be in a position of saying he doesn't know what we're doing," Watts interrupted. Youngblood nodded at this.

"I understand, Sirs," Lowe said.

"I think that's all we have right now, Lowe, unless you have something more to add?" Watts asked.

"That was all," Lowe said.

"Dismissed, Sergeant."

ELEVEN

Lowe was awakened at 2:15 by his phone. It was Walker. "Mike, there's another report of dead bodies in a vacant house on Jordan Street, 122 Jordan. Fortunately the FD has a station a half-mile away and has a sand-truck headed right over."

"I'm on my way," Lowe said, climbing from bed and putting on jeans and sneakers.

"Careful out there, Mike," said Lisa, who had been awakened by the phone. "God, I wish you'd just retire already."

"I'm too young for that," Lowe said, putting his holster on his belt. "Lord, what would I do with myself, Lisa? I'm a cop, used to be a soldier, and few of those skills are of use anywhere in the civilian world."

"Yeah, I've heard it all before," Lisa chuckled. "I love you, Mister. Be careful out there. I'm really hoping you die in bed here in about 40 years or so."

"The way I feel with my arthritis and all, I'm hoping for more like 20 and then God can parole my battered old self," Lowe cracked.

"Asshole," Lisa chuckled. At 38, she was still spry and vigorous and Lowe often wondered what she saw in him, but he knew he loved her like he'd never loved any other woman, and was in this with her for the long haul.

The thermite devices went off right as the dump-truck full of sand arrived, followed by two pickup trucks full of wheelbarrows, shovels, and firefighters. The truck dumped its load and the firemen hurriedly filled wheelbarrows and wrestled them into the house right as the devices started firing. The sand helped smother the thermite, and the other flames were readily contained. Lowe was excited that the fire was fairly rapidly under control and evidence could be collected. The CSU team assigned him was already standing by, simply awaiting clearance by the FD and bomb squad. The bomb people with their dogs found no explosives, and the CSU people were cleared to enter the building. Five minutes later, one of them staggered out, fell to all fours in the grass, and vomited violently. He spat a few times and stood weakly, and then found Lowe, marched up to him, handed him his badge, and wandered away. A few minutes after that, the lead CSU officer came out of the house, and beckoned to Lowe.

"This is fucked up, Sergeant," she said. "I think you need to see this now." She pulled the chip from her camera and stuck it into a laptop in the CSU van, and showed Lowe the pictures she had snagged. There were several pieces, of course.

"Jesus, our killer is equal opportunity, isn't he?" Lowe observed. "It looks like all races around, male and female."

"Yes, Sir, it does," said the tech, a woman Lowe's age with thirty years on the job. Her name was Kelly Brock. "But look at these. These six torsos – we're estimating parts of nine bodies, perhaps more, but at least the nine – but these have all been … Sir, they've been scourged. Savagely whipped. I wouldn't be surprised if several of them bled to death under these lashings. This isn't S&M,

Sergeant. This is just … I don't even know what to call it, but these poor fuckers were tortured to death."

"Scourged, like Christ," Lowe said, unaware he'd spoken aloud.

"Does this mean something to your case, Sergeant?" Brock asked.

"Yeah, it kind of does, or I think it does," Lowe answered. "Okay, am I needed in the house, Kelly?"

"No, Sir," Brock said. "By the way, just to save you a couple or three steps, I noticed tape cut away from the front door identifying the house as condemned, so probably the city owns this one, Sir."

"Thanks," Lowe said. He looked at his watch and saw it was 4:40 in the morning and knew there was no sense in running home only to sleep an hour, so he drove to his office and typed at a report and his impressions of the crime scene. Walker arrived at 6:00.

"This is bad, Mike," Walker said. "Christ, I swore off the booze three years ago and I swear right now I'd give my left nut for a half-gallon of vodka to blot this off my mind. When I was eleven years old I went to visit kin in Iowa and my cousin and I snuck into a slaughterhouse. I turned green then and I'm damn near that bad now, man. That's what it reminded me of, those people slaughtering and parting out pigs."

"It's worse than that, Jay," Lowe said. "Brock showed me initial photos. The bodies were scourged, skin flayed off of them like we read happened to Jesus Christ, or thousands of poor souls who ran afoul of the Cossacks in Russia once upon a time."

"God fucking damn," Walker said. "I was raised Baptist and I remember us seeing *Passion of the Christ* when it hit the theaters. You kept hoping at the last minute the cavalry would ride to the rescue. That one made me sick too. I think we're all going to need PTSD counseling when this is said and done."

"Probably," Lowe allowed. His cell rang and he saw it was Holmes, which came as no surprise. "Get on out of here, Jay. We're on this one now." Walker left and Lowe answered his phone.

"Chief Watts wants updates from you over breakfast every morning now," she said. "Can you be at his house at 7:00?"

"There was a third one overnight," Lowe said.

"Oh, shit," Holmes exclaimed.

"Yeah, that's just about my reaction too, Lieutenant," Lowe said. "I've been on the job since a little after 2:00 this morning. I'm just wearing jeans and a shirt. Do I need to climb into a suit first?"

"Not over breakfast," Holmes decided. "But after, you should go home and shower and change, yeah."

TWELVE

"I don't know what happened that the house didn't burn," the woman said. She was already naked and kneeling before the post, fully expecting another beating for her failure. "But I have no excuse to offer."

"The police and fire departments aren't stupid," the man said. "Once they knew it was thermite, they knew how to defeat it. They poured sand on the devices, which smothered them. I was taught to do that with fires when I was a Boy Scout. Put your dress on. You won't be punished for what isn't your fault."

"Yes, Sir," the woman said, rising and hurriedly dressing herself, grateful to the man for his mercy, which she thought she didn't deserve. "Thank you for your mercy."

"From this, they'll start learning of the cleansing we are doing, one bit at a time," the man said. "They might even empathize with us, but that won't stop them from trying to hunt us down and persecute us, especially since you killed five of their own."

"I deserved the flagellum for that," the woman said. "Maybe for my own pieces to be scattered with the others and a note saying it was me that killed the officers."

"Yes, you did, and still do, but I intend on doing far more and you're necessary to my plan," the man said. "But perhaps you need the flagellum, a few lashes to teach you further."

The woman didn't answer. She simply shed her attire and raised her wrists to the cuffs on the post. The man cuffed her and retrieved the flagellum, one that had seen a great deal of action. "Ten lashes," he said. The woman shivered and bit her lower lip. She'd seen many lashings with this item and knew this just might kill her. Two of their prey had died with but 12 strokes applied, although most of them lasted far longer, to their misfortune.

The beating was gruesome, and she screamed so hard at the first lash she could only groan and hiss through the next six, when she fainted. The man kept lashing her until the ten were applied, and then put coagulant and two trauma dressings on her back. And then he took her from the post and carried her to the cell. The woman weighed about 130 pounds and the man could bench press thrice that, so she was no effort. In the cage, he laid her gently on the cot and then went to the first aid box he kept there. He set up an IV bag of Ringer's Lactate and in a moment had an intravenous line dripping into her to help replenish volume. He taped it in place and then set the drip to 80 milliliters per hour, which meant the bag would last about 12 hours.

He had sprouted another erection and was starting to hate himself. When it had been that strumpet McCloud woman he had grown hard, and with two other whores he had executed, but that was to be expected. He'd even raped one of the women before lashing her to death. But it was wrong to get hard for the young woman in the cell, and he frowned, knowing he needed more discipline than he could self-inflict. But he was too tired right now.

He fell into his bed, swearing he would place a call to someone who would do what was necessary, and fell instantly asleep.

He was instantly with her in the barn, and put her on all fours, and fucked her like a whore he'd had several times during a long-ago shore leave in Po City, when he was a Navy Corpsman. He thrust in and out of her, hard and fast, and they came together, and he instantly woke, his seed still spurting into his underwear. It was the first wet dream he'd had in over twenty years, and he hated himself as he rose from bed, stripped, and showered himself clean. He returned to bed moments later. Yes, corrective measures would be necessary, he knew. He would have been astonished had he returned to her cage.

The woman, perhaps in spite of or because of her pain, masturbated, and went through three orgasms before exhaustion claimed her once and for all. She loved the man and wished she was fully his instead of just his servant. But she knew that wasn't possible. They both had a higher purpose to serve than one another.

THIRTEEN

Five minutes into the drive home, John Avery's phone rang. It was Sarah. "Look, now that we're away from the headhunters and all, we need to talk," she said in a nervous tone. "Meet me at Axton Park – it's about two minutes ahead. I'll park by the duck pond."

"Okay," John agreed, curious. He piloted the monster Ford F-250 through the park to the duck pond and parked it. He'd never driven a truck this big before, and indeed his personal car parked at his little one-bedroom apartment was a four-year-old Dodge Dart he'd bought for a song, with nearly 200,000 miles on it now, formerly the car of a road warrior of a route salesman. Already, with just a very few miles in the brand-new truck, he knew he liked the behemoth of a 4x4 and would miss it when this assignment ended.

Sarah exited her car and went to a picnic bench, looking contemplatively at the pond. About a hundred yards offshore, a couple was in a rowboat, seeming as though they were enjoying their afternoon. "So what's up?" John asked as he sat beside her.

"Bona fides," Sarah said simply. "It's something none of the IA people would suggest, even at gunpoint, but we have to look the part to these people. I mean, if we were going undercover as biker and bitch to infiltrate their culture, you'd need to shag out in a beard and long hair and get a few tattoos, and I'd have to tramp up in low cut shirts and tight jeans. If we were trying to infiltrate white-collar circles we'd be in expensive clothing and jewelry and those two Fords would be Beamers or Bentleys. Now, they got our sizes and have closets full of clothes for us, all things that the church would approve. From here on in, we're in a protocol like theirs, where I call you 'Husband' and not John. Are you tracking me so far?"

"I am," John said, but still curious where this was going.

"I've been thinking of all that stuff the CI told them, whoever he or she is," Sarah said. "The physical exams are specifically on my mind, as well as the video of that woman being horsewhipped. These people are big into discipline and husbands disciplining their wives. Now, my husband has just returned after a long stint working overseas, right?"

"Yeah, and?" John asked.

"After a year apart, do you think the wife in such a marriage would just be raring to go, or do you think maybe she'd have a few bumps in the road re-adapting to her husband's return and re-establishment of his rules?" Sarah asked, her tone making it clear she felt like she was talking to a backward child.

"Are you seriously suggesting I spank you?" John asked, shocked to his core.

"I am seriously suggesting you beat me hard enough that when they examine me, I'm wearing marks that I will have to explain in sheepish terms to whoever examines me, John," Sarah said simply. "Look, this assignment could be a career-maker, but if we're blown before we're allowed inside the doors, we'll be in uniforms writing parking tickets Monday morning and we'll probably never get the chance again to shine. I know this Inspector Reese would freak the fuck out, but a few welts and bruises fade a lot faster than a biker tattoo, John. I don't think five years down the line I'll need a laser to erase the marks of you taking a strap and some switches to me."

"Jesus H. Christ," John breathed, still shocked.

"John, I hate sounding like Yoda or Darth Vader, but search your feelings and you'll know it to be true," Sarah said, doing a comical Yoda voice coupled with a grin.

The truth was, John found her to be highly attractive and was already fighting with himself not to let the little head make decisions. And he'd long held fantasies, thus far unrequited, of bending a woman over his knee and paddling her thoroughly before ...well ...doing what men do. He felt himself growing erect and decided he had to be honest with his partner. No matter what may come, their lives could depend on it.

"Sarah, I realize I might be blowing this up before it ever launches," he said after a moment of gathering his guts. "But I know we need to know and trust one another fully and completely. If you decide to go right back to Reese and say no-can-do, I'll understand."

"Go on, John," Sarah said.

"First and foremost, I find you highly attractive and appealing, Sarah," John said. "I've been telling myself since we met not to make a pass at you and a fool of myself."

"I'm flattered," Sarah returned, blushing. The truth was that she found him highly sexy in return.

"And I've ... I've always had S&M fantasies," John confessed, unable to look Sarah in the eye.

"John, do you think you're the only one ever?" Sarah asked. "I think one hell of a lot more people try it than will admit it, but I agree it's not for everyone. Look, if you're worried you'll get an erection, stop worrying. You probably will, and that's flattering to me. And it's a safe bet if you stick a finger inside me before you start you'll find me quite wet. Maybe afterwards too. Believe me, this is new territory to both of us. That means me too, John. How often do you think I suggest something like this, after all? But ... I think it would cement us in their minds as legitimate, and I get the idea these sons of bitches are awfully paranoid. We already know one of their parishioners tried to disrupt that aspect of the investigation, someone tied in to the police department. I don't know why the secrecy since we're bound to find out anyway." And then her tone changed, became meek.

"But that's beside the point, Husband. I know I have disappointed you since you returned from away, and I deserve and expect harshness from you to put me on the straight and narrow path. I'm going to nudge this a bit further, John. It's going to happen one way or another, and I would far rather use it as trust-building with my partner than a cold business transaction with a dominatrix whose number I have."

"You've done this before?" John asked.

"No, but I looked some up on my smartphone when this idea dawned on me several hours ago," Sarah said honestly. "John, we need to know and trust one another, because I think one misstep is going to really fuck us up on this assignment."

"I ... Jesus, you go right for the jugular, don't you?" John remarked.

"My dad and big brother taught me to play poker and to kick ass and take names," Sarah chuckled. "But this is the highest stakes I've ever played for, John."

"How do you want to do this?" he asked.

"I'll be home in two hours, Husband," she said, then kissed his cheek, got into her car, and left while John drove home to oversee the last of the move-in. The house was beautiful, John thought, with five bedrooms spread across 3,700 square feet on a 2-1/2 acre spread, complete to a three-car garage and a big barn toward the back of the property. Several willow and oak trees were scattered about the spread, and midpoint between the back of the house and the barn was a monster of a pecan tree. In all, John loved the place and already knew he'd miss it when the assignment concluded. He remembered his brother Lionel, an EMT, had run a kid once who went with his parents to a seafood restaurant, and devoured a shrimp feast only to learn soon after he was allergic to shrimp. The kid made it, but Lionel remarked it was sad for the kid to find something he loved that much only to learn it would be forever denied him. John knew he'd never be able to afford living like this on a cop's salary and began wondering if he shouldn't explore other careers. Between VA and Hazelwood benefits he could go to college and get his degree. He knew it was a lot of time and work but even wondered about becoming a pharmacist. They made good money, but just looking at it, it looked like boring work. He had been courted by private security firms, but he honestly never wanted to see the Middle East again. But he'd left the Army with few marketable skills, as so many combat soldiers did, and the police seemed a natural fit.

The movers finished their job and left. He and Sarah would need to unpack things, but it was little of concern, a few boxes of dishes and kitchen goods, and a few boxes of clothing. The Department had even sent in people to mount a big-screen TV on the wall. He had been warned to only get basic service and make sure he was only running family-appropriate programming so that he wasn't suspect when the church loonies came by to visit and snoop about. Another thing they'd been warned about via the CI Lowe had cultivated was that these people would search their home to ensure John and Sarah weren't in current violation of church law, and they had studied photocopies of the church's law book, which John found unsettling. It was beyond intrusive. Reading between the lines, the church seemed to consider its members to be property. But then, John considered, so did the Mafia and street gangs and motorcycle clubs, and for that matter, the Police Department too. But the PD was unlikely to demand entry into his house without a warrant and then wander about the place.

Sarah arrived and whispered in his ear, and he nodded. They unpacked and he told her to start washing windows, and she snapped, on cue. "I'm tired. I'll do it tomorrow, Husband."

"Get to the barn out there," John said evenly. "I'm going to have to reassert my place and yours in this marriage. Go!"

In the barn he found items she had bought. "You sure about this?" he asked.

"It needs to be real," Sarah said. She'd hit an adult store, a feed store, and a hardware store, and probably parted with a huge amount of money. "I need to still be wearing marks in a few days, John, when they give us our physicals. There is a paddle in there, a riding crop, a rattan cane – I'm told those are notably painful – a razor strop, a quirt, or if you want, I can go cut willows and strip them. It's probably best if you get my back and my butt and thighs. Jesus, I can't believe I'm doing this, but ... I think it'll do a lot to make us look the part, so to speak. The last time my parents took some switches to me was when I was fourteen and played hooky with three friends from school. One of them boosted a bottle of Jack from her dad's liquor cabinet and we got drunker than old Cooter Brown in a park a half-mile from the high school. The truant officer found us and hauled us to the police station. They did a Breathalyzer on me and I blew a .215, which still astounds me. We all had to pay fines and do community service for our several misdemeanors, and we were all suspended from school for two weeks, but when I got home, I had to go cut twenty switches as long as I was tall, and they wore those switches out on me. I never misbehaved again."

"My old man never spared the rod either," John said, then flashed a wry grin. "But I have to admit I always had it coming."

"So did I," Sarah agreed, and then began stripping from her clothing. Once naked, she grasped the top rail of a stall gate, and then took a couple steps back to shift her weight to it, so that evasion would be clumsy. "Please, let's just do this before I lose my nerve, John."

John selected the paddle, a half-inch-thick fraternity-style paddle made of mahogany, and approached. He steeled his nerve and then spanked her with it, not counting, just spanking while she sobbed and howled and her butt grew red and started to purple, and then set the paddle aside.

"God, that hurts," Sarah wept. "My back too, John. I want them to believe one hundred percent in us. Just ... not something that will break bones."

John selected the strap. "I'm sorry, Sarah," he said, and then swept her blonde locks from her back and gave her fifteen lashes while she howled anew, doing her best to hold her place. He couldn't help noticing her firm and toned body and was mortified that he had grown erect by the time he was done, setting the strap aside.

"Thank you, Husband," Sarah said. "I will endeavor to be a better wife." Surprising him, she came to him and kissed him, and then groped him. And then she went to her knees and undid his pants. "May I take care of this, please?" John nodded, his mind awhirl, and in a second his member was deep in her mouth as she took him, taking her time to build him up, before finally going for the climax. He cried out as he came, erupting hugely into her while she desperately swallowed.

"Good Lord, that was amazing," John breathed a few moments later.

"Well, there was this one time at band camp," Sarah said, and then giggled, groaning. "It even hurts to laugh, Husband."

"Forgive me?" John asked.

"I … Husband, I deserved it, and it makes me a better wife if I am disciplined and obedient," Sarah said. "Forgive you? Husband, I thank you for this. Might I dress myself, Husband, and work on the windows now?"

"Yes," John said, wanting to talk more but understanding they could only be out of character far from here. Sarah dressed herself and went to the house, and got busy with Windex, polishing the kitchen windows to spotlessness. John went and showered, feeling uneasy in his role but knowing he needed to warm up to it very quickly, and went downstairs.

"You'll need to go grocery shopping tomorrow, but since there's no food here, we're going to go out for supper," he announced. "I saw a steak place out on the highway, Saltgrass or something like that. We'll go there."

"Yes, Husband," Sarah said, and followed him meekly to his truck. It was a magnificent steak, although John had to remind himself that he couldn't order a beer as he wanted to do, and limited himself to water. On the way home, Sarah asked if they could go take a little walk through Axton Park, and John agreed, piloting the truck in, and parking it.

"John, it's ... I've held a black belt since I was sixteen, and I'm 3rd degree now," Sarah said. "I keep current on it at a dojo near here. I've become pain tolerant, more than most people. I've been punched in the face a few times, and once got so battered up it took two weeks for the bruises to fade. But I mostly heal quickly. Cut my leg shaving and it's healed up the next day, for instance. There honestly is nothing to forgive, okay?"

"Thank you," John said.

"Besides, I guess I'm kind of kinky too," Sarah said. "I've never been that horny in my life as when you did that to me and then I sucked you down. Now, I know the church is death on what we did, the oral thing, and death on contraception, so we'll have to be careful. But I have a doctor appointment Monday. I've been getting quarterly shots for birth control and I'll get the shot updated and that will keep me safe for about three months. My husband is horny after so long apart from me and should fully enjoy his spousal rights." She grinned and gave him a little kiss.

"I think my wife has great understanding of husbandly needs," John agreed.

"Meanwhile, if this grows hard again, perhaps I can please you again with my mouth, Husband," Sarah grinned. "It's one way of keeping a wife from talking, right, Husband?"

"Indeed," John agreed, chuckling.

"Let's head on home," Sarah said. "One way or another I'm tired."

FOURTEEN

Lowe arrived to his office at 5:00 and reviewed his e-mail, and was pleased to see that all the bodies from the third incident had been identified, thirteen in total, with no leftover parts. All thirteen, unsurprisingly, had convictions on their records. One was a burglar, two were convicted of robbery, six were rapists, three had convictions for prostitution, including one transvestite, and one was a murderer. Lowe frowned as he considered this information. In a big way, most of these were good riddances, but the law didn't afford for executions of all criminals, and the truth is, if Lowe had it his way prostitution would have been long since legalized, freeing up cops for far weightier issues. And one way or another, all thirteen of these poor fuckers were murdered, and the murderers, no matter their motivation, needed to be brought to justice.

He sighed and closed his computer, and then drove to Chief Watts' house, uneasy to suggest what he was about to suggest, but pleased he at least had some place to hang his hat now. He arrived and was glad it was just Holmes and Watts this time and not an audience of other superiors.

"Did anything new come up?" Holmes asked.

"Actually, yes, Ma'am," Lowe said. "Every victim we've identified has been someone with a criminal record, heavy on rapists and murderers, but several prostitutes to include one transvestite. It appears – mind you, we know more from the third scene than we'll know about the other two – that these people were tortured to death, scourged like Christ was scourged. Considering the angles with Luden and the Church of God's Law, they bear closer watching. Reese has two officers undercover to penetrate the church, and I would guess she'll tighten surveillance on Luden in the meantime. But unless Luden proves to be our killer, he's not my problem, strictly speaking.

"This brings me to the victim pool," Lowe said uneasily. "We ... we need to find out who's missing among parolees in the area, but we also need to keep tabs on them, see if any get kidnapped. I know in a way the killers – this cannot be one person doing all this unless it's all he does and he has automation for his process – they're doing a public service in a way, but I'm afraid this is going to escalate more and more. Three of the victims lived in neighboring cities and two others were from neighboring counties, so our city limits don't mean anything to the killers either. But at the end of the day, these animals also killed five good cops, and I want them, Chief Watts. I want their heads mounted on my wall."

"One moment, please," Watts said. He dialed his phone and put it on speaker.

"Hiya, Aaron," a male voice said.

"Zach, I need some help here," Watts said. "How soon can you be to my house?"

"I'm actually in DC at a conference right now," said Sheriff Zachary Moore. "I won't be home for two days. But let me call Freda Thackery and see if she can be there. Give me a moment and I'll call back."

Watts waited quietly for two minutes when his phone rang again, and he put it on speaker again. "Chief Watts, this is Freda Thackery," the woman said. She was the undersheriff of the county sheriff's department, Moore's second-in-command.

"Freda, we have a situation here in the city," Watts said. "I need you to come out to my place as quickly as you can. It's something I'd rather not discuss by phone."

"Sure, Aaron," Thackery said. "I'm in my car already and ten minutes from you."

"If you haven't had breakfast —" Watts began.

"I haven't," Thackery said.

"I'll have the cook here handle that for you," Watts told her.

"It's a deal," Thackery said. "I'll see you soon, Aaron."

Watts asked the cook to prepare a fourth breakfast, and six minutes later his doorbell rang. Holmes answered the door and admitted Thackery. She was a striking woman, in her mid-forties, with white hair worn in a single braid halfway down her back, trim and beautiful in a skirt-and-jacket. She and Watts embraced one another and she took a seat at the table. "You already know Miranda," Watts said. "This other gentleman is Sergeant Mike Lowe. He's —"

"In charge of the investigation into those multiple murders," Thackery finished, her piercing green eyes appraising Lowe. "How do you do, Sergeant?"

"Very well, thank you, Ma'am," Lowe said.

"When I heard through the grapevine that you were running this case, I asked a few questions," Thackery said. "I figured the odds were high that Aaron would want us cooperating since crooks mostly don't give a damn about city limits. The word on you is you're a good investigator, a good cop with the right instincts. One of my people said we really should try to poach you over to the SO." She smiled and so did Lowe.

"You poach him and I'll skin you alive," Watts chuckled, and then turned serious. "Sergeant, go on and tell Freda what you told us."

Lowe told her what he knew, and his suggestions, while Thackery listened quietly, nodding here and there through his recitation. He finished and looked expectantly at her.

"I agree with you, Sergeant Lowe," she said. "I'll get people on this immediately, learn who's missing – I have good contacts with the parole officers throughout the county. I'll also contact the sheriffs of the neighboring counties and see what's what with them, but we'll be on his one. I think most of those criminals ... well, we're better off without them. But no way can we let cop killers walk away unscathed. These people need to be on death row and waiting for a date with a needle. Aaron, you know I speak for Zachary on this one. Whatever it is you need of the SO is yours for the asking. And he and I keep good relations among the neighboring county sheriffs, so I'll be tearing up the phone lines as soon as I'm in my office."

"Thank you, Ma'am," Lowe said.

"Many thanks, Freda," Watts said, the warmth and fondness for her manifest in his tone. The four ate their breakfasts and then parted ways.

Back in his office, Lowe read report after report that said nothing. The cops wearing out shoe leather were consistently coming up with nobody saw or heard anything, whether they did or not. Near the end of his day he heard from Thackery herself. There were thirty people in the county, outside the city limits, who seemed to have skipped parole. One, a former robber named Dirk Chatman, had been reported missing by his frightened wife. Chatman was one of those rare few who seemed to have straightened out in prison, learning carpentry skills in his four years there. On parole these last four years, he had a wife, a good job, a son two years old and another child on the way. He was well-regarded by his boss and coworkers. In six neighboring counties, five other parolees within the profile Lowe had developed were missing. It was harder to know about the prostitutes, who weren't altogether stable citizens in any event and just disappeared sometimes, often passed about from pimp to pimp to pay off debts, little different than livestock or trading cards.

He got a call from the coroner's office with a tidbit of interesting information. "Sergeant, your killer is a southpaw," the technician said. "I don't know how much it's going to help until you have a list of suspects, but you're looking for a leftie. Also, something else unusual … in what we've recovered, none of the skulls still had their right eyes, and we have yet to recover a right hand."

"Well, that narrows it down some," Lowe said, wondering why alarm bells were going off in his head at this news, but knowing the reason would bubble to the surface on its own in time. Tired from his day, he reached into a drawer of his desk and poured a small glass of Jack Daniels, then drank it, logged off, and drove home to Lisa.

FIFTEEN

While Lowe was reading reports, Dirk Chatman was dragged from a cage to a post, and tied to it. He was naked and afraid, but overpowered by three huge men. "Mr. Chatman, you broke with important laws, and one of God's Ten Commandments," a man said behind him. "You have rejected all goodness, and you are now to face the Lord's justice, made to understand what our Savior suffered for us before you are killed and dismembered."

"I'm not that man anymore!" Chatman protested. "Look, I accepted Christ in prison. I've changed. I have a wife, a son, and my wife is pregnant. I have become productive."

"Save it," the man said. "You may have been punished by man's law but not God's. But since you claim to follow Christ, you may have a moment to pray to Him to accept your soul into Heaven."

The man was surprised as Chatman indeed began to pray in earnest, citing many passages from the Bible, Old Testament and New, but the sentence was passed and would not be withdrawn. When Chatman ran out of air the lashing began, the flagellum effortlessly slicing his skin, as Chatman howled in agony, still praying to God to be delivered from this beating. But the die was cast, and the lashing continued, inexorable and cruel, as Chatman endured God's Justice. It took fifty-six lashes in all before he bled to death.

And then he was uncuffed from the post, and a hoist lifted him by his ankles as another man opened Chatman's throat with a well-practiced slash from a machete, letting the rest of the blood drain from the wretch.   Saws were brought in, and in moments, Dirk Chatman was in pieces, his right hand lopped off and his right eye was removed. These went into a burn pit and were incinerated to only ashes with a smaller thermite device, and then the ashes were scattered to the four winds. His parts went into a huge walk-in meat freezer, the contents of which had been emptied earlier in the day into a huge refrigerated truck.

Late that night, near 11:00, three men departed in the truck for a selected house, this time in a neighboring suburb, another condemned house. The house was entered easily enough – most locked doors were a joke to one of the men, a skilled lock picker – and the parts scattered about the three-bedroom frame house. Thermite devices were set throughout the house, and as the truck left, the woman dialed the phone number, and the devices all fired perfectly. Inside ten minutes, as the first call went out to the fire department, the house collapsed in on itself. It would be six hours before the fire was put out, and six more until bones were found and the police called, in this case a harried detective of the quiet bedroom community named Jim Dundee, who instantly saw his small department was overwhelmed. He called in homicide people from the sheriff near sundown.   Another four hours passed before someone remembered a memorandum from the undersheriff, and a call was placed to Lowe late in the afternoon. Uncertain what to do with a crime outside his jurisdiction, Lowe phoned Holmes, who reluctantly phoned Thackery and established a multi-county task force under the auspices of the PD, and under the general command of Sergeant Michael Lowe.

The task force got the call and Walker took the call, quickly ascertaining that the crime scene was ruined and there was little the task force could do. Thackery had promised thirty deputies to the task force in the morning, and Walker decided to let his boss sleep, pleased with his promotion but happy as could be that he wasn't in command, and doubtful they'd ever fully unravel this case. In fact, Walker knew, if the murderer stopped right now he'd get away clean with this. Walker had gotten the names of the deputies being assigned, and knew a half-dozen of them, including Sergeant Beverly Dawson, whom he had dated for a few months ten years before. He was untroubled by this. They had remained friends, and occasionally friends with benefits. Their careers and the hours demanded of them just seemed to make a stable relationship between them an impossibility. But he also knew Dawson was intelligent to the point of brilliance, and was very likely to be a huge asset to this task force, however seemingly hopeless their mission might be.

As to Lowe, Walker knew his boss was exhausted, and had scheduled the next day, a Sunday, to be off. Since there was nothing to do for it, and since Lowe was, frankly, worn out, Walker made the executive decision that his boss could learn the news Monday. Walker called Holmes and updated her, and she agreed there was no sense in disturbing Lowe with information he couldn't affect.

SIXTEEN

"I am sorry, but our church is for members only," Carl Drayton said to John and Sarah. "I cannot admit you."

"Then how do we join?" John asked.

Drayton reached into his pocket and handed John a business card. "That is Shepherd Quinn's card," he said. "I suggest you call him tomorrow and make an appointment, and he'll walk you through the process, and you and he can determine if you and our church are right for one another, Mr. ...?"

"Avery," John said. "I am John Avery, and this is my wife Sarah."

Drayton shook hands with John but completely ignored Sarah. "I am pleased to meet you, Mr. Avery," he said.

"And likewise, Sir," John returned, noting that the man hadn't given his name. "I will call Shepherd Quinn tomorrow. Sarah, let's go. We'll pray at home."

"Yes, Husband," Sarah said meekly, and followed him out to the truck.

"Well, we shall try to meet this Quinn fellow soon," John said a mile down the road, uncertain if microphones or listening devices had been placed in the truck. In truth, nobody had touched the truck, and they weren't yet being monitored, but better safe than sorry.

"Yes, Husband," Sarah said. "From their website, it seems the right place for us."

"Let's eat brunch – I know it's a bit early, but I'm hungry – and then go home and pray," John said.

They drove to an IHOP and ordered meals, and talked little throughout the meal, but a couple of officers in plainclothes stood beside his truck having a casual chat while surreptitiously scanning the truck, finding nothing suspicious. They wandered to their cars and a third officer made his way through the parking lot with several flyers for a rock concert at a warehouse the following Saturday, taking care to place one under John's windshield wiper. It would tell John and Sarah they were safe. A flyer for a jazz concert would have meant they were already under surveillance.

John took the flyer from underneath his windshield and tossed it in a trash can, muttering about sinners, and they couple got into the truck and then drove home. "We'll pray outdoors," John said. "It's a beautiful day."

"Yes, Husband," Sarah said. "May I go inside and retrieve the Bibles?"

"Yes, and then make us a pitcher of lemonade," John ordered.

"I did that last night while Husband showered," Sarah said, smiling, and then went indoors. "We should keep the Sabbath Day holy."

"I'm pleased you're starting to settle in again," John remarked. He removed the jacket of his Botany 500 suit and handed it to her, along with his necktie, and sent her indoors. She took the items inside and hung them, and then grabbed two well-worn Bibles (culled from estate sales) and the pitcher of lemonade and two plastic cups, and went outside to the picnic bench.

"Well, it went as expected," Sarah remarked. "It will be interesting to see who meets us in the office, and who they send to our home."

"Yes it will," John agreed. The two read their Bibles for a time, drinking lemonade.

"Two people, a husband and wife, tried to attend services, Shepherd," Drayton said to Quinn after the service was over. "Their names were John and Sarah Avery."

"Did you get a contact card from them?" Quinn asked.

"There were none," Drayton said. "Or if there were, I didn't know where. But I did give them your card. The wife seemed very meek. They were dressed well. His suit didn't come off-the-rack from Sears, and they were in a new-looking Ford truck, one of those big diesel ones, Shepherd."

"Disappointing that you didn't get a contact card," Quinn noted. "Did you get a license plate from the truck?"

"It was a paper tag, Shepherd," Drayton said. "As I said, it looked new."

"Send Elder Luden in here, please, and go join the fellowship," Quinn ordered.

"Drayton said you wished to see me, Shepherd," Luden said two minutes later.

"Close the door and have a seat," Quinn ordered, noting that Luden looked tired and drawn. He removed his suit jacket and sat on one of Quinn's chairs. "I gather night shift is a difficult adaptation."

"It's been trying, Shepherd, but I'm suffering less than did our Savior," Luden returned. "What can I do for you and our Lord?"

"Are the police trying to infiltrate our church?" Quinn asked.

"It wouldn't surprise me, Shepherd," Luden said. "Right now, there's not much I've been able to learn, but the murders are getting a lot of press attention, and sometimes tongues wag. I've heard they found bodies from the one scene the fire department defeated, and that they were beaten badly. Our church owned the house that was the first crime scene, but I don't think the police have figured out that one of our parishioners had owned another before he died intestate. That was the scene the firefighters managed to save. The house was condemned and probably would have been bulldozed in three or four months. But if the police did link the owner to us, then ... Shepherd, we look suspect. That's just how it is, so it's a safe bet we're being investigated in some measure to learn if we're involved."

"I know I'm not involved," Quinn said, then looked right into Luden's eyes. "You're the police officer, Paul. Who do you think is doing this?"

"I don't know enough to guess," Luden said. "And I'm hesitant to accuse anyone of things this horrible, Shepherd."

"A couple came here to attend services and Drayton sent them away," Quinn said. "He got their names – John and Sarah Avery – but little else, except they drove off in a brand-new truck still with dealer tags on it. If they show up, I'll want you to look into them for me."

"I'll need names, driver license numbers, addresses, everything you can tell me, and then I'll do what I'm able," Luden said.

"Very well," Quinn replied. "Let's join the fellowship. I could stand a big glass of apple juice."

SEVENTEEN

"Shepherd Quinn, there are people here to see you, a John Avery and his wife Sarah," Bridger said the next morning at 8:30.

"Oh, yes, I neglected to tell you to expect them," Quinn said. "Please show them in."

"I heard you came by yesterday, but I'm afraid our greeter didn't get a contact card on you," Quinn greeted them. "I'm Isaiah Quinn, the Shepherd of this flock, Mr. Avery."

"Just John, please," John greeted him, shaking hands. "This is my wife Sarah."

"A delight to meet you both," Quinn said. "What can we do for you?"

"Well, I just got transferred here after spending too long overseas," John said. "And my wife and I are interested in joining your church. By the look of the website, it fits in with our beliefs. I've never gone in for those feel-good religions that think sin isn't important and that Christ forgives all and doesn't keep score. Christians need discipline. Wives and children need discipline."

"Do you two have children?" Quinn wanted to know.

"We don't yet," John said. "But we're working on it. I only got home ten days ago and we've been busy getting housekeeping set up and the like. I just bought a house and cars."

"I think you need to understand that the church must be an overarching element in the lives of our parishioners," Quinn said.

"Of course," John replied.

"Husband, with your permission, may I visit the ladies room?" Sarah spoke.

"Yes, you may," John said.

"Thank you," Sarah said, and rose, and asked Bridger for directions to the bathroom, and then meekly went down the hall. In truth, she didn't need to pee, but planted a listening device behind the toilet. Women talked, notably in the bathroom, and she suspected a lot could be learned from this device, even if, without a warrant, the information couldn't be directly used in a court of law. She exited the bathroom and found the fellowship hall and kitchen, and placed a second device in the kitchen, doubting that many men wandered through here. And then she returned to Quinn's office, where she smiled at Bridger and casually planted a listening device behind a file cabinet, before knocking at Quinn's door and being admitted. She "tripped" as she walked in and put the fourth and final device under the seat of her chair before rising with a sheepish expression.

"My wife has been known to trip over air as a matter of routine," John joked, and Quinn chuckled.

"I trust you're not hurt, Mrs. Avery?" Quinn asked.

"Thank you, but I'm fine, Shepherd," Sarah said in a meek tone. "I am sorry I've made a spectacle of myself. But husband has caused me more pain with punishment than this little fall." She even managed to blush a bit, thinking not of the beating but of the post-session blowjob she'd given him.

"Quite," Quinn responded. "Sarah, John, you should both know we believe your bodies are important. We keep to God's laws on food, for instance, so if you're fans of pork or catfish, or crabs, shrimp … anything banned in the Bible, then you should give those things up now."

"I understand," John said. "I was in the Middle East as a contractor and those Halal laws aren't as rigid, but similar. I never cared for eating swine anyway, and never got much of a taste for most seafood. I'm a meat and potatoes man, beef and lamb mostly."

"It also requires that we send people to your home to inspect your home and perform thorough physicals on both of you," Quinn went on, as though John hadn't even spoken. "So if either of you, for instance, is wearing a tattoo, you may as well depart now."

"I have some scars," John said. "So does my wife, for that matter. But no tattoos. The very idea disgusts me, Shepherd."

"We also require that you tithe," Quinn said. "And this means you give us pay stubs. Christ told us to render unto Caesar what is Caesar's, and unto God what is God's, and our doctrine is that you tithe ten percent of your after-tax pay. But any extras, your health insurance, for instance, don't count. Let's say you get paid a thousand dollars and the taxes taken from it are a hundred fifty. You owe us $85.00, ten percent of that $850.00. If you paid a hundred dollars for health insurance, for instance, that's your problem, and the church requires your tithe."

"I have no problem with that," John said.

Quinn buzzed Bridger on the intercom. "Shannon, if you will, bring a male and female membership packet in here, please," he ordered.

"Yes, Shepherd," Bridger said, and in seconds was in his office with two manila envelopes, handing one to Sarah and the other to John.

"That'll be all, Shannon," Quinn said. "Thank you."

"Yes, Shepherd," Bridger said, and returned to the outer office.

"I'll take you to Fellowship Hall where you can fill these out," Quinn said. "Meanwhile, I'll set up someone to do the physicals on you two and we could introduce you at our next services."

John and Sarah, privately, each thanked God for the thoroughness of their handlers and the backgrounds and bios they both had, as they filled out the paperwork, which was deeply intrusive, asking for social security numbers, permission to run credit checks, and a variety of matters, including schools attended as children, right back to kindergarten, and four personal references. Using their cell phones, they found numbers for the "references" and were done with the paperwork in thirty minutes. The paperwork even specified their duties to the church and included blanket consent to the church's disciplinary regime, which they both dubiously signed.

Done, they went to Bridger and handed their packets to her. "We'll need copies of your driver licenses or ID cards," Bridger said, and both handed her temporary licenses.

"We just moved here," John explained. "We should have the regular licenses here in a week or two, they told us."

"Then when they come in, I'll copy those as well," Bridger said, smiling. "Now, if you'll stand in front of that wall, I'll get official photos of both of you."

"Will you two be available this afternoon for a visitation?" Quinn asked them, poking his head out of his office.

"I don't start my new job until next Monday, Shepherd, so our time is your time," John said.

"Outstanding," Quinn said, and smiled. "We'll be at your house at 3:30, John. Including me, there'll be eight of us."

John and Sarah left the church, where a man across the street was working on a derelict car with its hood up. He was wearing a green shirt, which meant nobody had come near the truck. The man behind the wheel of the car, in a red shirt, would have been doing the work if the truck had been molested.

"The hell of it is, Quinn seems like a really likeable guy," John said a mile from the church.

"More or less, yeah," Sarah agreed. "His sexytary seemed nice too."

"Did she get your motor running?" John joked.

"No, I don't walk those roads, but she is mighty attractive, and all but certainly the mole," Sarah said.

"Most likely," John agreed, then sighed. "I saw your marks this morning, so let's hope that satisfies them. It's 10:00 now. What do you want to do?"

"Go home, Husband," Sarah said, back in character. "If we are expecting guests we should make preparations for them. Let's go to the grocery store first. I'll make sandwiches for them and a lot of lemonade, maybe buy a gallon each of orange, grape, and apple juice."

"Yeah, we can do that," John said. "Good thinking." And then Sarah dug out her phone and placed a call to Reese.

"Ma'am, we were turned away yesterday, as expected, and met with this guy Quinn —"

"I know where you were," Reese interrupted. "What happened at the meeting? You were in there 90 minutes or so."

"We were," Sarah confirmed. "Ma'am, I placed the listening devices in the ladies room, the kitchen, the secretary's office and in Quinn's office. They gave us huge packets to fill out demanding almost everything in our backgrounds, so kudos to you for that. We also had to sign a huge consent form surrendering to the church's discipline. The packet was thorough, even asked for personal references, what kindergartens we attended, the whole nine yards. But the upshot of it is we're being visited by them this afternoon at 3:30. They're sending eight people to us, and I assume we'll be stripped down and examined."

"Good work, Sarah," Reese said. While uneasy about it, Reese didn't order the house monitored. She figured they were an attractive couple and if they grew intimate she would be better off not knowing, although she would have blown her top if she'd known about the beating Sarah had endured in the barn. But the only monitoring Reese was doing was still active. The house across the street from John and Sarah was full of cops doing surveillance and ready to blow cover and extract them at the drop of a hat, and Reese had seen to it that no matter what, a patrol car was always inside five minutes of the Avery house.

"We'll keep you posted, Ma'am," Sarah said. The IA people were so thorough that Reese was in the phone as Pearl Cottonwood, a cousin of Sarah's who lived one town over. This way if phones were examined, a distinct probability, nothing suspicious would be found there. The call ended and Reese offered up a prayer that these two would remain safe.

EIGHTEEN

John and Sarah parted with a chunk of change at Wal-Mart and then the grocery store and hit the ground running at home, building a platter of tuna salad and chicken salad sandwiches, and filling a 3-gallon glass urn with lemonade (which involved fresh-squeezing many lemons) and otherwise making ready for their honored guests. Their doorbell rang at 3:30 on the dot, and the guests were admitted. Quinn was in his minister uniform but the others were more casually dressed.

"Elder Luden is one of our most trusted members," Quinn said, introducing the man. "This is Elder Dan Calloway and his wife Louise. And these other gentlemen are Hollis Butler, James Thurston, Glen Marks and John Stowe."

John shook hands all the way around, and noted that Luden looked tired and in a foul temper, and wondered after that, but decided not to pursue it. "Sarah has prepared refreshments for everyone, sandwiches, lemonade and a variety of fruit juices," he said.

"Very kind but unnecessary," Butler said. "But I have to say a big glass of lemonade does sound in order."

"Yes, Sir," Sarah said. "Anyone else?" She busied herself filling glasses for their guests, and then brought out the tray of sandwiches and a stack of small plates. Louise Calloway opted for grape juice, and Quinn asked for apple juice. John opted for orange juice and the rest of the visitors asked for lemonade, making John grateful they'd mixed up a four-gallon batch of it.

"Please be seated, Sarah," Quinn said. "The choices are your husband's, and rightly so, but it is better that you know what to expect. Hollis is a physician and will give you both examinations in a few minutes. John, in the interests of modesty, Louise has agreed to be in attendance while Hollis examines your wife."

"Yes, Shepherd," John said. "I got checked out stem-to-stern when I got home from the Middle East, and they seem to think I'll live a while longer." He chuckled and Sarah grinned.

"What sort of work are you doing?" Luden asked.

"I am with a security firm," John said. "Hayes, Rollins & Flick, specifically. I was in charge of security and defusing IEDs at several oil fields in the Middle East. Those people over there ... so much savagery and godlessness ... anyway, my assignment there ended and they transferred me here. I'll be teaching here, technicians to go over there and do what I did."

"Would it be okay to visit you there?" Luden pursued.

"Probably not," John said. "I had to leap through a thousand hoops for Homeland Security to clear me for this job, afraid I was about to start my own bomb-making lab right here. The building ... it's about ten miles from here ... it's heavily guarded and nobody gets in or out without Homeland Security's approval. Even the janitorial staff has clearances from them, I was told."

"That sounds impressive," Luden said.

"It's just what I do," John returned. "It started in the army for me and ... I have to believe that's what God wants me doing, or

He would direct me down other avenues, Sir. What about you, Mr. Luden? What do you do for a living, Sir?"

"Until I retire, I'm a police captain," Luden said. "Earlier in life I was a Marine."

"Marines ... they're total absolutists," John said.

"How's that?" Luden asked, looking annoyed.

"They either absolutely loved being Marines or absolutely despised it, with virtually no middle ground," John said. "Air Force, Army, Navy, it could span the whole spectrum from 'it was ok' to 'I mostly didn't like it' to 'I kind of wish I'd stayed in,' but Marines, you get none of that. It's either absolutely loved it or absolutely hated it."

"I loved it," Luden snorted, and then smiled a bit. "Sometimes I wish I'd stayed in. I'd be retired by now with a decent pension, but then what would I have done?"

"The possibilities are endless," John said. "Between HRF and the VA and the Hazelwood Act, I think I'm going to go into college and get my degree. It would involve a nice pay boost, but would let me do more."

"I have a master degree in criminology," Luden remarked. "Like you, I deal with godless people all the time. Sadly, too many of them wear uniforms just like mine."

"Sarah, will you come with me, please?" Louise asked. "We need to go to your bedroom to do your examination. Dr. Butler, I will tell you when she is ready."

"John, these men also will need to search your house," Quinn said. "Why don't you and I step outside for a few minutes?"

"Let me refill my drink," John said. "Do you want a refill too, Shepherd?"

"Yes, please," Quinn said. A moment later the two men stepped outdoors and sat at the picnic bench, shaded by a monster of an oak tree that was, John estimated, a hundred or so years old.

"That looks painful," Louise said a moment later to Sarah, who stripped to the skin.

"Husband is retraining me after being so long away," Sarah said meekly. "I didn't want to polish windows and he took me to the barn. He paddled me and used his strap on my back, Ma'am."

"Your marks are far from the first or worst I've seen," Louise said. "And I've had worse too. A week ago my sister came to visit for a day and … I sinned when she took me to lunch. We drank our lunch. My husband took a whip to me that night and I'm still hurting from it. But better that than being lashed at services, in public."

"Sometimes it seems we women would self-destruct without our men keeping us in check," Sarah said.

"Probably," Louise snorted. "I'll tell Dr. Butler you're ready."

While John and Quinn had small talk over juice in the back yard, the other men thoroughly searched the house. Luden even brought along a device to determine if there were listening devices in the house, but found nothing. He turned on the TV and went through the channels and saw only local channels and family channels in their favorites list, and nodded, still unconvinced. But nothing contraband was found in the house, and he had nowhere to hang his hat on his suspicions. He'd looked up their histories online, unaware he was being monitored, and found nothing of huge interest. Calls and e-mails placed to their personal references had told them these people were as represented. But again, Luden didn't believe in coincidence, and wondered. A gun safe was found in one closet and Luden made a mental note to ask John to open it, and a pistol was found in John's nightstand, a .40 caliber Smith & Wesson. But the church didn't oppose to good men of God who defend themselves. Luden himself kept eight handguns in his apartment, as well as a shotgun and a Remington .30-06 rifle.

Meanwhile, Hollis Butler was surprised not that Sarah was healthy – he knew that at first glimpse of her downstairs in the living room – but that she was so well-toned, and asked about that. "I have little to do and Husband wants me to be fit and healthy, so we exercise," Sarah said.

"Where?" Butler pursued.

"There's a 24-Hour Fitness three miles away," Sarah answered. "We go there."

"Among heathens and the immodest," Butler remarked with distaste.

"Sometimes," Sarah said. "But Husband insists that I dress modestly. The bottom drawer of my dresser is full of my workout clothing."

"The church has a complete gymnasium, mostly for the men, but perhaps Shepherd will permit you to use it," Louise remarked. She began going through the room, even lifting Sarah's mattress and looking under it, and found a pistol, a .380, in her nightstand. "Why do you bear arms, Sarah?"

"Husband gave me the pistol shortly after we married," Sarah said. "He works long hours sometimes, and was away for a year, and didn't want me defenseless. He has a larger one in his bedroom but it's too big for my hands."

"And do you know how to use this pistol?" Louise asked, looking dismayed.

"I have fired over a thousand rounds through it," Sarah said. "Husband wanted me to be safe while he was away. I do pray often that I never have to use it, Mrs. Calloway."

"Okay, get dressed and you ladies go have a seat outside," Butler said. "And ask your husband to come up to his bedroom, please. I need to examine him as well."

"What's this scar on your arm?" Butler asked John a few minutes later.

"My purple heart," John said, honestly. "A piece of shrapnel from an IED got me."

"And this scar down on your left thigh?" Butler asked. "It's an older scar."

"That was from when I was a kid far more adventuresome than wisdom would decree," John said, and chuckled. "I fell from a tree and landed and skidded on sharp rocks."

"It left its mark, John," Butler said. "Okay, you're so disgustingly healthy that if everyone looked like you I'd have to take up driving a dump truck. Get dressed and head on down the stairs."

"I need you to open the gun safe there," Luden said when John got down the stairs.

"Sure," John said, and put in the 6-digit code, and then opened the door before backing away. John knew there was nothing of interest in the safe, just two shotguns and a Winchester .30-06 rifle, and ammunition for all, including Sarah's .380 and his .40. John wandered outside and saw Louise and Sarah some distance away, out of earshot, and sat back on the bench across from Quinn.

"You seem quite calm about all of this," Louise ventured to Sarah.

"I am," Sarah said. "My church growing up was a lot like this. To many it would seem intrusive or abusive but to me ... I don't know ... I guess it's comforting, knowing the church and Husband are always studying my spiritual welfare. I hate being whipped when Husband finds I've gone astray, but even that is ... comforting ... knowing he loves me so much."

"I understand," Louise said. "Come into the barn, please." Inside, Louise removed her blouse and showed Sarah her back, which was crossed in scars and wounds, many of which looked fresh.

"What did you do to earn this?" Sarah asked, hissing at the marks of a painful whipping.

"As I said, sinning with my sister," Louise said. "But I wanted you to see I do understand. Look, you should always be on your best behavior, Sarah. Members are lashed by the church as well. We're often made to witness this woman or that horsewhipped before the congregation."

"The men too?" Sarah asked.

"They are not whipped at services, but sometimes are taken to the post at a private assembly of the elders and perhaps others," Louise said. "Husband told me it would make the women lose respect to see our betters facing the lash, and perhaps he's right."

"What did he use on you to do that?" Sarah wanted to know, realizing that Louise's statements alone could see her husband jailed a very long time.

"A scourge," Louise said. "One very much like that used on our Risen Savior. It's agonizing, but it reminds me how much He suffered that my soul is saved. It … I hate it, but it's worth it to both of us."

"I see," Sarah said. And she did, intellectually, but the visceral end was lost on her.

As the women returned to the house, Quinn's phone rang and he answered it.

"Shepherd, this is Shannon," Bridger said.

"What's going on?" Quinn asked.

"Sir, I just got a call from Mary Nichols," Bridger reported. "Oscar Nichols had a massive heart attack. He was rushed to the hospital but he died."

"Lord, how sad for Mary," Quinn said. "What is her address?"

"Shepherd, she's on her way here," Bridger told him. "She wishes to discuss his funerary services with you, and get set up for a supervisor." The church frowned on single women, even widows, without oversight, and at 57 with over 25 years in the church, Mary Nichols knew no exception would be made for her.

"And so are we," Quinn said. "We'll be out of here in a few minutes."

"I'll wait," Bridger said. It was 5:00 and she wouldn't die for flagging an hour or so of overtime.

Quinn rounded up his party, and Dan Calloway noticeably grimaced as he stood, as though his back was hurting him. Hands were shaken and the party boarded their big van and returned to the church.

NINETEEN

"Louise Calloway seemed impressed with the marks, and there's no way Butler missed them either," Sarah said in the back yard when the visitors abruptly departed to attend a grieving widow, which impressed them both in spite of the lunacy they thought was the Church of God's Law. "Her husband ... Jesus Christ, he uses a scourge on her. She showed me her back when we went out to the barn. She's scarred and has several more open wounds from a few days ago.

"Jesus, I'd have quit this assignment in a heartbeat if you'd asked me to do that to you," John said.

"I'd have shot you with that .380 if you'd suggested it," Sarah returned, chuckling. "Do you think they left listening devices in the house?"

"I wouldn't bet against it," John said. "Reese will send someone by late tonight to take a look-see, but we need to be in-character at all times there in the house."

"Yes, Husband," Sarah said, and then flashed him a grin. "Would husband like to explore his spousal rights tonight?"

"Of course," John said, smiling back at her. Surprising him, a man ventured into their back yard, smiling and carrying a Playmate cooler. He was in his late 50s or so, built thinly, with grey hair and mustache. A moment later, a woman about his age followed.

"Hi, neighbors," the man said. "I'm Robert Ross. I live across the street from you."

"John Avery," John said, and the men shook hands. "This is my wife Sarah."

"A pleasure," the woman said. "I'm Jane Ross."

"Want a cold beer?" Robert asked.

"We don't drink, but thank you anyway," John said.

And then Jane flashed a badge. "Why don't you two come over for supper?" she asked. "We thawed out several chops from a deer Robert shot, and corn on the cob and potatoes."

"That sounds great," John said, and he and Sarah followed the Rosses across the street.

"Okay, for now you just know us as Jane and Robert," Jane said in the house across the street. "We're here and desperately hoping you're not in enough danger to need us. But if we're needed, we have people armed to the teeth to extract you. Meanwhile, we have the house under surveillance in case we spot anything amiss. Your house is not, I repeat not, under electronic surveillance from us. Luden is a smart guy and he'd see devices and wonder after them. I doubt they're going to do surveillance on you, not to that degree, because Luden damn well knows he'd be in the pen for a long time and his career up in smoke. But we don't keep undercover cops alive by taking stupid chances, so right now an officer is on his way with countersurveillance gear to see if they left any listening devices on you two. Christ, that church reminds me of tales of the KGB in the Bad Old Days."

"I never imagined a church going to these lengths with its membership," John said.

"These people are intense," Sarah chimed in. "I was just telling John the woman with them showed me her back. Jesus, her husband whips her with a scourge. These are dangerous people."

"You'll be wise not forgetting that, Sarah," Jane said.

"What's your take on Luden?" Robert wanted to know.

"He seemed annoyed and even hostile at first," John remarked. "But seemed to settle down, only a little but some, by the time they left."

"You two have a need to know that Luden is under investigation, and he's already doomed his career. He used his computer to access your records, and that's a huge no-no these days," Robert said. "We're watching to see what's what, but he's going to be fired and arrested when this all concludes."

"Yes, Sir," John said.

"Meanwhile, we're going to all become good friends," Jane interjected. "I'm a *hausfrau* just like Sarah here, so we'll have lemonade – well, she'll have lemonade while I have a pot of coffee – most mornings. Robert works in a building neighboring John's. He is an executive with the company contracting John's. Sometimes they interact. In truth, the building has a bunkhouse in it and you two may be spending much of your time sleeping, but we will be teaching you more and more about IEDs, John, and when this is said and done you can probably find the skids greased to get you into the bomb squad. Meanwhile, we have people checking your apartments and mail and all, and handling that end of things for you, so just settle in to being John and Sarah Avery and let's see what happens. Meanwhile, Robert has steaks to go on the grill and we can feed you a decent supper, at least."

"Sold," Sarah said, and laughed. "I was terrified we'd have to eat those tuna sandwiches, and I downright hate tuna salad."

TWENTY

"Sergeant Lowe, this is Jim Worth," Lowe heard over his office phone at 5:45. "I'm a sergeant in the 22nd. I was told you're the man to call. We have a house at 488 Lathrop, human remains in pieces scattered all over it. There are several bug bomb cans scattered about. The FD is putting those in special containers."

"Be Goddamned careful, Worth," Lowe warned. "And yeah, it sounds like this case is mine. I'll be there in … thirty minutes. Secure the scene, and other than the FD and bomb squad, nobody goes in our out of the house."

"We have it secure, Sergeant," Worth said, sounding annoyed. Lowe hung up and put the call out to his CSU team. Walker was due in an hour and he decided to let the poor bastard rest. And then he drove over to the scene. Lowe wasn't in a huge hurry. The dead would remain dead no matter how long he took, and he saw no reason to make a hazard of himself. On the way, his stomach twisting in knots, he called Holmes.

"I'm heading that way, then," Holmes said, not adding that she was bringing Inspector Johnson along as well, just to illustrate to the cops in the 22nd that this indeed had high-level interest. But Johnson had confided in Holmes and said his presence might terrify the captains of the precinct into being more cooperative than was ordinarily the case.

Lowe arrived, found Worth, and shook hands with him. "Jesus, I'm glad this is yours and not mine," Washington said. "What was the deal with the bug bombs? The FD was acting like they were nuclear devices or something."

"They're homemade thermite grenades," Lowe said. "Do you know what thermite is, Sergeant?"

"I've heard the word but … no," Worth admitted.

"It burns over 2,000 degrees, and we've lost bodies at other scenes that were reduced to ash," Lowe said. "The firemen defeated them at one scene with sand —"

"Can you explain that?" Worth asked. "I wondered why the FD dumped a load of sand and the wheelbarrows."

"Sure," Lowe said. Until the house was secure, he had nowhere to be. "Fires are usually fought with water, but thermite burns so hot that it actually, as I understand it, fractures water molecules into hydrogen and oxygen, which only make the fire that much more intense. So they use sand to smother the flames instead since that will just melt into glass."

"What the fuck?" Worth asked. "Are these terrorists?"

"If you mean Al Qaeda and Islamists, the answer is no, or I don't think so," Lowe said. "We haven't heard from these people, and we have no idea what their game is, except they get their jollies murdering people and butchering them."

"It's weird," Worth said. "I glanced in for a moment and it was a racial mix, at least by skin tones. Several were blacker than me and others were whiter than you, Sergeant."

"That's how the scenes have all been," Lowe agreed. "And hopefully this time they left some evidence that'll give us a place to hang our hat. What can you tell me about the house, Sergeant?"

"It's vacant, but nearly a fourth of the houses in this neighborhood are," Worth said. "Crime magnets for rape, crack abusers … I'm sure you know the song and dance. But I have no idea who owns it, or the like. I called Homicide, spoke with a lieutenant named Capps, and he said this sounded like your case."

"Capps was right," Lowe said. Just then a young patrolwoman approached.

"Sir, the neighbor across the street at 485 says she has information, a lady named Shirley Garcia," the officer said. "She's wheelchair-bound, so we'd need to go see her."

"I've got this one," Lowe said, looking at the patrolwoman's nameplate. "Officer Hebert, I'm Sergeant Michael Lowe, and this case is mine. Take me to Ms. Garcia and introduce us, please."

"Mrs. Garcia, I'm Mike Lowe, a sergeant with the police department," Lowe said to the lady a moment later. "May I take a seat?"

"If you want," she said. Lowe sat on a rickety folding chair and looked at the woman, guessing her to be somewhere in her 70s. She was thin, even scrawny, but her eyes were bright and intelligent, and Lowe doubted much got past this lady.

"I understand you saw something," Lowe said.

"I did, sonny," Garcia said. "I've been stuck in this wheelchair the last year after a car wreck, and there ain't a hell of a lot to do other than look out this window and hope I get a call now and again, or sometimes company other than those meals on wheels people or the kid delivers groceries. My son Mark wants to put me in a nursing home but I flat out told his ass that I'll roll this wheelchair off a skyscraper first. That shut him up. But enough about me. I don't have much else to do but look at drivel and bullshit on the TV or to look out the window. So last night my back was paining me and I was up. Around three in the morning, a big truck pulled up to that house. It was one of those 'frigerated trucks you see taking meat to restaurants. Not an 18-wheeler, but a big ... kinda like one of those Ryder trucks."

"What can you tell me about the truck?" Lowe asked, his calm tone masking his excitement.

"Well, it was nighttime," she said. "The truck ... the cab was a dark color, maybe dark blue or green, but that's all I can tell you. It used to have some kind of logo on its side, but someone went and painted over it. One way or another, another car pulled in behind it, a Chevy Cobalt that looked just like the car I had when I got ran over. Two men got out of the truck and three out of the Chevy, and they started toting stuff from the truck into the house. They worked quick. I think they were gone by 3:45. I figured maybe somebody bought the place and was moving in, and one way or another, there was nothing in the house. Margaret Lewis died three years ago without any heirs – her son Damon died in the Army and her son Ralph overdosed about three weeks before Margaret died, and she just gave up – but I didn't think much else of it until today, Mr. Lowe."

"You've been a huge help," Lowe said, and gave her his business card. "If you remember anything else, anything, please call me and let me know."

"I sure will, sonny," Garcia said. "Could you stay and have a cup of coffee with me? I know you're a busy man but I don't get much company here."

"Of course," Lowe said. "Do you need me —"

"Nope," she said. "I got a nice settlement from the wreck and had my kitchen redone for the wheelchair – had the whole house redone, in fact – and I manage very well, but thanks anyway." She rolled her power chair toward the kitchen while Lowe briefly wondered how she kept the simple house neat as a pin, correctly guessing she had money for a housekeeper to come in and keep it in order.

Just then the doorbell rang and Lowe answered. This visitor was about Lowe's age, Hispanic, with a lot of grey in his hair, and he looked curiously at Lowe. "Who are you?" he challenged.

"I'm Sergeant Lowe with the police," Lowe said. "And you are?"

"Mark Torres," the man said, looking suddenly intensely worried. "Is Mom okay?"

"Come on in," Lowe said. "She's making coffee in the kitchen."

"I saw a flash on the news that there was a murder here and got scared," Torres admitted, offering his hand to Lowe.

"She's fine," Lowe repeated. "We're interviewing people to see if anyone saw anything."

"You hear that, Mark?" Garcia said as she wheeled into the living room. "Here you want me in a gomer gulch somewhere and now I'm a star witness." She grinned and Mark looked alarmed, his eyes finding Lowe's.

"Nobody was murdered here," Lowe said. "But your mom was awake late at night and saw a truck pull up to the house."

"This isn't that thing where people are leaving body parts and setting the house on fire, is it?" Torres asked.

"I'm afraid it is," Lowe said. "The devices they've been using for burning the house down seem to have failed, but we don't know why yet."

"Mom, I wish you'd put this place on the market and move the hell out of here," Torres said. "Look, Carmen and I have been talking. What if we built a house on our place for you? You could have a hand in designing just what you want, and —"

"I love you and Carmen and the kids to pieces," Garcia interrupted. "But no. Mark, I've been nearly fifty years under this roof and I mean to die right in this house, God willing." Lowe sensed this was an old dispute between a loving son and a stubborn mother and that anything else he might have gotten from her at the moment wasn't going to happen now with her pestering son.

"I'll leave you two to your discussion on living arrangements," Lowe said. "Thank you very much, Mrs. Garcia, and it was nice to have met you, Mr. Torres."

Across the street, he learned the tally appeared to be eleven bodies, and he learned that these had been scourged like the others. And then he saw Holmes and Johnson and approached them. "Mike, we've got to get on top of this one, no matter what it takes," Holmes said. "Where are we on things?"

"It looks like the same setup," Lowe said. "Scourged to death and parted out. Right now they're telling me eleven bodies. I'll know more by morning. I was about to leave the scene and get Walker updated. I'm surprised you're both here."

"I wanted to see what was going on, and I figured perhaps Inspector Johnson's presence would inspire the crowd," Holmes said. "Or terrify them, whatever works," she added with a slight smile.

"That's probably a good idea," Lowe commented. "If I'm not required here, I'd like to get to the office and get balls rolling and get updates to Walker."

"Yes, dismissed, Sergeant," Holmes said.

In his office, Lowe hurriedly typed the notes of his interview with Shirley Garcia, and the first report of the crime scene. He sent it all to Walker and to Holmes, and wondered if Luden, now the night commander of the 22nd, would have to be brought in on these matters. But Lowe reasoned that the captains of the other precincts hadn't horned in. He wondered how long it would be before he found himself moved off to a rubber gun squad on the horns of what had thus far been a failure, and then logged out and drove home, stopping halfway home at a liquor store for a big bottle of tequila.

Home, he found Lisa waiting for him, and she knew by his look it had been a bad day. "I'll pour," she said. "You tell me what's going on."

That night, after downing a full eight ounces of tequila, the little fish that had been hiding behind a rock in Lowe's mind wiggled out, and he deftly netted it, and realized one suspect was suddenly looking far worse. But he was too drunk to even get out of bed and write a note, and a second later was sound asleep.

TWENTY-ONE

Lowe drove straight to Chief Watts' house the next morning, still gruesomely hung over but excited at his latenight realization. He arrived to find Walker's car there along with several he couldn't identify, and as he approached the door, Johnson pulled his car into the drive, and Capps right behind him. *Motherfucker*, Lowe thought, *I'm too late and I think this is the lynch mob that's going to send me to a rubber gun crew, hopefully not in the 22nd under that asshole Luden.* He took a breath and swore to take it like a man, and rang the doorbell as Johnson and Capps stepped up onto the porch.

"How goes, Mike?" Capps asked.

"Terribly," Lowe admitted, and was surprised to see sympathy in Capps' expression. And then Holmes admitted them.

"Ground rules," Watts said as all were seated and eating breakfast burritos. "Lowe, you're still in charge of this, so if you had hopes I'd transfer your ass back to Homicide and an easy life again, all hope abandon."

"Yes, Sir," Lowe said, surprised.

"Look, Mike, it's not 'fair' to you, whatever 'fair' means in this fucking job, but the fact is that sometimes really difficult cases get handed to us," Watts said. "Lieutenant Holmes has decided, like or not, that the FBI was brought in on this case, specifically a profiler

128

named Jeremy Hartz. He will be at your office at 10:00 to review your case and hopefully help us identify a suspect."

"Yes, Sir," Lowe said. "Sir, may I meet with you privately for a moment? Some information came to light that … I think I need your guidance on it."

"Yes," Watts said, ushering Holmes and Johnson into his home office.

"What is it, Mike?" Watts asked, not unkindly, a moment later.

"Sir, this … you know the bodies were scourged to death, yes?" Lowe began.

"So I've been led to understand," Watts said.

"Sir, CSU has led me to understand the person doing this was left handed," Lowe said. "The angles of the lash marks —"

"I understand the science," Watts interrupted.

"Sir, Captain Luden is a leftie," Lowe said. "I could hardly convict him on that basis. I couldn't even order his arrest, but he … he looks a little bit better for this."

"Jesus H. Christ, he does," Holmes said. "Mike, I got the message very late last night from Inspector Reese. The church looked at our people there, came to meet them – including Luden, if I have to say this – and our people had the feeling they'll be accepted into the church. So maybe Sunday will bring us somewhat better news. On the plus-side, Luden entirely ignored the crime scene on his overnight shift. One thing that's interesting – not really more than a data point, though – is that Luden owns a big property just outside town, but lives in a little apartment in the city. We're finding out what we can learn there."

"Assuming he's our guy, do you think he finally went off the deep end about all the parolees loose in the city?" Lowe asked.

"That's one thing I hope the FBI profiler can tell us," Holmes said. "Thus far he isn't behaving suspiciously, so it's hard to make guesses. He drives a battered Chevy Cobalt to and from his apartment, and other than church, seems not to have a life at all."

"Jesus fuck," Lowe muttered. "We found a witness yesterday. She gave somewhat of a description to us of a freezer truck, one of those that would deliver frozen food to restaurants and the like. It pulled up to the house at 3:00 yesterday morning, followed by a Chevy Cobalt, and unloaded the truck's contents into the house. She said the logos had been painted over on the truck. And all she could say was the truck had a dark cab since it was so late at night."

"A Cobalt?" Watts asked.

"Yes, Sir, it's one of the cheaper model Chev —"

"I know what the Chevrolet Cobalt is," Watts interrupted, and held up a finger, and then placed a phone call. "Reese, this is Chief Watts. How soon can you get to my house …"

The call lasted a minute and then Watts hung up. "Sergeant Lowe, Reese is on her way and will want to hear this and perhaps re-interview your witness," he said. "Captain Luden's personal car, not really befitting the august rank of captaincy, is a Chevy Cobalt. She'll be interested in knowing this."

"Sir, there's a bit more," Lowe said. "The coroner's people tell me the bodies were scourged by a leftie. Captain Luden is left-handed. This isn't enough to arrest him, but he's looking better and better for our killer."

"It sure looks that way," Watts agreed.

Reese arrived a few minutes later, and Lowe repeated his tale while she nodded thoughtfully. "We're going to start tightening the net on him, Aaron," she said to Watts. "Already we have enough to fire him, and even charge him under the statutes regarding official misuse of information. He's neck-deep in that church, one of the elders, in fact. And he was involved in 'interviewing' my undercover people and searching their home. I'm praying nothing blows their cover, because I could see them – they're good cops and nice kids, both – being dismembered and scattered about another abandoned house."

"If Luden farts, I want your people able to report the sulfur content and stench levels," Watts said. "Meanwhile, let's get someone to re-interview Lowe's witness this morning and see if there's more she can offer. God bless her for caring enough to step forward. Lowe, you look like hell. I want you to go your ass home and get more sleep. Lieutenant Holmes, Lowe isn't to be allowed into the HQ building before noon. Get lost, Lowe."

"Yes, Sir," Lowe said, too tired to argue. He was exhausted, and the veteran of enough hangovers to know he wasn't hung over, or at least, a hangover alone didn't explain how lousy he felt. He fell into bed at home and woke at 11:30 with a temperature of 101.6 degrees, and feeling more or less like he'd been handcuffed and tossed into the ring against Floyd Mayweather. He stumbled through the shower, which did little to make him feel better, and then dressed and drove to work. He was coughing and suddenly had to dash to the bathroom, where he had a round of explosive diarrhea, groaning throughout. He got to his office, jabbed his key at the door, and then fainted. He woke on the ambulance twenty minutes later en route to the hospital, and was hospitalized two days.

TWENTY-TWO

The elders met to discuss the membership application of John and Sarah Avery. "I can't say they're police officers sent to harass and betray us," Luden said. "But I can't say they're not, and my suggestion is to reject them. In fact, until the police have settled those murders, I would suggest we put a moratorium on new membership."

"Paul, let me ask you a question," Butler said. "Undercover cops ... are they excused from drug abuse? Let's say you put someone with a biker gang. Is it overlooked if the officer uses methamphetamine and/or deals it?"

"Of course not," Luden said. "Where are you going with this, Hollis?"

"We gave Mrs. Avery a physical and she has the marks from corporal punishment, on her buttocks and her back. Louise was with me and saw them too," Butler said. "Do you think the police would do that to her to cement her bona fides?"

"I didn't know about that," Luden answered, disturbed.

"Louise told me about it," Calloway said. "She said the bruises were real."

"I would imagine if some supervisor at the department suggested it, there would be a hundred lawsuits and probably the national news would be doing a huge feature on us, so … I guess it's possible, if they're officers, they did this outside the knowledge of their handlers. But … I'd say that's doubtful," Luden said.

"For my part, I like John," Quinn said. "I don't know enough about Sarah to make a decision but she seems as represented. I get the sense she's not altogether bright and couldn't fake this level of devotion."

"Brethren, I suggest we all pray on this and reconvene Thursday to decide," said Henry Melton. The elders agreed to this, and moved on to other business.

Meanwhile, the FBI profiler got on the case, and the police shifted into a higher gear. Holmes, using Lowe's information, put out word that any refrigerated trucks seen traveling at night where they didn't seem to belong were to be stopped. A re-interview with Mrs. Garcia turned up little that was new, only that the Cobalt was dark in color, like the truck. She shrugged and looked genuinely sorrowful that she didn't have more to offer.

"Ma'am, you've given us a whole lot more than we've had to this point," Officer Miguel Santos said to her. "It's been a complicated mess, this case."

"So I've seen on the news," Garcia said. "It sounds to me like you have a whole nest of psychos, sonny."

"Yes, Ma'am," Santos said, annoyed at being called sonny by the old *abuela*, but knowing she deserved a lot of respect and he needed to swallow some of his machismo. "But you may have given us a huge break in the case, Mrs. Garcia."

"I hope I did," Garcia said. "It's horrifying, what I've heard on the news, about those poor souls being butchered." She crossed herself and Santos surprised himself by doing the same.

The truth was, as far as Santos could tell, he'd wasted his time and hers with this interview, but he was a rookie and smart enough to know he hadn't the experience to make him valuable to the task force. He took his notes and returned to headquarters, where he popped to attention before Lieutenant Holmes, who was in full dress uniform, and gave his report.

"Thank you, Officer Santos," Holmes said.

"Ma'am, how is Sergeant Lowe?" Santos asked. He liked the grizzled old cop and hoped he was okay.

"No news is good news," Holmes said. "I think he just got hit hard by a virus while he was already worn down, Santos. As I get updates I'll post them."

"Thank you, Ma'am," Santos said.

"It looks like you're due in court in two hours," Holmes said. "Why don't you take your time getting to the courthouse? Go get a nice lunch or something? Otherwise I'll have to use you for a file clerk and I hate doing that to a go-getter." She grinned and so did Santos, who decided he liked the lieutenant.

"I'll see you tomorrow, then," Santos said, and departed.

"What color is the Cobalt?" Reese greeted Holmes on a phone call minutes later.

"The lady said it was dark, like the truck," Holmes said.

"Luden's Cobalt is black, and I would consider that a dark color," Reese sighed. "Jesus, I hope it's not him. He's a jackass, to be sure, but the Department absolutely does not need this kind of a black eye. Okay, I'm on it, Lieutenant. Thank you."

"Yes, Ma'am," Holmes said, ending the call. Reese sighed and phoned a DA in the Public Integrity section, and asked him to come to her office. They spoke for thirty minutes and then went to a judge to secure warrants for a whole battery of surveillance on Paul Luden. That night, a tracking device was planted on his car while it was parked at his precinct, and wiretaps were established on his personal cell phone, his home phone – Reese wondered why he had an apartment in town and didn't live at his ranch and made a note to bump that question to the task force – and his official phones, office and cell, as well as any and all online traffic, official and personal.

John's phone rang and he saw it was Robert, from across the street, and answered. "John, you and Sarah, wherever you are, go hole up somewhere," he ordered. "Find a diner or go see a movie. People just entered your home and a 'concerned citizen' phoned the police. The patrol car should be by any second. But you two don't come home until I give the all-clear."

"Okay," John said. He and Sarah were in Axton park and pondering supper when the call came. He told Sarah what was going on.

"Five gets you ten it's the Church of God's Law," Sarah said. "I say let the cops cart them off to jail and let's see how long it takes for a delegation of them to come to our house demanding we drop all charges."

"Yeah, that sounds wisest," John said. "How does Mexican sound for supper?"

As John was paying the tab at Oscar Ramirez' Comida Mexicana, the phone rang. "Come on home," Robert said. "Three are in custody and gone to the jail and a couple more officers are on-scene keeping the house secure until you're home."

"Be there in ten," John said, and drove his truck sedately home, making sure to be shocked at the officialdom surrounding his house. He was met by four uniformed officers, one of them female.

"What happened?" John asked, surprised.

"Sir, a citizen phoned in that people broke into your house," said an officer, a man in his forties named Gene Horner. "We arrived and found three individuals in your home, and took them into custody. They're at the city jail now. There was Edward Dorn, 33 years old, a Marion Lewis who's 37 and they were led by a Walter Zane, 35 years old. They were in a white Dodge Caravan, which we also towed away. Evidently, Zane is a locksmith, or so he says when we asked about the lockpicks in his pocket. Sir, do you have a moment to talk privately?" At the same time, John darted a look at the female officer doing the same with Sarah.

"Sarah, I'll be speaking with Officer ... Horner," John said, studying the officer's nametag.

"Yes, Husband," Sarah answered.

"Sir, this is the single weirdest burglary I've ever seen," Horner said a moment later, out of earshot. "Their van was plastered in religious bumper stickers, honk if you love Jesus and WWJD and the like."

"I have no idea who they are," John said, silently acknowledging the half-truth.

"They stole nothing that we can tell," Horner said. "If so, it was cheap stuff. They were all wearing cheap watches and their billfolds and pockets had seventy or so dollars between all three of them. No weapons. The only other jewelry any of them wore were wedding bands on two of the men and a steel cross on a chain on the third."

"That does sound … unusual," John agreed. "And in their thirties, I would think they're too old for frat-house pranks. But yeah, we'll press charges."

"Done and done," Horner said, and shook hands with John.

"What do you know about this?" Officer Patricia Cartwright asked Sarah.

"Only what you've told me," Sarah said honestly. "Are Husband and I in some kind of trouble?"

"Not yet," Cartwright said. "Mrs. Avery, does your husband hit you?"

"What goes on in marriage is sacred to husband and wife," Sarah said. "I would no more discuss that with you than I'd strut naked in the street, Officer Cartwright. I don't fear Husband. I love him with all of my heart, second only to our Risen Savior."

"Oh boy," Cartwright sighed, rolling her eyes. 31 years old and a cop since 21, Cartwright's instincts told her everything about this burglary and these kooks Sarah and John Avery was hinky. Something wasn't adding up. But Cartwright was smart enough to know she couldn't save the world, and she simply stopped giving a damn long since.

"What?" Sarah asked.

"Just never fucking mind," Cartwright said. "If you or your ... husband ..." she said the last word as though she had just vomited in her mouth, "... find anything is missing or wrong in the house, let us know soonest so we can add it to the report for your insurance claims."

"Officer, you seem to take offense to Husband and me," Sarah said. "Why is that? What have we done to you?"

"I don't like abusive or domineering men," Cartwright said. "We checked the barn and found a paddle, a strap, and other such items out there, so I think I have a good idea what goes on in your marriage, and it's sick and it's wrong and you can say the word and you're out of this mess this minute."

"Officer, if Husband ever laid a hand on me, it was laid on with his love for me," Sarah said. "And if it happened, it would probably be at my request. And I think I've said all I am going to say."

"Whatever," Cartwright sneered. "We're done here, Mrs. Avery. Have a nice evening."

In a moment, the officers all left, and John and Sarah entered the house, seeing slight signs of disarray but nothing of major importance. John knew the team from across the street would send in people to scan the house, but for now they were behaving as though every whisper was being monitored. John decided a homeowner would be upset enough to replace the locks on the house, and took Sarah to a hardware store, where he purchased new locks, all with the same code so they would take the same key, and then drove home. Halfway home his phone rang and he answered.

"John, it's Shepherd Quinn," Quinn said, even sounding sheepish.

"Shepherd, how are you?" John asked.

"Wondering where you and Sarah are, actually," Quinn said. "We're in front of your house and nobody answers the door."

John decided to play along. "Shepherd, someone broke into our house today and I went and bought better locks," he began.

"I know about that," Quinn said, still sounding sheepish. In truth, Quinn was furious but kept that buried deeply. "Come on home. We need to talk, John."

"I'll be there shortly," John promised, and hung up the phone.

"This oughta be fun," Sarah said, putting her game face on.

"I'm sorry for what happened today," Quinn said later in their living room. "Dale?"

"The men were good men of the church working at my orders," said Dale Rawson, one of the Board of Elders. "You will go to the police station with Elder Luden and release them immediately."

Sarah suddenly felt a burst of white-hot rage, and couldn't entirely contain it. "How dare you?" she snapped. "We're good followers of the Lord, we let you into our home, let you inspect every nook and cranny here, and now you dishonor God and us by sending men to break into our house? Get out of my house! Out!"

"Sarah, that is more than enough from you," John said in a calm but stern tone. "Go up to your bedroom and I will deal with you later."

"Shepherd, I hereby charge Mrs. Sarah Avery with insubordination," Rawson sneered, his rage obvious in his facial expression. "I will expect to see her punished for this outrage."

"I will deal with Sarah," John said. "But … now, I'm no lawyer, Elder Rawson, but you just admitted to me that you are a conspirator in this break-in, and that means if I raise cane about it, Elder Luden will have to take you to jail. I'd guess you'd do time for that, Sir."

"Gentlemen, cool down," Luden said. "Dale, I think Shepherd will agree with me that you should go wait in the car before you make a bad situation far worse than you already have."

"Shepherd?" Rawson asked, and Quinn quietly nodded and gestured to the door. "The charges stand," Rawson sneered, and barged out of the house.

"Insofar as the church is concerned, he is a male and an elder and your wife is in violation, John," Quinn said. "I will try to talk him out of it, but I think my hands are tied."

141

"John, the church … I'm going to tell you something that I had hoped we wouldn't have to tell the membership, and I hope you'll keep this confidence."

John raised a hand. "So long as you're not dragging my wife and me into criminal activity or things that will offend the Lord, I'll keep your confidence," he said.

"We're not a criminal enterprise," Luden said stiffly, and then softened. "But … I suppose we didn't make a good first impression, and part of that … let's be honest … most of it is my fault, John. Here's what's going on. A parishioner of ours died a while back and left his house to us in his will. Someone – we have no idea who – killed several people, threw the body parts about the house, which was vacant … anyway, they set off incendiary devices when police officers were in the house. Five good cops were killed just doing their job."

"How awful," John said. "I've seen something about it on TV, on the news."

"The most recent one was in my precinct," Luden confirmed. "Anyway, a police officer, a homicide sergeant named Lowe, came to visit the church and, frankly, raised some hackles. I tried talking sense to him and got nowhere, and our first thought was that you and Sarah were here undercover to infiltrate and persecute the church."

"You can't be serious," John said, acting surprised.

"I'm afraid I'm the one who rang the alarm on that," Luden admitted. "One way or another, my own paranoia was suppressed when Louise Calloway told us … well, you apparently punished Sarah recently. I've been a policeman a long time, and I know there is no way in the world undercover people could be assigned to do that, the same way the police could never order someone to use drugs or commit crimes. So I was satisfied that you and Sarah are as you represent yourselves to be. But Dale ... he wasn't. He sent that team here – one of them is a locksmith – and investigated your home again, stem to stern, thinking he'd find ... I don't know what he thought he'd find. But one way or another, the men arrested thought they were following the orders of the church. We would be grateful if you would release them to go home to their families."

"And I will promise you here and now that such an outrage will never happen again," Quinn said. "I know many see us as intrusive, and for good reasons of God's Holy Law, we are, but this ... John, you and Sarah were violated."

"We were," John agreed. "I assure you she'll go to bed tonight very sorry for how she behaved. But gentlemen, I want you both to know I agree fully with her. She'll be punished for speaking out of turn, not because what she said was wrong."

"I understand," Quinn said. "Look, as a favor to me, go easy on her. And I'll try to talk sense to Dale."

"Yes, Shepherd," John said, and then looked at Luden. "So how do I spring your jailbirds?"

Ninety minutes later, Luden dropped John off at his house. The men arrested had been released on dropped charges, and Walter Zane was given information on how to get his van from impound, which would hit him fairly heavily in his back pocket.

"Come to the barn with me," John said to Sarah, and she followed him out to the barn.

143

"Shortly after you left, the team came over and said we're clean," Sarah said on the way to the barn. "No listening devices, not even in the barn."

"That's good to know," John said.

"I know what has to happen in the barn," Sarah said. "And I honestly think I deserve it. I damn near blew our cover with that little tantrum, and thank you for intervening before we were clobbered. So I ... I really want you to lay it to me so I learn not to ever do that again in this assignment."

"As you wish," John said, feeling relieved. The truth was, she'd put them both at huge risk, and he agreed she had it coming. "You deserve it. Interestingly enough, Quinn feels badly about this and asked me to go easy on you."

"Wow, that is surprising," Sarah said. "John, at the risk of repeating myself, I deserve it."

"At the risk of repeating myself, I agree," John said. "Bare your ass in there, and bend over that table." Sarah stripped naked and obeyed, grasping the edges of the table. John picked up the cane, made of bamboo or something akin to it, and approached her. "Thirty," he said.

"Yes, Husband," Sarah replied, and grasped the edges of the table. John began lashing her, and Sarah began silently weeping, but holding her place.

"What in the hell is going on here?" Jane demanded, alarming both of them. "Put that down and put your hands where I can see them!" She produced a pistol and aimed it at John, surprising him.

144

"Jane, calm down," Sarah said. "I'm here voluntarily. Put the pistol down. John is on the right side of this one."

"This is going to take some mighty tall explaining," Jane said. "Get dressed, for God's sake. And then we're going to talk. I'm one heartbeat from calling Inspector Reese and terminating this assignment."

"Holy motherfucking shit," Jane breathed when Sarah and John finished telling her about the corporal punishment. "Goddammit, if Inspector Reese finds out about this, you two are off undercover work forever, and if she finds out I knew and didn't fucking tell her, I'll be fired retroactively until sometime before my grandparents were born."

"Then don't tell her," Sarah said, wincing as she shifted on her seat. "Look … I'm going to show all my cards here. The church is suspect in the murders of five police officers, and maybe it'll prove they're entirely innocent, but we all doubt that. When we were visited earlier tonight, one of the men, a Dale Rawson —"

"He's an elder of the church," Jane recalled from memory.

"Him," Sarah confirmed. "Anyway, the burglary team was acting on his orders. I lost my temper at him some, for real, and John sent me to my room before I totally blew our cover. Rawson is charging me in the church with insubordination and Quinn and Luden are going to try to talk him out of it, but indicated it was unlikely. So I'm very probably going to be whipped Sunday. But one way or another, I put John and myself at risk with that indiscretion. And again, if they see the marks – from what you told me, those to be punished get a pre-punishment physical – they'll see us again as legitimate."

"Look," Jane said after a long moment visibly thinking. "I wasn't here and I don't know jackshit about this aspect of your assignment and the discretion you two are employing. I'm not going to ask, I'm not going to tell, and if I'm subpoenaed I'll have the most profound dose of amnesia ever encountered in the justice system. But you both need to know that when the officialdom at the Department learns of this, you're both going to have your ass on the griddle. I assume you weren't quite done when I stuck my nose in here, so I'm going to go away now. Please wait a long moment so I'm entirely out of earshot on this." With that, Jane stood and marched from the barn.

"I think we just got a lesson in command-level decision-making," John said.

"Yeah, about trusting your people even if you disagree," Sarah agreed. "I believe I'm still under sentence of an additional twenty-seven lashes with that evil thing." She sighed, stood, and disrobed again, and then took her position back over the table. John picked up the cane and continued lashing Sarah until she'd taken all thirty strokes, sobbing piteously by the time it was done. Her right buttock was mostly purple by then. He helped her to her feet and she surprised him by falling into his embrace, and when the crying was done, even kissing him.

"Thank you, Husband," she said in quiet tones. "Will Husband want me in his bed tonight?"

"Of course," John said. Sarah rounded up her clothing and carried it under one arm, not wanting to dress herself this late at night only to undress herself in a couple minutes. They got to John's room and made tender love, and then fell asleep in a naked tangle of limbs.

At the church, Quinn called an impromptu meeting of the Board of Elders after he and Luden spent two hours trying to talk sense to Rawson, and finally gave up. The meeting convened and Rawson presented his charge against Sarah Avery, which required his revelation of what had caused her outburst. But the other elders, texted by Quinn, overlooked Rawson's culpability as they let him rail on about that uppity woman needing a comeuppance.

"Brethren, I suggest that Mrs. Avery did indeed forget her place and should be punished for her insubordination, but I would also suggest the extenuating circumstances and duress indicate she deserves a light punishment. I move that she be found guilty and awarded five lashes at the Sunday service," Butler suggested.

"Frankly, I know discipline is important here, but seeing how she was subjected to a felony crime, I would suggest she be reprimanded and this matter concludes," Luden said.

"Why are you going soft on her?" Rawson snapped. "She should receive forty lashes and ten years of probation."

"Dale, we've never given that many lashes to a first offender, and only very seldom to a second offender," Quinn said tiredly. "And if I had to bet, her husband already has her sleeping on her belly. And at the risk of repeating myself again, you subjected those nice people to a felony crime. A *felony*, Dale! Frankly, if Mrs. Avery had insisted you be arrested and charged, and your three minions all went to prison with you I wouldn't have blamed her. This is on you, Dale, not on her."

The talk went back and forth for ten minutes before Quinn interjected. "Brethren, I think we've all decided on this matter," he said. "I want you all to write your sentences on cards and hand them to me. The least and greatest punishments will be excluded, and I'll take an average of the rest."

One by one, the men wrote on cards and handed them to Quinn. Two went for reprimand, and Quinn eliminated one of those. One, certainly from Rawson called for nearly a death penalty, also excluded. Quinn did some quick math. "She will be given eight lashes Sunday and that will conclude this matter," he decreed.

"This is ridiculous," Rawson sneered.

"Oh, we're not done, Dale," Quinn said. "Brethren, Dale Rawson has risked the welfare of this church on a felonious fishing expedition, from which I'd be willing to bet his lackeys found nothing. I hereby move that he be found guilty of conduct unbecoming an elder, stripped of his elder status, and vigorously punished."

"What?" Rawson yelled, coming to his feet. His face had gone nearly purple with rage.

"Sit down, Dale," Luden said. "Shepherd Quinn has leveled a charge at you, as is his right to do, and if I have to say this, you're blessed that John Avery didn't want you arrested, because I would have had no choice, as an officer of the law, to have arrested you and put you in jail with your lackeys. I agree with the Shepherd. You should thank the Lord our God that you aren't cooling your heels in the city jail and contemplating prison time."

"Lackeys?" Rawson thundered. "They are good and strong men of God who are doing God's work. And you're the one who raised the suspicions about these people in the first place."

"Yes I did," Luden agreed calmly. "But Hollis laid my suspicions to rest. We've already been over that."

"I refuse to be railroaded by your sudden feel-good liberalism," Rawson said. "This is asinine, Isaiah. Asinine!"

"Dale, you need to wrap your mind around the fact that you orchestrated a felony today that could have destroyed our church," Quinn said, his own annoyance rising. "And right about now the last thing we can afford is stupid risks. You've been a longtime friend and a valued soldier of our church, but we're already under the scrutiny of the cops and you threw gasoline on those fires if our involvement in this came to light. Now, sit down and take it like a man."

"This is unconscionable," Rawson sneered. "Unconscionable. But fine. You want to punish me for doing right, well, our Lord was punished worse for doing better." He sat and glared at them.

"We've already talked this through," Quinn said. "What more do you have to say on your behalf?"

"Only that I did the right thing, no matter the laws of the godless beyond our walls," Rawson said. "I was willing to take the fall and be martyred in prison in the name of protecting our church. You men all know me. You've all been to my house, and we've mostly eaten at one another's tables. And where is Christ's mercy in all this, my friends?"

"You were quite willing to see Sarah Avery beaten half to death on the altar of your pride," said Dan Calloway. It was the first time he'd spoken. "Where is the mercy in that, Dale? Look, I'm going to throw this on the table too, just as an aside. John and Sarah are the first applicants for membership we've seen in six months, gentlemen, six months. They're young, healthy, active, and frankly none of us are growing younger. If we want our church to survive beyond our own lives before God calls us Home, then we need to add new and younger members like these two. And while I'm bringing up unhappy facts, about 40% of our youth leave the church between the ages of 18 and 21. How much of our paranoia is going to see John and Sarah giving up on us? And what kind of disservice will we have done to them as well in the process?"

"Dan makes a good point," Luden interjected. "Look, I like these two and we have accepted them into our church. I can't recall a single incident of us sending a black-bag team to a parishioner's house. Yeah, we do no-notice inspections from time to time, but I don't think we've ever sent someone to enter a house outside a parishioner's knowledge, and the more I think on it the more despicable I consider it to be. Dale, we've been good friends for years on end now, and as far as I'm concerned we'll continue to be good friends. But you ... you overstepped today, and that can't be overlooked."

"Paul, I'm disappointed in you," Rawson said. "Who stood beside you when your wife died? Who was with you when your sons disowned you?"

"You were," Luden acknowledged. "But this isn't about you and me, Dale. In or out of the church I think of you as my brother, and always will. But this isn't about us. It's about the church, a far greater concern than our friendship, or even our lives, if this must be said. Dale, if our chairs were reversed, I'm certain you would feel as I do."

"All for serving the church and our God," Rawson said bitterly. "Fine. What is my punishment?"

"Perhaps you should step outside while we discuss exactly that," Hollis said.

"Very well," Rawson said in a stiff tone, and then marched from the building to the parking lot, looking at his watch and wondering if maybe he had become too holy for this church. But he also acknowledged, at least privately, that he and his wife needed the church, at least for now, and he was embarrassed that he had behaved so foolishly in sending people to enter their home this early in. His secret was that he had done this with twenty other parishioners' homes over the past year, but what the Elders didn't know wouldn't hurt him.

Fifteen minutes later, Luden came out to meet him. "We've decided, Dale," he said. "Come inside, please." Inside, Rawson was sentenced, and felt nauseous at what he was to suffer. But he agreed to be there for a punishment after Sunday's service.

TWENTY-THREE

"The devices didn't go off," the man said to the woman. "But it wasn't your error. One of those people put the wrong phone on the device. The right one rang in the box. I have dealt with him. But this just exposed us to far more danger from the law."

"You said we were going to be caught in time," the woman said.

"So I did," he agreed. "But we have far more to do, and I'm afraid that's in danger now. The police are far from stupid, and this chief investigator ... Lowe, his name is ... apparently enjoys a very good reputation for getting the job done."

"Could he be turned?" the woman asked.

"No, not a chance, but I have a plan," he said, and explained for a few minutes.

"It would take a few days, but ... we could do it on the fly," the woman said.

"Yes, pick three men and let's get it done," the man said.

That night, parts of eight bodies, emptying the freezer on the property, were dumped in an abandoned storefront in an abandoned shopping strip in the 11th Precinct. This time the incendiary devices went off perfectly. No call was placed to the police. Enough body parts would survive to let the whole city know another cleansing had happened. The fire had blazed for nearly twenty minutes before a police cruiser spotted the flames and called the fire department. By then, the body parts were thoroughly incinerated.

The fire department threw sand everywhere, per orders, and calls went out to the task force. Lowe, fresh out of the hospital and over Lisa's howling objections, went to the scene. The truth was, he still felt like hell, but he had a fire in his belly that wanted to consume these sons of bitches once and for all. But he knew, looking at the scene, that little if any evidence would be forthcoming. Just the same, the CSU people were on standby and would work hand-in-hand with the arson investigators as well as the coroner to get all that was possible to get.

Six miles from the scene, the refrigerated truck picked up a nail in a front tire, which blew it out. The two men in the truck weren't worried. They had documents, and their leader took care to ensure that all the body parts had been wrapped in plastic never touched by bare hands, so the truck was entirely clean of criminal traces. It contained five cases of steaks and a like number of cases of fish, as well as about eighty frozen fryers, all earmarked for various restaurants. Uncertain what to do, the driver used his iPhone to look up heavy wreckers, found one, and called. The wrecker would be there in an hour, he was told. The car of others had gone a different route. Reluctantly, afraid of his temper, the driver called their leader.

"We have a flat tire and a wrecker on the way," the driver said. "Where do we take the truck?"

"Give me a moment," the leader said, groaning with pain. He tapped on his computer for a moment. "Okay, there's Stroud Tire and Wheel. They deal in heavy truck tires. Have it taken there. The refrigerator runs on a generator, so leave that running. I'll send someone to pick you up there."

"I understand," the driver said, and their leader hung up the phone, groaning in more pain as he placed a call for one of his people to go meet the truck at the tire center.

Fifteen minutes later, a police car stopped behind the truck and turned on his lights. "Exit the truck from the driver side and keep your hands in sight," the officer commanded. His name was Frank Parton, a seven-year veteran of the Department. It was Parton's first day back after a week of vacation, and he was glad he'd read the various memos before beginning his shift, and was grateful that he had a near-eidetic memory. The men, both unarmed and in a truck that wouldn't go far on the flat, exited the truck, keeping their hands in view, and wondering what went wrong. In a moment, three other police cars appeared, and the two were handcuffed and taken to jail. The wrecker arrived soon after, and was directed to take the truck to impound.

Lowe, excited for the first time in a very long time, made a beeline to the jail, eager to interrogate the two suspects, but realized he wasn't going to make the right impression in jeans and a stained t-shirt. He diverted home, placing a call to Walker, who said he'd get the DA in on it immediately. Lowe hurriedly dressed in a suit and made his way to the jail, where a DA was waiting, this one a woman he knew, Margaret Flame. She had been fifteen years with the DA, the last ten prosecuting murders, and enjoyed a very good reputation among the police. The subjects were identified as Luke Waterford and Matthew Lipton, both 32 years old and both with clean records. Both claimed to be employed by GGTB Frozen Foods, whose offices were closed until 8:00 AM. Flame said she would interview Waterford with Walker behind her. Lieutenant Holmes showed up in full uniform, looking fresh as a daisy, and would be in on the Lipton interview.

"Mr. Lipton, I'm Sergeant Michael Lowe," Lowe introduced himself. "This lady with me is Lieutenant Miranda Holmes. I want to re-read your rights to you for the record, before we speak."

"Save it, Sir," Lipton said. "The guy that cuffed me done did that, and I don't want to hear it again. And I'll save a lot of your time too. I want a lawyer and don't want to talk with you."

"That is your absolute right," Lowe said. "So I won't ask you anything, but you need to know you're in a heap of trouble, son. And by that, I mean we have enough on you to strap you to a table, put a needle in you, and put you down like a mangy dog. Here's where we are ... your truck was seen by a witness at the scene of the murders before this one. And now, lo and behold, here you are in this truck just a few blocks away —"

"Save it," Lipton interrupted. "Lawyer."

"Very well," Lowe said. "Do you have one, or will you require a court-appointed attorney?"

"I need to make a phone call, but I should have one," Lipton said.

"We'll have an officer take you to a telephone," Holmes told him.

"Son, one way or another – and I don't care if you drag in OJ Simpson's Dream Team into the courtroom – you're screwed," Lowe said. "I'm telling you right now that the DA is prepared to make a deal with you and your buddy Waterford. I don't have to be a rocket scientist to know you're a cog in the wheel here. Roll over on your bigger bosses and it'll go a lot easier on you."

"Sir, I want a lawyer," Lipton repeated.

"As you wish," Lowe said. "Lieutenant, I think we can proceed with capital murder charges against Mr. Lipton."

"I agree, Sergeant," Holmes said, rising. "Mr. Lipton, someone will be by shortly to collect information from you on how to contact your attorney."

They met Flame and Walker in the hall, and Flame clucked her tongue. "Waterford was barking for a lawyer the second we walked in," she said.

"Ditto with Lipton," Lowe told her.

"I'll be interested in knowing who's going to represent these two clowns," Holmes said.

"Worry no more," Flame returned. "He has indicated his lawyer is Walther Kurberg of Kurberg, Martin, Willis & Jordan."

"Well, now isn't that fascinating?" Lowe said, then looked around. "Let's all step in this empty interview room, shall we?"

"Walther Kurberg is one of the elders," Lowe said, and Holmes' brows rose at this.

"Fascinating," Holmes said. "But in and of itself it's not enough to convict someone."

"No, but it's another link in the chain, Ma'am," Lowe said.

"Hold on," Flame interjected. "I feel like I walked into the middle of a movie here. What's going on?"

"Shit," Holmes said. "Let's all go to the chief's conference room. It's more comfortable and private than this interview room. Maggie, this is about to be a huge career-booster for you if we do it right."

TWENTY-FOUR

In the conference room, Holmes called Reese and Watts, who both said they would be there shortly. "Maggie, this is going to be far-ranging, so you might want to call Blake Hamlin and get him on this train. I think he'd be pretty pissed off at you if he learned about this meeting after the fact."

"You're serious?" Flame asked.

"Maggie, the chickens aren't even going cockadoodledoo yet and I'm here," Holmes said. "Do you think I'd be here at this ungodly hour in full uniform to run a practical joke on you?"

"I'll call him," Flame said, and dialed a number on her phone. "Sir, I'm in Chief Watts' office suite with Lieutenant Holmes and Sergeant Lowe ... yes, Sir, but I'm not certain what this is all about ... I ... yes, Sir. I'll see you soon."

She hung up the phone, looking shellshocked. "I'll be Goddamned," Flame said. "He's on his way."

"Maggie, Sergeant Lowe is in charge of the task force trying to chase down those multiple-murder-arson scenes," Holmes said.

"Jesus, I heard about those, but ... I didn't know," Flame said.

"We've kept a tight lid on it," Holmes said. "One captain is going to be fired, and might be involved in the murders. If so, he's going to death row. We think a church is involved in this as well, one of those one-off charismatic ones out on the lunatic fringe. The captain is a member of that church. And if I had to bet, Misters Waterford and Lipton are members as well."

"I think we best get coffee started soon," Flame said, and went to the big Bunn coffeemaker in the kitchenette off the conference room.

"Jesus, it's all leading to Luden," Hamlin said a half-hour later. "But … no judge I know would put out a warrant on him on the basis of what you have. It's all circumstantial. Suggestive as hell, I agree, but it's still just circumstantial. What about the two clowns in jail down there?"

"Both of 'em hollered for a lawyer first shot out of the barrel," Flame said sourly.

"And the lawyer is an elder in this nutbag church," Hamlin said, more in distaste than surprise.

"I am not going to get into this in detail," Reese contributed. "My experience is the fewer people who know a secret, the better. But I have people working to infiltrate this church and see if more can be learned."

"Okay," Hamlin said. "I'm sure Margaret can get a warrant to inspect the truck. If we can find one shred of DNA that links that truck to the victims, then we're golden and they're going to death row. Meanwhile, I think we can keep them remanded on suspicion of capital murder. We also need to see if Mrs. Garcia can more positively identify the truck. Maybe also get some good photos of Luden's car and see if she can identify that too. I looked into this lawyer they're consulting, and these people are damned good. Not as flashy as some of the others, and awfully expensive, but … I think we can beat them if we build good evidence."

"Where is Luden now, Inspector Reese?" Watts asked.

"He's off duty tonight, and got to his apartment around 11:00," Reese said. "The lights were on until around 3:00 and then went off. As far as my guy can tell – I talked to him right before you arrived – he's sound asleep. I need to see what's up with his living arrangement, though."

"How do you mean?" Watts asked.

"Well, his permanent address is a farm just outside the city, yea many acres with a simple house on it, but he's lived in this apartment a few years now," Reese answered. "Probably an oddity, but why leave the house vacant, you know?"

"Yeah, that's worth a look," Watts said. "Get in touch with Undersheriff Thackery since that's in the county not the city. Find out what's going on there."

"I'll call her when she gets to her office," Holmes promised.

"Inspector Johnson, I want you to bury Luden in hours, at least twelve hours daily, seven days a week, to keep him too busy to murder anyone," Watts said. "Figure it like this. If more bodies turn up, then he has plausible deniability if he was on duty. But if the killings stop, he looks better for this. I know it's circumstantial but we need somewhere to hang our hat on this one."

"I'll write the orders this morning," Johnson promised.

"Lowe, you look like hammered shit and I don't have to be clairvoyant to know there's no way your doctor cleared you to return to work this morning," Watts said. "Get your ass home and see if you're more up to it tomorrow. I appreciate your devotion and work ethic, but I need you more later than now. Scram."

"I'm fine, Sir," Lowe protested.

"Lowe, you lie like old people fuck," Watts pointed out. "Scram!"

"Yes, Sir," Lowe said. The truth was, he felt like hell and wasn't doing well being dragged out at oh-dark-early, and the coffee was doing little, virtually nothing, to revive him. He drove home, weaving with exhaustion, and was embarrassed when a patrol unit pulled him down.

Lowe flipped his badge at the officer, but it seemed to cut no ice with her. "Sir, have you been drinking?" she asked.

"No, just exhausted," Lowe said. "And sick."

"Please step from the car," the officer said, and after a field sobriety test, was mostly mollified that Lowe wasn't drunk. Just then, another patrol car pulled up, and a crusty old officer stepped out, and Lowe chuckled.

"Mike Lowe, as I live and breathe," said Sergeant Darren Joplin.

"Hey, Darren," Lowe said tiredly.

"Sir, he's passed the field sobriety test and says he's exhausted," the female officer – her nametag read J. Latimore – said.

"Considering the way this man works I'm not the least bit surprised," Joplin remarked. "Okay, I'm going to park my cruiser in this lot and then you are going to follow me as I drive Sergeant Lowe home and then return me here. I'll call dispatch and put us both out of service.

Lowe was sound asleep two minutes into the ride home, and Joplin and Latimore had to half-carry him into his bed. Joplin sent Latimore from the room and removed Lowe's shoes and then loosened his belt, and left his old friend to sleep. Lowe wouldn't wake until his alarm went off the next morning.

TWENTY-FIVE

Quinn rang the doorbell at the Avery house, and Sarah answered. "Good morning, Shepherd," she said, smiling slightly at him. "Won't you please come in?"

"Thank you," Quinn said. "Is John around?"

"He'll be home shortly," Sarah said. "He went to the hardware store for something or other. But he called a moment ago to tell me he's on the way home. Please have a seat. Would you like a refreshment?"

"If you have apple juice, a glass of that would go down very nicely, please," Quinn said.

"Of course," Sarah replied with a slight curtsy, and then went into the kitchen and returned with a tall glass of juice for the shepherd. Quinn drank half the juice at a draught.

"Thank you so much," he said. "I was parched when I got here."

"It is a warm day," Sarah agreed.

"Even worse when the air conditioner in my car conked out this morning," Quinn returned.

163

"Oh, no," Sarah said, honestly feeling sorry for him. She was surprised to find she liked Quinn, even if she thought his religious leanings sounded insane. But it took all kinds, she knew.

"Yeah, at this point I'm probably going to have to get another car," Quinn said. "It's pretty beat up and mechanics are spending more time under it than I manage in it."

"I'm sorry," Sarah said. "That has to be a huge hit in your back pocket."

"Yeah, but not as bad as you'd think," Quinn said. "Greg Savage owns a used car lot and will sell anything he has to me for five hundred dollars above cost. Since I always buy something simple, it's not all that harsh on me, and I'm paying cash. He has a five-year-old Lincoln that he thinks I'll like, but probably a bit ostentatious for my tastes, and a half-dozen or so two-year-old sedans."

"We did that with our truck and car," Sarah said. "The house too. John and I both believe usury is sin, so if we can't buy it with what we have, we figure we don't need it all that badly. God will provide what we need. Besides, he made a ton of money working overseas, and we're far better off only paying the regular monthly bills, insurance, water, gas, that sort of thing."

"It's the wisest way to live," Quinn agreed, right as John opened the door.

"Well hello, Shepherd," John said. "How do you do?"

"I'm well," Quinn said.

"Sarah taking good care of you?" John asked.

"She is indeed," Quinn said, holding up his quarter-full glass.

"Would you like a refill, Shepherd?" Sarah asked.

"No, I'm fine," Quinn said. "I came here to tell you what the elders decided regarding your outburst, Sarah."

Sarah felt a genuine burst of butterflies in her belly as she sat on the sofa and looked wide-eyed at Quinn. "How bad, Shepherd?" she managed to ask.

"Not as bad as it could have been if Dale Rawson was the decision-maker," Quinn said. "Mrs. Avery, it is my duty to inform you that the elders have sentenced you to receive eight lashes of the horsewhip to your bared back at Sunday's service."

"Horsewhipped," Sarah breathed. "I've seen photos of slaves, gnarled on their backs for life."

"If taken to that extreme, it could happen, I suppose," Quinn said. "But this happens in our church, and I've never put scars on someone for a first offense, nor a second offense. The objective is to punish and make you a better follower of our Risen Savior, certainly not to destroy you. I know your husband disciplines you —"

"He did last night," Sarah interjected.

"Tell me, is it done to terrorize you or to make a better helpmate of you, Sarah?" Quinn pursued.

"To make a better wife and person of me, because he loves me, of course," Sarah said. "It was no different when I was a kid and my parents took me to the woodshed. Or when Dad took Mom out there on occasion, I suppose."

"Exactly," Quinn said. "The church loves you. If I have to say this I'm growing fond of both you and John. I won't go easy on you, but neither am I trying to break you like a glass dropped on a stone floor. This is to make you consider self-control. But I also … Sarah I want you to think of how much our Savior suffered for you, for all of us, and realize you are paying far less of a price."

"Yes, thank you, Shepherd," Sarah said, actually a bit relieved and wondering if she'd lost her mind.

"You'll be picked up Saturday afternoon and taken to the church," Quinn said. "We maintain dormitories there, for people needing a place to sleep. But once you are picked up, John can have no contact with you until after you've had your punishment. You will be summoned to the dais, your sentence will be read, and you will turn your back to the church and remove your blouse – the parishioners will only see your back, not your breasts or belly, which are rightly reserved to your husband's eyes, and your physician's. You will then have your whipping, and will be led directly from the chapel to the infirmary, treated, and then you'll be free to come home with your husband. John, another matter has come up – you're in no trouble – but I would be pleased if you'd return to the church Sunday at 5:00 for about an hour."

"Certainly," John said, curious but sensing he'd only annoy Quinn with questions.

"Well, I think it's time to take myself to the car lot," Quinn said, rising to his feet. "You'll be okay, Sarah. Just … please learn from this matter Sunday."

"Of course, Shepherd," Sarah said.

"I'll talk with you later," Quinn said, and departed.

"I hope I shame you no further, Husband," Sarah said.

"You'd be well-advised to stay on the straight and narrow," John returned.

"What does Husband wish to do today?" Sarah asked.

"I think I'm going to light up the pit and cook those lamb ribs we bought yesterday," John said. "I was thinking corn on the cob and baked potatoes with it."

"I can make an apple pie, Husband, if I may go to the store and buy apples," Sarah said.

"Go to the store, then," John said, smiling. "And a big tub of Blue Bell vanilla with it, please."

"Done and done, Husband," Sarah said. She grabbed her purse, and in a moment she was darting off to the grocery store.

TWENTY-SIX

"You have arrested my clients for nothing but being in a truck at night, which isn't a crime," snapped Clinton Dawes, a lawyer Kurberg had dispatched from his firm to defend Waterford and Lipton. "I'm already going to file civil suit against the city for false arrest, and every minute they're in here only adds to the award they'll receive. I demand you drop these charges and let them go right now."

"Dude, this isn't Hollywood and you're not going to get an Oscar for this performance," Flame said. "We have an eyewitness who identifies the truck, which was found not at all far from the last murder-arson scene —"

"Identified by a painted-over logo," Dawes interrupted with a snort. "I'll tear her to pieces on the stand, and we both know that, Ms. Flame."

"Sit down, Clint," Flame said calmly. "I'm not a juror likely to be impressed. I was prosecuting schmucks like your boys when you were still learning to hit the toilet with your first squirt." Blushing, Dawes shrugged and then sat. "Now, ordinarily, I'd agree. There's no way I could take this case into court on just what my witness has to say. But look me up. Look up my conviction record and ask yourself how careful you think I am, kid. I have far more than my eyewitness. We all know in spite of a thousand TV shows, eyewitnesses aren't all that great anyway, right? But the truck – we got warrants to search every centimeter of it – we've found blood traces in a couple parts that are human, and I figure DNA is going to match that blood to at least one, probably more, of the victims. And your boys – Jesus, they're so stupid they need to be locked away for stupidity alone – when they turned the corner from one scene, they drove across the corner of the yard and left some perfect tire impressions, and they match the truck to a tee. Now, I think we both know what that means, don't we? Tell your boys to roll over on the rest of their gang – I doubt those two morons acted alone and I suspect they're just hired muscle in any event – but tell them to roll over and I'll take the death penalty off the table and will make no huge deal about life with the possibility of parole.

"But the clock is ticking, Clint," Flame continued. "If we catch up to their partners – and that's going to happen, and we both know it – my offer is off the table. And if we find more damning evidence against them than we already have, my boss is going to tell me go for broke on these two, and with the climate in this county, you know come ten years, maybe fifteen if you get really slick, they'll be strapped to a table and get lethal injections. Right now, your boys are young, and could be free men in fifteen or so years. It's up to you and them, Clint. The discovery items thus far are being forwarded to your office later today, but let's face facts. They're fucked, your boys. Just how fucked do you want them to be? Have a good day, okay?" Flame rose and so did Dawes. They shook hands and Dawes returned to his office, where he had two messages telling him to come immediately to Walther Kurberg's office.

"Ah, Dawes, thank you for coming up," Kurberg said. "Tell me about your case with Mr. Waterford and Mr. Lipton."

"Sir, they're barely talking to me, and not at all to the prosecutor or police," Dawes said. "But the evidence against them ... if it went to trial this week, they'd probably go to death row. Human blood was found in their truck, which is being tested now for DNA to see how many victims it'll link to. And they cut a corner wrong and left perfect tire impressions in one of the yards. The DA is sending a discovery packet today. I can fuck up an eyewitness on the stand, but physical evidence ... since *CSI* and the like came around, jurors are really impressed with it, and ... yeah, my clients are going down, more especially in this guilty-until-proven-innocent climate of the area. What would you think about leaking to the papers, trying to build hoopla, and then going for a change of venue?"

"Absolutely not," Kurberg said. "Clint, I think the best thing you can do is to make the best deal you can for your boys, even if it means a guilty plea to capital murder, which would take the death penalty out of the equation, and send them to prison. I mean, unless God Himself comes down from Heaven with an Eleventh Commandment that exonerates your boys, they're finished."

"Yes, Sir," Dawes said. "I'll look through what the DA sends to see if I can find any holes, but they tend to be meticulous with murders, so I doubt there's going to be any chinks in the armor there. Thank you, Sir."

"I wish we could talk more but I have another client I need to go meet," Kurberg said. The men shook hands, and Dawes returned to his office while Kurberg went to his Mercedes, and drove to the Church of God's Law with the bad news.

"Look, I could be disbarred in a heartbeat if you mishandle this information," Kurberg said a little while later. "But sooner or later the cops are going to tip to the fact that those men are members of this church. If I had to bet, they already know this. They got search warrants for both of their houses, and – neither of them is very bright – there's bound to be the odd program from Sunday services or the like there, and then what? Paul, I looked into your Sergeant Lowe —"

"He's not mine," Luden interrupted. "If he was, I'd have pointed him anywhere but this church. We didn't do this, Walther."

"The truck is registered to a meat company owned by a holding company which is owned by another holding company," Kurberg said. "I had my corporate people look into it and they tell me it's anyone's guess who really owns it. But I'd suppose sooner or later the DA is going to report the company to the IRS, and they'll get to whoever owns it, one way or another, and God help us all if that ties back to the church, even with spider silk."

"Who's directing Brothers Waterford and Lipton?" Quinn asked.

"Shepherd, if I knew I'd tell you, no matter the consequences to my license," Kurberg said. "I sent one of my sharper guys, relatively young but smart, a man named Clinton Dawes, to represent them. He says they won't even talk to him. It's like they ... Dawes said it reminds him of tales of the mafia or biker gangs, foot soldiers so loyal they're even willing to be executed for their cause to protect their masters ... or maybe their greater cause."

"I see," Quinn said.

"I'm surprised they're not talking," Luden remarked. "Most people facing serious charges would give up their mother for a reduced sentence."

"It is surprising," Kurberg agreed, noting that Luden looked sick, and wondering why this was, but not pursuing the matter.

"Thank you for bringing this to our attention," Quinn said. "If you have a few minutes I want to call the elders and discuss excommunication of Waterford and Lipton at least until this matter is resolved.

"Shepherd, may I interject?" Luden asked. Quinn nodded. "Shepherd, perhaps until we know more, we're best not acknowledging those two. Right now, nothing implicates the church, so if we 'don't know' they're in jail it makes us look innocent not paranoid."

"He makes a good point," Kurberg agreed after a moment to digest this suggestion.

"Then we'll wait off a bit," Quinn said. "You can head back to work, I guess, Walther, unless you have something more?"

"No, that was all," Kurberg said, and left.

"You know something about this," Quinn said to Luden. "Spill it, Paul."

"Shepherd, please trust me that there are things you're going to be happier, and better served, not knowing," Luden returned.

Quinn thought this over for a long moment. "Very well," he said at length. "I'm sure you've got to be wiped out from working all night."

"When this case is done, I'm going to file for retirement," Luden said. "The truth is, I would already have done so if not for this. The 22nd ... it's a disgrace retirement, Shepherd." He was silent a moment. "I'm sorry. You have more to deal with than an old man feeling sorry for himself. But yes, I need to go try to sleep some."

Luden was almost home when his phone rang. "Captain Luden," he answered.

"Luden, this is Inspector Johnson."

"Yes, Sir?" Luden replied.

"Captain, we have a situation at the 18th Precinct," Johnson said. "Captain Terry Oliver took a sudden leave – it's a long story – but you're the man available. You're going to be covering his evening shift for a couple weeks and then your night shift at the 22nd. I need you there today at 1400, at the 18th."

"Inspector, I've been awake since 9:00 last night," Luden protested. "That would give me about one hour to sleep before pulling sixteen hours."

"Captain, I know it sucks, but you're the one picked for the job," Johnson said. Luden knew refusal would very probably see him forcibly retired before the end of the day, and Johnson knew Luden knew this. "The job at the 18th is mostly at a desk, Paul. And I know for a fact they keep coffee going twenty-four hours daily there." Johnson knew the church's stance on stimulants, but decided to play stupid just to stick the needle in Luden.

"I'll be there," Luden said sourly. He got to his apartment and took a lengthy shower, and then climbed into a uniform, noting that two of his uniforms were growing threadbare, and then he went to his car, ate at a diner, stopped at a drugstore for caffeine tablets (he knew he would have to confess this lesser sin to the Shepherd) and drove on to the 18th, where he worked until nearly 10:00 before driving off to the 22nd and working through the night in a patrol car. He got home at 6:00 in near-delirium, and had to fight to get out of bed at 1:00 to go report to the 18th again. He checked the schedules and learned he would be working seven days weekly. Oliver's nights off were Tuesday and Wednesday and his own nights off were Sunday and Monday, but one way or another, he was eighty-hour weeks, and wondered if this was the message that he should prepare for immediate retirement. But he didn't want to retire. Certainly, he didn't want to retire now when he might be in a position to assist the Church of God's Law, but honestly, he never wanted to retire, even as miserable as his assignment was. But he felt the chill on the wind and knew that sooner or later it would be forced upon him, and then what?

TWENTY-SEVEN

The doorbell rang at his house, and Lieutenant Capps, now on his seventh drink, answered, seeing a patrol officer, and wondering what was wrong. Capps had been celebrating the results of the captain exam, on which he had placed 5th, which should see him promoted very soon, perhaps inside the coming month.

"Yes, Officer ... Bekins," Capps slurred, despite how carefully he tried to enunciate. His boyfriend was out of town on a business trip, and Capps was alone.

The officer quick-drew his taser and zapped the lieutenant. In a moment, Capps was loaded into the back of a panel van, and he woke in a stinking stall somewhere, disoriented and angry. And naked. And with a hangover. And still mostly drunk on his excesses. And then fear settled in. He had no idea where he was. His hands were cuffed behind him and it became apparent a hood – actually it was a navy blue pillowcase – was over his head.

"Help!" Capps yelled loudly.

"There is no help, sodomite," a voice said, taunting him. "The wages of sin is death, and your payday has come around. If you believe in God, you should use this time for prayer. Ordinarily you would have a few days to get right with your Maker, but I am afraid your time is to be far closer, Mr. Capps."

"Who are you?" Capps demanded in his drunken anger, but the adrenaline was making fast work of the alcohol, and the hangover was likewise fast forgotten.

"I am God's righteous hand," the voice said. "And the world can no longer afford the godless. Pray if you wish, or don't pray. We'll begin soon on you."

Capps, raised Southern Baptist, never lost his faith, but once he understood and accepted he was, as his captor put it, a sodomite, he had given up on church. The confusion was too great for him, feeling right in the life he lived and loving God nonetheless, but being told in frequent sermons that he was doomed to Hell for what he was.

"Who are you?" Capps demanded.

"I think you know who we are, Mr. Capps," the man said. "In an hour, probably less, you'll be dead, whipped to death for your perversions and offenses to God. Soon after that, your body will be in pieces while your soul catches fire in Hell, and the pieces will be scattered for your buddy Lowe to find. We'll make sure he sees your head."

"Jesus fucking Christ," Capps groaned. "Let me go, right now! Murdering a police officer is a one-way ticket for your ass to death row!"

"Mr. Capps, that die was long since cast," the man said. "We killed five officers – it was a mistake, but it happened – at the first scene, that house on Drew Estates. So we will suffer no greater penalty from man's law for keeping up with God's holy law."

"All is in readiness," the woman said from behind the man.

"Excellent," the man said. "Bring him out of the cage."

Still cuffed and hooded, Capps was unable to put up effective resistance, but he mounted a valiant resistance anyway, to no avail. In a moment he was placed in a chair and his head was clamped in place, immobile. And then a knife pierced through the pillowcase, and he screamed in agony, fighting to no avail, as his right eye was deftly removed. A moment later, someone came along and used a saw, and his right hand was gone.

"If your right eye sins, pluck it out," the man said. "If your right hand sins, cut it off. That's from the Fifth Chapter of Matthew, holy law spoken to us by our very Lord and Savior Jesus Christ. And now you have something else driving you to sin, don't you, Mr. Capps?"

Barely conscious from the pain, Capps could only groan, and then screamed out as his captor quickly castrated him, and then cut his penis off, packing the wounds in coagulant to prevent him from bleeding to death. A moment later, his left hand was removed from its cuff, and another cuff was used to hoist him up by his left wrist from a chainfall mounted above. His clothing was cut away and the tatters dumped in a burn barrel, along with the parts cut off of him. And then the flagellum came into play. Capps cried out, but was soon too weakened, only whimpering as his right stump, tied off with a tourniquet, flailed about. He lasted through nearly fifty lashes before he bled to death, and then he was expertly pieced out as had been dozens of other sinners.

"Put his head in a box and get a courier to deliver it to this man Lowe," the leader ordered. "It's somewhere at police headquarters. I'll print off a note to send along with it. Wrap the parts and freeze them, and then let's call this a night."

The man went into a shower stall and thoroughly washed himself and then put on fresh clothes. He went into the house and wrote a letter on his computer, and then put on medical gloves and folded the paper into a Ziploc bag and took it to the barn, where the head was in a big Playmate cooler. He included the note in the cooler, and then the cooler was filled with dry ice and sealed in more plastic, and then into a cardboard box. A taxi would be hired in the morning to take it to Lowe's office in police headquarters.

TWENTY-EIGHT

Sarah slept poorly on the lumpy mattress in the dormitory, and woke gritty-eyed and grumpy for it. A woman named Laura Porter had stayed the night in the room next to Sarah. She was in her late thirties and seemed kind and concerned. "I've been right where you are," she said. "I won't lie, it hurts like you won't believe, but it's only a moment in your life, and it straightened me out once and for all, and it will straighten you out too. But you're forgiven with it, forgiven by the church, by God, by any and all, and that's an easy price to pay."

The women ate a simple supper of Arby's sandwiches before Sarah tried to sleep. And now, it was morning, and doom was very close to hand. "Go on and shower, Sarah," Laura said. "Once you're out, only put on your robe. Elder Butler will want to examine you. I, of course, will remain as matron."

"Okay," Sarah said, and then she went to the shower, taking only a small bag of her toiletries and her bathrobe. In a few minutes she was clean and did her hair as best she could, and then returned to her room, knowing she and Laura were locked into the women's dorm and there was no point now in trying to escape.

Butler arrived a few minutes later, rolling a big trunk, and Sarah disrobed in her room. Butler was thorough and professional, taking an ECG reading with a Lifepak monitor-defibrillator, and then her vitals and weight. "Your blood pressure and pulse are up a bit, but all things considered, not nearly as high as I might expect them to be," Butler said. "But I recall from your original physical that you are an amazingly healthy woman. What happened to your buttocks, Mrs. Avery?"

"My husband punished me after my outburst, Sir," Sarah said.

"I'll be on hand immediately after your punishment to tend to you," Butler said. "I'm sorry, but our doctrine is that you are not to have any analgesics for at least 24 hours, not even a Tylenol. And I will say that unless you want the marks to last longer, you should avoid aspirin in any event. You can put your robe on now." Sarah did so, tying the sash tightly.

"Laura, will you give the two of us a moment to talk privately?" Butler asked. Laura nodded and left. "If I have to say this I will, Mrs. Avery. You were the topic of a fairly heated discussion among the elders of the church. For my part, I wanted you to be merely reprimanded, considering what you'd just undergone. Dale Rawson wanted you whipped forty strokes. Ultimately it was decided that you couldn't go unpunished for this, but that it should be a relatively minor punishment. Now, I shouldn't be telling you this, but I like you and I think you deserve justice too. Dale Rawson was removed from the board of elders for his excesses, and is going to get a far worse punishment than you did. He was very nearly excommunicated, and that will be step next if he steps out of line here again. For my part, I'm sorry he did what he did, young lady. And I'm sorry you reacted as you did. But ... I think Dale Rawson will no longer be a problem to you. We have three men who'll sit with him at services, and then his wife will be told he needs to be in an important meeting. She'll get a ride home and ... why not? ... we sentenced him to fifty lashes, fined him a 20% tithe for the next six months, and again, removed him from his elder status."

"Wow," Sarah said. "Elder Butler, I might be speaking out of turn, but ... would it be possible to suspend the whipping and fine? I don't want the man hating me."

"I assure you he'll leave you alone from here on," Butler said. "If he runs afoul of our rules again, he will very probably be excommunicated or lashed until his body is crippled and fined until he's financially crippled. This brings me to excommunication, Mrs. Avery. You have the option of refusing your punishment and taking excommunication. Do so, and you're out of here and on your way home in a minute. But that's permanent. We won't entirely shun you like the Amish do to their children when they go out into the world and decide they like the world better, but ... let's say you and John need a sawbones to be your family doctor ... I would refuse you as patients."

"I broke with the rules and I will take what I deserve," Sarah said. "You needn't even tie me. I'll take it because I know I deserve it."

"Admirable of you," Butler said, standing. "I need to go. Please, as a favor to me, don't reveal to others what I revealed to you. But I thought you deserved to know."

"May I ask a question?" Sarah asked.

"Sure," Butler said.

"Are you ... satisfied ... that we're us and not up to no good here?" Sarah asked.

"Yes, we're satisfied," Butler said. "I couldn't envision an undercover cop or reporter going to these lengths, Mrs. Avery. I don't know how much you were told, but a number of human body parts were scattered throughout a house the church owned, given to us in a will. The killers put thermite devices near the gas fittings and set them off when the cops were in the house, and killed several police officers. And then right on the heels of that, you and John applied to join the church, and it ... I'm afraid you were suspected of being police officers, notably by Paul Luden. He's a good man and a good friend, and when I told him you had welts and bruises from a punishment, he agreed there's no way in the world the police would do that to you. But Dale ... I guess he was still paranoid about it."

"Thank you," Sarah said simply. "It sounds like a gruesome murder."

"From what I understand, it was horrible. I'll see you after services," Butler said, and left the dormitory.

The routine service at the Church of God's law began at 9:00 and lasted for two hours. John sat on a pew and listened to Quinn's sermon, which he had to admit was thoughtful and eloquent, if rather narrow-minded for his own philosophies. But he only halfway paid attention, worried about Sarah. Finally, the time came. "Brothers and sisters," Quinn said. "I am afraid there's some unpleasantness that has to be dealt with now. I think all of the details are best kept in confidence, but two matters have arisen. First, Brother Dale Rawson has stepped down from the Board of Elders. We will publish a list by Wednesday's service of who is qualified to run for the open seat, and those qualified can announce whether they are interested in running, or not. Next Sunday, we will hold the election of those running, and will ultimately choose your new elder.

"Secondly, Sarah Avery, our newest member, has offended," Quinn continued. "She will be whipped in a moment. Again, I think this isn't time or place to go into the details, but she committed an act of insubordination while under great duress. Even simply reprimanding her was seriously discussed, so great was her duress. But the elders and I ultimately agreed to eight lashes for her. Sister Laura, will you bring Mrs. Avery to the dais?"

The two women walked onto the dais. "Sister Sarah, you understand you are sentenced to eight lashes on your bared back?" Quinn asked.

"I deserve it, Shepherd," Sarah said quietly.

"Yes, you do," Quinn said. "You will approach the cross, remove your blouse, and then you will be bound and whipped."

"Yes, Shepherd," Sarah said, and then sighed and stepped to the cross, and did as bidden.

"We love you," Laura whispered as she cuffed Sarah in place and stepped aside. Quinn uncoiled his well-used whip and took his position. Without further preamble, he lashed her. Sarah groaned and hissed from the pain of the first lash, and yelped at the second one, grinding her teeth against further outburst through the next five as her eyes blurred with tears, and then crying out and sobbing as the eighth lash found her and Quinn coiled the whip.

John thanked God she wasn't bleeding, but his heart ached for his partner, who was getting the shit end of the stick on this assignment. *But who knows what's going to happen to me this afternoon,* he considered. *It may well be that I'm going to get far worse for not controlling her better. Christ, if so, I hope I take it as well as she has.* Laura uncuffed Sarah and helped her into her blouse, and then led the weeping woman out of the cathedral, through a side door. Butler was waiting for her and examined her welts, checked her vitals, and told her she was going to be okay. John was summoned and led her to his truck, and drove her home. There, she asked if they could talk outside for a time.

"How bad was it?" John asked.

"Husband, I would rather ten times the whipping you gave me than what I got in that church," Sarah said, rubbing her face with her hands. She was still red-eyed. "If they suggest ever doing that again to me, I will blow cover on this. The hell of it is, they're sincere, and I think under most other circumstances I'd really like these people. I genuinely like Isaiah Quinn. The matron … Laura, her name is … was very sweet and kind. Hollis Butler is as well. He had a little talk with me after he examined me. He even explained the worry that we're police undercover, which we already knew. But he told me this man Rawson is going to be severely beaten this afternoon and fined."

"Define 'severely' for me," John said. "Or quantify it."

"He is to be whipped fifty lashes and his tithe doubled for the coming six months," Sarah said.

"Wow," John remarked, shocked at the sentence.

"These people are harsh," Sarah said. "I ... it's confusing, John. I can't help liking a lot of them, because down deep they're really good people. But I think their religion is nothing short of insanity and I can't wait for this assignment to end."

"Lowe," Lowe answered his cell phone.

"Sergeant, this is Rich Kennedy," Lowe heard. Kennedy was a patrol sergeant left in charge of the task force for Sunday. "You have a package here that was delivered by taxi courier. I called bomb squad and they took it, but they determined it wasn't a bomb. But I was asked to phone you and have you report to the CSU lab. They only said you need to see it."

"Fuck," Lowe muttered. "Okay, Rich, I'll be there in an hour."

"They said it wasn't a huge rush but need you there today," Kennedy said.

"Tell them I'll be there in an hour," Lowe repeated.

"Will do," Kennedy said, annoyed. He'd been a sergeant eight years, didn't particularly like Lowe, and thought it was a load of horseshit that Watts hadn't given command on a seniority basis, which (he had looked into it) would have made him second in command behind Sergeant Lionel Patrick, and Lowe about sixth in command. But Kennedy knew better than to cross Chief Watts, knowing his own career could be derailed by making waves, and even understanding that this was a case that called for a detective not a patrolman. Kennedy had served two years as a burglary detective and had cleared exactly one case in all that while, and was routed back to

185

patrol, and assumed he was on a blacklist for any kind of flashier assignment since he'd spent the entire sixteen years since in uniform. But he had tested for lieutenant not long ago and had hopes that he would be promoted soon.

One way or another, Kennedy called down to CSU and reported that Lowe would be on-hand in an hour, and hung up. So far nobody had turned up anything, and Kennedy was seeing the case as a huge waste of time. But on the other hand, he knew nothing about the IA element of the investigation, something Lowe had shared only with Walker. Kennedy looked at the time and picked up his personal cell phone and called Paul Luden, unaware that he was throwing his own career into the abyss.

"Hello, Rich," Luden said, sounding exhausted. He'd slept little and was showing the signs of burnout from the killer hours he was logging. "What's going on?"

"Just checking in with you," Kennedy said. "Lowe ... Paul, a package arrived for him and we handed it off to bomb squad. And now CSU wants him to come look at it. Nobody down there is talking, but by the sound of them, whatever arrived here is important."

"Thanks, Rich," Luden said. "Keep me posted."

"Will do," Kennedy said, ending the call.

"So what's up that you needed me here?" Lowe asked when he arrived to CSU.

"Sir, this is pretty damn gruesome," said Kendra Maxwell, the lead technician on duty. "You'd best have a seat, Sergeant."

"Okay," Lowe said, taking a seat.

"Sergeant, the package was an Igloo Playmate cooler," Maxwell said. "In it was a human head packed in dry ice, and a note in a Ziploc bag for you. We examined the note but there were no fingerprints on it, and the ink on the note appears to be from a Hewlett-Packard printer, which tells us exactly nothing. But here is a scan of the note, Sir."

Sergeant Lowe,

You are a worthy and honorable adversary, but it's sad we're on opposing sides because we have the same objectives, to keep the world clean of criminals and … well … sinners. It's regrettable that several of your police were killed in the initial scene, and the miscreant (the devices were to have gone off far sooner than they did) has been thoroughly punished. The errant person was punished less than Man's law allows, but we are, as I am sure you've learned, doing God's work. This package is a gift to you, someone poisoning the atmosphere of your own department. Perhaps you will accept it in good faith and realize we are on the same side. Sodomites are to be put to death.

Sergeant, it is hoped that this will make you and your masters understand that we're doing what has to be done, and that you will back off your investigation and permit the unimpeded continuance of God's work on earth. Prayers are that you will let this duty to God happen rather than escalating the matter, and be blessed in Heaven for your wisdom. Leviticus tells us that a man lying with another man shall be put to death, and this one has held a long-standing open and notorious homosexual relationship. God laid Sodom and Gomorrah to waste, and hopefully you will agree this is necessary for the betterment of all mankind. You have likely learned by now that those we have killed are criminals, one and all. Rapists. Whores. Murderers. Thieves. Sodomites. These are hardly people you'd invite to a family picnic.

God bless you, Sergeant, but do not oppose us, because His finger may lay upon you.

In Christ's service,

Anonymous

"Okay, I don't think you brought me here to read a note," Lowe said. "What was in the cooler?"

"A human head we haven't identified yet, Sergeant," Maxwell said. She tapped on her computer and Lowe saw the head on the monitor.

"Holy fucking shit," Lowe breathed.

"Gruesome, yes, Sir," Maxwell said.

"I can ID the head," Lowe told her in a toneless voice. "That is the head of Lieutenant Darrell Capps, of the Homicide Unit."

"Holy fuck," Maxwell, ordinarily unflappable, breathed. She hurriedly brought up a basic profile of Capps, and in seconds the computer firmed up the match. "We were looking through criminal files, Sergeant. But yeah, it seems that's indeed Lieutenant Capps."

"I didn't know he was gay," Lowe said. "Shit son of a bitch. Sit on this information, Maxwell. I need to call Lieutenant Holmes about this, and probably Chief Watts."

"Goddamn," Holmes breathed a moment later. "Where are you, Mike?"

"CSU at HQ," Lowe answered.

"Go on up to the chief's conference room," Holmes ordered. "Sergeant Toland is on duty, or ought to be. "I'm going to call the chief. He's a cop's cop and will probably want to come in on this. Tell Toland we're on our way and go get coffee ready for the conference room. I'll call him and we'll both be there soon."

"They killed Capps," Watts said, working his way to a full fury. "I had no idea he was queer, but he didn't deserve to die for that. The hard reality is that his proclivities are legal and as long as he wasn't buttfucking his subordinates or underage kids I don't give two hoots in hell what he was doing in his personal life. The fact is, he was a good cop, and his record was nearly spotless. And these shitheads have now murdered six good cops amidst all the other criminals and sinners. They can wrap themselves in the Bible all they want, but they're just murderers, Lowe. I want their heads on this wall." By the time his oratory ended, he was shouting, spittle flying from his lips.

Holmes had been in the corner talking quietly on her phone and hung up, then came to the table. "Captain Worth is coming up from S&T with two people," she announced. "Inspectors Reese and Johnson should be here any minute. Worth thinks we might have found a break in the case."

"Alright," Watts said. "Let's all take five. I need a cigarette or forty – Goddamn anti-tobacco Nazis are making me insane – and I suspect we could all do with a visit to the john. I don't know how long we'll be in here today, but if it's more than another hour or two, supper's on me."

Lowe went to the john and relieved himself, and then to the chief's kitchenette. He was overdosed on coffee and opted for a Coke from the fridge, and then sat at the table. Two minutes later, they were joined by Reese, Johnson, Worth and two other officers from S&T. "Captain Worth, what do you have for us?" Watts asked.

"Sir, Officers McDonald and Stark had the idea to look into Capps," Captain Thomas Worth said. "McDonald scoured the internet for him and Stark went through the police computers. McDonald was able to find many records on Capps, and even found out he went three years ago with his partner on a gays-only Caribbean cruise. McDonald is looking into his partner, a car dealer named Jim Fisher. Fisher has been out of town on a family emergency and according to Southwest Airlines, he flies home tonight."

"Poor bastard," Lowe muttered.

"What was that, Lowe?" Watts asked.

"Sorry, Sir, just thinking out loud," Lowe said. "I said 'poor bastard' regarding Fisher. I feel sorry for him coming home to this kind of news."

"I understand," Watts said. Lowe noticed Holmes looking at him with sympathetic eyes, and Johnson with more or less a sneer.

"In any event, Stark found out that a number of inquiries from within the department have been made into Capps," Worth continued. "Stark?"

"Thank you, Captain," said Donna Stark. Lowe studied her for a moment as she stood and gathered her thoughts. She seemed mousy and bookish, but he sensed an alertness in her and doubted much snuck past the woman. She was short and slim, indeed petite, and Lowe wondered if a waiver had to be brought to the table to permit her to be hired at all. She didn't look tall enough to meet department minimums for female officers, nor heavy enough. He guessed her height at five feet and doubted the woman weighed a hundred pounds. The pistol on her hip looked like she could fire it downward and be launched skyward. Lowe stifled his amusement at the imagery.

"It seems Captain Paul Luden has been making inquiries into several officers, including Lieutenant Capps," Stark said. "Sergeant Lowe, he also got into your personnel file several times. The strange thing, however, is that while several of them came straight though his official department computer – we have a trap that records the IP numbers – but many of the inquiries have come from hairball IPs. We're still tracing all of that, but one was from Alaska, one from Sierra Leone, another from Venice, Italy … you get the picture?"

"There's no way he was in those places," Lowe said.

"Absolutely not, Sir," Stark said. "I took the liberty of looking into Luden's file and he hasn't had a vacation in two years. He could retire tomorrow and be on vacation nine months before his pension kicked in. So we're left with two possibilities here. One, he has skills to use IP dodges, but that seems unlikely. The second, more probable, scenario is that his ID and password were hacked."

"I have something to say here," Reese piped up. "But first, at the risk of sounding like an iron bitch, I have to give you all a warning. If any of you don't know me, I am the head of Internal Affairs. I want you all to understand that if you interfere with IA or if you talk out of school and it derails our investigation, you will be charged with obstruction of justice. I have two cops working undercover on this matter at great risk to their lives and you don't want to know how much money we've poured into this investigation so far. Are we clear on all of this?"

"Yes, Ma'am," Worth said, looking annoyed.

"Yes, Ma'am," McDonald and Stark said simultaneously.

"We've had Luden under investigation for a while now," Reese said. "And by that, I mean he's been under tight surveillance. His every move is watched, and he's on double duty, so he won't be going far. He will all but certainly be prosecuted and will absolutely be fired when this investigation concludes. But what I'm saying is he's barely been away from work, and we looked into it and his computer at home is still dial-up, for God's sake, and is barely being used. He logs on to look at his personal e-mail, of which there is precious little, and goes to bed."

"Okay, so he's been hacked, or gave his login information to someone," Stark said. "May I have a moment?"

"Sure," Reese said.

Stark brought a laptop computer out of a briefcase and spent a few minutes furiously typing, reading, and then typing some more. "Hmm," she said after a long moment. "The time of the inquiries opposed to Luden's activities … yeah, getting off work at 6:00 in the morning and knowing he has to be back on at 2:00 in the afternoon makes a 9:00 in the morning search improbable. So someone else is using his login, which he seems not to have changed in … Jesus H. Christ … over five years."

"Where is he now?" Watts asked.

"Sir, he has this evening off but is due back at the 22nd tonight at 10:00," Johnson answered. "He's probably at that psycho church of his getting jiggy with Jesus."

In spite of it all, Lowe barked a short laugh at this comment. "Nice turn of phrase, Sir," he chuckled.

"Can you get a location on him, Ma'am?" Stark asked Reese.

"Sure," Reese said and dialed a number on her phone, spoke a moment, and hung up.

"He is indeed at the Church of God's Law," Reese said, and snorted. "Still being jiggy with Jesus, I suppose."

"Well, someone logged in from an IP in Sofia, Bulgaria," Stark said. "This is interesting. This time it's going through violent parolees in the area."

"Okay, what do we want to do about this?" Watts asked. "I'm still hoping Luden isn't a party to all this and he was somehow duped. It won't save his career, but I'd rather the news not tell the entire world that one of our police captains was involved in mass murder including the fratricide of six police officers. I swear, if this turns out to be fratricide I'll kill that asshole all by myself. With my bare hands."

"Right now we don't know," Reese said. "Sure, he's suspicious and for good reason, but suspicious and guilty aren't the same thing, Sir."

"I know, I know," Watts said.

"Sir, unless I'm mistaken, I think I know what Officer Stark is about to suggest," Worth announced. Watts gestured to him to

193

speak. "Sir, I believe Officer Stark, who is a stone genius, is about to suggest that we do nothing right now, since this does give us a window – admittedly a narrow window – into their activities. We can't unring a bell, so the information they obtained is already in their pocket. While our routine is to give a new password to hacked officers – it happens sometimes – and we could do that right now with Luden, if we act stupid we might be able to get a better handle on who's doing this and, frankly, where they are."

"Captain Worth must be a mind-reader," Stark said with a slight smile.

"I also do card tricks and sometimes pull rabbits out of hats," Worth returned, chuckling. "But the last time I sawed an assistant in half, it got gory."

"Sir, I think Captain Worth … sorry, I mean Officer Stark … is right," Reese said. She smiled and winked at Stark, who blushed and smiled back.

"Then we'll do it your way, Officer Stark," Watts said, playing along. "Christ, we might need a smaller chair behind my desk when you become chief."

"I don't think the PD is ready to be led by a 26-year-old munchkin," Stark joked.

"Alright, I think we've done all we can do for today," Watts said. "Let's call it a day."

"Sir, with your permission I would like to meet Mr. Fisher when his plane lands and break the news to him, and find out if he or Capps suspected anything," Lowe said.

"He should be notified by an officer of equal or superior rank to Capps," Watts ordered. "Holmes, why don't you and Lowe meet Mr. Fisher? And take a patrol car with a couple of uniforms in it, and one of them can handle getting his car home."

"Yes, Sir," Holmes said. "Mike, I'll be to your house to pick you up at 7:00. The plane lands at 7:45 and that should give us plenty of time. Let's go in Class-A uniforms, okay?"

"Yes, Ma'am," Lowe said.

TWENTY-NINE

John arrived at the church a few minutes before 5:00. Uncertain what to expect, he put on a fresh suit after getting Sarah into bed, and then showering fresh. "Oh, good, you're here," Quinn said. "Come on in, John."

"Hello, John," Butler and Calloway said in unison.

"Good afternoon," John said, shaking their hands.

"John, ordinarily we wouldn't invite others to this sort of event, but we all agreed you had every right to be here," Quinn said. "The fact is you and Sarah were violated by that break-in, and the church will not tolerate that, no matter the motivations of the violator. We've removed Dale Rawson from the elders, of course, but we have also given him a fairly stiff sentence of fifty lashes to his back and doubled his tithe for the coming six months as a fine."

"Wow," John said. "Shepherd, we are taught by our Risen Savior to forgive —"

"I understand that," Quinn said. "And we overlook a number of minor sins in the name of greater causes. But whatever we could to do him would be of far lesser consequence than him doing three years in state prison for this, and if the police – I'm sure they're watching us like a hawk – went to the federal people and we

196

suddenly got charged under their racketeering laws … even if we won, the damage would be devastating. This isn't you punishing his wrongdoing, John. You're merely to bear witness. This is the church, God's right hand, punishing him. Come with us."

John followed the men into a courtyard, and saw Rawson chained to a cross, much as Sarah had been several hours before, wearing only underwear. "Dale Rawson, you are sentenced to a whipping of fifty lashes across your bared back," Calloway intoned formally. "You are also to be saddled with a hefty fine for the next six months of a doubled tithing, and you are put on notice that you are on probation and may soon find yourself excommunicated if you cannot adhere to our standards."

"I only served God," Rawson said, sounding terrified.

"Fifty lashes," Quinn said, as though Rawson hadn't spoken at all. And then the lashing began. John instantly saw it was a far harsher whipping than Sarah had gotten. Rawson was bleeding from three welts among the first eight strokes, howling and sobbing, and by the time he'd endured twenty, he fainted from it. He was aroused with smelling salts, and the whipping went on unabated. Rawson had no voice left for screaming, and only grunted his way through the last twelve strokes, many of which were bleeding, as Quinn cut the cracker from the whip and Butler examined Rawson, pronouncing him fit. Calloway and Quinn placed Rawson belly-down on a stretcher and rolled it toward a garage, where he was placed on his belly on a mattress in the rear of a panel van, and then driven home by Calloway.

"I hope you're satisfied," Quinn said to John.

"Shepherd, that didn't have to be done," John said. "I was angry with him. I suppose I still am —"

"He wanted Sarah whipped as badly as he was," Quinn interrupted. "There's no room in our dogma for hatred or vengeance, John. I would have resigned before doing to Sarah what I just did to Dale, simply to appease his anger. Now, if Sarah was caught in adultery or breaking other commandments, that would be a whole different ball of wax, but she lost her temper after you and she were violated. Your home is your castle, and you two had every right to be angry with him for his intrusion."

"Yes, thank you, Shepherd," John said.

"Would you like to break bread with us?" Quinn asked.

"That sounds great," John said. The men went into the fellowship hall and did precisely that, holding a brief communion of bread and wine (just Welch's grape juice) and offering prayers that Dale would find his way again soon, and that John and Sarah would grow stronger with the church and the Lord.

"How was it?" Sarah asked John when he got home.

"Awful," John said. "He was whipped bloody and was barely conscious when they took him home, and … I'm ready for this to end, Sarah. I think I could like these people – well, most of them – very easily, but to be honest they scare me to death. On the other hand, the point was made that Dale Rawson, if we'd pressed charges, would have easily done a stretch in prison, and they're right. And the point was also made – I don't know the legalities of all this – that it didn't stretch the imagination to see this handed off to the feds as a

RICO case. I suppose it could pass the sniff test for organized crime."

"Jeepers creepers," Sarah breathed. "Robert and Jane invited us over for supper, by the way. He likes to fish and caught some redfish and is grilling them. I told them we'd go over there once you get home."

"Then let's go," John said, and the two wandered across the street.

"Where did you go, John?" Robert asked.

"Back to the church, where I bore witness to the comeuppance delivered to Dale Rawson," John reported. "I know they're in a legal grey-zone and ... holy shit."

"What?" Robert asked.

"Sarah, did you notice there were no children at the service?" John asked.

"No, but you're right," Sarah said. "There weren't."

"We learned a bit from the listening devices," Robert said. "The church maintains a nursery for the kids still in diapers. Evidently the others, up to the age of about fourteen, are sent on Fridays to a weekend camp about thirty miles away, where they spend their weekends being indoctrinated or brainwashed or whatever the hell happens to holy roller kids. At fourteen, they go to another place for services, and then at seventeen – the legal age of consent – they are brought fully into the fold. So you probably saw some teens there. Something else we just learned, John, is that right after you left, Quinn got a call from another parishioner. His daughter is eighteen and about to graduate high school. She begged off church today, pleading she was ill. But she ducked out and saw a movie with a few school friends and got caught. The father is not only charging her in the church for her offense of idolatry and not keeping the Sabbath Day holy, but ... by doctrine there, parents still have rights over their children until the kids graduate high school ... he has offered her to marriage, and it sounds like she will leave the chapel next Sunday with a nest of whip-marks and a wedding ring on her finger. In short, her parents disowned the girl. Her name is Marjorie Stoddard."

"Surely they can't do that legally," Sarah said, looking outraged.

"They have a slick lawyer on their board of elders, a guy named Kurberg, who's also defending the two men arrested in the truck that was delivering body parts," Robert said. "Long and short, nothing they do is outside the consent of the subjects. Miss Stoddard has every right to opt out, but at eighteen, her parents have every right to eject her from their home and completely disown her. So it's coerced since she'd be homeless, starving and probably turning tricks just to live. But ... the truth is she can make that choice. Interestingly enough, the husband Quinn wishes her to have is Paul Luden, but Luden vehemently declined."

"Jesus, he's old enough to be that girl's grandfather," Sarah said.

"A point Luden himself made," Robert confirmed. "Luden lost his wife to cancer several years gone, which triggered his new religious leanings. By all accounts, he loved her very much and was devastated when she died, and he pointed out to Quinn he promised her on her deathbed that he would never again marry. But the fight is ongoing and we'll see what happens."

"Damn," John said. "I don't know the kid, but damn."

"We'll see what happens," Robert said. "But arranged marriages aren't your problem. Paul Luden is your problem, and ascertaining what, if any, involvement he has in those murders. Come on, let's eat."

Luden hung up with Quinn, and was annoyed, and called Hollis Butler and asked to come visit. "You look like I feel," he greeted Butler at the door.

"I've been through a lot lately," Butler agreed, admitting his old friend. Butler grimaced as he sat. "I've been having a lot of back pain lately."

"Physician heal thyself," Luden cracked, and Butler chuckled.

"It's a good thing we're godly men or I might have made a rude hand gesture at you, you know," Butler said. "What's going on, Paul?"

"I need some high-level protection," Luden said. "Chuck Stoddard seems to have disowned his daughter Marjorie. Shepherd Quinn wants me to marry her."

"She's a beautiful girl," Butler said. "She's tall, slender, and would probably give you a flock of healthy babies."

"That's disgusting," Luden said. "Hollis, I'm a confirmed widower. I promised my wife I would never marry again. And I sure don't want a wife younger than my two sons. I'd look like a pathetic old man. She'd only be in my way."

"Look, Isaiah Quinn's word is pretty much law, Paul," Butler said. "Marry the kid already."

"And leave her widowed before she's thirty?" Luden scoffed.

"Why not?" Butler reasoned. "Look, Paul. Your only way out of this is to marry someone else. My niece Anna is available, for instance, but … well, you know. Besides, I know the kid. In fact, I am her family doctor. She's healthy, and very sweet-natured. And I agree with one of Quinn's philosophies, that people should be married."

"Hollis, I don't want to be married, especially not to a kid eighteen years old," Luden said.

"When did our wants become more important than the church's?" Butler asked. "I wish I could help you out of this, but if Shepherd Quinn laid his finger upon you, then … yeah, you're out of choices, Paul."

"What am I going to do with a snotnosed child bride?" Luden asked, irritated.

"Make babies with her," Butler told his old friend. "You indicated you're retiring soon, and you wouldn't believe all the articles and real studies I've seen outlining the benefits of an active sex life."

"I guess I need to talk to the leasing office about a bigger apartment," Luden said. "Or maybe just purchase a simple house."

"That reminds me," Butler said. He reached into his desk and produced a check, which he handed to Luden. "That should cover the next three months. I heard a police lieutenant was murdered. What's the news on that?"

"I hadn't heard about the murder. Who was it?" Luden said. He pocketed the check.

"I think his name was Capland or something like that," Butler said.

"I hadn't heard, but the hours I'm working are killing me," Luden repeated. "Should be interesting to find out what's what. Thanks. I'll talk to you later, Hollis."

The men shook hands, and Luden left. Home, he logged into the HR and benefits section of the city website and found information about health insurance coverage for his impending and unwanted wife, and found it wouldn't be horribly expensive to insure her. Knowing he should sleep, he nonetheless looked up the Stoddard family in the church roster, and drove to their home.

"Elder Luden, what a pleasant surprise," Maura Stoddard said when she answered the door. "Please come in and I'll let Chuck know you're here."

"Hello, Paul," Chuck said a moment later, shaking hands. "What can I do for you?"

"Chuck, I understand you and Maura disowned your daughter today," Luden said.

"It's time," Chuck told him. "Shepherd Quinn says he has a husband chosen for her, and she can go be an adult now."

"He chose me," Luden said. "Chuck, I like you and Maura. I even like your kid. But I have sons older than Marjorie. I can't resist Quinn's order, but you can re-own her and let us both off a hook here."

"I'm sorry, Paul, but what's done is done," Chuck said, and snorted. "Frankly, Quinn is marrying her off far better than I thought she deserved. You're a good man, an elder in the church, you earn a good living and will be a good provider to her —"

"My sons hate me so badly they haven't said a word to me since the day I laid their mother to rest," Luden interrupted. "Yes, I have the love of the Lord with me at all times, but people who know me well mostly don't like me, Chuck. Undo this, please."

"I'm sorry, but I cannot," Chuck said.

"Very well, Dad," Luden said sarcastically. "I'm sorry I wasted your time."

"Marjorie," Chuck said, raising his voice. "Come in here!"

Marjorie, terrified of what was coming her way, came down the stairs, eyes cast downward, praying her father was bluffing. "Yes, Dad?" she asked, wondering why Elder Luden was here. He'd always been nice enough to her but she'd never liked him, sensing a coldness in him that alarmed her.

"I want you to meet your fiancée," Chuck said. "I believe you know Paul."

"Dad ... oh, God, please no!" she exclaimed, surprised to see Luden smile at this.

"You see, Chuck? I don't want to marry her and she doesn't want to marry me," Luden said. "Spank her or ground her or whatever, but don't do this to us, please."

"I'm sure you two have a lot to discuss," Chuck said, rising and leaving the room.

Luden grumbled, wanting to give Chuck Stoddard a good old-fashioned ass-kicking, but knew better. "Come with me, Marjorie, please," he said instead.

"Look, neither of us wants this," Luden told her in his car, driving aimlessly about. "I think you're a good kid ... okay, a good young woman ... but I've been widowed a long time now and would as soon remain so until God takes me away from this life. I know you don't like me. I've been a cop since your parents were in diapers and I hardly need to be told you think I'm an ass, for whatever your reasons."

"That sums it up," Marjorie said.

"And if I had to guess, I'd guess you're not that big a fan of the Church of God's Law, am I right?" Luden pursued.

"You like asking dangerous questions," Marjorie said. Luden looked at her, really looked at her, for the first time. She was tall, nearly six feet, with long legs and an hourglass figure, and he didn't need to undress her to know she had a tight and toned body that most men would kill or die to plunder. Back in his younger days he'd have done things to her that would have featured in porn films. But now, widowed all these years, Luden had to think to remember when the last time was that he'd even had an erection. But being this close

205

to her, to the knowledge he could have her as his own in only a week, suddenly had him growing erect, and even a bit dizzied by the excitement.

"Yeah, I do, I guess," Luden said. "Call it an occupational hazard, Marjorie. Look, I love the church, but I'll be the first to say that our doctrine isn't for everyone. It's why we vet member applications, for instance. So ... you have two choices, and I'll support you either way, Marjorie. First, you can marry me. I know you don't like me and I regret that, but think on it this way at the same time. At most I'm going to live twenty years further, and probably more like ten, and then you're a young widow with a handsome estate that will include my pension the rest of your life and social security benefits for children of our marriage. Seen through that lens, it's not a bad deal for you, Marjorie.

"The next option is you can refuse," Luden went on. "I wouldn't blame you if you did. Now, I know your parents have disowned you and you feel coerced into marrying me. So I'll sweeten the pot for you if you want. You can refuse. You will be excommunicated from the church and shunned by your family and most everyone in the church. But you won't be homeless, Marjorie. I am prepared to give you a stipend of two thousand dollars monthly to see you through graduating high school, and will provide you a one-bedroom apartment, all for one year. The utilities and all the rest are your problem, but you can get a job and do decently on your job – I have a bit of pull with the city HR department and might be able to get you a decent clerical job – and have a good life, however lonely at first. Don't decide now, but ... you need to decide quickly so I can get ducks in a row on Option B."

"Why are you being so good to me?" Marjorie asked with a suspicion that tore at his heart.

"I was a terrible father, so much so that my sons disowned me years gone," Luden said. "I've really only ever loved one woman in my life, and that was my wife. I was destroyed when she died, Marjorie. I guess a shrink could make a living off me clinging to my grief the way I do." He snorted and Marjorie chuckled.

"Can we stop somewhere and get a Coke?" Marjorie asked. "I know, I know, it breaks the rules."

"Yeah, why not?" Luden reasoned, stifling a yawn.

"Am I that boring?" Marjorie asked, looking a bit stung.

"No, not in the least," Luden said truthfully. "I'm working awful hours, 80-hour weeks, and simply worn out. I guess if we marry I'll have to bring you in on that as well. I'm in hot water with the Department and they're trying to force me into retirement. And I'm probably going to file for that retirement within the next couple or three months. I may seek out another job. There're at least four small towns near here looking for chiefs of police, for instance. But … well, anyway, there I am, warts and all, Marjorie."

The two parked at an IHOP and found a table, and ordered patty melts and Cokes. Luden was in his suit, still, and Marjorie was in a flowing dress that stopped at mid-calf. Luden realized she was very highly attractive and was feeling urges that he had thought were long since dead. But at the same time he felt like a pathetic old man for this. The overarching problem was that the Shepherd had made his edict, and defiance was unthinkable. So in many ways, at his ripe old age of 63, his fate was in the hands of this 18-year-old girl who had yet to finish high school. He found it as distantly and darkly amusing as it was infuriating.

"Either way, you'll get the car I'm driving," Luden said. "It's a Simple Simon machine but gets decent mileage and will get you around. I'll get another car for myself. Either way, Marjorie, I mean to treat you decently. This isn't fair to either of us, however it turns out. But I don't enjoy mistreating people and I don't intend on mistreating you."

"Amazing," Marjorie breathed. "An hour ago I'd have leapt off a bridge before marrying you, but now, getting to know you, I could see being Mrs. Luden."

"Because of the money?" Luden asked.

"No, because of you," Marjorie said, and blushed. "You're a far nicer man than you let on with your forbidding demeanor and all."

"Another occupational hazard of police work is we're always cops, even at the lofty rank of captain," Luden chuckled. "I think when my wife died ... I forgot how to be happy, Marjorie."

"I don't want to compete with her ghost," Marjorie said. "I never knew her, but I know ... Mr. Luden —"

"If we're 'engaged,' I think it's appropriate that you call me Paul," Luden interrupted. "If you're about to tell me you know she must have been very special because I love her even now, you're right." He held up his left hand, still bearing his wedding ring, and Marjorie nodded.

"Paul, Christ told his disciples to let the dead bury the dead," Marjorie said. "There are so many platitudes, life goes on, she's in a better place … they're all true, but … my grandma was very special to me, loved me, was always there for me. Then when I was eight, she died in her sleep, unexpectedly. I was crushed. And it still hurts ten years later if I let myself think about it too much. But she's gone and we're still here, and how much honor do we give them by wrapping ourselves in grief?"

"Wisdom from the mouth of babes," Luden said. "I just … I've gone through hell trying to let her go. I don't know, maybe I should see a shrink."

"Paul, let it go, is my advice," Marjorie said. "I obviously have a lot of soul-searching to do, but whether it's you or somebody else, I hope someday someone loves me as much as you love her."

"Thank you," Luden said, flattered. "Look, I know it's a school night, but if you want to go do things and get to know one another better, we can. There's a public aquarium not far from here. I've never been but I understand it's dazzling."

"That sounds great," she said, grinning.

THIRTY

Lowe and Holmes, considering it all, decided to stake out Capps' house while another officer staked Fisher's house, uncertain where Fisher was going. They mutually decided that meeting the man at the airport wasn't going to prove wise or sensitive. Fortunately, Fisher went to his own house, ten minutes from Capps' house, and Lowe drove Holmes over to Fisher's house, and they knocked at the door. Fisher answered, looking wiped out tired, but suddenly alarmed at two cops at his door. "Mr. Fisher, may we come in?" Holmes asked.

"Sure," Fisher said, admitting them. "Am I in some kind of trouble, officers?"

"No, Sir," Holmes said sadly. "Mr. Fisher, I am sorry to have to tell you this, but Lieutenant Darrell Capps is dead."

"Oh dear God," Fisher breathed, and fell heavily onto his sofa, and then loosed a wretched wail. "I tried to tell him so many times to get the hell out of homicide, but he kept telling me it wasn't dangerous since he was a supervisor, not in the field much, and homicide officers showed up way after the violence ended. What happened? Did you arrest the bastard that murdered him?"

"Sir, he was targeted," Holmes said carefully. "His house is a crime scene. He was seized there and killed somewhere else."

"My God, I know who you are," Fisher said, looking at Lowe. "Darrell ... he told me you had a big case. Said you two never got along but he was hopeful that you'd succeed. Is ... is this his killer?"

"Yes, Sir, it is," Lowe confirmed.

"Jesus, I need to call his parents and his brother," Fisher said. "I believe he listed me as his next of kin, but was otherwise ... he was afraid the homophobes would have killed his career if he came out of the closet."

"I'm afraid he may have been right," Holmes said.

"What do I ... how do I arrange for the funeral home to retrieve his remains and prepare him?" Fisher asked, and Lowe winced.

"Sir, he was mutilated like the other victims," Lowe said. "I'm sorry, but ... we don't have his body, and I don't know when we will."

"Then ... how do you know he's dead?" Fisher asked.

"Sir, we haven't released a whisper of this to the press, and ... Christ, I hate dumping this on you, Sir," Lowe said.

"Do you mind if I have a drink to settle my nerves?" Fisher asked.

"I'll pour it for you," Holmes said. "What would you like?"

"Fill an old-fashioned glass with ice and Jim Beam, please," Fisher said. "God, how I'm going to miss him. I know you two didn't get along – he told me it distressed him because he admired you as a police officer – but he was a really wonderful man, Sergeant Lowe."

"I had hoped when this case ended that we could have mended fences," Lowe said. "Mr. Fisher, in many investigations there's what's called a 'holdback.' Did Darrell ever explain that to you?"

"He told me that sometimes the police will keep information secret so if someone spills with knowledge of it, you know he's your guy," Fisher said.

"Yeah, that," Lowe agreed. "Right about now, very few people know Darrell is dead. We had hoped to have your cooperation in this."

"If it helps catch those sorry fuckers, I'll do anything," Fisher said as Holmes handed him his drink.

"We're going to tell the Homicide Division that he's on emergency leave and we have no idea when he will return to duty," Lowe said. "Can you play along with that?"

"I can," Fisher said. "His family disowned him when he came out to them. I have their numbers but I don't think he's talked to any of them in maybe five or six years. So yeah, I can sit on the news. But I think my sales manager at the lot is going to have a lot on his plate this week. Jesus, I ..." he trailed off, lost in his own thoughts, and took a huge slug of his whiskey. "Yeah, I'll sit on the information, but what are you doing about his house? I can't imagine it's going to stay secret long if you've wrapped it in crime scene tape."

"CSU has already done their thing," Lowe said. "Once that was done we changed the locks, emptied the perishables, and removed his cars – the Department unmarked and his Camaro – to storage."

"That Camaro," Fisher said. "I bought it for a song at auction and it was in terrific shape, and I gave it to him for his birthday two years ago. It wouldn't have sold well on my lot, but Darrell was so excited. He loved that car."

"Mr. Fisher —" Lowe began.

"Please just call me Jim," Fisher said.

"Call me Mike," Lowe returned. "Jim, we're … Darrell is the sixth police officer these clowns have murdered —"

"How do you know he's dead if you don't have his body?" Fisher interrupted.

"Mr. Fisher, these people … they kill their victims and dismember the bodies," Holmes said.

Even in his grief, Fisher was very intelligent and insightful, which was why Jim's Jalopies turned over a hundred used luxury cars monthly with a sales force of only six salesmen, all cars that had priced new at or above $50,000.00. "They sent you a part of his body," Fisher said. "Maybe one of his hands for fingerprints, but I'd guess … Jesus, they sent his head to you, didn't they?" Lowe solemnly nodded and Fisher began to sob and wail for his murdered lover. Holmes sat beside him and hugged the man. For his part, Lowe didn't understand gays or their culture, and was honestly shocked to know that Capps had been homosexual, but he knew grief and bereavement all too well, and he felt sorry for Fisher, widowed of a sudden.

"I think I'm going to drink this whiskey until I pass out, and pray this is just a terrible nightmare," Fisher said when the emotional storm passed. "I'm sorry, but can you see your way out?"

"Yeah," Holmes said, standing. Lowe could see she'd been weeping as well. "We'll keep you in the loop, Jim."

"Thank you," Fisher said, and went into the kitchen in search of his bourbon. Lowe and Holmes let themselves out, and returned to headquarters.

"God, I hated having to do that," Holmes said. "I always liked Darrell. I found out he took the captain's exam and passed high on it. He would have been promoted in no more than another two or three months, and on his way to bigger and better things."

"How did you do on the exam?" Lowe asked.

"I didn't take it," Holmes said. "I like my current assignment and I didn't want to transfer. Chief Watts is retiring in a couple years and I figured I'd take the test then to move up. Or move out. The problem with a high-profile assignment like mine is that there're a lot of people who wind up hating my ass and can't wait until they can stick a knife in my back. Some of it's jealousy, and some of it's just being hated for carrying out his orders, but one way or another I'm trying to time the test so I can be promoted captain about the time he's leaving. I figure I can gut it out for two years in any assignment so I save my pension at captain, even what they're doing to that asshole Luden. One thing seems certain, though. He might be eyes-deep in this but he's not our killer. Luden was on-duty and we can account for pretty well every minute of it, enough to know there's no way he directly attacked and killed Darrell. That doesn't necessarily mean he's not involved but ... killing him would have taken at least thirty minutes and he hasn't been out of our sight that long."

"For the sake of the Department, that's good news," Lowe said. "For my sake as lead investigator, it's lousy. I'm right back to Step One."

"Maybe it's wishful thinking, but something tells me this case has hit critical mass and is about to break," Holmes said. "People willing to do this are always willing to escalate, and sooner or later trip over their own dicks. Anyway, go home and enjoy your night with Lisa. I think I'm going to go do about what Fisher is doing. G'nite, Mike."

THIRTY-ONE

Luden and Marjorie had fun exploring the aquarium, and a decent dinner afterwards, before he drove her home and she went inside, straight up the stairs, and to bed. All throughout, Luden felt something niggling at the back of his mind, but it wouldn't quite come into the light. Meanwhile, he found that Marjorie interested him but he worried it was his sexual desire interrupting higher thought processes. To put a point on it, at sixty-three he was suddenly as horny as a teenager Marjorie's age, and went into the private john off his office and jacked off for the first time in maybe forty years, just to get her off his mind.

He figured he'd have a quiet night and could figure out what was bothering him, but he figured wrong. Shortly after 11:00 there was a mass disaster wreck out on the Interstate. An 18-wheeler overturned and its tanker trailer full of gasoline exploded, instantly killing twenty people, with nearly a hundred injured, thirty of whom requiring transport to the hospital. The injured were treated. Of the thirty transported to hospitals, seven were admitted, one with a closed head injury and four broken ribs from the violent inflation of his first-generation airbag, and a goodish amount of lung damage. The upshot of it all was that the disaster was an all-hands-on-deck operation and Luden got off at 6:00 exhausted, and his niggling issue was on a high shelf, not even in sight.

He got to his apartment dog tired, sweaty and stinking like a skunk, showered, and dropped into bed dead-tired, so tired that his alarm took ten minutes to wake him. He was pleased, exiting his apartment, to see that UPS had delivered an order of uniforms for him. He had ordered ten of them with this new assignment, a waste of money in some ways since he intended on filing for retirement as soon as he could, but he didn't want to waste his time running back and forth to the washing machine to wash the four usable uniforms he had. His Class-A uniform was still in plastic from the dry cleaner, hanging in the closet, and unworn these past three years. He slid the box into his apartment and left his apartment, enjoying the "Sunday" of this forced evening shift. He arrived at the Stoddard house a little after 4:00 and found Marjorie waiting for him. She got into his car and the two drove to Axton Park, where Luden produced a loaf of stale bread and they fed the ducks for a little while.

"I haven't told any of my school friends about this, Paul," Marjorie said. "And I know this isn't the answer you want, but yes, I will be your wife."

"Then I suppose we should go to the jewelry store and get you rings," Luden said. An hour later they walked out of Helzberg with rings. They didn't even have to be sized. He got her home by 7:00 so she could get on her homework, and then drove himself home via McDonald's, wondering if he could Big Mac himself into a heart attack before Sunday. But he removed his wedding ring, one he had worn forty years, and set it in a jewelry box, preparing for a new ring for his finger all too soon. His worries of the night before still teased him but wouldn't step into the light as he ate his burger and fries. He called Butler and told him it appeared the marriage was going forward and would Butler be his best man?

"I'd be delighted," Butler said on the other end. "What's going on with the murders now?"

"Hollis, I'm on this horrible assignment because I stuck my nose into it once, and they're trying their best to force me to retire," Luden said. "I just don't know, and I doubt I'll know about it before anyone else does. This sergeant is good at what he does, very good, and he and the chief are keeping a very tight lid on it."

"I'm just worried since there was a peripheral church involvement," Butler said.

"I ... Hollis, I think the house was just one of opportunity, and it just happened to belong to the church," Luden said. "Sergeant Lowe has left the church alone, hasn't he? He had questions about it and I think we overreacted in circling our wagons, if you want the truth. It cost me my career and God knows what I'll do when the PD finally takes my badge, gives me the gold watch, and tosses me out on my ear. But ... I don't think we're central to the investigation."

"Did these people kill that policeman?" Butler asked.

"Hollis, we had a huge wreck in my district last night, multiple fatalities and injuries," Luden told him, trying not to let his annoyance show. "I never heard anything and don't dare look into it. You know more than I do about it."

"I guess it's a morbid curiosity," Butler said. "I need to take care of a few things before bed here, Paul. Talk to you later."

THIRTY-TWO

The doorbell rang and Sarah Avery answered, seeing a woman on the other side dressed modestly, and almost certainly a member of the church. John was off at work, probably learning all there was to learn about IEDs and other bomb stuff. The housework was done, Sarah had eaten her lunch, and she had mostly decided on a trip to Axton Park to feed the ducks and just get fresh air. "Hello," Sarah said, smiling at the woman.

Shocking her, the woman punched her in the eye, staggering her as she waded into the house. Sarah had been punched many a time, and quickly regathered herself as she wondered who this woman was. So she asked. "Who are you and why are you doing this?"

"I'm Alice Rawson and you had my husband beaten to a pulp, and now I'm going to make you wish you were never born!" the woman screamed, launching herself at Sarah. Sarah easily sidestepped and punched the woman in her ear as she went flying past, dazzling her.

"I don't know what he told you and I don't know what you're talking about," Sarah said as the woman bounced to her feet, glaring at her. She shook her head and then charged Sarah again, who went to the floor and punched her feet into Alice's belly, lifting her up and over to sprawl on the sofa. Sarah heard wood cracking and knew the sofa would have to be replaced as she sprung to her feet and wondered how bad of a pounding she was about to have to give this psycho woman, and what it was going to cost either or both of them at Sunday services. Already she'd been careful not to really hurt her, even intentionally hurling her at the sofa rather than the wall or through a window, but Sarah decided it was time to go for the knockout as Alice produced a knife and launched another attack. Sarah was wearing leather-soled shoes and piston-kicked into Alice's face, hearing teeth shatter, and perhaps her jaw, and Alice fell unconscious to the floor, blood leaking onto the area rug in the living room. She hurried to the phone and called 911, groaning and hoping this didn't upend her mission. And then she called Quinn.

"Shepherd, this is Sarah Avery," she began.

"And how are you this afternoon, Sarah?" Quinn inquired.

"Not good, Shepherd," Sarah said. "Sir, I was just attacked by a woman who said she's Alice Rawson. She said I beat up her husband ... was making no sense."

"Did she leave?" Quinn asked.

"Shepherd, I ... she's unconscious on the floor and an ambulance and police are on the way," Sarah said.

"Oh no," Quinn said. "I'll be there quickly."

"Goddamn, what happened?" Officer Leonard Jensen asked when he arrived. Sarah told her tale and wasn't quite finished when EMS arrived.

"What happened?" the lead paramedic asked.

"She attacked me," Sarah said. "I just answered the door and she went nuts, gave me this black eye. She was out of her head and I didn't have much choice. The third time she attacked, she had a knife, so I kicked her in the face and that knocked her out."

"Christ," the medic muttered. "Yeah, I'd say so. We're calling in a helicopter. I don't know if she's going to live. You fucked her up bad, Ma'am."

"You're the resident here?" Jensen asked Sarah.

"I am," Sarah said. "My husband bought the house only the other day, Sir."

"And you don't know the victim?" Jensen pursued.

"Sir, she's a member of my church and was screaming at me about her husband," Sarah said. "There was somewhat of a dispute with him that as far as I know was resolved. And then this."

"Ma'am, we'll see what happens in all this," Jensen said, withdrawing a laminated card from his breast pocket. "You're not under arrest, but I should read you your rights at this stage. You have the right to be silent ..."

"Then I think I'm wisest not answering questions and consulting an attorney," Sarah said when Jensen finished the Miranda recitation.

"As you wish, Ma'am," Jensen said, and radioed for a supervisor.

"My Lord, how terrible," Quinn said when he arrived.

"I need to call John and have him get me a lawyer," Sarah returned. She'd filled a Baggie with ice cubes and had it pressed to her left eye, which was rapidly swelling shut. Whatever else, Alice Rawson had a killer right punch.

"She's half again your size," Quinn remarked. "How … how did you win?"

"I took up karate when I was a kid and earned a black belt," Sarah said. "Husband likes me to stay healthy, so I frequently attack a punching bag at the gymnasium."

"Wow," Quinn said. "Sarah, you'll be in no trouble with the church for this. But I think Dale and Alice just got excommunicated."

"If she lives," Sarah said. "Apparently when I finally decided I had to put her down, it destroyed her mouth and she … the paramedic says she has a blown pupil, whatever that means … she might not live, Shepherd. I … Sir, I was just trying to protect myself, not to really hurt her. I still don't know what I did to deserve this."

"The long and short of it, Sarah, is that Dale was removed from the board of elders, and got a far worse whipping than you did," Quinn breathed. "John was on-hand to bear witness to it, and I figured he would have told you —"

"Jesus Christ, what happened here?" Jane interrupted. "My Lord, are you okay, Sarah? Who did this?"

"I'll be okay, Jane," Sarah said. "Someone knocked at my door and attacked me."

"Jesus, just like you read about all over the internet with the knockout game stuff?" Jane asked.

"Not quite," Sarah said. "Shepherd Quinn, this is Jane Ross, my across-the-street neighbor. Jane, Shepherd Quinn is the minister of my church."

"Howya doing, Reverend?" Jane asked, smiling.

"Very well," Quinn allowed, and shook her offered hand.

"What happened to the woman who attacked you?" Jane asked.

"I knocked her out," Sarah said. "I called 911 and then the Shepherd. The ambulance guys put her on the helicopter."

"Good for you," Jane grinned. "Girl power!"

"No, not really," Sarah said. "The poor woman … I think she was unbalanced or fighting a demon. I had to protect myself but I feel awfully about it, Jane."

"I … wow, I'm sorry," Jane said. "Look, your place is a mess and all, so why don't you let us pop for supper tonight? Steaks and potatoes and some steamed veggies. You too, if you like, Reverend Quinn."

"I'm afraid I have other plans," Quinn said. "But thank you, Mrs. Ross."

"Mrs. Ross was my mother-in-law," Jane returned. "I'm just Jane, buddy. Glad I met you, and honey, I'm glad you're okay. I have some arnica at my place that might help with that shiner, too. We'll dab some on there after supper. Did you call John?"

"There's no way to call him," Sarah said. "He's in a secure area and … he'll be home soon enough, I think."

"Okay, then," Jane said. "I'll see you two for supper and I won't take no for an answer!" Jane went back across the street to her place and Quinn chuckled.

"She seems like a character," he remarked.

"She's goodhearted but … I try to keep her at arm's length," Sarah said. "They're nice to us, invited us over for dinner the other night, but … well, you heard her blasphemy and she and her husband drink like fish."

"Sinners aren't automatically bad people, but yes, I understand how she could make you … uncomfortable," Quinn agreed. "I need to get some things handled, Sarah. I'll talk to you later, but call me any time you need, even at 3:00 in the morning, okay?"

Quinn drove straight to Rawson's house, but Rawson wasn't there, and neither was his car, a battered relic of a Pontiac he'd purchased new in the 1980s and had driven ever since. But he felt sorry for Rawson in a way. He'd earned a good living as a butcher and owned his own meatpacking plant until an injury damaged his right hand. He kept the hand and could do some things with it, but spent three years really learning to be left-handed. In the meantime, creditors seized his business while he was in therapy, and other than the odd job here and there, Dale Rawson had never worked again, and lived from investments his grandparents and Alice's parents had left in their wills to them. Quinn drove on to the hospital and found Rawson in the ER waiting area.

"What's the news?" Quinn asked.

"Get away from me, Isaiah," Rawson said with a quiet but controlled fury. "I know you're here to make Alice and me back off of prosecuting that woman, but I'll see her in prison or dead before I consider forgiving her for this."

"Dale, she attacked Mrs. Avery in Mrs. Avery's own house," Quinn began. Rawson erupted from his chair. Even weak and pained from his beating, his fury pushed him through and he punched Quinn in the gut and then kneed him in the face before the security guard tackled Rawson and subdued the man.

"Let him go," Quinn groaned. "Have it your way, Dale. I'm sorry, but … you need help the church can only provide if you allow it. You and Alice can consider yourselves excommunicated."

"You can shove that church right up your fucking ass, Isaiah," Rawson snarled. "Burn in hell, asshole."

"Sir, do you need to be seen before you leave?" a nurse asked, looking with concern at Quinn's bloodied nose.

"I'll be okay," Quinn said. "And I'll be gone. Dale, your wife was the aggressor, not Mrs. Avery. Check your facts before you go off half-cocked again and get yourself into trouble that I can't get you out of." Quinn left to the church, where Bridger, seeing him, sprung from her chair, shocked.

"My God, what happened?" she asked.

"It's a long sad story," Quinn said. "Get me an ice pack for my honker, please." He chuckled sardonically and realized his shirt was ruined. He looked in the mirror in his office and saw he was a mess. Angry, even furious, at first, by now he was sad and wondered what had happened in the Rawson family, and if they could somehow be led back into the fold. Bridger brought him an ice pack, which he applied gingerly to his proboscis, and he leaned back, instantly learning this was a mistake as blood trickled down his throat and he suddenly flung himself forward and vomited into his trash can.S

"Shepherd, will you let me take you to the hospital?" Bridger asked.

"Yeah, I think this is worse than I'd first thought," Quinn said. "We'll take my car. There's no sense in me bleeding all over yours too, is there?"

THIRTY-THREE

"Okay, what happened over there?" Jane demanded when John and Sarah arrived.

"She's apparently the wife of Dale Rawson," Sarah said. "She knocked at the door and I answered, and she immediately sucker-punched me. We fought ... well, she kept attacking wildly and I kept fending her off. First time, I punched her in the ear, hoping to stun her. Second time I flipped her up and over onto the sofa – we need a new sofa now, by the way – and the third time I kicked her in the face. She came up with a knife on that third attack. Maybe I overreacted but ... I don't think she was going to stop until one of us was disabled, and I ... Jane, I think she meant to kill me."

"There was another huge butcher knife in her purse," Jane said. "I think she meant to either kill you or really fuck you up to make an example of you or get revenge or ... anyway, I think you're on the side of the angels in this, but I want to tell Inspector Reese this has gone too far —"

"No," Sarah interrupted. "How many undercover officers get their ass kicked being jumped into gangs, Jane? How many get their ass kicked just proving their mettle? This isn't much different. Frankly, I think the poor woman has some serious mental problems, and I feel like shit over this. But ... we're in now, and that took a lot of time and effort, to say nothing of God alone knows how much money, Jane. So no, I say let's keep doing what we're doing."

"I agree," John said. "We're in, and there is no possible way we could infiltrate this church again."

"You two are gutsy," Jane said. "Come on and let's eat and then I really do have some arnica to put on that eye, Sarah. It's supposed to help with healing bruises faster."

"So what was with you needling Quinn over there?" Sarah asked as they sat at the table.

"I'm trying to get my own feel for him, and figured I'd bait him some and see if he'd go full Christian on me and hellfire and brimstone and all that jazz," Jane said. "He … he wasn't what I expected."

"This sounds fucked up, but I like the guy," Sarah said. "He's hard, but I get the sense he honest-to-God gives a damn about people."

"Dale Rawson kicked his ass, I've found out," Jane said. "He went to the ER to see how Alice was going and Rawson … Quinn left there probably with a broken nose. He got back to his church and his secretary took him to another hospital. The last we heard, they're still there."

"I hope Alice makes it without permanent damage," Sarah said. "I didn't want to fuck her up. But I wasn't about to get my ass kicked to appease her."

"I'd have shot you myself if you had," Jane grumbled. "I'll be glad to extract you from this assignment. Fucking psychos at that church."

"They're really not," John said. "I mean, I know they're out of step with the zeitgeist, but they're reasonable men and women. They just take a very narrow view from a religious standpoint. But they're not like … say … those nutcases from that Westboro church. Nobody has proposed protesting at soldiers' funerals, for instance, but yeah, they take a dim view of homosexuals. But most traditional churches do that."

"I learned something interesting from our surveillance of Luden," Robert interjected. "He does not, I repeat, does not, want to marry this girl Quinn has set up for him. He … he has a lot of grief still about his wife and thinks he'll look pathetic at his age – he's 63, I think – marrying a girl young enough to be his grandkid. But … they seem to be growing a genuine fondness for one another and will be married Sunday, like or not. I still think he's a misogynistic asshole, but I feel sorry for him, how conflicted he is."

"I've wondered about that, and I guess it doesn't matter, but I wonder if grief over his wife has poisoned him toward women," Robert suggested. "My mom died when I was seven years old and I remember my dad hating women for a long time, several years, before he dated again. He never remarried. He died three years ago."

"I'm sorry," Sarah said to Robert.

"It's okay, but thanks," Robert said. "Like I said, it doesn't matter in the whole mess surrounding Luden. Just food for thought."

"Mr. Rawson, I'm afraid your wife is hurt very badly," said Dr. Amelia Croix.

"What's going on with her?" Rawson asked, already hating this young woman for doing a man's work.

"Sir, from what we were told she was kicked in the face," Croix said. "Her jaw is broken in two places and she lost seven teeth. Her nose is shattered, and a bone shard took out her right eye. And she has what's known as a coup-contrecoup brain injury."

"Explain that," Rawson ordered.

"When she was kicked, the brain hit the skull hard and was bruised, and then when she hit the floor, another bruise was inflicted, but we also found an inoperable tumor in her brain that ... I expect she was behaving irrationally much of the time," Croix said. "We'll do surgery on her and try to get her back to you, but ... one way or another, the outlook is bleak. The oncologist ... he says your wife has a year at most, and probably only four or so months."

"No," Rawson said. "No! Jesus wouldn't approve and neither do I, missy. Let her go."

"Sir, she's not brain dead, just brain damaged," Croix said.

"Get another doctor and ... I just ... I don't want my wife living on machines," Rawson said, choking back a sob. "She belongs with our Lord in Heaven and not down here in a coma. And that rotten bitch who did this to her needs to rot in jail."

"Code Blue to Trauma Three, Code Blue to Trauma Three, Code Blue to Trauma Three," the loudspeaker announced.

"Come with me, Mr. Rawson," Croix said, and led him to Trauma Three, where work was underway to resuscitate Alice Rawson.

"Stop," Croix ordered loudly. "This is her husband and he tells me he wants to let her go."

"Are you sure, Sir?" a nurse asked.

"What do I need to sign?" Rawson asked, weeping. "God, I love you, Alice. I'm so sorry. I'm so, so, sorry."

"Come with me, Mr. Rawson," the nurse said. She led him to a small office and produced DNR forms, and showed him where to sign. "I'm sorry about this," she said. "Is there someone you'd like us to call?"

"No," Rawson said. "When ... when she's ready, call Griggs & Murphy Funeral Home."

"Sir, she will have to be autopsied," the nurse said. "That's state law, and our hands are tied. But I promise her remains will be handled with respect and dignity through and through."

"I ... yeah," Rawson said. He opened his mouth again, but couldn't speak, and instead wailed in grief. The nurse tried to hug him but he pushed her away and wandered blindly from her office, sobbing piteously. He found his way to his car and then went home. There, he loaded his .45 Colt, one he'd stolen from the Army long since, and got back on the road.

"Oh shit," Officer Delbert Fuller breathed at 1:00 in the morning. "Robert, that man Rawson is across the street, just pulled up in an old car. He's approaching the door."

"Call John and Sarah, and tell them to lock and load," Robert ordered. "I think their cover is about to be blown."

Sarah wasn't sleeping, too tormented about Alice Rawson, and instantly answered her phone as the pounding on the door began. John was instantly awake and fetched his pistol. "Stay up here," he told Sarah, and made his way down the stairs, and opened the door, wary about Rawson.

"You win," Rawson said, and drew his pistol, stuck it in his mouth, and pulled the trigger seemingly all in one motion, scattering his brain all over the porch. The bullet went right through him and punched through the front door of the Ross house across the street.

"Jesus Christ," John said, right as Fuller called 911 for shots fired.

THIRTY-FOUR

"Okay, here's what happened," Jane said a few hours later. She'd consumed a whole pot of coffee and was worried sick about this matter, but thought this was isolated and John and Sarah were still relatively safe in their assignment. "Our people asked some questions around the trauma center. Alice Rawson had an undiagnosed brain tumor, inoperable. We'll know more but it seems the tumor was fueling her madness. Rawson signed DNR paperwork on her and she died."

"I'm going to prison," Sarah said wonderingly.

"No, you're not," Jane countered. "Look, self-defense killings happen all the time and get referred to the grand jury without charges and then the grand jury rubber-stamps them. But this is important, Sarah. We're going to get you a lawyer. But you will not take the stand to testify. As soon as you use your cover name in testimony, you have committed perjury. So you're going to sit there prim and proper while the DA lays out his case, and then your lawyer will present your case, and you're out of this. Sarah, I'd feel just the same as you, but you had no choice. If you'd been a street cop and this had happened, you might have used a taser, but you probably would have shot and killed her. You're not here to be martyred, Goddammit."

"Yes, Ma'am," Sarah said.

"Meanwhile, John is going to set you up with a shrink for stress debriefing and further visits if necessary," Jane continued. "But there's no question ... Christ, we need to order a new front door here too! ... there's no question Dale Rawson was straight-up suicide. Officers are working on locating next-of-kin on them, but they had no children. We executed a search warrant on their house and found a will that pretty well gives everything to the Church of God's Law since they're both dead."

"So how do we play this out?" John asked, yawning some.

"In a moment, you're going to call your guy Quinn and tell him what happened, and see what kind of reaction we get," Jane ordered.

"My Lord, I wonder if he had a demon," Quinn breathed a moment later after John told him Rawson had beaten at his door and committed suicide on his porch.

"You sound like you have an awful cold," John said to Quinn.

"No, Dale attacked me at the hospital yesterday and broke my schnozz," Quinn said. "As parting gifts go, I think I'd have rather gotten a basket of fruit. How are you and Sarah holding up?"

"My next call is to our lawyer, and then to a stress debriefer for both of us," John said. "She needs it more than I do. One officer told us Alice Rawson died in the trauma center."

"Lord have mercy," Quinn said. "I need to do some praying, John. But whatever you and Sarah need from the church is yours for the asking. One of our elders owns a law firm, so if you decide you need him – who knows what the police and DA are about to try? – you put the arm out to me and I'll see to it that Walther Kurberg personally represents you two."

"I don't think that's necessary yet," John said. "From what we're being told – a DA was sent here to meet us around 4:00 this morning – unless the autopsy on Mrs. Rawson shows something unexpected, this will be referred to a grand jury without charges."

"As well it ought," Quinn said. "I wish I knew what happened to them. It … well, anyway. I have a lot to do today with all this and preparing for a wedding. If you need me, call me immediately, John."

"Thank you, Shepherd," John said.

"Okay," Jane said, handing John a business card. "This is Dr. Louis Grey. He works with a lot of police officers. He knows you two are undercover and knows not to ask too many questions. He is also strictly confidential. Probably a third of his business is debriefing cops from shootings and other traumatic events. He's expecting you, so high-tail it over to him now."

John and Sarah went to Grey. John was okay with things. He'd seen some horrors in his military service and was a bit more insulated than Sarah. But this was Sarah's first true foray into real violence, and the poor woman was shaken badly. Five minutes into the visit with Grey, Sarah was sobbing out a river of guilt while John held her. The debriefing lasted an hour, and Grey set them up for two more appointments together, and Sarah for three more solos beyond that.

Later in the day the coroner gave a preliminary report. While Sarah had certainly badly hurt Alice Rawson, the fact was that Alice's brain was a mess, and the death was the result of the brain tumor infiltrating her brainstem. The case would indeed be referred without charges.

THIRTY-FIVE

Getting a new freezer truck wasn't at all problematic. This one was registered to a meat company whose only address was a post office box an hour from the city. The leader wanted to dispose of more filth, and began lashing them to death. He had six captives, and killed five of them, and gave addresses on eight others to his people.

The parts were wrapped in plastic and put into the huge walk-in freezer off the barn. "How many more will be in this delivery?" the woman asked him.

"As many as it takes," he said. "Ultimately I want to rid this city of sin and filth, a city truly dedicated to God. I have no illusions. It will be the work of more generations to follow me, but hopefully my example will be ... inspirational ...and others will gird their loins and do God's work on earth."

"It will be beautiful when it comes to pass," the woman said.

"Indeed," her leader and master returned.

"I need to shower and go to bed," he said, dismayed that he was growing aroused near her, and deciding to remove himself before his member grew fully erect.

Two officers knocked at the door of the tenement, and waited for an answer. One of them produced a nightstick and hit harder at the door, and a man answered. "Demetrius Simms, we have a warrant for your arrest," one of the officers said.

"Why?" Simms asked, his arms crossed angrily. On parole for another three years for statutory rape, and a registered sex offender for the rest of his life, he wasn't at all in a cooperative mood. When he got out of jail his first stop was at a courthouse to marry Deanna Long, and they had a son and a daughter. Simms earned a decent living as an electrician, a trade he had learned in prison, and damn well knew he'd broken no laws.

"They just told us to come pick you up, Mr. Simms," the other officer said. "Turn around and put your hands behind your back so we don't embarrass you worse in front of your family."

"What is it, Demetrius?" Deanna asked nervously.

"Apparently they think I broke another law," Demetrius said sourly, and offered his hands behind his back, which were cuffed.

"Ma'am, you'll be able to see him tomorrow at the main jail in police headquarters," the first officer said. They took Demetrius to the elevator and then down to the street. They got no further as they were surrounded by seven real police officers from Lowe's squad.

"Hands on the car, both of you," a patrolman demanded. "Right fucking now!"

The officers knew they were in trouble, but both did as ordered, knowing there was no way they'd win a gunfight surrounded as they were. They were hurriedly cuffed, and another officer uncuffed Simms and led him to a panel van.

"Thank you for your cooperation, Mr. Simms," DA Flame said. "I am sending the report in and asking the governor for a full pardon in your case."

"What's going on with this?" Simms asked.

"These are fake cops that 'arrested' you up there," Flame told him. "We think they're vigilantes trying to clean the streets of anyone and everyone who ever ran afoul of the law."

"The hell of it is I'm on their side," Simms said. "I made a bad mistake, let my little head do the thinking with Deanna, and paid a terrible price. But … Ms. Flame, I've been a good citizen before that and since that. I love Deanna, love our kids … shit, I sound like I'm running for office here, don't I?"

Flame chuckled. "Look, we studied you carefully and that's why we asked for your cooperation," she said. "The governor's office can be slow as hell, but I'll personally go to the capitol and build fires under their asses there if that's what it takes. But I think in six or so months you'll be fully pardoned and off the sex offender list, and can have a better life for you and your family. So again, thank you. As far as I' concerned you're square with the house, Sir."

"Thank you, Ma'am," Simms said, and returned to his apartment and family, hugging Deanna tightly and glad the kids were still in bed and didn't see any of this.

"Scott Davis and Leon Martin," Lowe said, sneering at the two men in interrogation. "You two have really fucked yourselves to the floor. You want to dig yourselves out of this hole, or at least into a hole not as deep?"

"We're not answering your questions," Martin said.

"We want a lawyer," Davis chimed in.

"That's on you, boys," Lowe said. "But you two are going to prison for a very long time, and if you're doing what I suspect you're doing, you may well be going right to death fucking row. Here's what I think, boys. I think you're pretending to be police all in the name of being vigilantes for God's justice, cleaning the streets of these sinners to prove yourselves to God. And that's up to God, whatever He thinks of you two. But I think you're fucking murderers, and I damn well know you're facing hard time for impersonating police officers and for kidnapping. But you're also involved in the murders of six police officers. You two … I'm the only chance you have, but if you want a lawyer to tell you that and then find out what I can do for you is off the table, go ahead."

"You're bluffing," Martin said.

"If you want to think that," Lowe returned. He saw on Davis' face that the young man – both were in their mid-20s – was scared.

"I'd rather talk with my lawyer," Davis said, though.

"Let me guess," Lowe said. "You boys, who probably don't have a hundred bucks between you, wish to employ the law offices of Walther Kurberg, right?"

Both men looked disturbed at this announcement, but Martin decided to brazen it out. "He's the one," Martin said.

"Jesus, you morons think he's going to help you?" Lowe asked. "He's on the board of elders at the Church of God's Law and if you think he won't sell you down the river to protect the church and pocket his thirty pieces of silver, you're out of your minds. But okay, we'll have someone bring you a phone to call Kurberg."

Lowe shook his head disgustedly and left the room, joining Walker and Holmes and watching them through the two-way mirror. "Good job shaking them up," Walker said. "I'm curious now as to whether these two shitheads are dumb enough to talk in there."

"Maybe … maybe we should take the deal," Davis said. "I mean, we got Kurberg's number —"

"Shut up," Martin said, cutting him off. "Look, do you see that mirror? Do you? I'll guarantee you half the police department is watching us through that thing and waiting to pounce. Just shut your mouth, call Kurberg, and let his people handle all this."

"I think that cop Lowe is right," Davis said. "We see Kurberg sitting with the elders at services, but he's never shared a word with me, and I doubt he's ever noticed you either, Leon."

"I said shut up," Martin repeated. "Scott, we don't matter. We serve God, and whatever goes on in this life doesn't mean anything. Take it like a man. We both knew what we were getting into."

"How did I let myself get talked into this?" Scott asked.

"By seeing the world as it is, going straight to hell," Martin snapped. "Now shut your mouth already."

"What about locking them in a cell with their other cohorts?" Lowe suggested to Holmes. "We could monitor their cell – which is our right to do – and see what kind of pillow talk opens them up."

241

"Yeah, let me talk with Major Shard over at the county jail and see what he can arrange," Holmes said after a long moment. "Meanwhile, send someone in there with a phone and let these dickheads call their shyster."

THIRTY-SIX

"Master, we were set up," one of the men reported to the leader. "Scott Davis and Leon Martin were just arrested in a sting operation. They've called Mr. Kurberg so I hope they're just keeping their mouths shut."

"I guess it's time we changed our game a bit," the leader said. "What about the others?"

"We brought three to you, a whore, a robber, and a murderer," the man said, still in his police uniform.

"Bring the whore to me," the leader said.

"Luetta Jefferson," the man said a moment later, growing aroused. "I'm going to enjoy this."

"Da fuck are you?" she demanded.

"I'm the man who's going to send you home to God," he said.

"Ain't no fuckin' God," the woman said. "Da fuck you want?"

"A whore really has to ask a man?" he asked.

"Jesus, you went through a lot of trouble just to get laid," she said. "Two hundred for a straight lay —"

She yelped as he punched her in the face, staggering her. "Shut up," the man said.

"Tyrone gonna kill you for damagin' one of his girls," the woman said, spitting blood at him. She was rewarded with another punch to her face.

"Tyrone is on our list too," the man said, fetching scissors. He held her down while she fought in futility with her hands cuffed behind her, and scissored her clothes to tatters.

"Now you can cooperate or I can hurt you," he said. "Which is it, whore?"

"I been rape before," she sneered. "Jist get it over with, assho'." She was rewarded for this with a hard punch to her kidney and another hard punch to the back of her thigh, making her writhe in pain, gasping.

"What's that delightful phrase, again?" the man said. "Oh yes, face down ass up, whore. Do it now before I decide to hurt you more."

Groaning, and for the first time afraid, Luetta obeyed, hoping this asshole didn't last long, but still she muttered "asshole" under her breath and swore to herself he would be made to pay. Tyrone would probably gut this son of a bitch like a fish, but she was sure he'd let her participate. She'd done it twice before with clientele who'd crossed Tyrone. One of them punched her in the chest and the other robbed her. Both men were dead and the bodies would never turn up. And then she howled in fresh agony as his huge erection went into her ass, something that had never happened before. And he pumped it into her hard, sparing no mercy. To her misfortune he lasted a while before he came, pulling out of her and chuckling at the trickle of blood that flowed from her rectum. He shoved a tampon in there and then told his helpers to do what had to be done. They dragged her out into the barn, and he heard her fresh screams as they dug her right eye out and he skinned his condom and tossed it in the toilet and flushed. He decided against a shower just yet, dressing as she screamed anew at the loss of her right hand, and screaming and begging them to stop as they hoisted her high.

He wandered into the barn and retrieved the flagellum. "Christ suffered terribly for your sins and you don't care," he said. "Not only are you a dirty whore, but you're an apostate, an atheist. So you shall suffer as did Christ before you suffer far worse in hell." He began lashing her with the flagellum, seeing a somewhat alarming flow of blood leaking from her rectum, where he supposed he tore something. Well, no matter. Luetta Jefferson was dead seventeen lashes later, and in wrapped parts in an hour.

"Jackson Wayne Smith," the man said to the murderer cuffed to a chair. "What is it with the middle name Wayne? Seems like a third of the nation's prisoners have the middle name Wayne. When your parents gave you that middle name, did someone just paperclip a parole card to the birth certificate?"

"What the fuck do you want?" Smith asked.

"What do you know of our Risen Savior?" the man asked.

"You can't be serious," Smith said. "I don't give fuck-all about religion or any of that bullshit, just making my way in this world. Let me go now and maybe I won't kill your ass."

"Oh, it's gone too far for that," the man said. "I am afraid God's justice has caught up to you since man's justice is insufficient. A moment later, Smith howled in agony as his eye was removed. And then he screamed when his right hand was severed, and screamed anew as one of the helpers used a blowtorch to cauterize the stump. And then Smith, a big man who seemed to spend much of his time in a gym, was hoisted up for his flogging. He screeched through the beating, and to his own misfortune had a strong constitution. It took 67 strokes to kill him, shattering the record by eight lashes.

The big man was parted out and frozen, and then it was time for Steven Dupree, who had done four years of a six year sentence for armed robbery, and had been on parole these past six months. "Thou shalt not steal," the man said to Dupree, whose blue eyes widened at this announcement. "Have you heard that one before? It's one of God's Ten Commandments, Mr. Dupree."

"Yeah, I've heard it," Dupree said nervously. Unlike much of the criminal element, Dupree was highly intelligent. "You're the killer who's been leaving body parts all over town, aren't you?"

"I am indeed," the man said. "Tell me, do you know who Dante was?"

"Yeah, I heard of him," Dupree said, struggling with his bonds. "He wrote a bunch of shit about Hell. We had to read some of it when I was in high school."

"Then you maybe heard about the sign above the door to Hell," the man said. "It read 'all hope abandon, ye who enter here,' or words to that effect. Sometimes translations vary, but that's what it boiled down to. And it applies to you. Consider this … Hell's lobby. That's where you're going from here, Mr. Dupree."

"Look, what do you want?" Dupree asked, at the edge of panic. "Money? I can have money in your hands tonight if you let me go!"

"I don't want anything from you, Mr. Dupree, but to send you to Hell and clean this planet of you and sinners like you," the man said. He approached Dupree and, with a special tool he'd made, deftly removed his right eye while he screamed and fainted from the panic and pain. But something didn't seem right, and the leader saw that this one had gone wrong.

Steven Dupree, known to some as Lightfinger Stevie, had been born with a bad heart, and the terror of the night had overtaxed him, and his heart seized. He was dead but had avoided much of the suffering of his fellow captives. Even so, his body was parted out, wrapped, and frozen.

"Let them freeze overnight and take them to the next site in the morning," the leader said. He worried about Scott and Leon and hoped they wouldn't talk. More to the point he was worried about Leon, who always seemed a weak link to him. He would have been surprised to have learned that Leon had become the strong one in handcuffs and Scott the weakling. One way or another, he saw they had contacted Kurberg, and through another lawyer, he made funds available for bail for them, which seemed more attainable than with Waterford and Lipton, caught not a mile from one of the scenes in a truck with bloodstains from an improper wrap job, and with tire marks left behind at another scene. There was no way Waterford or Lipton would be given bail, and that was that. But whether they were too stupid or too loyal to make a deal, one way or another they maintained their silence and that was what was most important. He had more to do, a spectacular finale. But this man Lowe was relentless and hurrying the agenda. The implied threat of the queerboy's head sent to him apparently did nothing to throw on the brakes, and the leader knew more had to be done.

THIRTY-SEVEN

Davis and Martin were arraigned, but only on charges of impersonating police officers and aggravated kidnapping. Both worked for low pay, Davis as a trash truck driver and Martin as a construction-site laborer, and both were assigned bail of thirty thousand dollars. Clinton Dawes, representing these two in addition to Waterford and Lipton, was prepared to post three times the bail, and had them out of jail and in his car inside an hour, and drove them to a greasy spoon diner fifteen minutes from the courthouse.

"I don't know what game you two clowns are playing, but you'd better both Goddamned well keep your noses clean," he said to them. "If you violate your bail there won't be extra chances for you two dickheads. Now, I'm telling you the evidence against you is damning, and this guy you were trying to kidnap is more than willing to play ball with the police and DA, especially since a full pardon was dangled under his nose and he swallowed it whole. Now, I'll do all I can to trip up the cops on this, but the hard reality is you two are going to prison and the DA doesn't have to take a plea bargain."

"Whoa, hold on," Davis said. "You mean to tell me a godless rapist gets a full pardon and me and Leon are going to take the fall?"

"Jesus, how can you be so stupid and live?" Dawes asked.

"You stop taking the Lord's name in vain or you'll be —"
Martin began.

"What?" "Dawes asked. "Chopped up like a rough-butchered hog and dumped in a building to burn to the ground?" He saw by two shocked expressions that he had their attention. "Now you two listen to me, and you'd best listen very Goddamned good if you want to avoid death row. Right now, all the cops have on you is impersonation and kidnap, and that's bad, but you can hopefully be back out on the streets in six or eight years and back to living your lives. I have a good idea what you were into and I don't want to know, so don't fucking tell me. But the fact of the matter is that the cops know what you're into even if they can't prove it, and it's a stone guarantee that they're watching you like a hawk and hoping you lead them to breaking this case. Christ, they didn't even put up a fight at the bail hearing. So you two clowns stay away from any and all such activity. Now, your benefactor, whoever he or she is, has arranged your bail, but you two need to go to your fucking lives and not even consider so much as making an illegal left turn." Dawes reached into his pocket and produced a sheaf of twenties, and peeled off four for each of them. "I'm sure you can see your way home. One of you cover the tab here."

Dawes left, driving straight back to the law firm, where he wasn't the least bit surprised to find a summons to Kurberg's office. Dawes had a bad feeling about Kurberg's interest, and hoped the old lawyer wasn't involved in the notorious murders.

"Congratulations on getting your boys sprung," Kurberg said.

"Sir, the prosecution barely put up a fight," Dawes returned. "I think they're probably watching those two clowns very carefully."

"Why would that be?" Kurberg asked.

"You sure you want to know?" Dawes asked.

"I am," Kurberg said, masking his anxieties behind a cultivated poker face he had used in his practice for years and forever.

"Sir, there's no question at all in my mind that Waterford and Lipton —"

"I'm asking about Davis and Martin," Kurberg interrupted.

"I'm getting there, Sir," Dawes said, trying not to let his irritation show. Kurberg gestured for him to go on. "Sir, one way or another, Waterford and Lipton are involved in those multiple murder butcher crimes. Two of the victims had been my clients and I got word about them. And now here we have Davis and Martin pretending to be police officers to arrest and kidnap another criminal on parole." Dawes sighed. He knew he was about to infuriate his boss, but had bigger worries than that right now. "Sir, I looked into the discovery packets and learned that all four of them are members of some offshoot church called the Church of God's Law."

"Holy smokes," Kurberg said, dismayed. "Are you seriously telling me the church is committing these murders?"

"No," Dawes said. "But I'm telling you there's something mighty fishy there and I could see it blowing up in our face at trial, and us all winding up with a lot of egg on our faces. It could be a small clique in the church. I doubt it's the entire church because there's no way that many people can maintain a secret. But it's bound to involve this church to some degree."

"I see," Kurberg said, his calm demeanor putting lie to the twist in his gut that had him ready to shit his pants. Or puke. Maybe both, he considered, suddenly feeling quite grim. "What's your strategy?"

"I don't know if there's going to be one with Waterford and Lipton," Dawes said. "They won't even talk to me, for God's sake, and I suspect those two morons are headed to death row in a year or so, and in maybe twenty years, probably less – keep in mind they killed five cops, Sir – they're going to be executed.

"Davis and Martin are in less trouble," Dawes went on. "But the case against them … they were caught red-handed in police uniforms with a man in handcuffs. They're going down, Sir. My best hope is that something gets screwed up in the evidence and the prosecution offers a deal. But so far this looks open-and-shut for those two. They're fucked."

"If the police link them to the murders, do you think they'd turn state's evidence to cut a deal?" Kurberg asked.

"I don't know if they're that smart," Dawes said. "And it puts me in an ethical dilemma, Sir. I'd probably have to recuse myself from both cases on the basis of a conflict of interest."

"I get the feeling that wouldn't give you any sleepless nights," Kurberg ventured.

"Sir, if it came to that, it would be best if this entire firm dropped all four of them like hot potatoes," Dawes said.

"You might be right," Kurberg agreed. "Okay, head on out of here. I have to meet a client shortly."

"Shepherd Quinn," Quinn answered his phone.

"Isaiah, it's Walther," Kurberg said. "I think we definitely need to talk, my friend."

"I'm at the nursing home with Bethany," Quinn said. Quinn's wife Bethany had suffered a savage stroke ten years before and was debilitated in Jonas Harbor Convalescent Center. She hadn't uttered a word in years, but beyond the brain damage, Bethany was altogether very healthy, and Kurberg wondered if the poor woman would ever pass and set her husband free.

"Let's meet at my house," Kurberg suggested. "It's not far from there."

"Thirty minutes?" Quinn suggested.

"Yeah, sounds good," Kurberg agreed.

"What's going on?" Quinn asked a half-hour later in Kurberg's study.

"That's what I'm here to ask you," Kurberg said. "Isaiah, I am your lawyer, and the church's lawyer. The other day, Mr. Waterford and Mr. Lipton were arrested on suspicion of murder. Last night, two other parishioners were busted wearing police uniforms and with someone 'under arrest,' a pair named Scott Davis and Leon Martin, also members of our church. Isaiah, do I need to prepare a defense for you and/or the church?"

"God save us," Quinn breathed. "What do those four have in common?"

"You tell me," Kurberg said. "Isaiah, the church has nearly 500 members with more or less compulsory attendance at services. I don't know any of the four. Their faces are familiar from the mug shots but ... I don't think I've ever spoken with any of them."

"I know them, and I don't think all four of them put together have the intelligence of a houseplant," Quinn said.

"Do you think Paul Luden is involved in this?" Kurberg asked carefully.

"No, I don't," Quinn said after a long moment of thought. "When that police sergeant visited me I called Paul and ... he sounded sick at what had happened. Why are you focusing on him?"

"Well, two of the dead were ID'd as clients of one of my attorneys, and a pair of moles I have in the department have indicated that all the victims identified – barring those five police officers – were convicted criminals. And the uniforms they were wearing were genuine, although the badges were counterfeit. Unfortunately, the city uses a standard stock badge and they can be purchased online from vendors. But the uniforms are from the same vendor the police use. Officers have to provide their bona fides, but then get an account and can order all the uniforms they want. I think Paul is the only police officer in the church, Isaiah. I'm not saying he's the killer or involved with this, but I am saying it's ... suggestive."

"Paul Luden is no murderer," Quinn said. "I'd stake my life on it, Walther."

"I think you need to take a hard public stance about these killings," Kurberg said. "Not in the news, but from your pulpit. God help us if the church is implicated in all this mess, Isaiah."

"I think you might be right," Quinn said. "Interestingly enough, I set up a marriage for Paul with Marjorie Stoddard. They'll be married Sunday."

"I never pegged him for a cradle robber," Kurberg said, surprised.

"He's not," Quinn said. "I set it up. Paul isn't the least bit happy about it."

"Then why did you do it?" Kurberg asked. "Marjorie seems like a good kid."

"I have a variety of reasons," Quinn said. "There's strictness with your children and then there's abuse of them, and I think Chuck and Maura all too readily cross that line. For whatever their reasons they seem to hate Marjorie. There was nothing I could do about it, but she's eighteen now. So Chuck called me to disown her, and I considered it. So here's the deal. I think Paul needs to be dragged kicking and screaming out of that shell of grief he's occupied for thirteen years, four months and nine days. Maybe he'll exercise spousal rights and make babies with her. It would do him a world of good even if he's sterile by now. But I figure it like this. He might live twenty more years but probably not. His sons have disowned him, and as a widow, Marjorie Luden would have a strong position to live her life. I think she's one of those young women who's going to decide sooner or later that she doesn't want to be a part of our church."

"That's still ... wow," Kurberg said.

"Well, what's done is done and I wish them all the best," Kurberg said. "I suppose if you thought he was a murderer, you wouldn't have arranged the marriage."

"Of course not," Quinn said. "Next item of business, and this is going to involve you. Dale and Alice Rawson."

"Is he still angry he was punished?" Kurberg asked.

"It's far worse," Quinn said. "Alice drove to the Avery house and attacked Sarah. She gave Sarah a black eye, but Sarah won the fight. She has a black belt, did you know?"

"No," Kurberg said.

"Neither did I," Quinn responded. "One way or another – I don't have all the details yet – Sarah karate-kicked Alice in the face. The upshot of it is that I went to see her and met Dale in the ER waiting room, which is how I got the nose splint. Alice died sometime later, and then Dale … he drove to the Avery house with a pistol and killed himself on their front porch."

"Oh, my dear God," Kurberg breathed.

"I don't know if they had demons or … I just can't even guess," Quinn said. "One way or another, Dale told me a few years ago that their will gave the entire estate to the church, 'right down to the trash in the cans,' as Dale put it. So we'll have to deal with that in due course."

"I recall it was a nice house, just outside the city. Two or three acres, little ranch-style place?" Kurberg asked.

"Yeah, out there near Highway 5 and Lineman Road," Quinn confirmed.

"He was a client of my firm," Kurberg said. "I'll see if we have a file copy of the will and get started on things."

THIRTY-EIGHT

The scene was a house near finished with construction, in a neighborhood being built by a McMansion builder. It was a remote area, two square miles of virtually nothing. Only a dozen houses were in the area, none completed and none occupied, although signage was out advertising the neighborhood from the low 800s.

The freezer truck backed up to the house, and in moments, body parts were scattered everywhere, letting the blood soak into the carpet to ruin it. This time there were no incendiary devices, but a letter addressed to Mike Lowe was tacked to a wall. The men, two in the truck and two in a Chevy Cobalt, got back on the road. They got to a rally point, and one of them opened a disposable cell phone and placed a call to the hotline the police had established.

"You will find parts of several bodies and a letter for Sergeant Lowe at 15338 Eagle Peak Lane," the man said. "It's in that new neighborhood off Highway 5. Hurry up before the evidence is gone." He hung up and tossed the phone into a half-filled ditch, and then the men wandered to their base, taking different routes.

Any hotline in the world gets its crank callers, so the operator didn't get excited at the call, but passed it to the sergeant manning the call center. In a few minutes, two officers arrived at the scene, and one shine of the flashlight through the window told them the scene was for-real, and called it in.

"Lowe," Lowe answered, struggling to wake. He shot a glance at his clock and saw it was closing in on 3:00 AM.

"Mike, this is Jay," Walker said. "We have another scene, 15338 Eagle Peak Lane, in the 10th Precinct. There are eight heads, and this time no incendiaries. But there is a note for you pinned to the wall."

"Christ," Lowe muttered. "Okay, Jay. I'll be there as soon as I can."

"I'll text you the address," Walker said. Lowe went into his bathroom and washed his face to wake himself. He was glad he kept his hair chopped into a military burr, so he had no worries about bad hair days. He dressed in jeans and a T-shirt, and put a light windbreaker over it to conceal his pistol, and then put the address Walker texted into his GPS.

"Okay, so what do we have?" Lowe asked.

"More of the same," Walker said. "CSU is doing their thing. But this time they left a letter for you, Mike."

"What does the letter say?" Lowe asked.

"The CSU van has a photocopier," Walker said, handing Lowe a folded sheet of paper, which Lowe opened.

Sergeant Lowe,

It had been hoped that with the death of that sodomite Capps that you'd have accepted we're on the same side, yet you still pursue us. This is disappointing. We are relentless, Sergeant.

The police are not to blame for the godlessness surrounding them. Your hands are tied by courts and three generations of decisions that have cast God to seeming irrelevance, but God is the most relevant being anywhere, ever. His laws are His laws, and mortal man is foolish and evil to ignore this inescapable fact. It is regrettable that you have chosen man's law over God's, and the consequences of this misjudgment are yours to own.

You can still turn from this. You could even join us in doing God's work and making a better environment for us all. But God is not tolerant of irreverence or disrespect to His decrees. The card attached to this note has a contact for you to message. Don't bother wasting your time on trying to figure out who we are. The contact will bash you through several clouds to Moscow. Consider carefully what we're doing and ask yourself if we're of benefit, irrespective of the five officers killed in the first scene. The error was punished severely, and it is hoped that you will accept that, and accept us as agents of God doing work you are not permitted to do. In truth, you are a respected adversary, but you shouldn't be at all opposed to us.

Lowe folded the note and grunted, and then Walker handed him a copy of the card with the contact information. "I suppose I'd best go to HQ and see what this is all about," he said to Walker, and stifled a huge yawn.

"There's nothing here that requires you," Walker said. "Head on to HQ and I'll be along soon. Christ, what a mess."

"I somehow doubt Christ is smiling at these fucking assholes," Lowe growled. "Okay, see you at HQ."

Lowe arrived to his office and booted up an off-network computer, and then followed the link from the card. It asked him to identify himself, asking questions that surprised him, to include his mother's maiden name (Jameson) and his city of birth, as well as the first car he'd ever owned, and the last four digits of his driver's license and the last four of his social security number. Each question took a moment for the cloud to digest and return an answer to him. A timer popped up to tell him he could get into the cloud in two hours, and he let the timer run, drinking coffee and going through reports. But finally, he was in, and clicked on the new message. It was an audible message, not text. The voice was male, but heavily accented.

"Sergeant Lowe, there are consequences to your conduct and opposition, and you are soon to discover the first of those consequences. You can only execute someone once, so at this point, it doesn't matter what else we do. Our demand is simple: back off of us, and let us do God's work. If you do not, consequences will escalate to an unacceptable level. As a show of our sincerity in this, we want you to go to 104 Maxtonwell Avenue. The key is under the flowerpot to the left of the door. We're not going to give you the long runaround like a bad movie, or tell you to come alone and unarmed. Bring every SWAT officer you have, but it's a guarantee you'll enter and leave the address unmolested and with no physical harm.

"We are sincere and dedicated to God, Sergeant," the voice continued. "In truth, we need men of your caliber who understand the situation, the crisis of crime and godlessness, and are willing to do what has to be done to these godless people for the benefit of the rest of us."

The message ended and Lowe finished his coffee, and then dispatched his bomb team and CSU team to the address, and rounded up a half-dozen of his task force and went with them to Maxtonwell Avenue.

Lowe had been gone an hour and Lisa was back into deep sleep when the doorbell rang. She went to the door, annoyed, thinking it had to be Mike having trouble unlocking the door. She was wearing thin pajama pants that clung to her, and a tank-top shirt over no bra. She looked through the peephole and saw a police officer, and grew instantly alarmed as she opened the door.

"Mrs. Lowe, I'm officer Hansen," the man said. "I need you to come with me, please."

"Is … is it Mike?" Lisa asked. The officer with Hansen shot her with his taser, and in under a minute, Lisa Lowe was zip-tied into submission and tossed into the back seat of their car. There, Hanson gave her a shot of a sedative, and then they drove to their base. She was planted in a chair in the barn and photographed with the morning's newspaper, and then the photo was messaged to another device via a dozen routing stations, to mask its source. And then Lisa was deposited into a cell in the barn, wearing a pillowcase over her head.

The bomb squad cleared the house, a rickety old structure, and reported it was vacant but for a desk, a chair and an iPad with a Post-It note directing Lowe to open the text messages.

Lowe did so, and was staggered seeing the photo of Lisa with the newspaper, and a message telling him to open his e-mail. Lowe, feeling like he was in a horrible nightmare, brought up his Department phone and saw an e-mail three minutes old from God's Justice, whoever that was.

Sergeant Lowe,

As we've tried to tell you, there are consequences to opposing the laws of our Lord, and those who do His work in this world. We require that you stop interfering with us, stop investigating us, and let us do our work. We expect by 5:00 this afternoon that the mayor and chief of police will publicly embrace our work and grant us immunity. Your wife will endure punishment if this does not happen. In one hour, you will receive a photograph and see her first lash marks. She will be executed by flogging tomorrow night if our demands are not met. Her fate is in your hands, Sergeant.

GJ

Lowe suddenly dashed out of the house and fell to all fours, vomiting up coffee onto the grass. He dry-heaved several times before he could struggle to his feet, and looked into the intelligent eyes of Lieutenant Holmes. "Jesus, what happened, Mike?" she asked.

"They have Lisa," Lowe said. "God help me, they have Lisa." He handed her his phone, which still had the email open. "The iPad in there has a photo of her, with today's paper."

"Jesus God," Holmes said. "Okay, Mike, let's get to HQ and start sorting this out. Officer Lundgren will drive you."

"Sergeant, you have to understand we can't give in to these people," Watts said gently a half-hour later.

"I know, Sir," Lowe said. "I just want her back safe and sound."

"You know I have to remove you from this case, yes?" Watts continued. "You have a personal stake in this, an emotional stake."

"I understand that too, Sir," Lowe said, considering an idea but not putting voice to it. "Sir, I would rather this wasn't announced to the department or to the public, please."

"I'll do my best on that," Watts said. "Lieutenant Holmes, you are temporarily relieved of your current assignment and given operative command of the task force, which means direct command. I will have the spokesperson announce today that command has passed to Inspector Johnson, but that a arrests – plural – are expected very soon."

"Chief, in conjunction with this, I request up to thirty days of leave," Lowe said. "Sir, I have just short of 300 days built up."

"I understand," Watts said, but he didn't. "Sergeant, this in no way will reflect on you. If your wife hadn't been kidnapped by these people you'd still be leading this task force. But I know when we recover Lisa you're going to need some time with her, and God knows this assignment has seen you wrung out anyway. Yes, take all the leave you want, Sergeant."

"Thank you, Sir," Lowe said. He hooked a ride home and got on his computer, curious about an idea he had. Lisa was an iPhone junkie and kept it within arm's reach at any and all times.

Indeed, when the doorbell rang, Lisa had, as a matter of habit, swept her iPhone from her nightstand and put it in the pocket of her pajama pants, and when she'd been tossed into the back seat of the car, it had fallen out, unnoticed, on the floorboard of a car parked not 200 feet from where Lisa languished. And now Lowe knew where she was, and wasn't even surprised at the address.

He considered his options and decided to do a driveby of the place and try to figure out how to penetrate it. But if they'd been to his house, they damn well knew his car, so his first call was to Enterprise at the airport, where he rented an SUV available for immediate pickup.

THIRTY-NINE

"Good morning, Paul," Butler said over the phone.

"Hollis, I'm not trying to be rude here but I'm dead tired," Luden slurred, dragged from his sleep. "How important is this?"

"I heard that your Sergeant Lowe's wife was kidnapped," Butler said. "Doesn't he live in your precinct?"

"No, I think he lives in the 30th Precinct," Luden said as his eyes popped wide open and a hundred things seemed to connect all at once. "That's too bad about Lowe. Whoever did this has really crossed some serious lines."

"From what I'm seeing and hearing, this guy Lowe is all-thumbs," Butler said. "I guess I get morbidly curious about things."

"Why aren't you in your office today, Hollis?" Luden asked.

"I have three residents from the hospital covering," Hollis said. "I figure if they need me they can call me, right?"

"Oh, okay," Luden said, and faked a yawn as he sat at the edge of his bed. "Look, I'm due in at 2:00, so I'm going back to sleep. Thanks for letting me know about Lowe. I'll pray for him, Hollis."

"Me too," Butler said.

Paul Luden hung up and rose from bed, donning jeans, hiking boots and a shirt and vest. He went to his closet and got his shotgun, and put his pistol and four magazines in a holster, praying he was wrong and making a fool of himself. He suspected he was being watched, and placed a phone call to a friend of his.

"Phil, this is Paul Luden," he said to Philip Kale, a sergeant in the 11th.

"Yeah, what's happening, Paul?" Kale asked.

"Look, can I borrow your truck today?" Luden asked. "I have some furniture I need to move and —"

"Yeah, that's fine, Paul," Kale said. "I'm swamped in a project here at home. Can you come get it here?"

"On my way, and thanks," Luden said.

Ten minutes later he was at Kale's house and exchanged keys, and then was on the road, promising Kale he'd fill the big truck's tank when he was done. And then he hit the highway to his farm, which Hollis Butler had been renting from him the last several years. Hollis and his wife did not have a happy marriage, Luden knew, and so Hollis left her at the house they'd bought and lived on the farm with his niece. Luden never got clear on the backstory of the strange young woman, now probably 20 years old, but Butler seemed devoted to her.

Luden knew an alternate back entry into the farm and figured it would be wiser to go in that way than another. Even so, he fervently prayed to God that he was mistaken and about to make a fool of himself, but in his heart he sensed he was right, and felt heartbroken about it.

Lowe drove past the front gate and knew there was no way he could charge in with guns blazing and any hope of Lisa surviving his attack, and so he circled the property in his huge rented Expedition and found a spot where the barbed wire fence wasn't clogged with brush and he could enter unobserved.

He fetched his shotgun, a Remington pump action tactical weapon loaded with buckshot, and his .45 pistol, and then pulled two wires wide and entered the property. He'd learned much of woodcraft as a kid hunting small game in the woods, and as a young soldier as well, and figured he would easily get to the house on the property, and more importantly the barn. He suspected the goings-on were in the barn after studying an overhead photo on Google Earth. It was a large property and he figured he'd be hiking at least an hour through the thick woods to get to the barn, but kept his head low and on a swivel for the enemy.

Luden was also skilled in the woods. A couple hundred yards in, he found a man peeing against a tree, and snuck up behind him, then butt-stroked him with his shotgun, addling the man. Luden grabbed zip-ties from his vest and hurriedly bound the man, and then gagged him with a bandana he grabbed from the man's back pocket, and then rolled him over. He recognized the man as Harlan Majors, 30-something years old, but didn't know what Majors did or what his involvement was in this. Linking a dozen zip-ties together, he bound the man to a tree by his ankles, and then made sure the man was unlikely to choke or strangle, and then went toward the house.

It was early afternoon by the time Luden found the guest house on the property, and at a glance he recognized the three cars parked there. One was a dark blue Chevy Cobalt, nearly identical to his own black one, which belonged to Hollis' nephew George, a shiftless ne'er-do-well who Hollis employed as a laborer here. Another was a Chevy Impala, light blue in color, which Hollis had purchased as a "just-in-case" car at a police auction, and the third was a BMW 5-series that Luden knew was Hollis' personal car.

The problem, Luden saw, was that there was about 300 yards of open ground between the woods where he was hidden and the guest house, and he knew if he was caught he'd be killed and buried immediately. He studied his watch and something in his belly told him he couldn't wait for sundown, and then he heard a piercing scream coming from the barn, and hoped it wasn't Lowe's wife. He crept up to the guest house and found George sitting on the back porch with a drink in his hand, reading a comic book. He butt-stroked George as he did Majors, and quickly zip-tied the big man before he could put up a fight, and then dragged him into the house, tied him to a bed, and buried him in blankets that would muffle his protests.

And then he made his way to the barn, finding that fury was quickly supplanting his sickness at the scene he beheld. Hollis was raping Lisa, and finally erupted into her, Luden observed from behind some boxes, and then his niece dragged the poor woman to a post and chained her to it, and Hollis lashed her several times with a horsewhip while the woman screeched in agony. And then Luden saw Hollis' other assistant come into the barn, and he sprung out of his hiding place. The young man – Luden had seen him at the church but didn't know his name – went for a pistol in his belt, but Luden blasted him with his shotgun. Anna dove for the young man's pistol and Luden shot her as well.

He looked at Butler, who had his hands raised. "You figured it out, I guess," he said. "I surrender, Paul. But God's work will not stop."

Luden saw a pistol sitting on an old barrel within arm's reach of Butler, and for the sake of his church and sanity and soul, shot Butler between the eyes with his pistol, and then put the other pistol in Butler's right hand, using an old rag to keep his prints from it.

"Sergeant Lowe coming in," Lowe called from behind another cluster of boxes.

"Come on, Lowe," Luden called back. He and Lowe hurriedly uncuffed Lisa from the post. She was sobbing hysterically and scurried away from them, hunkering in a corner, looking at them hollow-eyed, and Lowe felt his heart break.

"Call the cops and your task force," Luden ordered. "God forgive me." Luden, who looked like he'd aged ten years in the last several minutes, put the safety on his pistol and handed it butt-first to Lowe.

"Yes, Sir," Lowe said, guessing his own ass was on the griddle too about thirty seconds after Holmes' arrival. He wandered toward Lisa but she cringed from him, glaring balefully. He removed his own shirt and gave it to her to cover herself, and then called Holmes' number and gave her a brief encapsulation, and she said she'd handle it. Moments later he heard the sirens wailing their way to the farm while Luden went to the gate and opened it to let them in. In twenty minutes the property was filled with all kinds of officialdom, and Luden led officers to the two suspects he'd subdued.

Lisa cringed so badly from the first paramedic that a pair of EMS units were called in, each with a female medic, to form a new team, and they transported the traumatized woman to the hospital. Lowe wanted to go with her but he knew she wanted no part of him, and wondered if she somehow held him to blame for this.

"What happened, Mike?" Holmes asked. "How the hell did you and Luden hook up to do this?"

"We didn't," Lowe said. "Luden ... I didn't even know he was here. Lisa ... she's addicted to that iPhone of hers, so I took a chance and did a 'find my phone' on it, and located it here. I was too afraid the police would show up in a raid and this clown Butler – I had no idea it was him, or even who he is ... well, 'was' since Luden killed him – and I figured I could reconnoiter and either extract her or coordinate things better from here. Luden ... I don't know why he was here or anything, but he stepped out and ... Lieutenant, whatever happens to him, he's a hero, Ma'am. He stepped out, shot the man over there, and when the woman leapt for the gun he shot her too, then dropped his shotgun and drew his pistol right as Butler turned around, and did for Butler too. He risked his ass and saved Lisa's life."

"How did Luden tip to this?"

"I honest to God don't know, Miranda," Lowe said.

"And you never fired a shot, Mike?" Holmes pursued.

"Ma'am, I didn't," Lowe said. "I was hiding over there when Lowe burst out and took the situation in hand. I was drawn and ready to join the fight if needed, but from my angle, Lisa was in the line of fire. Sweet Jesus, that was the hardest thing I've ever had to do, hiding quietly and waiting for my moment while that animal did that to her."

"It's a fucking mess here," Holmes said. "There's a walk-in freezer down the hall and it's full of dismembered body parts, and I expect CSU will be busy for a month on this fucking place." Holmes sighed, and then her tone changed. "A few things here, Mike. First, I'll try to fade the heat that's liable to come down from Chief Watts for you going cowboy here, but you'll probably pick up a suspension for this. Second, I ... I agree with you that Luden was a hero in this mess, but he's still in very hot water and may well do time. Third, go your ass to the hospital and be with Lisa. I know how to find you, and God knows there'll be ten thousand questions that pop up in this. Where did you park?"

"Out that way," Lowe said. "I snuck in. Even rented an SUV so I wouldn't be recognized so easily."

"Get in my car," Holmes said. "I need to get out of peoples' way so they can do their jobs, and go see Watts and try to save your ass from his wrath. Christ, what a fucking mess this is going to be."

Lowe got to the hospital and was allowed to go back and see Lisa, who had been lightly sedated. She had been told that it was likely two or three of her wounds would scar. She was being prepped for surgery to repair tears in her anus.

"How are you feeling?" Lowe asked gently.

"Mike, this is your fault," Lisa hissed in a furious tone. "You could have refused this assignment, but no, you had to be Supercop. And now, for the rest of my life, every time I see my back in the mirror, every time I go number two, I'm going to remember this. I'm going to remember I was beaten like a nigger slave from some bad movie and raped in my ass, because of you." She groaned as she shifted. "I want a divorce, Mike. This has been bigamy on your part. You're not married to me but your Goddamn job. Please ... just go away. I won't be a bitch in the divorce but I never want to see you again. Please move out before I get home."

"Lisa —" Lowe began.

"Get the fuck out!" Lisa screamed. "Out! Out! Out!"

"I ... I'll look in on you later," Lowe said. He left and drove about aimlessly for a while before returning the Expedition to Enterprise. He prayed to a God he seldom consulted that Lisa would calm down and absolve him of blame, but long experience with her told him that she was unlikely to do so, and that he was headed headlong into his third divorce. He parked at a shopping center lot, now in his own car, and pulled his pistol, looking at it and considering just putting it in his mouth and calling it quits. After a long session of contemplation, he decided against, reholstered his piece, and then simply drove home.

FORTY

"Captain Luden ... may I call you Paul?" Reese asked. She was astonished, from the tale she'd heard, that Luden had been the hero.

"Sure, whatever," Luden said. "I guess the 'Captain' bit has come to an end anyway, hasn't it?"

"Yes it has," Reese said. "Captain, we'll get to other matters later, but I want to know what happened today."

"I figured out Hollis Butler ... it's a long story and if I'm going to be honest I may as well say I feel like a fool," Luden admitted. "I suppose a lot of it is denial. If he had been someone I hadn't known and considered a good friend for ten and more years – honestly, my best friend – I think I'd have figured it out several days ago. Tell me, if you can, is Lieutenant Capps dead?"

"Yeah he is," Reese said.

"I figured his whole case was a holdback, and well-played, Inspector," Luden said.

"What I want to know is ... how did Butler learn this and why did he murder Lieutenant Capps?" Reese asked.

"Because there's no fool like an old fool," Luden said. "Hollis was my friend. Friends sometimes confide in one another.

273

And … God forgive me, I made a lot of mistakes regarding him, but Inspector, I will put my hand on a stack of Bibles and promise on God's Word a thousand times that I didn't know what Hollis was doing."

"Start from the top," Reese ordered, suspecting that this was going to be a very long night debriefing Luden.

"That farm has been in my family about 200 years," Luden said. "I grew up here, in the bedroom on the southeast corner of the house. The house came to me when my mother died – Dad died when I was still in the Marines – when I was just starting my second year in the Department. Anyway, I was in an apartment in town and then moved in after Mom died. When I married it was our home and I raised my sons there. But … when Ruth died, I couldn't bear being in that house. Honest-to-God the night of her funeral I moved into a residential hotel and put a hurry-up on getting an apartment. I got the apartment, bought furniture for it – I couldn't bear being surrounded by memories of my wife – and took only my clothes. Anyway, Hollis talked with me about the place a time later, told me his marriage wasn't at all a good one, and asked me if he could rent it from me. He wanted to try his hand at a bit of farming, live off the land, you know the deal. To be honest, I was a lieutenant then and needed the money, so we shook on it, no contracts or anything, just a gentlemen's agreement, and I seldom went to the farm again."

"Captain, I think at this point I should read you your rights," Reese said. "You've been under investigation and surveillance from IAD since you got transferred to the 22nd. You may as well know you're fired for making illegal inquiries. But I'm going to flip up a card and tell you we're pretty sure Butler hacked you – Jesus, for the first time in my career, the Butler did it, oh my God – and was using

274

your login to do a great deal of the inquiries." She pulled a card from her purse and began reading his rights to him, but Luden interrupted.

"Ma'am, I know all of that," Luden said. "I've been reading rights to people as long as you have. Let's get on with this." Surprising her, Luden reached into his pocket and produced his badge and then handed it to her. "Nothing matters anymore."

"What do you mean?" Reese asked.

"I have to say you IA people outdid yourselves this time," Luden remarked. "One way or another, I didn't kill those people, but I think Hollis was setting me up to take the fall for it, and today I shot and killed my best friend. Put me on death row. It doesn't matter. He had the wool pulled over my eyes for years now. I saw it, couldn't believe it, so I unsaw it."

"Explain that, please," Reese said.

"It started the other day, when I should have tipped over to it," Luden began. "He asked me what I knew about Lieutenant Capps being killed. Something rang a distant bell in my head but I was in the middle of a lot of things, to include a marriage planned for this Sunday – I guess that's off the rails now – and that night at work we had that huge pileup, and I never returned to thinking about Capps. Nobody'd said anything around the department but ... I guess I filed that aside so I could stay in denial."

"Lieutenant Darrell Capps' head was delivered by courier to Sergeant Lowe," Reese said. "It was news to all of us he was gay."

"I was shocked too when I found out a couple or three years ago," Luden said. "I went to dinner at a place out of town, and there were Capps and another man billing and cooing together. I don't think he recognized me, but … yeah, I was outraged. Hollis was my best friend. We vented to each other about things, and I vented to him. I had no idea he … well, I guess we've already established the depth of my denial, haven't we? Anyway, there I was in denial when he called me early today – well, it was around 10:00 this morning, but with the hours I've been working, I was dead asleep – and asked me what I knew about Lowe's wife being kidnapped. That's when the dam burst, Inspector. I got dizzy and really thought I was about to have a stroke. Even then, I hoped I was wrong, and figured to reconnoiter the place, and honestly hoping I was just making a fool of myself. I found the two men, one in the woods taking a leak on a tree and the other on the back porch of the guest house, and subdued them. I snuck into the barn and was hiding behind boxes. Hollis was just … he was finishing raping Mrs. Lowe." Luden fell silent, sickened at the memory. "It was an anal rape, Inspector. And then his niece dragged the poor woman to a whipping post and Hollis began using a horsewhip on her."

"What happened next?" Reese prompted.

"I came out and told him to stop and another man came in with a pistol," Luden said. "I shot him and then Hollis' niece went for the pistol and I shot her, and then dropped my shotgun and brought out my pistol. Hollis spun around and had a pistol as well, so I shot him too. Lowe came out then. He had a bad angle from his position and might have shot his wife from where he was. I can't imagine how that was for him, being forced to witness that and not able to intercede."

"We're going to set him up for counseling," Reese said. "Lisa as well."

276

"I'm going to be praying for them, as well as all the poor wretches Hollis killed," Luden said. "And to think he used me unwittingly. My God, I don't blame you for firing me."

"Did you give Hollis your login information?" Reese asked.

"No, but … Inspector, I'm one of those old people who got dragged into computers and the like really late in the game. You have to have a login for this, a login for that … a lot of it is very hard to keep in my mind. So I wrote all the logins into a notebook that I left in my desk at the farm. When I moved out, I totally moved out, and figured Hollis would box it all up. Mostly, he did, but I guess he got the book and used it."

"We're looking into it but that's probably how he got police uniforms," Reese said.

"Uniforms?" Luden echoed.

"We arrested two of your church members, both in police uniforms, with a paroled felon in handcuffs," Reese told him. "We took them in on charges of kidnapping and impersonating the police. But if he had your login information for the uniform supplier, that would explain how he got genuine uniforms."

"Why would he need them?" Luden asked, knowing he was missing something here.

"Yeah, I guess you wouldn't have known," Reese said. "He was killing parolees, Paul. We think the MO was to send people dressed as cops to arrest them for parole violations or other warrant issues. But he was rooted in religion. He flayed them to death with a whip like the Romans used on Christ, and then parted them out."

"Did he have a demon?" Luden asked. Reese guessed correctly that Luden was asking himself this, and unaware that he'd put voice to the thought.

"Paul, we know you indeed made several inquiries into people, including a John and Sarah Avery," Reese said. "We've been watching you closely, like I said."

"I did that," Reese admitted. "It was a background check for my church."

"It was illegal," Reese pointed out. She found herself feeling sorry for Luden rather than scornful or contemptuous. "Look, you're a police officer and that means the union will pop for a lawyer for you. Cop to cop, I'm telling you that you're best calling the union rep and getting a lawyer to protect your interests."

"Like it really matters," Luden said. "Okay, let's do that, Inspector."

FORTY-ONE

"Jesus Christ, you are not going to believe this, Lieutenant," Walker said to Holmes. "This dude Butler was totally gone. He honestly seemed to think that he was God's agent on earth, like a second Savior. He had a manifesto we found, detailing all they'd done, and naming names. He even recorded some of the kills on video, planning someday to take credit for all this shit. We have the cohorts dead to rights, though. There are several others who seem to be in the wind but I think they'll turn up. All of them are members of that church, but Butler wrote disparagingly of Quinn. Quinn and the other elders were entirely in the dark, as best we can tell, Ma'am. He also had a list of over forty other parolees and prostitutes they were planning to seize. He also had an area where he wrote about Luden, Ma'am. He apparently had that poor son of a bitch hoodwinked all along. He wrote that he was really fond of Luden, thought the world of him, but freely admitted he was using the man like a tool."

"Get the manifesto copied and bring the DA in on it, and we'll re-arrest Davis and Martin on capital murder charges," Holmes ordered, and yawned hugely. "Goddamn, I'm tired."

"Yeah, I understand," Walker agreed. "How's Lowe's wife doing?"

"I haven't gotten word," Holmes said. "I had to suspend Lowe earlier, and haven't gotten to talk with Chief Watts about him. Reese is with Luden now, probably arresting him."

"Considering his heroism today, good luck finding a jury that'll convict him," Walker snorted.

"Yeah, you're probably right," Holmes agreed. "God, there's no goodness to be found in this case."

"This is Clinton Dawes," Dawes answered his phone.

"Maggie Flame here," Flame said. "Clinton, I'd like to meet with you. Can I buy you a drink?"

"You know, a glass of forty-year-old Scotch sounds like just the ticket, as long as it's on your dime," Dawes chuckled.

"Shanahan's?" Flame suggested.

"I'll be there in twenty," Dawes promised, wondering what was going on.

"You probably get paid three times what I do," Flame greeted him at Shanahan's Pub, a popular hangout for lawyers. "But I have bad news for you, so this is on me."

"Okay," Dawes said dubiously, but he took her at her word and ordered a glass of Scotch that listed for thirty dollars. Flame, surprising him, ordered the same, and they small-talked until the waitress brought their drinks.

"The case broke on your boys, all four of them," Flame said after a sip of her Scotch. "We've issued warrants for Davis and Martin for capital murder, and barring divine intervention, your boys are going to death row, Clinton."

"Oh, really?" Dawes asked.

"We have a detailed manifesto from the ringleader, naming names, including all four of your boys, and video recordings of them all taking part in the killings," Flame said. "You'll be officially notified tomorrow. Clinton, they're only going to avoid the death penalty by confessing to their parts in the murders and accepting life without parole."

"You can't be serious," Dawes said.

"Ask around about me, buddy," Flame said. "Any defense attorney in this county will tell you I'm a straight shooter and I don't play bluffing games."

"I guess you want something more or you wouldn't be getting me drunk on this outstanding whiskey," Dawes said.

"It'll go far better on Davis and Martin if they turn themselves in," Flame said. "Three of these people, including their leader, were killed today. The leader had anally raped a woman – the wife of the sergeant leading the task force – and was busy horsewhipping her when an officer intervened. He was shot at, and the officer killed three of them, two with shotgun blasts and when their leader spun around with his own pistol, the officer shot him between the eyes. I need you to understand, Clinton. These people have killed six police officers, including the lieutenant commanding Homicide Division, and the cops on the street are bloodthirsty. Now you know and I know sometimes street executions happen, and I'd rather put your boys in prison than see them shot full of holes."

"Let me try to get in touch with them," Dawes said. "I'll do my best to talk them into turning themselves in, but … I can't promise they will, Ms. Flame."

"Just call me Maggie, dammit," Flame said. "We're on opposing sides but that doesn't mean we're enemies, Clinton. We both want justice. We just see it differently."

"Yes, Ma'am, Maggie dammit," Dawes shot back with a grin, and Flame laughed.

"Smartass. Okay, now that we've cleared that up, let's have another drink," Flame said. "This is really good Scotch."

When they parted company, Dawes returned straight to his office and called up the files on Davis and Martin. He called Martin first. "Leon, you and your buddy are fucked to your knees," Dawes said. "The case broke and there are fresh warrants on you and Scott for capital murder. I met with the prosecutor a few minutes ago. You need to go to the nearest police station and turn yourself in. I don't mean in the morning or even in a couple or three hours. I mean you need to go right now to the police station because the prosecutor is worried the cops – you're accused in the killings of six of them, I'll remind you – are going to be a bit jumpy and trigger-happy. There's no sense dying sooner than you must."

"What are you telling me?" Martin asked, starting to panic.

"I'm telling you that you and your buddy are fucked," Dawes said, his patience slipping. "And I'm telling you that if you don't want to die in a hail of bullets tonight, you need to turn yourself in."

"Okay," Martin said. "I'll go there now."

"I'll see you tomorrow," Dawes said. "Don't talk to any of them unless I'm there and tell you to talk." He hung up.

"Hello," Davis answered a minute later.

"Scott, this is Clinton Dawes."

"How are you, Mr. Dawes," Davis asked.

"Scott, I'm going to cut the bullshit here," Dawes said. "You and Leon both have warrants for capital murder, and the cops are coming for you. You need to go straight to the PD and turn yourself in."

"Why should I do that?" Davis asked.

"Because there's a good chance, after you and Leon killed six cops, that the police are going to come up with a way to kill you tonight," Dawes explained. His clients weren't the sharpest knives in the drawer, he realized anew. It probably made them easily led, he considered, wondering how that would play to a jury. "I'll see you at the jail tomorrow morning. Don't talk to anyone unless I'm there. Get over there now." Dawes ended the call and hoped his due diligence would keep the two dummies alive.

Leon Martin panicked. He'd been ready to accept the consequences of his conduct until it came right down to facing those consequences. He had two thousand dollars in cash salted away, and hurriedly grabbed that and three changes of clothes, hopped in his car, and spun out, dashing away from the city. He'd go to Arizona, he decided, where he knew the church owned property and would give him sanctuary.

He stopped at a hotel a little after midnight, tired to the point of delirium, and checked in. He was spent, and terrified. The next morning he got forty miles before he was surrounded by the cops, easily tracing his cell phone with a warrant. Unarmed, he surrendered, and was transported the following morning to the county jail. He was remanded without bail, and the bail paid for his original charge was seized by the court since he had indeed jumped bail the second he'd crossed the county line.

Scott Davis was ready to make a stand for God. He got a shotgun and three boxes of shells, and climbed up onto his roof, ready for the cops to arrive. He would rather die on his own terms than strapped to a table like a sick old dog and injected with poison. Always afraid of needles, Davis honestly envisioned crucifixion as a lesser cruelty than lethal injection.

When three police cruisers arrived, Davis took position behind the chimney of his house and fired at them with the shotgun. The cops were unharmed and took positions behind their cars, and called for backup. While every one of them wanted to return fire and kill this little fucker, orders had come down from On High that every effort was to be made to capture this one alive. The DA wanted to make an example of him and not have the press going wild nationwide about the police having their own killing spree. Paul Luden had already capped three earlier in the day, and while it looked like a righteous shoot, the press was good at making a story where there was none, and the press generally hated the cops.

Seven more police units and SWAT were called in, surrounding the little row house that Scott Davis had called home the past seven years. In truth, Davis was little danger with his shotgun, loaded with birdshot since he was an avid hunter of dove and quail. He popped up, standing on the peak of the roof, and fired three more rounds from his Remington 1100 shotgun, and was then toppled from the roof when he was hit in the upper back with a beanbag gun, staggering him. He hit the ground and broke both arms and a leg, and got an ambulance ride to the hospital. Surgery was required on his right humerus and shoulder, which had also broken in the fall. He woke with the right arm in traction and the left in a cast and sling, and his left lower leg was also in a cast. His right ankle was handcuffed to the bed, and he knew he would never again be free.

FORTY-TWO

Luden had been arrested and released on his own recognizance, and called Quinn to tell him it was an emergency and they needed to talk. "Do you know what time it is, Paul?" Quinn asked irritably.

"I do, Shepherd," Luden said. "It's 11:48 PM. Shepherd, if you think two minutes into our talk that I wasted your time, then excommunicate me."

"I'll do no such thing, Paul," Quinn said, reining in his temper. "Come on over."

"Shepherd, I pray the church isn't damaged," Luden said as he walked in. "The killer was Hollis Butler, and a flurry of church members. I discovered them earlier today."

"Whoa," Quinn said. "How do you know it's them? Is he under arrest?"

"Shepherd, I'm relying on your discretion here as my clergyman," Lowe said.

"Of course," Quinn replied.

"Hollis … he asked me the other day about a police lieutenant named Capps," Lowe said. "He told me Capps had been murdered and asked what I'd heard about it, which was absolutely nothing. Capps was a sodomite, and they somehow got his boyfriend to keep a lid on his murder, and I didn't think any more about it. But then Sergeant Lowe's wife was kidnapped last night, and Hollis called me this morning to ask if I'd heard any news, and it dawned on me he had too much inside information, so I went to the farm – he's rented it from me for years – to find out what was what. Honestly, I had high hopes I was wrong and would wind up feeling like a fool."

"But that's not what happened?" Quinn asked, feeling sick.

"That's not what happened," Luden echoed. "Shepherd, I entered on him anally raping Lowe's wife. I made a call to the hospital and she's in surgery repairing the damage he did. Anyway, he ... he had his niece, that girl Anna, bind her to a post and was horsewhipping her when I stepped out. One of his people pointed a gun at me and I shot him. His niece went for that gun and I shot her too. And then ... Shepherd, this is where I committed a crime. I shot Hollis between the eyes and then put a pistol in his hand."

"Why, Paul?" Quinn wanted to know.

"Shepherd, I didn't want a big trial for him humiliating and ruining our church," Luden said simply. "But it's torturing my soul. I have no doubt he would have gotten the death penalty and been executed someday for what he did. But I didn't want the church damaged, Shepherd. God help me." Luden sat heavily and began to weep.

"Paul, I don't quite know what to say," Quinn said. "If you were a danger to yourself or others, or told me you were going to go out from here and kill someone I would have to stop you, but what's done is done, and you did what you saw as right and true. I suppose if we were Catholics I would tell you go say Hail Mary and Our Father a hundred times each and tell you go forth and sin no more, but we're not Catholic. All I can tell you is through Christ you are forgiven, and if my forgiveness matters, I forgive you too."

"Thank you, Shepherd," Luden said. "I got fired tonight and arrested for misuse of information. Or, well, I got instantly retired. Contractually, I'm on leave for the next several months, and when that expires I go on pension."

"Then you and your new wife will have a good deal of time to enjoy one another," Quinn said.

"You sure you want to marry her off to a murderer?" Luden asked, surprised.

"Yes, now more than ever, Paul," Quinn said. "People aren't made to be alone. Oh, we survive it – God knows I have, right? – but we're not made for it. Men and women need one another."

"I'm old enough to be her grandfather," Luden objected.

"And old enough to be her husband," Quinn countered.

"Alright, then," Luden said. He wasn't worried about jail time just yet. His attorney from the police union told him he could probably cut a deal for probation and an agreement never to work in law enforcement again. The lawyer pointed out that at his age, Luden was unlikely to be hired in a hurry by anyone anyway, and should think about enjoying his retirement. "I think I'll look like a pathetic old man with a thick wallet and a thin wife 45 years younger than me, but I have to confess the thought of sex with her excites me just the same, Shepherd. It's confusing."

"Paul, if Bethany died tonight I'd take a bride," Quinn said. "Do you think being the Shepherd relieved me of a man's urges?"

"I guess I never thought of it," Luden admitted.

"It's really okay, Paul," Quinn said. "How often have people been thoughtless around you because of your career?"

"Good point," Luden said, yawning.

"Look, why don't you bunk here in the guest room tonight, and hit it fresh in the morning?" Quinn suggested. Luden nodded and stumbled to the guest room and fell into the bed. He slept nearly sixteen hours.

FORTY-THREE

Lowe woke the next morning and went to the hospital only to be rebuffed again by Lisa, and then he called an apartment hunter, looking for a one-bedroom available for immediate move-in. He got a call back fifteen minutes later with three possibilities, and Lowe immediately ruled out two of them for high crime in the areas, but the third, a place called Pike's Ridge, was in the relatively safe 5th Precinct, and he drove over to look at the apartment. It was nothing spectacular, Lowe instantly saw, but would suffice. He'd always been one to work long hours anyway, and figured once he was reinstated, he'd be back to working long hours, so it was just a place to sleep and shower, a hotel suite of sorts.

Lowe paid the deposit and decided to pay the entire six month's lease up-front for a 5% discount, and got the keys to the apartment. He then called a 2-men-and-a-truck mover and met them at his house, boxing the guest bedroom in its entirety, and then leading them to the apartment, where they set him up. He drove to Sam's Club next and got a television, pots and pans and a few other odds and ends, and then to a furniture store where he bought an amazingly ugly sofa and coffee table on clearance, and then back to his apartment, where he paid a pair of maintenance men to drag it all up to his apartment. He returned the truck and got home, and was surprised to run into Paul Luden.

"I didn't know you lived here," Luden said.

290

"I didn't until today," Lowe told him, offering his hand. "Lisa blames me for what happened and said she wants a divorce, and asked me to get out of the house before she comes home from the hospital, so here I am."

"I'm very sorry," Luden said. "Hopefully she'll come around. Do you need a hand pushing furniture around?"

"I think it's good," Lowe said. "But can I take you to supper, Captain?"

"It's just 'Paul' now," Luden said. "They fired me last night and filed charges against me."

"Charges?" Lowe asked. "What did they charge you for?"

"Oh, it's a long story," Luden said. "But long and short, they've accused me of misusing the computer system to do a background check on someone."

"Come in for a moment," Lowe said. "I want to change shirts before I go out. Mexican sound good for supper?"

"Yeah, sounds really good," Luden said.

Lowe changed his shirt and went back into the living room. "I'm going to tell you one thing that I'll never tell anyone," Lowe said to Luden. "I owe you and I'm damn sure not going to betray you, Paul. I don't think anyone is going to notice, and if they do it might not matter anyway. The pistol was in Butler's right hand, but he was a southpaw."

Luden's eyes went wide and he sucked in a deep breath of air. "It's okay, Paul," Lowe said. "That stays entirely between you and me. I think you did the right thing, okay?"

"Thanks, Sergeant," Luden said.

"You saved my wife's life, Paul, and even if she hates me I still love her, more than I can say," Lowe said. "I owe you. And just call me Mike. Let's go get some supper. I could eat a horse right now."

Luden was up late, half readjusting to being retired and not having to keep late hours, but doing a huge measure of soul-searching. He had found a very unlikely friend in Mike Lowe and was thinking about the Asian tradition of being responsible for someone if you saved his or her life, and wondered if it would somehow atone for at least a teaspoon of the guilt burdening his heart.

He woke early and ate a quick breakfast, and then drove to the hospital, and found Lisa Lowe in her room. "You look familiar," she said. "Do I know you?"

"You ... we haven't met, Mrs. Lowe," Luden said. "My name is Paul Luden. I ... I shot the people abusing you."

"Then I owe you my life," she said.

"Do you think we can talk for a few minutes? May I sit down?" Luden asked.

"By all means," Lisa said, trying to smile.

"Ma'am, I was retired from the police department immediately after that shooting, but until then I was a captain," Luden said. "Hollis Butler was my best friend."

"God, I'm so sorry," Lisa said. "That must have been horrible for you."

"Hollis … I had no idea until then what he'd been doing," Luden said. "Mike … he found out and got to that farm minutes behind me. He didn't have the angle to get a shot at Butler. The risk of hitting you instead was too great. Life isn't a Hollywood movie, and at distances, especially with adrenaline and emotion added to the mix, pistols are notoriously inaccurate. As things turned out he moved into my apartment complex and I ran into him there. He tells me you want a divorce."

"And he asked you to talk me out of it," Lisa concluded.

"Mike has no idea I'm here," Luden said. "He'd probably want to box my ears if he knew. But … he's crushed, although he won't show it. He loves you, and he's grieving, and confused."

"The hell of it is, I love him too," Lisa said. "I even know he never wanted this to happen, Sir, but … it happened because of him. My God, he could have turned away this assignment."

"Technically, yes, but he would have been … look, because I pried into this case I got sent to the worst assignment a captain could have, an assignment that the only way out of it is to retire or die. I was forcibly retired last night, in fact. It had nothing to do with you, Mrs. Lowe, but with … well, I did something I shouldn't have done and that's the price I paid. But if Mike had turned away the assignment he would have gotten a similar transfer until he took the hint and retired, and then what? He's a lot like me, Mrs. Lowe. All he knows is being a police officer, and he enjoys a good reputation as one of the best. Nobody could have predicted that Hollis would behave as he did."

"You know his excuse for raping and whipping me?" Lisa asked bitterly.

"No, I don't," Luden said.

"I answered the door at 3:00 AM wearing pants and a tank-top, dressed like a strumpet, which made me a whore deserving of the lash for being a temptress," Lisa said.

"Well, if it means much, he's answering to a far higher law than any institution of man affords," Luden said, feeling his eyes growing wet.

"I'm sorry," Lisa told him. "I … Mike's told me about police officers who've killed people, and the stress they undergo from it. I can't imagine how horrible this is for you since he was your best friend."

"I don't know how I'll live with it," Luden admitted, surprised he was opening up to a woman, particularly this woman. "But I don't regret doing the right thing, Mrs. Lowe. And usually the right thing tends to be the hardest. God knows the Bible tells us that over and again. But I didn't come here about me. I came here about you and Mike. I know his career was an element in what happened, but let's say he was a brick mason and this had happened to you. He'd be just as blameless. Hollis tried to use you to blackmail Mike and the city, so he could keep killing, Mrs. Lowe. And Mike was immediately pulled from the case and put on leave. He's in hot water for riding in to your rescue now. He was prepared to die for you, Ma'am."

"Call me Lisa, please," Lisa said, chewing her bottom lip in thought. "I guess if my heart ever listens to your logic the problem is solved, Mr. Luden —"

"Just Paul, please," Luden interrupted.

"Paul, then," Lisa said. "You make a lot of sense. I'm still coming to terms with what happened, and Mike's the only one alive to blame."

"What about me?" Paul asked. "Hollis was doing these things right under my nose on a farm he'd been renting from me for ages, Lisa. He got my login information and was using my accesses to find and kill these people. He even used it to find out your address."

"Jesus," Lisa said. "How did he manage to hack you?"

"He ... Mrs. ... I'm sorry ... Lisa," Luden choked out. "My wife Ruth died thirteen years ago. I loved her very deeply, and her last two years were a horror. When she passed, I couldn't bear the thought of being in that home that she and I had shared for so long. The memories were haunting me. So I just left. I got an apartment, bought some cheap furniture, and left just about everything. That included a little notebook full of passwords, and a huge walk-in freezer in the barn – I had a few head of cattle long ago and would kill and butcher one occasionally, and kept other frozen goods in there, and I hunted a lot in those days, including a yearly trip to New Mexico where I always brought back an elk and a deer or two. Anyway, he went through the notebook and he was in like Flynn, and nobody had any idea until I got into trouble and the Department started checking up on me."

"How did you and Mike find me?" Lisa asked.

"Separately," Luden said. "Hollis asked me some questions and seemed to know far more about the case than anyone should, including stuff that nobody should have known, and ... I finally emerged from the denial, I guess. Mike told me – he recovered your phone, by the way, and it's at your house – that he noticed your phone wasn't around the house and that you pretty much always had it on you, so he used that 'find my phone' feature. Apparently it was on the floorboard of the car those men used."

"I'll be damned," Lisa chuckled.

"No, I don't think you will," Luden said. "I need to get going soon. Is there anything I can do for you?"

"I think I'm good," Lisa said. "They're keeping me stoned out of my gourd on Demerol, but told me I should be going home in another day or two."

"Then I'll be off, Lisa," Luden said. "Thank you for hearing me out."

"Thank you for saving me," Lisa said.

"I think in a way you might be saving me in return," Luden told her. "Thank you for your time, Lisa. May I visit you again?"

"I hope you will," Lisa said.

"Then I'll do that. I hope you recover fast."

"I hope so too," Lisa said. "Jesus, that reminds me. I need to call work before I get fired for job abandonment. Will you hand me the phone, please?"

Luden handed her the phone and then left the hospital. He knew Marjorie was still in school, and wondered how the church would react when the news got out. The police had only said that several suspects were killed in an exchange of gunfire, and that identities were being withheld pending notification of next of kin.

"Jenna, this is Lisa," Lisa slurred into the phone to her office receptionist.

"Lisa, oh my God, where have you been?" Jenna asked. "Mollie wants your head on a plate."

"Go ahead and transfer me to her," Lisa said. She worked well under Mollie, but this wasn't to say that Mollie was a good boss, and Lisa had been actively job-seeking for six months, but the right one just never came up.

"This is Mollie."

"Mollie, it's Lisa Lowe," Lisa said.

"You know you're at the edge of being fired," Mollie said.

"I think I have a good excuse, so back the fuck off," Lisa snapped, a sudden burst of anger dispelling the narcotic haze.

"Okay, let's hear it," Mollie shot back, her own anger rising.

"I'm in Mount Jordan Hospital," Lisa said. "Room 313 here."

"What happened?" Mollie asked. "Nobody could have called sooner?"

"I was kidnapped and raped," Lisa said.

"Oh, Christ!" Mollie exclaimed. "Are you okay?"

"No, not really," Lisa said. *Goddamned moron cunt*, she raged inwardly. *Is anyone okay that's in the fucking hospital?* "I'm probably going to be on medical leave for a while. I … Jesus … he raped my bottom, and then horsewhipped me. They had to do surgery, and I've been stoned until a few minutes ago."

"God, I'm sorry, Lisa," Mollie said. "I hope your husband is helping you through this."

"He would be if I let him," Lisa said.

"Did he do this to you?" Mollie asked, sounding suddenly furious.

"No, Mike didn't do this," Lisa said. "I'm … I don't think I should give you many details. The case is under investigation, still. Another cop shot the rapist. Mike was in the wrong position and might have shot me. But … it's just a fucked-up mess, Mollie. I … I need to go." Lisa hung up the phone and began crying inconsolably, and a moment later a psychiatrist consulted arrived.

"It looks like I got here right on time," said Dr. Elaine Grogarty. "So let's talk, Lisa."

They spoke about Lisa's ordeal for nearly an hour, and Grogarty made a note that Lisa would require PTSD counseling, and set her up for several regular appointments over the coming three months.

FORTY-FOUR

"Look, I'm going to be blunt here," Flame said to George Tarkin, another of Hollis Butler's lackeys. "You could possibly get paroled in a few years and maybe make a decent life for yourself, George. I don't think you're the type to do this on your own hook, but right now my bosses are bloodthirsty and want you and your cohorts all on death row. Confess and tell us what all happened, and I'll tell my bosses that we need to cut you a deal." What she really meant was that Tarkin was too stupid to have done these crimes on his own hook.

"I ... I don't ... I don't think so," Tarkin said.

"George, that's your —" Flame began.

"Ms. Flame, I would like a moment alone to confer with my client," Dawes interrupted.

"As you wish," Flame said. "I'll go get a cup of coffee, then." Flame left the room and went down the hall to the coffee maker, and poured a cup of the foul coffee, took a couple of sips, then poured it down the water fountain drain, and waited for Dawes to call her back.

She had another meeting planned with Scott Davis, and had been tipped off that he had a pathological fear of needles and would quite probably be receptive to a deal that would save him from having a needle slid into his vein.

Surprising her, Dawes came out of the interrogation room, and while he struggled to keep a poker face, Flame could see the look of disgusted dismay on his face. "My client has instructed me to decline your offer. He wishes to pursue an alternate defense, centered around your Captain Luden's brutal assault of him. He seems to believe that he will be released by the court on the civil rights violation."

"Yeah, good luck with that," Flame said sourly. "Okay, when do you want to meet your boy Scott Davis?"

"Mr. Davis is in the infirmary here," Dawes said. "Let me meet with him and find out if he wishes to speak with you."

"You know where I'll be," Flame said.

Twenty minutes later her phone rang and Dawes asked her to come to the infirmary. Davis' bed had been moved into a private room, but with two broken arms and a broken leg there was little worry he'd escape.

"Mr. Davis, I'm Margaret Flame from the district attorney's office," Flame introduced herself. "I'm not going to take up much of your time, but here's what's going on. You're going to trial in probably about four months. For us around here, it's unquestionably the Trial of the Century, and for us, it's also a slam-dunk case, Scotty. We have a detailed memoir from Hollis Butler and your name is up in lights there, and he also video recorded you in some of the activities. So I think you should warm up to the fact that you're going to be found guilty, and there is no question in my mind that sooner or later, possibly as soon as six or eight years, but certainly no longer than twelve or so years, they're going to strap you to a table, stick needles in you, and inject a variety of poisons in you. They're going to kill your ass like a mangy dog, Scotty. And you have one, and only one, way out of this mess, my boy. If you plead guilty and agree to turn state's evidence against your cohorts, we'll give you life in prison. I'll even up the ante and you can be eligible for parole in thirty years. I need to step into the ladies room for a moment, and you and Mr. Dawes can discuss your predicament. I'll be back in a few moments."

Flame left the room and indeed had to go to the bathroom. She fetched a Styrofoam cup and filled it with water from the tap, drank it, and refilled, and decided Dawes and Davis would have an answer by now, and returned to the room.

"So what's it going to be?" Flame asked.

"My client will cooperate and testify in exchange for immunity," Dawes said, as instructed by his moron of a client.

"No deal," Flame said. "See you on death row, Scotty."

"Hold on!" Davis exclaimed.

"Mr. Davis, I am here as a courtesy to Mr. Dawes," Flame said. "And shame on you for taking advantage of my better nature, Clinton. The long and short of this is that you will strengthen this case a bit, but our case against you and your companions is open and shut. So my offer stands for about one minute more." Flame consulted her watch.

"Life with a possibility of parole in ten years," Dawes said.

"Twenty-five," Flame returned. "That's the best deal you're going to get. To be honest, Scotty, it makes me want to puke, making this deal. I'd like to put the needle into you myself. My God, your friends kidnapped, raped and whipped a police sergeant's wife."

"I had nothing to do with that," Davis said.

"Do you know what the law of the west was about horse thieves?" Flame asked, and Davis looked at her in confusion. "The long and short of it was that if one rider in a gang was on a stolen horse, the whole gang hanged for it. So I blame you as much as I blame Hollis Butler for this. But he left you twisting in the wind when he got shot. So what's it going to be, kid? I have a busy day and I'm not going to waste time on you anymore."

Dawes nodded almost imperceptibly to Davis, who nodded. "I'll take the deal," Davis said.

"Very well, let me call some people and start interviewing you," Flame said.

Three hours later, a complete confession was signed crudely, in more of a scrawl than letters, and witnessed by two witnesses, in addition to Flame and Dawes, and people would start preparing him for testimony. She and Dawes left together and rode the elevator down.

"Jesus," Dawes said. "You know, I defend criminals for a living, but I never considered this level of ... well, of evil, that Scott described. I honestly figured he'd stay clammed up. I'm surprised he finally saw the light."

"Lucky for him, I suppose," Flame said. She elected not to tell Dawes she'd learned of Davis' fear of needles and used that against him. It was cruel and she felt a bit guilty about it, but at the same time, his testimony would cement their case, and it was worth jailing this little dickhead rather than executing him. Besides, he would be sixty years old before he made parole, if he could make parole, and with luck he'd be too broken down by then to be a threat to anyone.

"What about the rest of my clients in this?" Dawes asked.

"Clinton, I only needed one weak link," Flame said. "The rest of them … we're seeking the death penalty, and we'll get it. Your only chance with them is to persuade them to confess fully and accept life without parole in exchange."

"Come on, Maggie, you have to give them a carrot at the end of the stick," Dawes said.

"Clinton, ordinarily I'd agree, but your people killed six cops and forty others," Flame told him. "To be frank, I'm glad the cops didn't kill Martin and Davis when they took them down, and God help the other three who are in the wind. Chief Watts wants them alive, but other agencies might not feel so charitable in subduing them."

FORTY-FIVE

It was decided to leave John and Sarah Avery in place, to see if there was more to learn. They were given a full debriefing but were to play dumb and act surprised if word was out about Hollis Butler and his cohorts. The news shook Sarah, who'd genuinely liked Butler, and she was grateful she didn't get in his crosshairs. She felt terribly for Sergeant Lowe's poor wife, and even felt badly for Captain Luden. John found himself admiring Luden for having to make such a tough decision, and wondered if he'd have the intestinal fortitude to kill a friend in such a circumstance.

The two woke Sunday morning, ate breakfast, and dressed in Sunday finery, and then drove to the Church of God's Law. Shepherd Quinn shook hands with them, but looked grave. Luden shook hands with John and nodded to Sarah. A very pretty, even beautiful, young lady was standing beside them, who he introduced as his fiancée Marjorie. Marjorie blushed and smiled at them. "I'm pleased to meet you," she said.

"And you," said Sarah, smiling. "And congratulations, you two."

"Thank you," Luden said, smiling.

"So how goes the business of protecting our fair city?" John asked.

"I retired this week, so that's someone else's problem," Luden chuckled.

"Then congratulations, Paul," John said. "And congratulations on your impending wedding. When is it?"

"Today, at the end of services," Luden said. "It's a good thing I retired because we're going to be busy. She'll graduate soon and I'll be overseeing construction on a new house."

"Oh, excellent," John said.

"It's my family farm," Luden told him. "I grew up there. But the house and ... well, there's a house, a barn and a guesthouse on the property. I'll have movers remove the sentimentals and valuables, but then the fire department will torch them for practice. After that, I'll doze it all flat and build fresh. I don't mean to keep cattle so there'll be no barn. But we'll build a nice house with room for children if I'm able to father more children. I ... well, my sons and I are estranged. But maybe this is a new lease on life for me, for what time I have remaining."

"Good luck, Paul," John said, surprised to find he meant it.

"Brothers and sisters, I'm going to be frank with you today about some terrible things," Quinn began his sermon. "You may have noticed that two more elders are absent today, Dale Rawson and Hollis Butler. And several of our congregation are also absent this day. This has been a very distressing season for me personally, and now for our church, but I pray that season is passing. I don't know if they had demons, but Alice Rawson attacked another sister of this congregation and the sister fought back and won, as was her right to do. Anyway, Alice was taken to the hospital where they learned she had a cancer in her brain, and the fight aggravated it. She died in the emergency room. In the midst of it, Brother Dale attacked me in the waiting room, which is why I'm wearing this fashionable splint on my schnoz."

The congregation chuckled at Quinn's little joke, and Quinn did too, and then continued. "Dale … he must have been torn apart inside when Alice passed. Not long after this happened, he committed suicide."

Many in the crowd gasped at this, and a buzz of quiet prayer erupted among the congregation. Quinn frowned and then drank a glass of cold water from the pulpit, and let the congregation have a moment to pray. "This is not the most distressing news I have to offer," Quinn said from the pulpit. "Some of you know that a house willed to the church was the scene of a crime. Several people were murdered, dismembered, and their body parts were scattered about the house. The people who did this called it in anonymously to the police, and then waited until police officers, five of them, were in the house before setting off incendiary devices that murdered those good police officers as well. A policeman came to see me and ask questions, and I cooperated, certain that it had nothing whatsoever to do with our church. I was wrong. God forgive me, I've never been more wrong in my entire life.

"A few days ago the case unraveled," Quinn went on. "I won't go into all of the details because it's altogether possible some of you may be subpoenaed to offer testimony, but the upshot of it was that Brother Hollis Butler was the murderer. He was kidnapping people with criminal records, flogging them to death as Jesus was flogged, and then dismembering the remains and scattering them in vacant properties. This was terrible, but it went even further. A few days ago he had his men kidnap the wife of the policeman leading the investigation. He raped her and was whipping her when the police arrived. Two of Hollis' assistants were killed in a gunfire exchange, and then Brother Hollis tried to shoot an officer and was also killed.

"Now, my brothers and sisters, these are not unsubstantiated allegations," Quinn spoke, his voice ringing true in spite of the splint on his nose and the agony in his soul. "I was met by another police officer and a representative of the district attorney, presenting me irrefutable evidence of their guilt, and asking the whereabouts of several others of our flock who are wolves in sheep's clothing. I don't see them here today, but an e-mail blast has gone out to all of you detailing who these three are. I cannot bear to even say their names in this holy place. But if you know the whereabouts of any of these people, you will report this to the police so they can face charges for their crimes. Any of you found protecting them will be arrested and charged for aiding and abetting, I'm reassured. And I will reassure you that, man or woman, anyone I learn has protected them will be whipped harshly every week for several weeks, in this very chapel."

A loud buzz rang among the crowd, and Quinn let them chatter for two or three minutes before he spoke again. "Because the church itself … brothers and sisters, this is such a gross violation of our dogma that I can't even put my dismay into words … but because of this, the DA has no intention on smearing our church. I am afraid the church will be mentioned in the trials since these people were mostly members of the church. But at the risk of repeating myself, the church will demand full cooperation from you. These men who committed these crimes are a cancer on the body of our church, and cancer must be removed for the body to live. We cannot countenance such crimes, no matter the madness people might employ to justify them. And now let's move on to other, far happier, business. Paul Luden and Marjorie Stoddard, come to the dais."

Both were seated on opposite sides of the chapel, and approached the dais. "Brothers and sisters, Paul and Marjorie have agreed to be united in holy wedlock," Quinn said. "They have been counseled and see helpmates in one another. Has anyone a valid reason why these two should not be joined in holy wedlock?" Nobody rose in objection.

"Paul, have you a best man?" Quinn asked.

"I do not, Shepherd," Paul said.

"Then I shall choose a best man, who shall be the godfather of your children," Quinn said. "Marjorie, have you a maid or matron of honor?"

"Shepherd, I do," Marjorie said. "Emma Southern, Sir."

"Emma, do you agree to being Marjorie's maid of honor, and to being the godmother of children she may produce from this union?" Quinn asked.

"I do, Shepherd," a young woman said, rising to her feet.

"Then approach the dais, please," Quinn said, and Emma approached, standing behind Marjorie.

"John Avery, will you agree to be Paul's best man, and to being the godfather of children of this union?" Quinn asked.

"Shepherd, I ... I cannot," John said.

Quinn looked surprised that the young man was declining this honor, but laid it aside. "David Lyons, will you?" he asked.

"I will, Shepherd," Lyons said, standing and approaching the dais.

The ceremony was a brief one, rather standard, and Paul and Marjorie were pronounced man and wife. They marched out of the church and to a new pickup truck Paul had purchased the day before, jet black in color and with a crew cab, and drove away.

"Being a best man and godfather is an enormous honor," Quinn said to John in fellowship hall following the services. "I'm surprised you declined, John."

"I'm afraid I wouldn't be able to fulfill those obligations," John said, thinking at a rapid-fire pace to protect his cover. "My bosses told me I may be transferring out of here soon to a more remote place in Nevada, far from prying eyes. If so, I might never return here again, and I felt Paul and Marjorie deserved better, Shepherd." The truth was, John found that he liked these people and was starting to hate himself for deceiving them. Sarah had confessed the same to him the night before.

"I hope we get to remain here," Sarah said. "But whither thou goest …"

"I understand," Quinn said. "We have a retreat in Arizona where you two could spend weekends, if you wish, though. If you get moved to Nevada I'll be certain to let you know."

"Arizona?" John asked, surprised.

"It belonged to a parishioner who willed it to us fifteen or so years ago," Quinn said. "It makes a good retreat, but we're also offering retirement housing to members who wish to relocate to the drier environs."

"That sounds nice," Sarah said. "I love that the church will see to the care of older members late in life."

"We do our best," Quinn said, leaving out the fact that people wishing to retire to the retreat had to trade their houses to the church for a lease on a bungalow in Arizona. "Feel free to stay and mix and mingle. I'm afraid I have an appointment soon."

FORTY-SIX

"Shepherd Quinn?" Flame asked in the lobby of the county jail.

"You must be Miss Flame," Quinn said, smiling and offering his hand. The two had made a bargain. Quinn felt uneasy about it, but at the same time, if it worked it would spare the church.

"I am indeed, Sir," Flame said. "Are you ready?"

"I am," Quinn said.

He went with her through a metal detector and had to shed most anything metal on his person, and then the two rode an elevator to Block B, where Waterford and Lipton were being held. Waterford had been taken to an interview room and Lipton to another. It was decided that it was better to meet alone with them.

Quinn entered Waterford's room and saw the look of surprise on the young man's face. "Good afternoon, Luke," he said, taking a chair across the table from the man.

"I'm surprised to see you here, Shepherd," Waterford said, looking like a scared schoolboy.

"I'm very disappointed to see you here, Luke," Quinn returned. "And I understand you're being difficult about not taking what's coming to you, and it's going to see you dead on an executioner's needle. I know you've pled not guilty at arraignment, but we both know you are guilty, Luke. The evidence is ... well, it's damning. And we need to talk about that, son. You have an opportunity, though, Luke. It's an opportunity to serve God, to serve the church, and perhaps to earn a bit of redemption."

"What is it?" Waterford asked. "Shepherd, I don't want them to kill me. I remember being there when the vet killed my dog that way, how gruesome it was to see that. How do ... what ... what is it I am to do, Shepherd?"

"Plead guilty, confess, and spread God's word in the prison," Quinn said simply. "Take what you have coming, and like Saint Paul, what you can do for God, even when confined by man. That would be a greater service to the Lord than you fighting this tooth and nail and pretending you didn't do it, lying about it ... and ... Luke, it would destroy the church to have us held up to ridicule throughout your trial. They have all the proof they need to send you to death row, Luke. I don't want to see that happen to you. Be a man, a penitent man, and take what you have coming."

"Shepherd, please, not this," Waterford begged.

"Luke, this is my order," Quinn said, rising. 'Take or leave it. But the Lord and the church expected far better of you." Quinn shook his head and walked out, and then down the hall where Matthew Lipton was waiting.

Quinn laid down the law to Lipton as he had to Waterford, and then emerged, telling Flame he was confident the two would change their pleas to guilty within the next day or two. He met with Leon Martin next, and said the same to him. Surprising him, Martin immediately agreed to confess, only asking the opportunity for parole, to which Flame agreed readily enough. She called for a court reporter, and placed a call to Dawes, and an hour later was questioning Leonard Martin through his complete confession. But by then, Quinn had long since gone home.

For Quinn, he saw it as a win-win-win scenario. The church won by not being dragged through the press and painted as psychotics for practicing a sterner version of the faith. Those who confessed would find their lives spared, given the opportunity to devote their lives to God's service. And the prosecution won, not needing to spend precious money on an array of long and convoluted murder cases. He drove to the home where Bethany was, and spent several hours there, praying fervently by her side.

Finally, exhausted, he drove home, but sleep was a long time coming.

FORTY-SEVEN

Lowe's personal cell phone rang at 6:00 AM and he answered. "Lowe, this is Chief Watts," he heard. "Where are you?"

"Honestly, still in bed, Sir," Lowe said, wondering if the axe was about to fall. "I figured I'd start getting a resume together today."

"Bull fucking shit," Watts countered. "Get out of bed, shower, climb into a suit and I'll send an unmarked for you. We'll have breakfast at my place."

"Yes, Sir," Lowe said and then his mind caught gear. "Damn. Chief, I'm in an apartment now. Lisa and I are separated."

"Jesus, I hadn't heard, Mike," Watts said. He got the address from Lowe and told him an unmarked would be there in thirty minutes.

Lowe hurriedly showered and shaved, and ducked into his best suit, and then walked to the parking lot, surprised to find Luden with a beautiful young woman. "Hi, Mike," Luden said. "Meet Marjorie."

"Miss," Lowe said, and smiled.

"Actually, Mrs.," Luden said. "The Shepherd decided I need a wife and she needs a husband." Lowe remembered hearing about that in one of the reports right before he got the boot.

"Congratulations," Lowe said, smiling. "I wish I'd known."

"Husband told me about you saving your wife from those people," Marjorie said. "I hope she's well, Mr. Lowe."

"It just takes time," Lowe said.

"I need to go, Husband," Marjorie said. "I should be home by 4:00." She got into her car and left.

"It's something the church does that ... I didn't think it would ever bite me, but now it has," Luden said. "Honestly, she's a very nice young woman and I like her, but ... it's hard to find much in common."

"She's in college?" Lowe asked.

"Finishing up high school, but she's eighteen," Luden said. "Her parents ... well, they don't seem to understand a kid at eighteen." He chuckled sardonically. "But then, neither do I."

"You sound like you'd rather not be married to her," Lowe ventured.

"I ... honestly, Mike, I don't know," Luden said. "I was widowed a long time back and didn't want to marry again, but our Shepherd is right. Men and women shouldn't be alone. But I think it stinks that she'll be a young widow. I mean, I'm 45 years older than she is. As far as I know I'm healthy, but I don't think I'm going to live to see a hundred."

"I understand," Lowe said. "I've thought about that a few times since I'm fifteen years older than Lisa. But I guess Lisa took care of that herself, huh?"

"She's still shut you out?" Luden asked.

"I haven't heard a peep from her," Lowe said. Right then the unmarked pulled up and Lowe got into the car, surprised to see it was Lieutenant Holmes driving.

"I didn't know you lived in the same apartment as Luden," Holmes said as they got out onto the streets.

"It was news to me too," Lowe allowed. "Lisa threw me out on my ear, and —"

"She what?" Holmes interrupted, torn between shock and outrage.

"Told me it was all my fault and she never wants to talk to me again and please move out before she gets home," Lowe confirmed.

"Jesus, Mike, you deserve better," Holmes said, frowning. "Pass her by, my friend."

"I always figured she deserved better than me," Lowe said. "One way or another, cops don't generally have stable marriages anyway. I guess you're going to fire my ass today and maybe she'll take me back if I'm driving a taxi for a living or managing a Burger King."

"Jesus," Holmes remarked. "Is she still in the hospital?"

"I don't even know that," Lowe said. "I'm respecting her wishes."

"I know you love her, but she's doing you dirt, Mike," Holmes said.

"No matter," Lowe told her. "I'm guessing the chief is about to fire me and —"

"He's not firing you, Mike," Holmes said. "He damn near fired me over suspending you when he heard what happened. He was out of town at a conference until yesterday, but when I told him everything … well, he ate my ass for a good hour. I guess he gnawed on Reese too about Luden. I don't like Luden and won't miss him, but he was a hero when it counted."

"He was," Lowe agreed. "It's kind of hard to dislike a man who saved my wife's life. And he has a new wife now."

"Wow, I didn't know he was dating anyone," Holmes said.

"According to him, the church arranged it," Lowe told her. "Jesus, the girl is eighteen and still not out of high school. Luden's not too happy about it himself, says he feels foolish with a child bride."

"He damned well ought," Holmes remarked. "Christ, this isn't 1910 anymore."

"I get the sense he's as unhappy about it as you are," Lowe repeated. "But she seems happy. Seemed like a nice kid."

"Lowe, your suspension has been lifted, on review of your situation," Watts greeted him a few minutes later. "Jesus, I just got off the phone with Maggie Flame and she's apparently secured a flurry of confessions after this preacher … Quinn, I think she said his name is …"

"Isaiah Quinn, Sir," Lowe said.

"Yeah, him," Watts agreed. "Anyway, Quinn apparently told them all to take it like a man and carry God's Word into the prison system, and several are doing just that. She thinks when the others get wind of it, they'll roll over too. None of them particularly want to go to death row."

"I'll be damned," Lowe said. "That's good news."

"Good for us, yeah," Watts agreed. "But the DA is quietly infuriated about it. He'd hoped to get this into the court and give the news a nice long look at his tough-on-crime face leading up to the elections. But he knows he can hardly intercede without getting his ass barbecued in the local news. One way or another, I think all of these clowns are going to quietly go away, so as far as I'm concerned, the Church of God's Law is on our side."

"Yes, Sir," Lowe said, making a mental note to ask Reese about the undercover people there.

"Lowe, let's talk about you, moving forward from this," Watts said. "Do you want coffee, by the way?

"Sir, I think I'd slap my mother for a big cup of joe," Lowe said, and Watts laughed.

"Then let's have some coffee and sit down and talk," Watts said. The men poured cups from the chief's Mr. Coffee and Holmes poured a cup for herself, and they all sat in the chief's living room.

"First, I'm sorry about Lisa reacting as she has," Watts said. "Because she's a material witness, we're keeping a close eye on her. She is home now but not cleared to return to work for probably another week or so.   She's seeing a shrink and working her way through this, I'd guess."

"Thank you, Sir," Lowe said.

"Smart move, using her phone to track her down, by the way," Watts said. "You should have told us —"

"Sir, maybe you're right, but I worried the police would show up in force and create a standoff," Lowe interrupted. "No matter what, I didn't want Lisa to be killed by those psychos."

"And Luden, one of our prime suspects early in, was the hero of the day," Watts concluded.

"And freshly remarried, Lowe told me a moment ago," Holmes said.

"I'll be damned," Watts remarked. "I had no idea."

"As I understand it, the church forced them to marry," Holmes said. "The girl is eighteen – Lowe met her this morning – and Luden is older than Methuselah."

"Just as I was starting to like that church, too," Watts muttered.

"From what I saw, the girl is happy as hell," Lowe said. "But I talked with Paul —"

"Paul?" Watts echoed.

"Sir, I've discovered much merit in the man who saved Lisa's life," Lowe asserted. "By happenstance, we live a few apartments away from one another, so we talk, and I've found I like the man."

"Maybe being retired will suit him," Watts said. "Because of his heroics – I wish Reese hadn't filed charges on him, but she did what she thought was right – the DA is going to offer him a slap on the wrist. A very light slap. In short, he'll be fined a hundred dollars and placed on deferred adjudication for one year, and then he's home free. They'll offer him that deal this week."

"Yes, Sir," Lowe said.

"Okay, on to you, Lowe," Watts said. "You're off homicide now. I've decided the Department needs a special investigation task force, and that you're going to lead it. You'll qualify in a couple more years to take the lieutenant's exam and when that happens, I'll reclassify the task force and leave it under you."

"Who is going to Homicide, then?" Lowe asked.

"Lieutenant Jeremiah Surrey will be tapped for commander of Homicide later today," Watts said. "I'm returning Jay Walker to Homicide and there's a hotshot sergeant in Robbery named Wanda Escobar who will replace you."

"I don't know either of them," Lowe said after searching his memory and coming up empty.

"I didn't think you would, Mike," Watts said. "You're on leave, and I know you need a rest. Take your thirty days and I'll see you in a month."

"Sir, I'd rather come back to work," Lowe said.

"Sergeant, take at least a week, preferably the whole month," Watts said. "Recharge your batteries. Go fishing. Fly to Reno and get laid in a legal whorehouse. Fly to Denver and get stoned for a week on legal weed, so long as you can pass a test when you get back. Mike, you've been killing yourself with work. It's probably why you wound up a couple days in the hospital with that flu or whatever it was. You're no good to me dead. Take a rest."

"Yes, Sir," Lowe said, wondering what the hell he'd do with himself. With Lisa, a leave would be great. All by himself, it promised to be an ordeal.

"Let's have breakfast – the cook is sick with the same crud you seemed to have – so it's on me at Cora's Diner," Watts announced.

Two hours later, Holmes dropped Lowe off at his apartment, and Luden came out to meet him. "How goes, Mike?" Luden greeted him.

"Oh, it's so-so," Lowe said. "The chief reversed my suspension – he told me to congratulate you on your marriage, by the way – and ordered me to take leave. Apparently my task force will be reduced but not disbanded, and I am to be its commander for special investigations that crop up along the way."

"That sounds promising," Luden said. "You're a smart cop and a gutsy one, Mike. I think you should definitely go for the lieutenant's exam next time they come up."

"I don't qualify," Lowe said. "I've only been a sergeant about five months now, so that's still nearly three years off."

"Late bloomer, were you?" Luden asked.

"I liked being a detective, and the overtime money was good," Lowe admitted. "But the pension for a retired lieutenant or captain is far better than that of a retired police officer, so I decided the time was right to try to advance. I figured if they threw me back into a uniform I'd do the extra jobs route."

"Did these people offer you a free apartment in exchange for doing security here?" Luden asked.

"Yeah," Lowe confirmed. "But I've been down that road and it's not worth it."

"No, it's not," Luden agreed. "So what are you going to do with this forced vacation?"

"I have no earthly idea," Lowe said.

"The police should be releasing the farm today," Luden remarked. "Marjorie and I talked about it. I'm going to move the sentimental and valuable stuff out and then let the FD burn it to the ground for drill practice, bulldoze it all, and rebuild."

"Why?" Lowe asked. "The house and all looked to be in good shape."

"Too many memories, and ... I don't go into mumbo-jumbo about ghosts and all, but it's psychologically haunting to me, Mike," Luden explained. "Besides, I don't think I'll be raising livestock there, so a barn is pointless. Marjorie wants to garden and likes to paint, so I figured I would put in a greenhouse there and maybe a studio for her. Shepherd Quinn isn't going to like it, but I'm going to enroll her in the local university in the fall. One way or another, whenever my time comes, I want her prepared to face the world,

Mike. She's not that enamored of the church, but it's the only social structure afforded her outside of school. So I suspect I won't be cold in my grave when she leaves the church."

"Paul, you're only 60-something," Lowe said. "You behave as though you're going to die in your sleep this week."

"I don't have illusions," Luden said. "Look, part of why I brought this up ... do you think seeing the barn burn would be beneficial to Lisa?"

"I honestly don't know," Lowe said. "And she ... she asked me not to contact her, so I'm respecting that wish. I wonder if I don't need to get out of town before I make an ass of myself, serenading her in our yard like some loser in a romantic comedy film."

"It seems to me she broke your heart pretty badly," Luden remarked.

"I love her, Paul," Lowe said. "I ... well, she wants to be rid of me and I can even see how she feels, but that doesn't mean I don't love her just the same."

"You don't seem the religious type, but consider praying on it," Luden suggested. "You want to go get brunch somewhere?"

"I had a huge breakfast, but I could stand a glass of OJ, and I'll even pay," Lowe smiled.

"Let's go," Luden said.

FORTY-EIGHT

"Who are you?" Lisa asked as she answered the door, this time with one of Mike's pistols in her hand.

"I am Miranda Holmes," Holmes said, looking Lisa in the eye. "Your husband worked for me, Mrs. Lowe."

"Did he send you here?" Lisa asked bitterly.

"No, he did not," Holmes said. "But I know what happened."

"No, you don't," Lisa countered.

Just then a car pulled up and another sleek and attractive woman emerged and came to the porch. "Hello, Mollie," Lisa said to her.

"Can I come in?" Mollie asked.

"Sure, both of you come on in," Lisa said.

"I'm Miranda Holmes," Holmes introduced herself to Mollie. "I work with Mrs. Lowe's husband Mike."

"I'm Mollie French, Lisa's boss," Mollie said, and the women shook hands.

"Coffee?" Lisa asked them.

"I'd rather a glass of ice water," Mollie said.

"Coffee sounds wonderful," Holmes answered.

"Sure," Lisa said, and disappeared into the kitchen.

"Okay, I'm here to do an intervention," Mollie said. "How about you, Miranda?"

"I think that's a good word," Holmes said.

"Lisa, this is a story I've never told anyone before," Mollie said. "I don't know if you're getting counseling to help you through this —"

"I am," Lisa interjected.

"Good, because you need it," Mollie returned. "Lord knows I needed it." She sighed. "When I was in college I was gang-raped. I went to a frat party, eighteen and full of myself. I don't know if they drugged me or what, but I was suddenly in an attic and six men had me tied down, and raped me. They drugged me again and I woke up naked in a park. The men ... they all got away with it. They were wearing masks and I was too drug-addled to remember any scars or tattoos. The police took me to the attic of the frat house where the party was, but it wasn't where I was raped. My old man said that's what I got for going off to college. It was a long struggle for me, Lisa, and it ... it turned me asexual. I don't even masturbate."

"I'm sorry that happened," Lisa said.

"Look, you deserve better," Mollie said. "So why did you shut Mike out of this? I've met him a few times and he seems like a good man, and you know how hard that is for me to say."

"Mike was the lead on that case where body parts were scattered over all those places," Lisa said.

"I didn't know that," Mollie remarked.

"He's a very good cop and a very good investigator," Holmes offered. "I don't understand your reasoning in blaming the man either, Mrs. Lowe."

"If he wasn't on that case, they wouldn't have done this," Lisa said.

"You can't be serious," Mollie said. "Goddamn, Lisa, people are raped and killed daily. Mike didn't do this to you, and I don't think for a second he could have foreseen or prevented it."

"He was riding to your rescue," Holmes threw in.

"But if he'd refused this case it wouldn't have happened at all," Lisa returned. "My God, that son of a bitch raped me in my butt and then horsewhipped me like … like some slave in a bad movie!"

"Hollis Butler did exactly that," Holmes reasoned. "Michael Lowe did not."

"Why did you fire the officer that shot Butler?" Lisa asked, trying to change the subject.

"That was another matter altogether, I'm afraid," Holmes deflected. "Look, if you called Mike right now he'd be here in seconds, Lisa."

"You think I don't know that, Lieutenant?" Lisa asked. "Look, there's no lack of love here. I don't hate Mike. I love him and this breaks my heart. But how … how can I look at him dressing for work, putting on his badge and pistol, and not be reminded of the rape? How?"

"I don't know if you can," Mollie said. "But you're robbing yourself of your best support system, Lisa."

"Look, I suspended Mike right after the matter," Holmes said. "It was a knee-jerk reaction, and on reflection, a stupid action on my part. The chief overrode the suspension but told Mike he is on leave for at least a week but hopefully an entire month. Frankly, he's physically and mentally exhausted."

"He's a good man," Mollie contributed. "Don't let him go, because this world is full of women who'd love to have him, Lisa, and you're always going to regret pushing him out."

"That man … Mr. Luden … he came to see me in the hospital," Lisa recalled. "It was right before I was able to call you, Mollie. He more or less told me what both of you have. I … I just …" she trailed off.

"Well, I did what I could do," Holmes said, annoyed with Lisa. "I'll put this cup in the sink and be off. Thank you for your time. Mrs. Lowe, when I was sixteen I was raped too, by my brother's best friend. My brother beat him within an inch of his life, and … the brain damage saw him locked away in an institution until he choked to death on his own puke and died ten years later. I was there too."

"Lieutenant ..." Lisa began, but it was too late. Holmes was gone. A moment later Lisa and Mollie heard the sound of her engine starting, and then fading as she drove away.

"She's right," Mollie said. "Look, I'm sorry I came. I ... well, I only wanted to help, but it doesn't matter. Take all the time you need, Lisa. I'll see you when you get back to the office."

"Why are you acting like I'm a horrible person?" Lisa asked.

"You're not, and I'm not behaving as though you are," Mollie said. "But tell me, if you see a friend of yours hurting herself by behaving irrationally, wouldn't you want to intercede? Anyway, I'm out of here, Lisa. Do whatever you fucking well please."

Mollie left and Lisa sat, shell-shocked, and suddenly burst into loud wails, and then ransacked the living room in a fit of fury until she doubled over with pain, suddenly praying the surgical repair wasn't undone. But she went to the bathroom and looked at her panties and saw there was no blood leaking.

And then she got into her car and drove. She didn't have a conscious destination in mind. She just drove, until she was hauled down by a patrol officer for going 95 in a 60. As the cop asked for her driver's license and proof of insurance, she suddenly burst into fresh wailing and tears.

"Ma'am, is something wrong?" the officer asked. Her name was Cathy Haley, a four-year veteran of the Department. She'd taken the sergeants' exam at the same time as Mike Lowe, but placed far lower, and figured if she got promoted it wouldn't be for another six or so months yet.

Lisa was unable to talk, just sobbing hysterically. Haley, uncertain how to handle this, put in a call for EMS on a psychiatric emergency. EMS arrived and found Lisa still an emotional mess, and transported her to the hospital while Haley arranged a tow truck, deciding not to ticket the poor woman as well.

Lisa Lowe was admitted on a 24-hour psychiatric hold, and Dr. Grogarty was called in. Michael Lowe was listed as next-of-kin in her records and the charge nurse called him as well.

"Lowe," Lowe answered.

"Sir, this is Gretchen Maybank, I'm a nurse at the hospital," the nurse said.

"What can I do for you, Ms. Maybank?" Mike asked.

"Sir, you're listed as next-of-kin for a Lisa Lowe," Maybank said. "She's been admitted to the hospital on the psychiatric unit."

"Oh shit," Lowe groaned. "What happened?"

"Sir, from what I was told, the police pulled her over and she was crying badly, so EMS was called and they brought her here," Maybank said.

"Damn," Lowe muttered, dabbing suddenly at his own tears. "Does she want to see me, or no?"

"Sir, I ... I don't know," Maybank said.

"Okay, backstory for you," Lowe said. "She was recently kidnapped and anally raped. She was rescued and the rapist and two of his cohorts were shot dead by the police. She told me immediately after that she wants a divorce and never wants to see me again. I love her ... but I don't want to make a bad situation worse. Please let her know you spoke with me and I can be there in minutes if she wants to see me."

"How awful for her," Maybank said, guessing that Lowe took part in the attack on her or was otherwise somehow to blame. Her tone turned cold and businesslike. "I will pass that along to her, Mr. Lowe." She hung up the phone and went about her shift.

Lowe felt kicked in the guts by the call, and sensed by Maybanks' tone that he was going to be persona non grata at the hospital. He drove to the liquor store and spent a ton of money on a bottle of tequila, and then drove to his apartment to partake of it.

"Hi, Mr. Lowe," Marjorie greeted him at the top of the stairs, smiling broadly. "Husband sent me to fetch you. He bought steaks at the market and wants you to have supper with us."

"Tell him I said thanks, but ... I shouldn't," Lowe said. "I'm going to drink my supper."

"If you don't mind me saying, you look like you have a lot on your mind, Mr. Lowe," Marjorie said. "Husband is fond of you and would like to see you."

"I do have a lot on my mind," Mike agreed. "Tell Paul that Lisa is back in the hospital, please." Mike turned toward his apartment and got inside, instantly filling a huge water glass with tequila. He tossed in a few ice cubes and drank half of it when there was a knock at the door. Lowe, guessing it was either Paul or Marjorie Luden, ignored the knocking, staring into space and drinking his liquor, when Holmes spoke up. "Open the door, Mike," she called loudly.

"Goddammit," Lowe muttered, and let her in. "Jesus Christ, I'm seeing as much of you on leave as I was on duty. What do you want?"

"How much have you had to drink, Mike?" Holmes asked.

"Not nearly enough," Lowe said, turning surly. "What do you want, Miranda?"

"We need to talk," Holmes said. "I went to see Lisa earlier."

"Jesus H. Christ," Lowe said, fury suddenly penetrating his self-pity. "It was your fault."

"What do you mean?" Holmes asked, baffled.

"She just got tossed into a rubber room," Lowe said.

"Oh, holy shit," Holmes breathed.

"Get the fuck out of here, Miranda," Lowe said. "With friends like you I don't need enemies."

"Mike ..." she began, but Lowe waved dismissively and filled his glass afresh, taking another deep drink of the amber *reposado* tequila. Holmes left, and was surprised to run into Paul and Marjorie Luden approaching.

"Good evening, Captain," Holmes said, forcing a smile.

"Hello, Mrs. Holmes," Luden smiled back. "This is my wife Marjorie."

"A pleasure, Ma'am," Marjorie said, shaking hands with Holmes.

"If you're going to see Mike, all I can tell you is good luck," Holmes said. "He's deep in the tequila in there. At least it's good tequila, but still, he's in a fury."

"What's going on?" Luden asked, and his genuine concern penetrated Holmes' dislike of him.

"His wife, in short," Holmes said. "I don't know the story because he threw me out, but she's apparently in a psych ward. I tried to go talk to her earlier today, and so did her boss. I got nowhere and left. But she's in the hospital now."

"How awful for that poor lady," Marjorie said. "Husband, should we go see Mr. Lowe? Or Mrs. Lowe?"

"I went and saw her when she was recovering from the surgery," Luden said. "I don't think Mike knows. I guess I feel a certain … responsibility … toward her, and a lot of guilt too for not figuring out what Hollis was doing before he … did what he did. I tried to get her to see sense, but I got nowhere too."

"That was very kind of you, Captain," Holmes said, surprised at his kindness. Luden had been known far and wide through the department for his misogyny and his bigotry toward non-Christians.

"They're both nice people and I feel terribly about what happened," Luden said. He frowned and visibly thought for a moment. "I guess there's no sense trying to talk to Mike while he's in his cups. I bought steaks to grill over at the park here. Would you care to join us?"

"That sounds very good," Holmes said, surprising herself. The apartment complex turned out to have a park with playground equipment, picnic benches, and grills set into the ground. Luden lit a bag of charcoal and once it turned grey, he threw steaks on the grill, and foil-wrapped packages of chopped vegetables.

"It seems like retirement and marriage suit you, Captain," Holmes remarked a few minutes later as Luden plated the food.

"Just call me Paul, please," Luden said. "But ... we'll see how the next few months go for me. Right now, we're honeymooning. I got called a couple hours ago that the police have released the farm to me. We're going to burn the buildings and rebuild, but I want to ask your opinion, if I may, Lieutenant."

"Miranda, please," Holmes said.

"Miranda," Luden repeated. "Thank you. Anyway ... I'm going to have the fire department burn the buildings, doze it all away, and we're going to build a new house, a place without the memories of Hollis, or of my first wife, God rest her soul. Tell me, do you think Lisa Lowe would be benefited by coming to see the place burn? Notably the barn?"

"Wow," Holmes said, caught off-guard as she thought for a long moment. "Honestly, I think you should invite her. That's very thoughtful of you, Paul."

"I only met her for a few moments, but she seemed a nice woman," Luden said. "I certainly understand what Mike sees in her. She's tough, but ... I don't know if anyone is tough enough for what she was forced to endure. One way or another, I figure it's somewhat of a closure for all of us, for a variety of different reasons. You and Mike ... anyone from the task force, for that matter ... will be welcome too, of course." He snorted and managed a chuckle. "Maybe we'll have a big barbecue. It'll be on a Saturday, of course."

"Yeah, that sounds great," Holmes said, enthused.

"Excellent," Luden said. "I'll get in touch with you after I've moved stuff out of there and made a date with the firefighters."

"Thank you," Holmes said, and turned her attention to Marjorie. "So tell me about you, Marjorie."

"There's not much to tell at my age," Marjorie grinned. "I married Husband after my parents disowned me. Shepherd Quinn thought Husband would be a good match for me. I'm graduating high school soon, and Husband is going to send me to college in the fall."

"Oh great," Holmes said. "What major?"

"I'm good with numbers, so I'm thinking finance and accounting, but maybe engineering," she said. "Horticulture interests me too but I don't think I'd want the hassles of owning a nursery."

"Small businesses are a great way of getting rich but a better way of going broke," Holmes acknowledged. "A girlfriend of mine from college opened a boutique and made good money, but she sold the business after about ten years because she realized the business owned her, not vice versa. An easy week for her was sixty hours, and often more like eighty or ninety."

"That's what would worry me," Marjorie acknowledged. "A lot of people think that's the American Dream and scorn being on someone else's clock, but at the same time, the wage earners ... their lives are their own. My daddy owned three convenience stores until about five years ago and ... his experience was like your friend's. Sometimes I could go two weeks and never see him at all."

"All my best to you, however it turns out," Holmes said. The three chit-chatted for another half-hour and then Holmes had to leave, thanking them for the meal and conversation before driving home.

"Husband, have I told you what a hero I think you are?" Marjorie asked later in their apartment.

"I'm no hero," he said. "I'm just me, another sinner trying to make his way in this world, Marjorie."

"Maybe, but you risked your life to save Mrs. Lowe, and you still are interested in helping her out of her darkness," Marjorie countered. "Something changed in you, and I think for the better, Husband. And you're my hero ... and I love you."

Luden's mind filled with the images from the barn, and suddenly he ripped her nightgown from her, flung her on the bed, and had her, consummating their marriage. Marjorie orgasmed twice and bled some on the sheets, and dragged her nails down his back before they fell asleep in one another's arms.

Lowe drank himself into a stupor and fell asleep in his chair, too drunk to wake up to pee. He woke in the morning with wet pants and a killer of a hangover, showered, and fell into bed, sleeping until early afternoon. He contemplated, and rejected, the notion of downing more of the Mexican liquor, and woke up, showered again, and built a ham sandwich. He sat for hours on end, his phone by his side, looking more through the television than at it.

FORTY-NINE

"Lowe," he answered his phone the next morning at 8:00. He still wasn't over his hangover and felt miserable.

"Mike, it's … it's Lisa," Lisa said. "Look, can you … I got hospitalized when I had a meltdown. I got pulled over by the police for driving like a bat out of hell. The car got impounded, wherever the hell it is now is … anyway, the shrink says I can go home. And I … I think we need to talk, to try to iron things out."

"Let me shower and I'll be there in thirty minutes," Lowe said, and they hung up. Lowe did his best not to be excited as he showered and dressed in jeans and a t-shirt. He put a .380 in an ankle holster and his badge in his left front pocket, and then went down to his car and drove to the hospital.

Lisa was waiting for him in the lobby, looking bedraggled and tired, and got into the passenger seat of the car. "I don't want to go home yet," she said. "Can we go to a park and talk for a bit, Mike?"

"Yeah, sure," Lowe said, and drove to Hartin Park, which was minutes from the hospital. He was grateful it was a school day and the park was mostly vacant but for an old man tossing bread to seagulls a hundred yards off.

"I have to say you have one hell of a legion of admirers," Lisa said. "You must be doing something right, Mike."

"I don't understand," Lowe said honestly.

"That man who saved me with you, Paul Luden ... he came to see me in the hospital after my surgery," Lisa said. "He tried to set me straight about things, about your career, about the good work you do, about how much you love me. I wasn't ready to listen. And then when I was discharged home, Mollie came to see me and so did your Lieutenant Holmes, both of them telling me I was being a fool for throwing you out. They both left, and seemed disgusted with me, and I had a meltdown. I got in the car and drove like I was insane and a woman cop pulled me over. Probably that was a blessing since a man probably would have schlepped me off to jail. I don't think I was consciously trying to kill myself, but ... Mike, I fucked up. Not just Monday, but with you. I know you'd have died before letting that happen to me. But that man Butler was dead and you were a handy target for my rage. I can't ask you to forgive me but I hope you do. I'm sorry."

"Don't be," Lowe said. "Lisa, there's no way to prepare for something like that."

"I know you've worked hard to keep me ... insulated, I guess ... from what you do," Lisa told him. "Maybe that was wisest or maybe you have the right to rub my face in it. I honest-to-God have no idea how you do it, Mike."

"My life prepared me for it, or for a lot of it," Mike said. "Yours didn't. And ... I'm glad you never went through such traumas, and wish you hadn't gone through this one. Lisa, I love you. I love you like I never loved anyone before, and I want you in

338

my life for the rest of my life. But if I'm harmful to you, I do love you enough to let you go. I'll be miserable – trust me, I hate my life without you – but I'll do it."

"You ain't getting rid of me that easy, Mr. Lowe," Lisa said, chuckling as some of her humor returned. "Besides, I need a strong back and a weak mind to set the living room straight. I seem to recall I trashed it in my rampage. Let's go home. I need you to fuck me good to get that son of a bitch out of my soul. And then you can clean up the living room while I'm Lady of the Manor."

Lowe took his wife home and did precisely that, making slow and tender love to her, kissing and touching her all over before entering her gently, taking her to the heights of ecstasy. Always a skilled and considerate lover anyway, this time he gave her his all, and by the time he came, she had already enjoyed four orgasms. The two fell sound asleep for nearly three hours before Lowe woke, needing to pee. He looked into the living room and groaned at the wreckage, which included a small granite statuette hurled into a 65-inch television.

Lowe began cleaning the mess, and taking a tally of the costs of replacement of what was destroyed. Somehow, Lisa had managed to not only undo a recliner in the living room, but to rip and shred the upholstery, for instance. The TV was irreparable, and ditto the recliner, so Lowe dragged them out to the curb. She had also managed to shatter a coffee table, but it wasn't a piece of furniture that held any particular meaning, and Lowe realized then that anything sentimental had survived the storm of her rage utterly undamaged.

Lisa came out a short time later and looked sheepishly at her husband. "I really made an ass of myself, huh?" she said.

"It's just stuff," Lowe said. "We can get more stuff. I was tired of that TV anyway." He grinned and Lisa blushed. It had been an expensive television when he'd bought it new three years before, and he agonized for a month over whether to spend that much money.

"I'm sorry, Mike," she said, weeping.

"Lisa, I repeat: it's just stuff," Lowe said, and a thought occurred to him. "Look, we owe ten grand on this house, so we have equity out the ass. Would you feel better if we sold it and bought a new one?"

Lisa looked at him, stunned. "Are you serious?" she asked. The truth was that Lisa didn't much like the house. But the thought of living debt-free within the coming year was a good thought.

"Like a heart attack," Lowe said.

"Yeah, I … I think I'd like that, Mike," she said.

They called a Realtor and looked at several houses, and made an offer on one about four miles from Luden's farm, a 2,800 foot 4-bedroom house on three acres – Lisa had always wanted to have a big garden – and an hour later the offer was accepted. The Lowes had always managed to live just fine on Mike's salary alone, banking Lisa's salary, and had only ever had the house as a standing debt. They decided to pay cash, fix the old house, sell that, and then re-bank the proceeds.

"We can close in two days and you two can move in," the Realtor said.

"It seems we have a lot of work to do, Mister," Lisa said on their way home.

"Yeah, we do," Lowe agreed. "I'm signed for six months on that apartment, and gotta get moved out of there, and then —"

"I mean on us," Lisa interrupted. "Look, let's go post bail on my car – I found out it was towed by Wheeler & Sons, and it's at an impound lot on Westhaven Road – and get the hell out of town. Let's go to the lake for a few days."

"I think I'd like that," Lowe said. "Let's stop at the apartment first so I can get clothes."

"It's good seeing the two of you back together, like you belong," Luden greeted them in the parking lot. He had just parked his truck, bearing boxes from the farm. "I hope it's permanent."

"It is," Lisa said, and hugged him, even kissing his cheek. Luden was disconcerted at first, but smiled at her. "And thank you … you talked sense to me even if I wasn't ready to hear it then."

"My pleasure," Luden said. He and Mike shook hands.

"So I guess I need to move out of the apartment and sublet it," Mike said. "We actually are closing on a new house in a couple days, not too far from your farm."

"Outstanding," Luden said. "And … wow … what if you move out and I use your place to store all this stuff from the farm? That would be a win for both of us."

"It costs more than a storage unit," Lowe said.

"I'm not worried about that," Luden returned. "I have a lot that needs moved here, and the apartment complex isn't going to care as long as the rent is paid."

"It's a deal," Lowe said. "I should have my stuff out in three or four days, and then have at it."

"It's mostly boxes of smaller stuff," Luden said. "But there's a kitchen table my grandfather made forever ago. Marjorie loves it. I think I'll try to make chairs to go with it, actually. Suddenly I have a lot of free time on my hands, so I might try my hand at woodwork. I wanted to ask you both something, so I'm glad we bumped into one another. I'm going to have the fire department burn the buildings on the farm as an exercise, the house, guesthouse, and barn. I figure the FD needs the practice, but I also figure we all deserve some closure, so I was thinking – I know this sounds strange, but here goes – I was thinking of making an event of it, a big barbecue, and inviting your task force and others to it, Mike. And Lisa, if you want to light them up since … well … I would be pleased. It'll probably be in a few weeks."

"I'd like that," Lisa said, and Lowe picked up a grim undertone in her voice.

"Then we'll do it," Luden said. He seemed also to have picked up on Lisa's slightly altered tone.

"I don't adhere to the same faith as you," Lowe said suddenly. "But I believe in God and I think things happen for a reason, and I'm glad He put us together, Paul. Thank you for … well … more than I can say."

"You free for dinner tonight?" Luden asked.

"We have a lake house and I want you to come there," Lisa said, surprising Lowe. "Bring the little lady —"

"That would be me," said Marjorie, towering four inches above Lisa. She grinned. "I hope you're Mrs. Lowe."

"Mrs. Lowe was my mother-in-law," Lisa said. "She passed before I ever met Mike. I'm just Lisa."

"I'm Marjorie Luden," Marjorie said, and the women shook hands. "I'm so glad you two are back together now."

"So am I," Lisa said. "I was shaken for a while, but I think I'll be okay. Anyway, y'all come to our lake house. We can fish or swim or just be bums in the shade."

"I can't," Marjorie said. "I'm in school."

"Oh, what's your major?" Lisa asked.

"I'm in high school," Marjorie said. "Fortunately it's almost done."

"Then y'all come up Friday evening and spend the weekend with us," Lisa said. "Other than signing papers on the house, I think we'll be there through Sunday and then come back and start moving. After … what happened, I don't want to stay in that house anymore."

"I can't imagine," Marjorie said.

"We're lucky women," Lisa told her. "We're married to a pair of heroes."

"We are," Marjorie agreed. Luden and Lowe exchanged a discomfited look, and Lowe broke the moment.

"Kissing our rings is not necessary. A slight bow is sufficient for our combined exaltedness," Lowe said. Marjorie giggled at this, and Luden looked gratefully at him.

"Okay, smartass," Lisa chuckled, and kissed him. "I love you anyway."

"You need help with this stuff?" Lowe asked.

"Sure," Luden said. "But not if it's holding you two up."

"We're happy to help," Lisa said, opening the tailgate and grabbing a box.

FIFTY

"We want you two to remain on this assignment another three or four weeks," Reese said to John and Sarah. "We're hoping the fugitives finally run out of resources and turn up needing help."

"Quinn mentioned the church owns a retreat somewhere in Arizona," John said. "He didn't say where and I couldn't exactly ask right then, but ... maybe?"

"Interesting," Reese said. "I'll have people look into that. Meanwhile, how are you two doing?"

"We're doing okay," Sarah said. "The shrink helped a lot."

"I ... I'm sorry this has happened," Reese said.

"Ma'am, I am too," Sarah said. "But the fact is, she was an isolated psychotic. It wasn't the church that attacked me, and if I had to bet, I would bet her husband had no idea about this. I feel more pity than scorn for them."

"I still think that church is full of dangerous loonies," Reese said. "But okay. Keep us posted. Jane and Robert are your new best friends, you two. Got it?"

"Yes, Ma'am," John said.

"Okay, get out of here," Reese said.

The lake house was in good shape after a quick half-hour cleanup, and Mike and Lisa went out on the boat to try to reel in some fish. They each caught two largemouth bass, and motored back to their dock, where Lisa fired up charcoal and Mike quickly filleted the fish, leaving the skins on so they'd hold together for grilling. Soon, the grill was ready, and they were eating grilled bass and corn on the cob. Lisa had stopped along the road and bought a watermelon and a tub of strawberries, which made for an excellent dessert. And then they went inside and made love again.

"This feels like a new beginning, or a honeymoon," Lisa said afterwards. "Lord, I don't ever want to go back to the world, Mike."

"I think I'm going to take the entire month off," Lowe said. "Alone, it would suck, but with you ... it's ... it's like I shed thirty years. I feel young again, Lisa."

"Mollie told me to take all the time I need," Lisa said. "I think I'm going to milk this one. To be honest I'm still hurting. I'm glad Butler died before he could finish whatever he planned."

"Your back seems to be healing," Lowe said. "How's your ... your ..." he trailed off.

"My ass," Lisa said, chuckling some. "It's still very sore and I think I'll be on stool softeners for a longish while. You know, all those blue movies have men hung like horses, and Butler was about that size. It would've hurt going into my vagina, even. I guess I should be glad I didn't bleed to death."

"I remember that happening when I was maybe two years on the job, still a patrolman," Lowe said. "A gay rapist caught a kid maybe nineteen years old and had at him. Someone called in about the screaming. I was the third officer on scene. The rapist wasn't there, but the victim was. He bled to death before EMS could arrive."

"You know, that's one of the only serious things you've ever told me about your job," Lisa said. "You sometimes come home and tell me the funny things, but almost never the serious stuff. Why is that, Mike?"

"I don't want you to feel dirty for what I have to do for a living," Lowe said. "And … too many cops … most of the ones I know, in fact, don't know how to take off the badge at the end of the day. They wind up hypertensive and hating the entire world, and too many of them eat their guns. I remember talking with a nurse once in the ER who was stressed out and taking a brief break. She told me she found that hospital in the parking lot and that's where she damn well left it, and I took that lesson to heart. Off-duty means just that to me, and I do my best to leave my desk in my office."

"I understand," Lisa said. "But I still feel … I guess it makes me feel excluded or unwelcome, and let's face facts, Mike. You spend far more time with them than you do with me in any given year."

"Butler … you know he was dismembering bodies and scattering them in buildings, and setting of incendiary devices, right?" Lowe asked. Lisa nodded. "Well, he learned how to make thermite for the incendiaries, which is too easily done for my comfort."

"I've heard the word," Lisa said. "But I don't know what it is."

"You mix aluminum oxide and iron oxide, and add a magnesium kicker," Lowe explained. "Iron oxide is just rust. Aluminum oxide is used in any number of abrasives, even a lot of common sandpaper. Magnesium ... you can get that at sporting goods stores. Campers and hikers use it to start fires, for instance. Thermite burns so hot that if you spray it with water, it fractures the water molecules into hydrogen and oxygen, which only intensifies the fire."

"Jesus," Lisa breathed.

"I want to believe Jesus was out of this one, and even disapproved. But the kicker was how Butler was killing his victims, Lisa," Lowe continued. "He was flogging them to death with a flagellum, like that used on Jesus Christ. The beating Jesus endured was sometimes called the Roman Half Death because roughly half the people beaten that way bled to death. This was what Butler considered God's Justice in his warped vision of Christianity. He'd have fit in great with those Wahhabi dickheads in Saudi Arabia or those ISIS dickheads in the Syria, or skipping back 500 years and joining those Inquisition dickheads in Spain. Things like this are what I have deliberately not told you, Lisa. That ain't Mr. Rogers' neighborhood out there and I sure the hell ain't Officer Friendly."

"How was he picking his victims?" Lisa asked.

"I don't know, except the ones we identified all had criminal records. Murders, prostitutes, rapists, thieves, you get the picture," Lowe said.

"It sounds like I'm very lucky I lived," Lisa breathed.

"He discovered Lieutenant Capps was homosexual," Lowe said. "I was sent his head. The letter was couched as a 'we're on the same side' song and dance, but it was a threat. And then he kidnapped you and … you know the rest."

"How awful," Lisa said.

"This … I don't like telling you things like this, Lisa," Lowe said.

"Mike, I'm better knowing than not," Lisa told him. "I'm know I'm younger than you but I'm no starry-eyed kid either."

"I hate reliving this stuff to you, but if it makes you feel better, then so be it," Lowe said, frowning. "You wanna just go take a boat ride?"

"Yeah, why not?" Lisa asked. A moment later they were motoring up a canal toward the main part of the lake, and just puttered around aimlessly.

FIFTY-ONE

The Lowe and Luden families spent much of their time together over the ensuing month, fishing many times at the lake and enjoying the company. Both couples had come across heightened sex drives, and Lisa and Marjorie discovered in the same week that they were pregnant. The news excited and terrified both husbands.

The fire department came to Luden's farm, as well as over a hundred police and a like number from the Church of God's Law. Luden had a barbecue caterer come out and there were briskets and sides in abundance. Luden had fashioned a torch for Lisa, and let her set all three buildings ablaze, the barn last. The fire department waited until the structures were fully involved before swinging into action.

Lisa stood beside her husband with a look of dour satisfaction on her face. Marjorie stood on her other side, holding her friend's hand while they watched the flames engulf the barn. Paul Luden circulated, shaking hands with several friends from the police and church, not wanting to watch it burn, but knowing it was necessary.

"I'm glad you could be here," Luden greeted John and Sarah.

"Thank you for inviting us," John said. "I hear you and Marjorie are expecting a little one. Congratulations."

"Exciting and terrifying all at once," Luden said. "Good Lord, what's an old man like me going to do raising a baby?"

"The best you can, Sir," Sarah tossed in, smiling.

"It's daunting," Luden confessed. "In my generation, men simply had no part in raising kids, and ... frankly, I think we're poorer from it. Maybe ... it doesn't matter. Just ... take a lesson from an old man, John ... when you and Sarah have kids, don't put your career and your own pursuits ahead of that. I did, and my sons and I have been estranged since my wife died. Alcoholism and selfishness."

"I understand," John said. "That's the culture of the Army – I think you were a Marine and I doubt it was any different – and I hear that's how it is with cops too."

"It is," Luden confirmed. "At least now I'm retired, right?"

"I just wish the fugitives would surrender or be caught," John said. "Why are so many cops here?"

"They were all on the task force that were working on the case," Luden said. He pointed to Mike and Lisa Lowe. "That man over there was leading the task force, and his wife beside him. Hollis had her kidnapped. He forcibly sodomized her and was whipping her when I ... when I stepped in and stopped it. That's why she lit the fires. They're good people. We've all become good friends since."

"I thought he was investigating the church and the reason we were so heavily vetted," John said.

"I think we overreacted," Luden said. "Looking through a policeman's eyes, we looked suspect, and nobody will come right out and say it but I think I was a prime suspect all by myself, mainly on the horns of my own foolishness. I rented this house out to Hollis and pretty much only took my clothes and a very few sticks of furniture, but ... I left it all, including a book with my login information. I suppose the Department could have seen me prosecuted for it, and I think I'd have walked into court and simply pled guilty. But I think public relations rode to the rescue. It's an election year and the mayor was catching a lot of heat for this case, and it would have done them in to have it revealed that the police shared any culpability in it. It ... well ... it probably helped that the doers were mostly white, but for Pablo Chavez, who's still a fugitive – our best guess is he spirited away to Mexico, or maybe El Salvador – so the mayor's competitors can hardly beat the racism drum, especially since so many of the victims were of varying races. Washington tried to make a big deal of us only interceding when the victim – Mrs. Lowe – was white, but that old dog didn't hunt either, and the press made a fool of him for once."

"Politics," Sarah said, the distaste plain in her tone. "How sad that it would get in the way of whether or not someone breaks the law. I suppose in a way it protected you, but it's still a sad state of affairs."

"I agree, actually," Luden said. "The mayor is here too, coincidentally." He pointed toward a black limousine and the mayor himself. "I made a point of not inviting him, or any of his competitors."

"I guess it's like that old joke about the 800-pound gorilla sleeping wherever he pleases," John offered.

"Yeah, about like that," Luden agreed. "The chief answers to the mayor. This was attended better than I'd anticipated. I think I need to get more refreshments. Enjoy yourselves."

"I parked outside the fence," John said. "Why don't I go get things? I have a ¾ ton truck. I think it'll handle a few flats of water and juice."

"I'd be grateful," Luden said. He handed John two hundred dollars. "Get ... well, you know what the church drinks. If the cops here want beer they can pop for that from their own pockets, but ... here's another hundred ... get Cokes and Sprites for them."

"I'll be back soon," John promised.

"Do you want me to come with you, Husband?" Sarah asked.

"No, stick around here and have fun," John decided.

"We have a lot of tubs and coolers, but ... ice too, please," Luden said.

"Two hundred pounds?" John asked, and Luden nodded.

John dashed off to a Sam's Club ten minutes away and loaded his truck with water and sodas, and found a gas station nearby that had ice cheap in 20-pound bags, and bought ten of those, and then darted back to the farm.

As soon as John left, Luden located Quinn and took him to the mayor, deciding the mayor was probably going to win the election and a personal contact couldn't hurt. "Mr. Mayor, I'm Paul Luden. I'd like to introduce you to Shepherd Quinn, who leads my church."

"A pleasure to meet both of you," the mayor said, flashing his politician smile. "How are you gentlemen?"

"Doing well," Quinn answered for both of them, shaking the mayor's hand. "I'm pleased you're here and that Paul has been so generous …" Luden quietly backed away and let them talk. He remembered lying to Lowe about the political activeness of the church, but just the same, he understood the importance and benefit of the church having a good contact with the mayor's office, especially now.

He saw readily enough that there was no way John was going to get onto the property in his truck, but Luden had purchased a little Kawasaki Mule truck the week before, as well as a little utility trailer, so he drove that toward the road and waited on John. When John arrived, the men hurriedly unloaded into the Mule, requiring three trips. The news arrived, annoying Luden, who chased them away.

"Sir, the First Amendment grants us the right —" some bleached-blonde bimbo started to protest.

"You haven't the right to trespass, and your First Amendment rights end at my property line," Luden said. "There are about a hundred cops on the property right now and I assure you they'll be more than happy to stuff you two in jail and lose your paperwork for a couple days while you get lost in the system, and since your van is parked on my property, I promise you I'll call an impound lot from all the way across Texas to seize it so you'll also be saddled with a bill for about four grand once you figure out where it is. Please leave before I have to take such steps."

"Look, asshole," the woman snarled. "So far we've played fucking ball with this bullshit story about —"

"If you're about to try to blackmail me, I'm not buying," Luden said. "I am now retired so you have no job to threaten. This is a private affair, so please remove yourselves. You are not welcome here, Ma'am."

"You'll be prominently featured on tonight's news, jackass," the woman snapped. "Let's go, Danny."

The fire department worked rapidly when their captain gave the order, but it was soon determined the buildings would cave in, and the firefighters were called out of them, spraying the buildings liberally from the pumper trucks. The house was about ninety years old, built by Luden's father and grandfather. The barn was even older, and the dried wood burned about as fast as kitchen matches. The guest house was newer, built by Luden's father (with Luden's involuntary assistance) when he was a boy of fifteen, a place for relatives and the occasional itinerant worker to stay. The barn was first to cave in, and fell into a surprising hole. The firefighters put it out and one of them found Luden.

"Sir, you need to see this," he said, and Luden approached, and gaped. There had been a basement or catacomb under the barn, and in it were a number of ancient coffins, several floating in the water the firefighters had dumped onto the blazing structure.

"Dear Lord," Luden breathed.

"What is it?" a fireman asked.

"This, I think, is an old family legend," Luden said. "My family has owned this property since 1810, over two hundred years. It was an old legend that a catacomb was built here and then ... I'm not a direct descendant of the original owner, one James Thurston. He had a brother and three sisters. Thurston died in 1826, and his son Tyler got the farm … long story short, his line died in the Civil War and my great … however many greats … grandfather got the property. There was a legend that there was a catacomb on the property but nobody ever found the entrance. I've been all over the place and never found it. But these, Sir, are my kin going back to … quite possibly Thurston."

"Holy shit," Chief Watts breathed, seeing it. "I don't even know what the law is about things like this."

"Easy," Luden says. "When these remains were buried there was no law, so it's grandfathered. We'll pump this out to the ditch and try to identify who's who, but I think that'll prove a waste of time, and then rebury them right where they lay. I'll probably get a monument for the spot and then fence this off. I would think anything left in those coffins is just bones and scraps of old cloth."

"Come to think of it, this is out in the county, isn't it?" Watts asked.

"Yeah, about a mile outside the city limits," Luden said.

"Good, then it's not the city's problem, is it?" Watts remarked.

"I suppose not," Luden said.

"So you're building new here?" Watts asked.

"I am," Luden told him. "Dozers and trucks will be here tomorrow. They're even going to take the slab, bust it up and cart it off. I'm having a huge pit dug out on the far end of the property to dump all that in it, and bury it over. And then an architect has plans done and construction will start Monday a week. The builders tell me they plan to be done in four months, which works nicely since my lease expires in six months, so I have time to move Marjorie and myself into the new house. She's pregnant now."

"Oh, congratulations," Watt said, meaning it. He too had noticed something noteworthy had changed inside Paul Luden, and sensed that he could really like the man under other circumstances than they had heretofore experienced.

FIFTY-TWO

John and Sarah had been instructed that their assignment was done, but it was decided, in case the church bore closer watching, that they would have a cover story for extraction. One of the fugitives had died after cracking up his car in a high-speed chase in Louisiana. The other two were suspected of taking sanctuary in the Arizona facility. It was learned that Quinn had ordered them to surrender the two to authorities, but the people there seemed defiant, for whatever their reasons. But it was learned that one of the fugitives, Nicholas Parsons, had all four of his grandparents there, and they were unlikely to give up their only grandson, no matter what he'd done.

A petition had been filed with the courts in Tempe, but the court had sided with the religious commune. The judge, Alphonso Morales, was known for protecting illegal aliens on the thinnest of constitutional rationale, and it was believed he was trying to hold consistency with other decisions protecting people illegally in the US and taking refuge on the grounds of various places run by the local diocese. The appeals process was in the works, but it was believed it would be years before authorities were allowed to access the community.

"So go and tell this clown Quinn that you're being transferred to Nevada," Jane relayed orders to them. "Your house is being handled by agents of the company, etcetera blah, blah, blah. You're leaving Wednesday in John's truck and the other goods are being transported to Nevada. Meanwhile, you're going to be able to occasionally visit the Arizona commune – yeah, we're flying you there – and hopefully find those two asshats and give the courts irrefutable proof that Parsons is there."

"Where will we be in Nevada?" Sarah asked. "We won't have legal authority there, Jane."

"You're not there to arrest them, just to find them," Jane said. "Get photos if you can, etcetera, but locate do not detain."

"Jesus," John said. "How do I get out of this chickenshit outfit?"

"Killed in the line of duty is about the only option," Jane said, annoyed. "Once you go undercover we own your ass."

"So we're supposed to do what?" John asked. "Just go traipsing into church Sunday and tell Quinn we're leaving and, by the way, how do we get to visit the community in Arizona?"

"Yeah, pretty much," Jane said.

"Shit fuck," John grumbled. "Okay, so be it. And when do we get to come home and have our lives back?"

"We think maybe a month, maybe six weeks, maybe just two," Jane said. "Reese told me she will recall you after no more than ninety days."

"Well, it seems we'll be wandering the desert, as was Moses, Husband," Sarah said.

"So it appears," John agreed. In truth, they were deeply in love by this point, and if their relationship became known to their handlers the assignment would instantly end. John had already asked her hand in marriage as soon as this assignment ended, and already they were making plans for a life together. This extension of their assignment put a delay on those plans, but both knew at the same time that they would be only very loosely supervised in Nevada and Arizona.

"Shepherd, bad news," John said the next day in the fellowship hall. "I have been transferred, immediately. Sarah and I will leave Wednesday for Nevada, in my truck. They have people who'll pack our house and get it listed on the market, and we'll be house-shopping up there."

"I'm very sorry to learn that, John," Quinn said. "Why don't you two come to my office, please?"

"Yes, Shepherd," John said, curious what it was Quinn might want but not concerned.

"I want you to look for Nicholas Parsons while you're there, as well as Jonas Luther," Quinn said a moment later. "I think those people are protecting those two, and I want them excised from this church and to the police after what they've done. They seem to think their remoteness makes them immune to our law, and I suppose to a point, they're right. But if those two are found there, I have good cause to eliminate those people from the church. We're not about murder of people. We are about discipline among our members – you've both seen that here – but we're not here … look, faith does not spread by the sword but by love, John. Hollis Butler was … I don't know if he had a demon or if he was evil or insane or mistaken … but we cannot in good conscience countenance such behavior."

"I don't know either of these men," John said.

"I figured you didn't," Quinn returned. "Give me a moment." He stepped from his office to Bridger's, and found the membership files on his two errant parishioners, and then scanned the images and printed them on photographic paper. He put each into a manila envelope and brought them back into his office. Unbeknownst to him, Sarah removed the listening device, undiscovered, that she'd left under the chair.

Quinn gave them the folders and John and Sarah looked at the photos, both of clean-cut young men, looking more or less to be in their late 20s. "They aren't standouts," Quinn said. "But I am fairly certain they are there, under protection, probably from Parsons' grandparents – all four of them are on that compound – and this cannot be accepted. I understand their love of their grandson, but ... these two young men need to be turned over to the authorities to protect the church. So as to who to call ... if you see them, call the Arizona authorities. I hope we don't have to excommunicate everyone there, but it looks like we might."

"If we see them we will report them," John assured Quinn, feeling a bit better about this involuntary evolution of his assignment.

"I had high hopes that you would be here a very long while," Quinn said.

"So did we," Sarah chimed in. "I like it here and don't think I'm going to be happy with the desert."

"Well, perhaps I'll see you there," Quinn said. "I don't get there often because of my business here, but ... I think the shepherd there isn't doing his job and might need replacement."

"We leave Wednesday," John said. "I doubt we'll be there for Sunday's services but perhaps the following Sunday."

"I wish you'd told me before our services, so I could have announced today and people could have had more of a chance to wish you well," Quinn said.

"I wanted to tell you yesterday, Shepherd, when we were at the fire," John said. "But you were talking with … was that the mayor?"

"Yes, it was," Quinn said. "Paul felt I should meet the mayor. I suppose he was right but I didn't like politics interfering on a good act."

"He told us the woman who went about with a torch was the one Elder Butler had raped, and who he saved," Sarah remarked.

"Lisa Lowe," Quinn said. "She was the wife of the lead detective investigating those awful murders."

"I was surprised Mr. and Mrs. Luden weren't here today," Sarah ventured.

"Paul called me early this morning," Quinn said. "Marjorie is deathly ill with morning sickness and he's helping care for her."

"I hear that's a nightmare for a pregnant woman," Sarah said. "I hope when I finally get pregnant, it doesn't hit me."

"I hope to see you when I visit Arizona," Quinn said, and shook hands with John.

"I hope so too," John said. "From what I understand I can hire a private plane to fly us there and back so we can attend services easily enough."

"That's going to cost a pretty penny," Quinn observed.

"It is," John agreed. "But the flip side of that is I'm not piloting that monster of a truck four hours each way. It gets decent mileage, but 380 miles … that's burning nearly 20 gallons of diesel, and time has to be worth something, right?"

FIFTY-THREE

The following Sunday, John and Sarah didn't go to Arizona, both too exhausted and butt-sprung from the drive to Nevada. But the Sunday after, they took a charter plane and flew down there, and a car from the community was at the airport to take them to the community.

Quinn wasn't there, which didn't surprise them. An e-mail blast had gone out a few days before that his wife Bethany had finally passed away. Her services were slated for Saturday. Paul Luden and Dan Calloway were to officiate. Marjorie was still feeling lousy with the vomiting and sickness, but Lisa offered to go and sit with her to free Paul to be at the funeral.

One way or another, while it was only a matter of time, Quinn was shaken by his wife's death. He'd devoted himself to her for years on end, and wondered what his life would bring him, moving forward.

John and Sarah shook some hands and were greeted warmly, mostly by elderly parishioners, and went into the chapel for services. They recognized all four grandparents, sitting together on the fourth pew back, but did not immediately see Nicholas Parsons.

The service started, conducted by Alonzo Rincon, and went very much as did the services back home, they quickly saw. Rincon spoke loudly and at length about obedience to the laws of man, as well as obedience to the laws of God. "You will see this every Sunday here," he concluded. "Bring him to the cross."

Two huge men approached the dais with Parsons between them. He was wearing pants and a gauzy shirt, and was chained to the cross and the shirt torn away. Sarah gasped at the gnarled wounds from God alone knew how many whippings he'd endured.

"Nicholas Parsons, do you choose to face our justice or to surrender to the police?" Rincon asked.

"I was only doing God's Will back there," Parsons protested.

"This is not an answer, Nicholas," Rincon said, seeming to lose patience. "We've all taken a huge risk in the name of protecting you, but we've all made it plain to you that you'll be whipped every Sunday until you agree to surrender to the police."

"I can't go to death row," Parsons said. "That's suicide to turn myself in. I won't surrender."

"As you wish," Rincon said, looking disappointed. "Brother Lionel and Brother Randolph, give him forty lashes each."

Lionel and Randolph took turns in ten-lash sessions with a whip that looked far more terrible than the one Sarah faced. Nicholas was screaming by the seventh lash, and before it was done, his back was a bloody mess and he was barely conscious as he was dragged out of the chapel.

"Brothers and sisters, this concludes today's service," Rincon said. "We shall meet in Fellowship Hall."

"Shepherd Quinn told us to expect you," Rincon greeted John in Fellowship Hall, completely ignoring Sarah.

"He's a good man, and we miss the church back home," John replied, shaking hands with Rincon. "I have to ask, what did that poor man do to encounter such a harsh lashing?"

"He's a fugitive, and it seems he took part in many murders back there," Rincon said, sounding annoyed. "I believe Shepherd Quinn – he knows Nicholas is here – wants to persuade him to turn himself in. So far I've gotten nowhere with him, and it was agreed that as long as he uses us, violates the tenets of sanctuary, and puts us at risk, he'll be lashed weekly."

"It seems like it would be simpler to just hand him off to the police," Sarah remarked.

"That came up," Rincon replied. "But the tenet of sanctuary is sacred. We would rather hold that inviolable than to set a precedent that the police can trample on our rights in this sacred community. So we're prepared to fight this to the Supreme Court, if we must. It's not to protect him – frankly, he needs to be in prison if even part of the allegations hold water – but to protect the church and our right to offer sanctuary to the persecuted."

"Interesting premise," John said. "I can see the quandary."

"Indeed," Rincon returned. "To be frank, we haven't even admitted he's here. I guess sooner or later the police will tip to that. God knows they get way too much latitude in surveillance. Sooner or later they'll be in a position to say they know he's here, and the courts will probably ultimately decide in their favor. Honestly, I hope Nicholas loses his nerve and surrenders before it comes to that."

"I took eight lashes back home," Sarah said. "I think I'd rather death row than facing eighty weekly."

"He's gutsy," Rincon allowed, his facial expression making it plain that he didn't like women speaking on such weighty matters. "And he honestly thinks he was doing the right thing in killing those wretches. But he was wrong. We're not about murdering anyone. Never. We're not about disciplining the nonbelievers but leading them to the fold. Our own discipline ... the outer world would see it as harsh ... but we've never laid a punishment on anyone who doesn't consent."

"I understand," John said. "Sometimes I have to punish Sarah but it's always done with love, not to terrorize or harm her."

"Exactly," Rincon agreed. "Why don't you enjoy a good lunch here? There's plenty, as you can see."

"Thank you, we will," John said, smiling. The men shook hands and Rincon wandered off, and then John and Sarah went into the serving line. The food was delicious, and they ate heartily before asking for a ride back to the airport. An hour later they were in the sky. Sarah wanted to talk but John gestured to her to hold it until they were on the ground.

"Holy shit, he's there," Sarah said. "But what do we do about it?"

"We call Captain Flagg at the sheriff's department and report a positive ID, and let them handle it," John said. "I worry that sooner or later that little bastard is going to bleed to death being whipped, or die of infection from the wounds. I guess in his mind, Rincon is doing the right thing, but … yeah, holy shit."

Home, John picked up a disposable cell phone, wandered outdoors, and placed a call to Flagg, who picked up on the first ring. "Jerry Flagg," he said in a rumbling voice.

"Captain, this is John Avery," John introduced himself. "I believe you were told to expect my call?"

"Yes, I was, Mr. Avery," Flagg said.

"My partner and I have positively identified Nicholas Parsons," John said. "He was at the chapel and they actually … Captain, what have you been told about this church?"

"Only that they're another lunatic fringe group of Jesus freaks," Flagg remarked.

"Sir, they are trying to persuade Parsons to surrender to the police," Avery said. "No, the truth is they're trying to coerce the poor fucker. He is being horsewhipped at every Sunday service until he agrees to surrender to the police."

"Horsewhipped?" Flagg echoed, astonished. "Are you serious, Avery?"

"Sir, my partner and I saw him enduring eighty lashes at the conclusion of today's service," John said. "Then they took him away, but no idea where. I could hardly ask."

"Why in the red, white, and blue bleeding fuck don't they just hand him over?" Flagg asked.

"I asked that," John told him. "Long and short, they think sanctuary is sacred and would rather not surrender that right for anyone, even someone they agree belongs behind bars."

"Nutcases," Flagg muttered. "I swear, he's getting worse there than he will in jail."

"He thinks he's going to be executed as soon as the courts allow, and sees surrender as suicide," John explained.

"Jesus, how can people exist being that fucked up?" Flagg asked rhetorically. "Okay. I'll let the DA know he was positively identified and see what they do from there. You take care of yourselves before they horsewhip you too, son."

John ended the call and tapped his fingers together in deep thought, and then e-mailed Isaiah Quinn substantially what he'd told Captain Jerry Flagg, deciding the poor man could address the matter at his leisure rather than have it drag him from the sure and certain circus that would be surrounding his wife's death.

FIFTY-FOUR

Nicholas Parsons was never one to sleep on his belly, and his back pained him too much to sleep on his back. His grandparents put him in a small room in their house, but made it plain they wished he'd face the law and take it like a man, and more or less grounded him to his room like an errant little boy. He knew he needed to run, and made his decision. He rose from bed and dressed, seeing by the bedside clock it was 2:21 in the morning. He groaned in pain as he moved, the stiff scabs protesting. He had been on antibiotics since the whippings started, but was refused so much as Tylenol for the pain.

He'd learned when he was fourteen the combination to his grandfather's gun safe, although his grandfather never found out that Nicholas knew, so he went into the garage and opened the safe, and drew from it a 9-millimeter Browning Hi-Power pistol, three magazines which he loaded fully, and two boxes of ammunition. He also grabbed a survival knife and sheath, and put the holster and sheath on his belt. He had arrived with a backpack and it was still in the garage. He grabbed it and went through the kitchen, filling the pack with various canned goods, and hissing in pain as he slung it over his shoulders. And then he left his grandparents' house for the final time.

The community wasn't particularly patrolled or guarded and most of these people were dead to the world by 9:00 at night, so

Parsons was able to make his way south, off the property. Thirty minutes later, with huge difficulty, he climbed the south fence, and dropped clumsily to the ground, groaning with pain as he landed.

With great effort he rose to his feet, and began walking southwest toward the highway. Three hours later, as the sky was starting to lighten, he found a rock overhang and slid into it, deciding to try to sleep a while and move at night while it was cooler. He opened a can of Ranch Style Beans and devoured it, and then used his spoon to dig a hole and bury the can before bundling up his backpack and using it for a pillow. Around noon, he was still asleep, his body spent as he healed from the beatings he had endured. He rolled some and flopped his hand onto a copperhead seeking the shade. The snake bit him and he woke up screaming from instant searing agony in his arm. The snake released him and slithered off while he fired four clumsy shots in the serpent's direction, but the snake went off unharmed as the venom began its work on the young man.

He knew copperhead bites could be bad and could see his skin blackening, and undid a shoelace to tie around the arm, just beneath the elbow, and wondered where a hospital was, and how to get to one. He began walking, consulting a compass in his backpack. Parsons made it seven miles before collapsing. Four days later his body was found. The medical examiner would determine that the whippings he had suffered had weakened him enough that the snake venom was able to do more damage than it ought. One way or another, Nicholas Parsons was dead, and his participation in the murders was now to be judged by a far higher authority than mortal man could provide.

Nicholas' remains were released to this grandfather, Terrence Parsons, and a funeral was planned, the remains to be cremated and scattered over the community.

"I suppose my trip here is pointless now," Quinn remarked to John and Sarah. "I'm sorry Nicholas died like he did, but ... at least the police will leave us alone now. Or, I hope they do."

"You seem like you don't like the cops much," Sarah remarked.

"Actually, I do like the police," Quinn said. "But any churches that hold any beliefs out of step with the modern mainstream ... well, you see how they get treated in the news. We're not lunatics howling at the full moon. We simply hold a stricter version of religion. I can even step outside and see how we look suspect to them. But we're fortunate that their Sergeant Lowe has, honestly, treated us with respect. I don't think he likes us much, although he and Elder Luden have become close friends since ... well, you know the story there."

"We were grieved to hear about your wife passing," John said.

"Thank you," Quinn replied. "It was her time, but it's left a big empty spot in my life. I visited her several hours at a time several days weekly. And now I'm a widower. It's a strange feeling. I ordered the marriage of Paul and Marjorie without a second thought, over his howling objections, and I thought he was being selfish, clinging to solitude and grief. But I understand a little bit better now. Sooner or later the elders will suggest, strongly, that I take a new wife. And they will suggest that she be of child-bearing age, which means, honestly, a girl of 19 or so years since anyone older is already married. Paul told me he thought he looked ludicrous with a child bride on his arm, and I dismissed him." He chuckled without humor. "I suppose God is about to hand me my comeuppance."

FIFTY-FIVE

Lisa Lowe was delivered of a baby boy, named Thomas Michael, weighing in at seven pounds two ounces. Lisa's father was named Thomas, and the boy was named in the gentleman's honor. Three days later, Marjorie Luden was delivered of a baby girl, named Erica Elizabeth. Mike applied for six weeks under FMLA to have time to help Lisa and to bond with his new son.

The Lowes and Ludens spent a good deal of time together during this period. The new house was built on Luden's farm, and his attorney, Kurberg, had processed about nine miles of red tape to get the family plot certified and grandfathered. Construction was underway for a studio and a greenhouse and potting shed for Marjorie. She had enrolled in online classes for the semester so she'd have the ability to be there with Erica. Luden was proud of her that she was thus far maintaining a 4.0 GPA.

A lot was done to keep the children together so they'd be friends. Lowe enjoyed his time with Tommy and Luden took delight in Erica, which surprised him, but a lot had changed in him.

Since all the suspects had rendered full confessions and guilty pleas, the trials were moved up to get them into the prisons and out of the county jails. The hearings were short and sweet, and in every case, Dawes represented the miscreants and Flame represented the state. In spite of their opposing views, the two had become friends,

374

often meeting in the afternoons for a glass of whiskey and conversation and venting. And life went on.

With no reason left to pursue their assignment, John and Sarah were returned home. There, they were assigned to undercover training. A month after they came home, John asked Sarah to marry him, and she agreed by flinging herself into his arms and kissing him hungrily. Three months after that, they married, and Sarah surprised John on their honeymoon by bringing along handcuffs and a riding crop. Their pay was banked while they were on their assignment, and they had enough to buy a house, and did so.

Four months after moving into the house, Sarah, off her shots, peed on a stick and learned she was pregnant. They later had a son.

FIFTY-SIX

Three Years Later

Lowe was surprised to learn that he had placed fourth on the lieutenant's exam, and was immediately promoted lieutenant. That was the good thing. The bad thing was that Chief Watts had retired eighteen months before on the heels of a massive heart attack.

The new chief was named Earl Zane, and he wasn't interested in Lowe's record or Watts' promise that Lowe would keep the task force. Zane wanted his own cronies in charge, and Lowe was rotated to the 7th Precinct in a uniform. Maybe or not by happenstance, the day commander of the 7th was Captain Miranda Holmes, and she saw to it that Lowe got the day shift. Lowe wasn't happy about going into uniform, but the pay was good, and he figured he would pick up extra jobs here and there, even pondering the merits of buying a police motorcycle and doing escort work here and there. But he balanced that off against time with Tommy, and knew he didn't have to work so much. Lisa had gotten a juicy promotion a year before and was making more money than his base salary.

So Lowe just accepted life as it was, although he wanted to get back into the detective game. Meanwhile, he spit-and-polished the officers under his command, and was pleased with how they performed. His arrest records of his unit were good, and there were few citizen complaints. In the first three months, crime in his area went down 4% and he got a letter of commendation in his file. Lowe appreciated that, but at the same time he grumbled inwardly, knowing that if he really shined in patrol, that was where he was likely to stay until retirement.

Luden wasn't doing well. He had been plagued more and more by nightmares, tormented about his murder of Hollis Butler, and wondering what made him better than Hollis. No answers came to him. A murderer was a murderer, and while Lowe had covered for him, his own conscience did not.

While Marjorie was in class – the college had a daycare where they enrolled Erica – Luden began visiting coin shops and making purchases. It wasn't as easy as one would think, but he had a specific idea in mind. It took three months before he finished the collection, and then he went to the hardware store.

Home, he felt at peace with his decision as he hastily typed a note on his computer and sealed it in a plastic Ziploc. It was raining and that was a shame, but he accepted it for what it was. And then he picked up his phone and dialed Lowe.

"Hey, how's Paul?" Lowe asked.

"Same as ever," Luden said. "Look, Mike ... I need you to come over here straight from work, please. I need a favor."

"In uniform?" Lowe asked, surprised.

"Yeah, I don't think you'll get dirty," Luden said. "But I need you here before Marjorie gets home, please."

"This job is a dead bore," Lowe said. "Yeah, I'll be there around 2:30."

"Sounds good," Luden said. "Thanks, Mike." The men hung up and Luden broke down crying for a while, and then wiped his tears, wondering if God would forgive him or if he was hellbound. Either way, what was done was done, he knew. He went into a closet and donned his uniform, absent the badge the department took from him when he retired. And then he got a sack and climbed a big oak tree beside the house, in plain view of the driveway. He tied a rope off to one branch and then went up higher. There, he retrieved a drawstring bag and put it around his neck. In it were thirty pure silver dollars, all from the year of his birth. The note was in the bag too, confessing to the murder of Hollis Butler. Luden had fashioned a noose already, and tied it to his neck. And then, so he wouldn't chicken out if death wasn't instant, he cuffed his hands behind his back, and then leapt from his branch. The noose worked fine, and his neck broke at C-2, as planned. Paul Luden was free of his nightmares forever. The nightmares for his loved ones were soon to follow.

Lowe arrived on the dot at 2:30 and instantly saw his friend's body dangling from the tree. Luden had done it well, Lowe saw. His feet were about seven inches above the ground. A ladder was leaning against the tree, and Lowe hurriedly went up the ladder and then cut the rope, letting Luden's body fall to the ground. Lowe checked a pulse, knowing in his heart he was wasting his time, and saw by the angle of his friend's neck that he was dead. Lowe called 911. He knew he wasn't in the city, and knew he would be in trouble if he was found out, but he cut the drawstring bag and took it to his car. He kept a blanket in the back seat of his personal car and took that to cover Luden's body, and then went to the car and opened the bag.

He saw the letter in the plastic envelope, and counted out the coins, not the least bit surprised there were thirty of them. Thirty pieces of silver, what Judas was paid for betraying Christ to the Romans. Lowe began to weep as the ambulance arrived, who immediately concluded that Luden was indeed dead. A deputy arrived soon after, and called Homicide. Lowe stood by in his car, weeping some for his tortured friend, and called Lisa.

"What's up, Mike?" she asked.

"Lisa, Paul just hanged himself," Lowe said.

"Oh, God," Lisa breathed.

"Look, I think Marjorie gets home around 6:00," Lowe said. "It's 4:00 now. Do you think you can come here, to their house? I think Marjorie is going to need us in a big way."

"Of course," Lisa said. "I'll go snag Tommy from day care and I'll be there in twenty minutes." She hung up and Lowe sat quietly in his car until the homicide detective approached his car.

"Lieutenant, I'm Ron Sheffield," the man said, offering his hand. "What can you tell me about this?"

"Paul called me earlier today —" Lowe began.

"Is that the decedent?" Sheffield interrupted.

"Yes, Paul Luden," Lowe confirmed. "He was a captain with the police department until a few years ago when he retired. Anyway, he phoned me and asked if I'd come over and do him a favor when my shift was done, and so I drove over here. And I found him hanging from the tree. I went up the ladder and cut him down but it was too late."

"I'm very sorry, Lieutenant," Sheffield said.

"So am I," Lowe returned. "We'd become very good friends the last few years since his retirement. He saved my wife's life right over there." Lowe pointed to the family plot, carefully tended, with a marble obelisk on it listing what names could be gleaned from the coffins discovered below the barn."

"I think I heard the story," Sheffield said. "The guy chopping up all those people?"

"Him," Lowe confirmed. "Anyway, you know about cops and suicide, right? You look old enough to have been all over the place."

"Yes, Sir," Sheffield said. At thirty-six, he was a fifteen-year veteran of the sheriff's department, and was already looking forward to retirement. Like so many police officers, he wanted to be a lawyer. Unlike so many police officers, he was actually in law school, finishing his second year.

"But as to specifically why Paul did this, I don't know," Lowe said. "My wife is on her way here and his wife should be home in a couple hours or so. Christ, I don't want to break this news to her."

"We can handle that for you, Lieutenant," Sheffield offered.

"No, we'll do it," Lowe said. "Marjorie is … she and Paul are like kin to us. Lisa and I think of her as a little sister to us. Our kids are the same age. And Marjorie is young. It's better if the news comes from us."

"I understand," Sheffield said. "The coroner will take his remains but this looks like there was no foul play. Thank you for your time, Lieutenant."

Lowe nodded and thought for a moment, and then looked up the church on the phone. "Thank you for calling the Church of God's Law," Bridger answered. "This is Shannon. How may I direct your call?"

"Miss Bridger, I don't know if you remember me, but my name is Mike Lowe," Lowe began.

"And how are you today, Sergeant?" Bridger asked, smiling. And then her voice lowered. "I think I'm getting a job offer from City Hall soon."

"Congratulations," Lowe said, happy for the woman. "Miss Bridger, it's very important that I speak with Mr. Quinn. Is he available?"

"Give me a moment, but I believe he is," Bridger said.

"This is Shepherd Quinn," Quinn said a moment later.

"Sir, I'm Mike Lowe —" Lowe began.

"How are you, Mr. Lowe?" Quinn asked. "Paul tells me you were promoted recently to lieutenant, so let me be among the last to congratulate you."

"Thank you, Sir," Lowe said, then took the bull by the horns. "Sir, there's no easy way to say this, so I'm just going to say it. Paul is dead. I'm at his place now waiting on Marjorie to get home."

"How awful," Quinn breathed. "What happened?"

"Sir, I'm not at liberty to say much more, but it looks like a suicide," Lowe said.

"God rest his soul," Quinn breathed. Paul had been plagued with a good deal of guilt about Hollis Butler, frequently seeking Quinn's counsel in recent months. But Quinn wasn't about to betray that confidence, not even with Luden dead. Quinn dabbed at tears leaking from his eyes, and spoke in a huskier voice. "I'll be there presently, Lieutenant. Marjorie will need the church in this difficult time."

"Hold this information for now, Shannon," Quinn said to Bridger in her office. "Lieutenant Lowe just told me that Paul Luden has passed away."

"Oh dear," Bridger said. Since his retirement, something had changed in Luden and she had come to genuinely like the man. "Should I head over there when the office closes?"

"No, I don't think there's much you could do there," Quinn decided. As far as he knew, his secretary was only slightly acquainted with Marjorie Luden. Besides, Quinn, always good at reading people, suspected that Marjorie would resign from the church before Paul was cold in his grave. He bemoaned her loss, but wouldn't try to coerce the girl to the contrary. As it was, her parents quietly seethed every time they saw her, and perhaps it was best for all if Chuck and Maura simply didn't see her again. Quinn suspected it was jealousy. Chuck and Maura were having huge financial troubles after a business venture failed, and the relative affluence of Paul and Marjorie irritated them, especially when Chuck went to Paul for money and was declined, right about the time Erica was born.

"Let me know if there's anyone I should call, please," Bridger said. "I'll stay here late if you need."

"Would you?" Quinn asked.

"Yes, Sir," Bridger said. "I didn't think I'd ever come to like Elder Luden, but since he retired, I really have come to like him. I don't particularly know Marjorie, but she seemed head over heels for him and ... this is heartbreaking, Shepherd."

"Yes, it is," Quinn said. "I'll keep you posted, Shannon. But if you haven't heard from me by 7:00, go ahead and close up shop here. There's not much to do for this tonight."

Lisa arrived, handed Tommy off to her husband, and then parked by the gate to intercept Marjorie. Quinn arrived and spoke briefly with Lisa, and then drove in and found Lowe in his car with Tommy. The ambulance was long gone and the body had been placed in the coroner's van, which left right as Quinn parked his Dodge sedan. Lowe got from his car with Tommy clinging closely to him, and the men shook hands.

"I'm very sorry, Lieutenant," Quinn said. "I know how close you two were."

"It's hard," Lowe admitted. "Jesus, I'm going to miss him."

"So will his church, but I don't think anyone is going to miss him more than Marjorie and Erica," Quinn said. "She's estranged from her family, so she's really all alone."

"Pardon me for saying so, but bull shit," Lowe said, pronouncing each word. "That young woman and Erica are family to Lisa and me. I have her back, Sir."

"I'm glad to hear that," Quinn said, meaning it. "I don't think she's enamored of the church, and if I had to guess, I'd guess she'll leave the church soon."

"I have no idea," Lowe said, honestly. "Paul and I didn't go much into religion, so I ... I just don't know. I remember him venting to me about her parents trying to put the bite on them for money about when the kids were born, but none of the particulars."

"Kids?" Quinn asked. "I thought they only had Erica."

"Oh, they did," Lowe said. "But our son was born three days before Erica. We've always called them the twins."

"I remember hearing that now," Quinn said, kicking himself mentally for the lapse in memory. "And this is Thomas, I gather?"

"In the flesh," Lowe said, smiling fondly at the boy.

"Cute little scamp," Quinn said.

"Yeah, I love him to pieces," Lowe confessed. "Marjorie should be here about 6:00. We'd all planned on dinner at our place tonight. I have a fryer all seasoned up in my fridge and was going to toss it on my pit, and let the kids go nuts together. They babysit each other and that's sure a lot easier on all our old bones."

"I'm certain," Quinn said. Bethany had been barren, so Quinn had very little experience with the ins and outs of children, but had always found them fun to watch in their antics. The elders had told him he should take a bride, and after a good deal of debate, he had reluctantly agreed. Elizabeth Lewis was eighteen and available, and had agreed to marry him in three weeks. But he wasn't as enthused, wishing he could convert Shannon Bridger to the church and marry her instead. He had developed feelings for the young woman over the years, redheaded and pretty. But he knew it was foolishness to pursue her. If he'd known she was a lesbian he would have been shocked to his core, but Shannon had hidden that fact quite well from him. Meanwhile, he knew that he and Elizabeth would be expected to make babies, and he worried about what kind of father he would be. But he was nothing if not honest with himself, and looked forward to plundering the black-haired beauty soon to be his bride.

"What's going on, Lisa?" Marjorie asked as she pulled up. Lisa was leaning on the hood of her car, and Erica was having a fit in the back seat. Marjorie could see that Lisa had been crying.

"It's Paul," Lisa said somberly. "He passed on."

"Oh God!" Marjorie howled in sudden agony. Lisa hurriedly got into the passenger side of the car and held Marjorie clumsily, but tightly and comfortingly.

"I'm so sorry, Marjorie," Lisa said.

"What ... what happened?" Marjorie asked, steeling herself.

"He called Mike and asked him to come over," Lisa said. "Mike told me he hanged himself."

"Oh Jesus," Marjorie moaned, sobbing anew. Lisa's heart broke for her young friend. "He's been planning this for a while, I think. He never said anything to me, but I noticed he was suddenly collecting old silver dollars. I counted them last night, out of curiosity, and there were thirty of them. But … I don't understand who he thought he betrayed."

"I don't know," Lisa said. "Mike is up by the house, and your minister too."

"Let me drive up," Marjorie said.

"You sure you're okay to do that?" Lisa asked.

"It's only 300 yards, so yeah," Marjorie said.

"I'll follow you," Lisa said.

"Marjorie, I'm so sorry," Lowe said.

"I … thank you, Mike," Marjorie managed to say.

"I think it goes without saying that whatever you need from the church is yours for the asking," Quinn said.

"Thank you, Shepherd," Marjorie repeated. "I … I want to bury him here, among his ancestors and relatives. Mr. Kurberg told us we could do that when he did all the legal stuff, that we could be buried here."

"Of course," Quinn said. "I took the liberty of calling Walther. He should be here soon. He told me Paul saw him not long ago and updated his will. He'll see that your interests are protected."

"Why don't you bring Erica to our house?" Lisa suggested. "We can see to you there."

"I'll take care of the yellow tape and stuff tomorrow," Lowe said. "I'm sure the captain will give me all the off-time I need."

Lowe stepped off to call Holmes. "Mike, I just heard about Paul Luden," Holmes greeted him on the phone. "One of the deputies on the scene was an old friend of his and an old friend of mine. He let me know."

"I need some time off," Lowe managed to say.

"Take all you want," Holmes said. "To be honest I was about to read you the Riot Act about how much time you have built up. And ... I'm sorry about Paul. I know how close you two have become."

"Thank you, Captain," Lowe said formally.

"Miranda," Holmes corrected. "I think we've been friends at least that long, Mike."

"Thank you," Lowe said.

"So are you going to tell me what's bothering you?" Lisa asked Mike when they were at home. Marjorie wanted to stay home and didn't want company, and Mike and Lisa accorded her wish.

"What do you know about spousal privilege?" Mike asked her.

"I think it means I can't be compelled to testify against you in court," Lisa said, after a long moment searching her memory.

"Yeah, that's what it means, but it doesn't mean you can't voluntarily do so," Lowe returned.

"Mike, I swear to you that if you tell me you're about to dynamite all of Washington DC I won't testify in court," Lisa returned.

"Paul ... he murdered Hollis Butler," Lowe said haltingly. "He planted the pistol in the doctor's hand after he shot him. It was an execution, Lisa. I saw him do it and even told him later he should have put the gun in Butler's left hand not his right, since Butler was a southpaw."

"And you sat on that all this while?" Lisa said, shocked. "Mike, I don't give a flying fuck that Butler was murdered. He deserved it."

"I agree," Lowe said. "As far as I was concerned, he'd just raped and beaten my wife and I'd have done the same thing Paul did, but Paul had the angle and I didn't. But ... it weighed on Paul. Good people never rest easy with killing, no matter the necessity, Lisa. A lot of cops – the news only tells us things that make cops look bad – but one hell of a lot of cops involved in justified shootings ... it fucks them up, Lisa. Some kill themselves. Some resign. Some take up drinking. And the police department is as bad as the military about overlooking PTSD until someone crams it in their face. The cultural standard is that it's a weakness and too many good cops who seek help find their careers in shambles. The smart ones don't go through EAP but go to a private shrink. I think ... I think Paul couldn't make that leap, Lisa."

"That poor man," Lisa said.

"I removed it from his body since I don't think he deserves dishonor in his death, and Marjorie and Erica sure the hell don't deserve it," Lowe said. "But he had a drawstring bag around his neck with those thirty silver dollars in it, and a note."

"What was in the note?" Lisa wanted to know.

"I haven't grown the balls to look at it," Lowe admitted.

Cops tend to gossip like widows around the village well, so by noon it was known by virtually every cop in the Department that Paul Luden, a retired captain, had hanged himself. Inspector Johnson, near retirement, called Marjorie and offered a police funeral with all honors, and Marjorie accepted, but suggested a meeting of herself, him, and Quinn, to iron out the arrangements.

She set up a 3-way call and arranged to meet at Quinn's office, and then drove Erica to the day care and herself to the church. Already, she knew she was going to have to withdraw from her classes this semester, but if the college didn't know that yet, then Erica could remain enrolled in their daycare. Paul had counseled her since they were married to think practically, and she blessed him for making clear to her parents that they were unwelcome.

The meeting with Johnson and Quinn, with Bridger taking notes, wasn't a long one. The church, Quinn said, was closed to non-members, so the chapel – probably too small anyway – was unavailable for Paul's service. The local Police Athletic League owned a huge gymnasium, Johnson said, which would seat around 2,000 guests, and the service could be conducted there. Quinn would officiate the service and agreed the pall bearers should all be police in

Class-A uniforms. Marjorie asked that Lowe be the lead pall bearer, and Johnson agreed.

Johnson had never liked Luden, but admitted to himself that Luden's last act as a police officer was one of painful heroism, and had heard through the grapevine that Luden had mellowed a good deal in retirement with his new marriage and daughter. He thought Marjorie was ridiculously young to be Luden's wife, but he could see what Luden saw in the young woman. She had poise and class, and he instantly saw she was nobody's dummy. He realized he almost immediately liked the young woman, which surprised him.

"I understand you wish to bury him in your family plot," Quinn said. "I'm going to call Jeremiah Lott and suggest that a contingency of boys from the youth group could show up with shovels and prepare a grave for him."

"I hadn't even thought that far ahead," Marjorie said, dazed. "Yes, thank you, Shepherd. I'm sure Mike and Lisa will see that they're fed well." She said this with confidence. Both had taken leave and made it plain they were at her disposal. She knew it would make them feel good to do something for her, and thanked God for their friendship.

Quinn immediately placed the call and Lott said he'd have ten people on hand first thing in the morning, and have them on standby to bury Luden when the graveside service concluded.

"Then I'll call Mike and see that they have food on hand for the young men," Marjorie said. "Thank you, Shepherd. And thank you, Inspector Johnson." Marjorie and Johnson left, both with Xerox copies of Bridger's notes, and Quinn brooded for a few minutes about his old friend and the guilt he must have felt, and then placed a call to Mike Lowe.

"Lieutenant, I want to ask you a few questions," Quinn said. "Would it be possible for you to come to my office?"

"Sure," Lowe said. "I'm not far from there anyway. I'll be there in ten minutes, Sir."

"Lieutenant ... can we be Mike and Isaiah here?" Quinn asked Lowe in his office.

"Sure, Isaiah," Lowe said, curious.

"I find it odd that Paul didn't leave a note behind," Quinn said. "Was one recovered and the police haven't released it to his widow? For now, let's say I'm your minister, so anything you say to me is strictly between us, not unlike a Catholic priest and confession."

"He left a note," Lowe said. "I decided that Marjorie had enough going on. I haven't opened the note and it's in a safe place. It was in a bag with thirty silver dollars. That's something I didn't tell anyone, Isaiah. But while I'm not the most religious man on this planet, I understand the significance."

"Thirty pieces of silver," Quinn said, more to himself than to Lowe. "But who does he think he betrayed?"

"Isaiah, I have a good idea but I don't think I'm at liberty to say," Lowe returned.

"I think I do too," Quinn said. "Did it have to do with a throw-down pistol?"

"I'd rather not answer that question," Lowe said, unsurprised and more or less expecting the question.

"Then consider it withdrawn," Quinn said. "How are John and Sarah Avery these days, by the way?"

"Who?" Lowe asked, at first confused, and then grateful his memory slip made it look more genuine.

"Mike, we could sit here for hours trying to outsmart one another, but why?" Quinn asked. "We're on the same side, on Marjorie's side. I figured the Avery family was a plant. At first we suspected them, and then Hollis Butler gave her a physical and saw marks from a whipping, and we figured there's no way the police would do that. And then they suddenly got transferred to Nevada right as Nicholas ran away to Arizona, and then disappeared into thin air right after he turned up dead of that snakebite."

"They're both in a special unit teaching undercover operations," Lowe said. "But if you quote me, I'll deny it like Peter denied the Lord."

"I understand, Mike," Quinn said. "As I said, we're on the same side in this. Paul even told me back when that he was certain the church was undergoing surveillance, and even I can admit we looked suspect. And let's face facts, Mike, the doers were all members of the church.

"But getting back to Paul, he ... he felt tormented by the killings, or at least about killing Hollis," Quinn continued. "I can't imagine how horrid it was for him, Mike. Hollis was his best friend and he ... he executed the man."

"It was tragic," Lowe agreed. "But I'm afraid I can't see it so dispassionately. I'd have shot Butler if I'd had a good angle, but I'd just seen him raping my wife and then horsewhipping her. I've been in combat and never felt that kind of fury, Isaiah."

"Turning the other cheek isn't as easy as it sounds," Quinn said. "But there was only one Jesus Christ who ever walked this earth."

"What did Paul's note say?" Quinn wanted to know.

"I haven't opened it," Lowe said. "That's God's honest truth."

"Maybe that's wisest," Quinn said. "Let the man be buried with all the honors due him, and you can do so with a more or less clean conscience."

FIFTY-SEVEN

"Let us all gather in the name of Christ to memorialize a good soldier of our Savior, who dedicated his life to the service of Christ our Lord, and his fellow man," Quinn began the service two days later. The gymnasium had, Quinn guessed, about 1,500 people in attendance. "Paul Luden lived his life in service of his fellow man. He served as a very young man as a US Marine, where he was decorated for his merit, and for being wounded in action. But when he left the Marines, his courage remained as strong, and he entered the police department, enduring a thousand dangers along the way as he rose to the rank of captain. He was a courageous soldier for this life and the new one on which he has just embarked. Let us pray. Our Father, Who art in Heaven, hallowed by Thy name …"

Quinn gave a good sermon, with many quotes straight from Scripture. Lowe noted that the man didn't use notes, and delivered it all from memory, and then Quinn handed the podium off to Lowe.

"I'm Michael Lowe, and in the years since his retirement, Paul and I became the closest of friends," he began. "It's easy to see all kinds of merit in a man who saved my wife's life." A small waved of chuckles went up at this.

"But it went deeper than that," Lowe said into the microphone. "Paul was there for both of us doing all he could for us in the most difficult season of our lives. He even saved our marriage when it was in shambles after that awful day. My wife and I got through it, with his help. We even had children three days apart, and these last few years spent much of our time together cooking a lot of chickens and steaks and catching who knows how many fish. Lord knows the man had some sort of fish radar. I once saw him catch a limit of largemouth bass in an hour, and we ate like kings and queens that night, the four of us.

"Marjorie, I can't imagine how this is for you, but I swear to you for the rest of our lives that you have a branch of your family named Lowe, and we're always going to be here for you," Lowe continued. "Erica has an Aunt Lisa and an Uncle Mike who are going to be here to support and help through and through." This wasn't just empty talk. Kurberg had met with Marjorie, Mike and Lisa the night before. Luden's will gave it all to Marjorie, but for a thousand dollars to each of his sons, but set it up as somewhat of a trust, putting Mike and Lisa in charge until Marjorie turned 30. He reasoned that Marjorie – Paul had remained in charge of finances and bills throughout their marriage – needed to be brought up to speed about the money, and needed to gain some years and wisdom. Still hoping to finish out college and begin a career, Marjorie had no problem passing off details to trusted friends.

"I pray that Paul has found peace on the other side, and if it means much from this side, I promise I'll take care of what you left behind," Lowe went on. "Paul, we didn't meet well at first, but God blessed me with you, my friend ... and my brother. God rest your soul, old friend."

Lowe departed the podium red-faced and doing his best to swallow back the lump in his throat. Quinn opened the microphone to anyone who would like to speak, and a small line formed, surprisingly including Reese and the chief of police. Several spoke for a couple or three minutes each, and then the chief spoke for about ten minutes on the courage of police officers and the icon that Paul Luden should have been.

Quinn took the podium for the final time, leading the assembly through three hymns, and then the Lord's Prayer, and finally eight police officers, Lowe in the lead, took the coffin to the hearse, and rode with Marjorie and Lisa in the lead limousine.

Marines were on hand to play *Taps* and perform the 21-gun salute, but it was decided the police would fold the flag to present to Marjorie. Lowe had drilled with them the day before and knew the commands to bark when the time was ripe. The service at the graveside was otherwise short and sweet. The chief personally presented Marjorie with the flag, and she began sobbing as the rifles fired and the twin bugles, just out of sync, played *Taps*. The coffin was lowered into its vault, and the workers stood by, waiting for the crowd to disperse before filling the grave.

Most of the attendees at the graveside service left, but closer friends stayed, and Lowe noted that Marjorie's parents had remained, and began bolstering himself for that confrontation.

"Daddy's here," Chuck Stoddard said to Marjorie a short time later.

"You have no business here," Marjorie said. "My father died the very moment he disowned me. Please leave."

"How about you honor your father and your mother?" Stoddard asked. "You need us and we need —"

"All you want is money from me," Marjorie interrupted. "Husband told me all about you trying to put the bite on him. The answer then was no, and that is the answer now, Mr. Stoddard. Leave."

"I will charge you in the church with violating the Sixth Commandment, and you'll be horsewhipped," Stoddard threatened, and was suddenly on the floor gasping as Lowe quick-stepped to him and kneed him in the crotch.

Lowe hunkered down before the groaning man. "Listen closely to me, Buckwheat," Lowe said in a gentle tone that nonetheless carried plenty of menace. "If I hear you gave Mrs. Luden any trouble ... if I hear you ever approach Marjorie again ... if I hear a whisper of trouble from you with regard to her ... you're going to wish I killed you today. Now, you get the fuck off this floor and you get the fuck out of this house, and don't you ever come near here or her again. You got that?"

"I'll sue you —" Stoddard gasped, and then Lowe casually popped him on the nose with the heel of his hand, and he cried out. It wasn't a hard pop. No bones broke and there was no blood, but it didn't have to be harsh to put the fear of God in this moron, Lowe reasoned.

"I'm fairly certain – I know memory is an iffy thing – but I'm fairly certain that Lisa and Marjorie are prepared to testify that you came in here threatening and then took a swing at me when I told you to leave, and I was merely defending myself. Added bonus: I'm a policeman in uniform, Buckwheat. Your assault on me is a 3rd degree felony. That means if the court clerk picks the right judge, you could get all five years, my boy. Now, pick yourself up and get the fuck out of here before I beat you so bad you'll be in ICU for the coming month."

"Hell awaits you all," Stoddard groaned.

"If you're not there, I'll be happy with it," Lowe remarked. "Get lost, asshole."

Just then, Quinn entered the study and clucked his tongue. "Chuck, I told you coming here was a bad idea," he said. "Marjorie is a grown woman and a widow now, and you disowned her right after she turned eighteen. This means your problems are not hers, now or ever. I am guessing by this scene that Lieutenant Lowe has remonstrated with you about this and that you have been asked to leave. I suggest you round up Maura and do so before you wind up in handcuffs and jailed for who knows what charges, but I would guess criminal trespass would top the list. Let me help you up and then you get going." Quinn did exactly that, and shushed Stoddard as he started to talk, and the man left.

"I don't need to ask what happened," Quinn said. "In about two weeks his house is going into foreclosure. He's in deep financial trouble and ... well, I feel sorry for him in a way but in another way, he was unwise with his money and investments, and we all know that old saw about whipping dead horses, right?"

"We do, Shepherd," Marjorie said, still furious with her father.

"I need to go," Quinn said. "Marjorie, I'm available around the clock, okay?"

"Shepherd, I ... I may as well tell you now that I am resigning from the church," Marjorie said. "I just don't see it as my path."

"I pretty well guessed as much," Quinn said. "And I understand. But in or out of the church, you're a daughter of our Lord and the widow of one of my dearest friends, so you're stuck with my help if you need it, okay?"

Marjorie managed to smile a little bit at this. "Thank you, Shepherd," she said.

"Just Isaiah," Quinn returned. He smiled, shook Lowe's hand, and left.

FIFTY-EIGHT

"This is Lowe," Lowe answered his phone that night. He was tired and on his third drink after a long and stressful day. He was on the back porch of the Luden house. He and Lisa decided to stay there with Marjorie for the time being.

"Lieutenant, this is Amanda Reese," Reese said.

"How are you, Inspector?" Lowe asked, suddenly wary and wondering if Stoddard filed a complaint on him anyway.

"Mike, I need you in my office tomorrow morning first thing," Reese said.

"Am I in some sort of trouble?" Lowe asked. "Should I have the police union attorney on hand?"

"Oh ... no, nothing of the sort," Reese said. "Mike, someone is copycatting Butler's murders and we're putting you in charge of the task force the chief wants to quietly assemble. Be in my office at 7:00."

"Inspector, I'd rather refuse this assignment, even if you send me to the 22nd," Lowe said.

"Mike, you know better than that," Reese countered. "Why don't you want this assignment?"

"Jesus Christ, you saw what happened the last time," Lowe said. "I won't ever put Lisa through that again, Inspector. I'm sitting here not fifty yards from where that all went down and … no."

"Mike, we're prepared to move Lisa and Tommy to a safe house," Reese said, leaving out that it was the home John and Sarah Avery had occupied, sold and repurchased by another shell company owned by the state. "I can have them in there tomorrow morning."

"No," Lowe said. "Goddammit, Inspector, I won't put Lisa through that kind of danger. And I sure the fuck won't put Tommy through that. No."

"Be here at 7:00," Reese ordered. "I'll show you what we have. If you still want to refuse the case, you can do so and your career will remain as it is, without negative impact. Mike, I think in your shoes I would knee-jerk like you have. But I think when you see this one you're going to want it."

"I'll be there," Lowe said sourly. He poured a fourth drink from the bottle on the table beside him, drank it, and then went in and showered. The kids were in the same bed and sound asleep. Lisa and Marjorie had gone out and bought a fortune in new clothes for Marjorie. Dressing like she was Amish was now and permanently in her past. She arrived home with several pairs of slacks and jeans, polo shirts, blouses, t-shirts, and even a revealing swimsuit. Lowe was astonished when she modeled the clothes, including the swimsuit. She had a hard and sleek figure too hidden under the simple dresses her church required that she wear, and Lowe found her simply stunning.

Lowe took a long shower and climbed into bed beside Lisa, setting his alarm to wake him early. The alarm went off at 5:45 to Lisa's growls of displeasure. "What the fuck, Mike?" she asked.

"I need to go to the office for a meeting," Mike said evasively. "I'll be home soon, I think."

"Supercop rides again," Lisa grumbled, and rose. "You're not leaving here without breakfast. Let's go to the kitchen."

"Thank you for coming in, Mike," Reese said in her office. Inspector Johnson was there as well.

"Ma'am, Sir," Lowe said.

"Have a seat," Reese said. "Do you want coffee?"

"Yes, thank you," Lowe said. Johnson poured a cup from a big Bunn coffeemaker in Reese's conference room and handed it to Lowe. "So why do I want this case, Ma'am?"

Reese pointed to the big television mounted on the wall and Lowe watched, transfixed, as a video came up. The villains were in clothes and masks. Race was indeterminate, but by the size of them, Lowe assumed they were male. A woman was chained to a post, her right hand missing, and Lowe watched, sickened as she was whipped to death as Butler had done. Once she was dead, the men used reciprocating saws and knives and cut the woman into pieces, tossed the pieces into a wheelbarrow, and rolled it away.

And then a man sat in front of the camera, his face invisible in his mask, and flashed a badge at the camera. Lowe saw it was a captain's badge, and had a sick suspicion whose it was. The voice had obviously been processed through synthesizers, and Lowe knew it would almost certainly be impossible to reverse the thing and get a voice print.

"A police captain betrayed us, and then killed himself in the style of Judas Iscariot," the voice said. "He should have had red hair as a warning to us. Hollis Butler was a saint, and we are picking up where he left off, ridding ourselves of whores and killers and thieves until our city shines as an example of how we are to live our lives on this earth. We hope to save this fair city from the fate that Sodom and Gomorrah endured. Do not interfere with us, or you will be punished for obstructing God's justice. The body of this ... whore ... will be found at 7702 33rd Avenue Southwest. We aren't going to plant incendiaries, just the body. A curse on the betrayer, and a curse on any who would defy us. What happened to Detective Michael Lowe's wife was, we agree, inexcusable, and the lives of family members are off-limits to us, but the lives of those who directly interfere ... well, you just saw how serious we are."

With that, the video ended, and Lowe trembled with emotions he couldn't begin to sort out and identify. "The video arrived yesterday, addressed to Inspector Johnson," Reese said, breaking Lowe's reverie, if only briefly.

"I only saw it once I was home from the services," Johnson said. "We dispatched officers there and recovered the body parts. And the badge. The coroner is still working to ID the body, but right now we have a Hispanic, probably, female in her mid-twenties."

"So why is IA on this one?" Lowe asked.

"Because ... Mike, the night Luden retired he handed in his badge," Reese said. "You get a new badge when you're promoted.

You know that. You got a new one when you made sergeant, and another new one not long ago when you hit lieutenant – congratulations, by the way – but when you retire or resign you are made to hand in your badge. That's been policy going back about 25 years. That badge was worn by Captain Luden, and he turned it in to me hours after he shot Hollis Butler. Per regulations, I handed it off to Personnel, taking their receipt for it – it's in my files, in fact – and they stored it and their records said they had it. I went and looked, thinking maybe the one these people used was counterfeit, but it's gone and there's no record of it being checked out."

"Christ," Lowe muttered. "How well is that storeroom protected?"

"Unfortunately, not very well," Reese said. "Anyone going into those offices has to have reason, but that includes any number of janitors and other senior brass. Pretty much any captain or above can waltz in and out of there at will, Mike."

"Super," Lowe said. "So you have another group of holy rollers – I think there were four on that video – trying to prove a point like the Manson Cult, and a bottomless well of suspects, pretty much anyone who believes in God. Does that sum it up?"

"The four all appear to be righties," Reese said.

Just then the door opened and the chief of police came in. Lowe, in a Pavlovian response, popped to attention. "Sit down, Lowe," the chief grumbled. "This ain't the army and I never went in for most of that paramilitary stuff one way or another."

"Yes, Sir," Lowe said to Chief Earl Zane, as he sat.

"Lowe, I've been in supervisory work at one level or another since I got promoted sergeant of the Little Rock PD 35 years ago," Zane said. "It's a job you never stop learning. One of the lessons I learned back when was to admit to myself that I'm human and all the decorations on my walls and uniforms don't make infallible. When Harry Truman was president he disbanded the OSS, realized soon after that he shouldn't have done that, and then created the CIA, for instance. Well, Reese and Johnson were gentle about it but made it clear that I fucked up with regard to transferring you to uniform duty. Fortunately, I can unfuck that right here and now. You're in charge of the chief's special task force, in plainclothes, starting now."

"Sir, I don't know that I want the assignment ..." Lowe began, but silenced himself at a gesture from Zane.

"Inspectors, I'd like to speak privately with the lieutenant," he said. Reese and Johnson immediately left Reese's conference room, closing the door behind them.

"You know, I called up the Butler file right after I got word of this new case," Zane said. "I know you're a smart man, and little escapes your attention. Now, I couldn't get with this anywhere in court, but one thing caught my attention. Hollis Butler was a leftie. But he died with a pistol in his right hand. I somehow doubt that escaped your attention, Lieutenant. Now, I don't think anyone else picked up on it. This world is littered with righties, and it was otherwise an airtight case. But ... I don't think you'd have missed that fact. Reese's notes on it even indicate that you were aware you were looking for a southpaw and that Luden marched in those ranks."

"If the Chief expects a reply, I'm afraid I'm empty," Lowe said.

"No, I don't expect a reply, Lowe," Zane said. "The case is closed and I can hardly dig Luden from his grave, no matter how fresh, and accuse the man of murder. In truth, any clown in his second year of law school would rip that case to mincemeat. I suppose what I'm saying is you're an observant and intelligent man, Lieutenant, and you're wise enough to know when to look the other way. No good would have come to anyone from putting Butler on trial, and he would probably have been found not guilty on an insanity plea, and right back out there murdering people again. Lowe, I need you on this. The Department needs you on this. We'll protect your family – I understand your worries there – but ... we need you, Lowe."

"Christ," Lowe muttered. "When do I meet my command?"

"We have Homicide on this case, a detective named Judy Simons," Zane said. "She'll be transferred to you ... shit, let's do it for Monday. And we'll quietly transfer in another fifty or so detectives and patrolmen. It'll be the same office suite you had before, Lieutenant. Head on home and we'll see you Monday. I'll see to it that Captain Holmes is notified of your transfer.

"Sir, do you know how I found out where Lisa was being kept?" Lowe asked.

"Yeah, I read that in the report too," Zane said. "You found out where her phone was."

"That hardly makes me the Sherlock Holmes you seem to think I am, Sir," Lowe said.

"I disagree," Zane returned. "Look, I know you don't want the case. I know your worries. I know you feel overwhelmed and out of your element, but all kinds of cases unravel on the thinnest of loose ends. Look at ... I think it was the Son of Sam killer ... he got popped because some cop stumbled across a parking ticket, and those walls came tumbling down just that easily. You don't think you're all that great at this, but looking at your record, and the last such case you headed, I think you're just the guy, Lieutenant Lowe."

"Yes, Sir," Lowe said simply, and then drove back to the Luden house, where Lisa eyed him suspiciously. Lowe cut his eyes toward Marjorie, and Lisa nodded, still looking dubious.

"I'm going to go outside and take a little walk," Lowe said a short time later.

"You okay if I go with him, Marjorie?" Lisa asked.

"Yeah, that's fine. I have the kids," Marjorie said.

"So what dragged you out of bed and to your office at oh-dark-early?" Lisa asked fifty yards into the woods.

"I just got co-opted into IA," Lowe grumbled. "Some copycat killer murdered a woman and sent a video to Inspector Johnson. It looks like the Department got infiltrated, so Reese is on it now, and the Jesus H. Chief Zane himself assigned the investigation to me."

"Shit," Lisa said. "I know you have to take the job, Mike. But I don't like it."

"Neither do I," Lowe said. "I've been promised high-level protection for you and Tommy, even a safe house, but ... I don't like it either. My only way out, really, is to retire. But to retire on a lieutenant's pension I have to hold the rank for two years, so if I walked in and retired, I'd get a sergeant's pension. So I'm going to leave this to you. I know of four small departments within an hour of our house that are looking for a chief of police, and I could probably land one of those jobs, or I can take this case and do my best on it."

"We don't have the choice, Mike," Lisa said. "Police chiefs are political animals, and you and I both know you'd be in a political job like that no more than three months before you pissed on someone's shoes and got fired and probably blacklisted. But I'm ... I have a permit to carry, Mike, and I'll be going about armed from here on in."

"Then I'll take the case," Mike said. "I start Monday."

"You want to see if Marjorie wants to go up to the lake and get away from this for a couple days?" Lisa asked.

"I like that idea," Lowe agreed. Life went on for those who remained here, and God alone knew when he'd get much time off. "Let's head back and toss her ass in the car."

4 March 2015

AFTERWORD

I hope you enjoyed this novel. I'm working hard on a sequel and it may turn into a trilogy of Mike Lowe before it's said and done. I finished it in March 2015, and now it's in your hands.

If you want to follow me online, here's where I can be found on the Internet:

Facebook:

www.facebook.com/PTHeffernan

Twitter:

@ptheffernan

Amazon:

http://author.to/PTHeffernan

ACKNOWLEDGEMENTS

You know, first and foremost, I claim the lion's share of the credit, researching all kinds of crap like how to make thermite and pipe bombs, so now the NSA is tracking my every move, most likely. At least now I know this somewhat unsettling information, huh?

I'd like to thank my wife Grace for her infinite patience as I was off being God in this world where Mike Lowe and a number of other fascinating people can be found. God knows I was far more a citizen of that world than this while I wrote this novel.

I would also like to thank my long-term friend Don Puryear for taking one hell of a lot of time I know he can ill afford to spend on reading this and giving me many long and thoughtful insights and much advice on *Pieces*. So, many thanks to you, Don.

I would also like to thank N.D. Taylor, another author who writes some amazing material, for her talents in making the amazing cover in which this novel is dressed. I'd casually mentioned to her that I needed a cover, and I swear to God, she sent me an example of this and I flipped for it. An hour later, the entire thing was in my hot little hands and I was a seriously happy camper. So thank you, N.D.

Perhaps most importantly, I need to thank Lee Ann Kanowsky and Kim Lehnhardt for far too many long days and nights guiding me through a thousand rocks and shoals, and working incessantly to help promote this novel in your hands. Thank you both from the bottom of my heart.

Last, but absolutely not least, I'd like to thank you, my readers, for taking the time to read *Pieces*. It makes this otherwise lonely and thankless pursuit worth it to know you read and liked what I gave you. I'd write anyway, because it's a passion to me. But I publish for you. It's symbiotic. So thank you from the bottom of my heart. And keep your eyes peeled for more. You haven't heard the last of me, nor of Mike Lowe, nor of other brainchildren my noggin has hatched.

PH